Inside the Hatboxes

RC Marlen

iUniverse, Inc.
New York Lincoln Shanghai

Inside the Hatboxes

iUniverse books may be ordered through booksellers or by contacting:

iUniverse
2021 Pine Lake Road, Suite 100
Lincoln, NE 68512
www.iuniverse.com
1-800-Authors (1-800-288-4677)

Historical events and information about St. Louis and the United States are portrayed as factually as possible. How the two families, the Bartletts and the Scagliones, relate to these historical events is completely fictitious. Any similarity to people in these two families is coincidental with one exception: the personality and characteristics of John Bartlett were patterned after my father, Thomas W. Marlen, Sr. The incidents in the story built around this character, however, were not real events.

Caption under photo of Al Capone from November 18, 1932, St. Louis Post-Dispatch newspaper. Used with permission.

Excerpts of lyric from song, **FIVE FOOT TWO, EYES OF BLUE**
Lyric by SAM LEWIS and JOE YOUNG Music by RAY HENDERSON
© 1925 (renewed 1953) EMI FEIST CATALOG INC.
Rights for the Extended Renewal Term in the United States controlled by RAY HENDERSON MUSIC COMPANY, EMI FEIST CATALOG INC.
and WAROCK MUSIC CORP.
Rights outside the United Stated Administered by EMI FEIST CATALOG INC. (Publishing) and ALFRED PUBLISHING CO., INC. (Print)
All Rights Reserved Used By Permission

ISBN-13: 978-0-595-36323-0 (pbk)
ISBN-13: 978-0-595-80759-8 (ebk)
ISBN-10: 0-595-36323-7 (pbk)
ISBN-10: 0-595-80759-3 (ebk)

Printed in the United States of America

Dedicated to My Children

S. Bryon Cariss
Carolyn Cariss-Daniels
Kim C. Halilovic

ACKNOWLEDGMENTS

In the process of writing this novel, I found that while I could complete the first draft alone, I needed friends to help me finish the book. Without their comments and support, *Inside the Hatboxes* would have been much less. I must thank Kristi Negri for her editing and insight. I want to thank my reading team of carefully chosen women and men; I am grateful to Cindy Bond (Thompson), Susan Boyovich, Karen Cristobal, and Linda Gilbert, and indebted to Larry Bills, Kevin Johnsrude, Charles J. Marlen, and Mark Wigg.

Special thanks must go to Todd Silverstein, who painstakingly combed through the manuscript and then spent more time giving advice for discrepancies in logic, overall readability, and more. I mustn't forget Richard Silverstein who was my *farther* and *further* expert. My two friends Pat Bingenheimer and Andrea Whalen are to be thanked for helping to maintain my health and sanity; Monday through Friday they pulled me from the computer to go on a power walk. Also, I am grateful to my sister-in-law Regina Schele, who was the first to read my novel; her excitement and praise carried me to the end. And then there were the encouraging words by Greg Lawrence who said my work deserved to be published. Lastly, I want to thank my father, Thomas W. Marlen, Sr., who was the inspiration for *Inside the Hatboxes* and for my next book, *The Drugstore*.

PREFACE

Large murals that depict a cultural event or an era have always attracted me. I like to sit, look into each face, search for the underlying story, and try to visualize where in the mural the events began. Murals by Diego Rivera, full of color and passion, come to mind and have been among the ones that have affected me the most. Picasso's mural *Guernica,* with scenes full of pain, has remained with me since the moment I first saw it.

I would like to make a mural in words of a story of two families. Unlike a wall of pigments, which, once completed, enables a person to view any aspect of it at a glance, words must be read if the story is to unfold. Reading a book is like watching the mural being painted; as one reads, scenes and incidents are created in the mind, but the whole mural cannot be seen until the book is finished. Life is a bit like this. We all have our story—a mural of scenes about our pleasures and pains, painted day-by-day into our memories and on an ongoing basis until we die.

With this mural in words, I'd like you to think of the beginning as somewhere in the center of the painting, with the past being on the left and the future unfolding on the right. Remember that when a story unfolds, the events don't always accumulate chronologically. One day a scene will be painted, and you will begin to learn of someone's life. As this person develops, the colors of her childhood splash onto the canvas from memories of simple things, such as toys, a home, or a tree outside a window. Then the child asks her grandfather, "Where did you live when you were a boy?" and images appear to the left of the mural, to the far edge of the past. With time, more images fill the white spaces as the child grows and learns more of her heritage, until there is a whole scene revealing who she is and from where she came. As life passes, images are created to the right and to the left, blending into one another.

However, in a book, just as in life, it is possible for one area of the canvas to remain unpainted. Surrounded by the colors of other times and events in the mural, a white emptiness can appear, holding a secret. A person could reach the end of her life and never be able to paint the missing scene because she had never learned the secret. If she wants to complete her mural, she must want to know her past, search for its secrets, and ask someone who knows. A simple question could add a tiny dab of blue, a swirl of green, or a complex mixture of colors to create a final understanding of the mural of her life.

Come, turn the page, and see this mural of the Bartlett and Scaglione families living in St. Louis, Missouri. At times, their lives will evolve, entwine, and twist into a story of dark and tragic colors, while at other times, there will be bursts of yellow and pinks of happiness. Murals are not simple; they are to be studied and absorbed. Life is not simple; it is painted slowly and carefully with the decisions each family makes.

PART I

1932

CHAPTER I

1932

Unbeknownst to Tony, he was rushing toward a crime—which he himself would commit. But at the moment, he was burdened with another problem as the Packard coupe sped north through the darkness on US Route 66. Autumn in Missouri has the blackest of nights, with skies heavy with clouds that weep a silent drizzle. However, in the coupe, the blackness was not coming from the night. Tony stared ahead into the bright triangular swath of the headlights and felt a weight enveloping his whole being. He found it hard to breathe. He felt a pressure in his chest, and glancing into the dark nothingness in the rearview mirror, he had the bewildering sensation of slipping backwards, sinking into a void like a deep sea of pain. He was drowning. He sucked in air, not in a large gulp, but in several short gasps. Then he sighed with sadness and listened to Claire weeping softly next to him. She clutched the bundle against her chest, making no effort to wipe the tears dripping from her cheeks and nose.

Rolling hills and woods flew by, though they were indistinct in the rain. To Tony, the obscured view didn't matter because he knew these woods. He knew exactly how the woods would be tonight when he finally would stop to enter them. He dreaded that moment.

Passing a distant house, Tony was surprised to see a flickering gas lamp in a window. He hadn't expected to see any lights, it being almost two in the morning. For what he had to do, he preferred everyone to be sleeping. He sighed deeply again, and then returned to his concern with the wooded countryside and his search for the right place. During this season, the trees stood bare, adding pain to this night with the colorless displays of bleak gray and black bark. But this drab scene suited his task. He realized that he must stop before morning to find a place among these oak and hickory trees where the moist, leaf-covered terrain showed no trace of footsteps and where the woods were too dense for an intruder to see.

As he drove over a small bridge, willows and cottonwoods swayed in the wind along the gravel creek bed. He used to hunt here. *Right about here,* he speculated silently as he remembered how he and his best friend Louie once tramped through these woods hunting for squirrels. They always shot a couple squirrels, yet Tony went with Louie not for the hunting, but just to spend a day with his friend in the woods. That was what he had liked, being with his friend.

A thought popped into his head. *What was it Louie told me about those scrawny evergreen trees? Oh, I remember,* he mused, as if in conversation with another. *Yeah, Louie picked up one of the hard, bluish, pea-sized seeds and said that the birds must eat them and then crap them out before those trees can grow. I remember we were sitting in a field and noticed that those cedars were growing all along that barbed wire fence. We laughed so hard at the idea of birds sitting on the barbed wire planting those seeds.* In the past he had laughed and laughed about a seed that must pass through the stomach of a bird before it can grow. Tonight, he remembered this without any sensation of pleasure. His despondency turned the colorful memory to sepia.

Not one to dwell on abstract ideas, Tony continued to think and plan. When presented with a problem, his way was to work out a practical solution and then do what he must. He was a hard worker and one who analyzed how to work best at whatever job he had. He wasn't one to have profound thoughts, yet he often said, "I've got this rule. For me, Life is Work." He had always prided himself on having a job and on being conscientious and dedicated to his job. The year was 1932, and the Great Depression had herded the people of the world into joblessness, even Tony. He had lost his night watchman job at the bank when it went belly-up. In a world where banks on every corner were going under and workers in every walk of life were losing jobs, Tony found himself among the masses—a failure. For him, his failure was not that he had lost a job, but that he had not found another. The problem in the nation was that a man needed more than fate or luck to find a job.

One needed a bird to drop a seed.

And one had fallen into Tony's lap. He was heading home to St. Louis to apply for his old job at the St. Louis Fire Department. His Aunt Maria, who had helped raise him, had written many letters asking him to come home and live with her. He had always declined. That is, until her last letter when she said the department had asked if he wanted to return to work as a firefighter. He wired a telegram back the same day:

"IN 2 WEEKS TONY SCAGGLIONE WILL BE THERE TO FIGHT FIRES. Stop"

People knew Tony to be a man of hope and determination and a firefighter who brought zest and energy to the job, so when some older men were going to retire, the department thought of Tony. He had always known that he possessed the energy to fare better than the ordinary man. But tonight he wondered. His energy was trickling away like the few drops of water that slid to the bottom of the windshield wipers and dribbled down the glass before vanishing. Tonight he felt important parts of his life were seeping away.

In frustration he ran his fingers through his dark wavy hair. "Now, Claire?" he asked, and she shook her drooping head back and forth. He said no more because he knew she didn't like what he was going to do. There was another turnoff down the road a few miles, so he could go a little longer.

The drone of the engine and the rhythm of the wiper blades eased his mind into numbness. It was hypnotic, and he felt as if he could drive forever, he could drive through—and even out of—his sadness. Somewhere, buried in his mind, another sad memory stirred. The event unfolded, and slowly the silence in the automobile filled with street sounds that seemed to be located behind him. Traffic sounds emerged—a horn honk, a brake screech, some vendor on the street singing his wares, the hum of motors, and a laugh or shout here and there. In his mind Tony turned around and it all appeared. Time leapt backwards fifteen years.

Classes were out. The sidewalks were filled with a flurry of afternoon shoppers as Tony and Louie ran to catch a streetcar on Grand Avenue. Dodging people, Tony hollered over his shoulder, running with arms pumping right, left, up, down, "Come on, Louie, we can catch it!" They were full of fun and energy. Tony's knickers billowed as he maneuvered his short muscular body this way, and then a quick turn that way. The streets were jammed, too, with merchants unloading trucks at the curb, with smells of peanuts coming from pushcarts, with an irate driver shouting at a taxi, and with a muddle of motorcars going fast, then slow, and then fast again. Tony figured they could catch up with the retreating streetcar if they could wiggle and sidestep around the maze of vehicles. Louie followed with long strides, holding his cap to his head with one hand while his book bag spun in the other. The streetcar clanged and a few sparks spat and sparkled from the cables above the middle of the street. The open box-shaped streetcar displayed paper advertisements pasted on both sides, covering much of the oxidized whitish red paint etched with scratches and rust. To enter, in front near the conductor, black metal stairs hung down close to the street, and more stairs descended from the back where Tony was getting ready to jump and grab the railing. He leaped and, turning back to shout to Louie, swirled around the pole he clutched to see a truck about to collide with his best friend. Tony heard the screech of brakes and a sickening thud, then other screeches as more vehicles collided. The colorful bustle of

*the street froze into black and white. The sounds of street life turned to silence as
a scream of "No!" erupted from Tony.*

*They had been having fun and running across that street, like so many times
before. The truck had seemed to emerge suddenly from nowhere! Such a simple
mistake. He remembered thinking that an act with such complicated consequences should not be so easy to commit. Why should you die because of such a
small error? How could someone disappear forever because he didn't turn his head
one way or the other? Tony never could resolve the enigma of that simple mistake.
He still could feel how it was to hold Louie in his arms, both of them covered with
blood, and not to want the time to pass, or a time to arrive when he must put
Louie down and end that part of his life forever.*

Tony glanced at Claire. He was pained, thinking of what he had to do
tonight. He didn't want to end this part of his life either.

So the coupe sped on like his thoughts traveled on, both passing through
time—one going forward and the other back—the automobile and his mind
journeying their own particular ways.

His reflections passed to thoughts of Claire. *If I hadn't lost my job with the
St. Louis Fire Department, I never would've left St. Louis to go west. Things usually happen for the best.* In California, he hadn't found a job as a fire fighter as
he had hoped, but he had found another job, and most importantly, met
Claire. They were married within a year. Tony believed that you need to take
what life dishes out, the good with the bad. He had told one of his buddies,
"Usually I'm served potatoes, but since Claire's in my life, they taste better 'cuz
she's the gravy. Ha, and if I'm lucky enough to get a piece of cake, it's better,
too, 'cuz she's the icing." She was the best part of his life.

"I'm so lucky to have her," he whispered under his breath. He hurt more
knowing that she was going through so much pain, too.

Tony worried how all their problems would affect Claire. *She's a mere wisp
of a woman at five feet two inches. She's like the song,* "Five foot two, eyes of blue,
has anybody seen my gal"? He remembered how he used to hum it constantly
after they had met, but tonight there was no humming, only the words echo-
ing in his thoughts. *Turned up nose, turned down toes, has anybody seen my gal?*

"Has anyone seen my gal"? Tonight that question was fitting. Claire was distraught, not her usual self. Normally she was sweet and kind and happy.
Driving in the darkness with only his thoughts, Tony's face passed a glimmer
of a smile as he thought how people seemed to fall from the sky, like gravity,
to be near her; young men followed her, little kids talked to her spontaneously, and old people chose her in a crowd to ask for help. People liked Claire. Her
boundless energy and happiness filled the room when she entered. Everyone
seemed more alive when she was around, and even her clothes moved with her

as if they were alive, too. The edges of her skirt danced as she walked, slipping this way and that around her firm, round hips.

Before he knew Claire, he had gone to see a motion picture called *It,* starring Clara Bow. *It* was the rave. With the popularity of the movie, the term "It Girl" became a phrase people used for a modern young woman who was different from the ordinary crowd and spontaneous—a gal who flaunted a felicitous personality. He had been bored one night and recalled some of the guys at work talking about this new film, so he went to see it. The movie star, Clara Bow, made an impression on him as did her character—the "It Girl." He had felt foolish at being so taken by this film, being more of a pool-hall kind of guy.

Then Tony had met Claire. What had astounded him was that not only did Claire look like the movie star, but also she had the same name as Clara Bow's—just spelled differently—and, more importantly, Claire's personality resembled the character in that movie. Tony had decided that she was his very own "It Girl." Claire was so much fun to be with, a delight to see, and she made him feel important. Their love was special. Yes, Claire was his "It Girl," without a doubt, but…not tonight.

"Claire, we've got to stop now. I just saw the sign for the town called Bourbon. We passed all the other places I thought would work. It's coming up soon and this is where I want to stop. It's fifty-five miles to St. Louis, so we better do it soon. I don't know how long it'll take me with my small shovel, so we got to stop."

It wasn't a coincidence that Tony stored a collapsible shovel in the space under the seat. In his automobile, he stashed rope, matches, an extra fan belt, a tool kit, and a first aid kit, too. Tony was an orderly person.

"Isn't this against the law?" Claire asked. "Couldn't we wait 'til tomorrow and do it right, with your family and some of your old friends?"

"You know we ain't got money for that. Heck, we decided not to spend our last few dollars to stop at a motel last night. How would we pay for a funeral? Do you know what they cost? Anyway, I don't see that this is anybody's business but ours, Claire." His hand went through his hair. "We're doing what's best. Why, what do you think people used to do? Like those who lived out west back when your granddaddy was alive?" He hesitated, and then with a softer and sadder voice, he told her the real reason. "I can't arrive and cause such pain to my family. I'll explain everything to everyone and they'll understand." But in an angry voice he told himself, *This is so hard to do!* He wanted to pull out his hair!

Claire began to sob. Though looking straight ahead at the road, Tony saw his wife's shoulders shake and he saw her head droop to the little blanket covering Sue Ann as she pulled her daughter to her face.

Tony reached over and put his arm around Claire's shoulders. "To die after a life of merely fourteen months," he lamented, "it's just not fair." Sue Ann's fever had started on the second day out of Los Angeles. They knew that babies got fevers a lot because they had experienced many sicknesses throughout those fourteen months. Many a night they had spent holding their sick Sue Ann to calm her. "She'd always got better before," he whispered, "just not this time."

"I knew it wasn't right to be so happy," Claire said. "Sooner or later something has to go wrong to bring you back to being more respectful. We were too happy, Tony. This trip wasn't right for us," she said between sobs. "We should've been saving our money real good instead of having fun."

"Don't do this, Claire. You know that kind of talk don't make no sense. This trip wasn't a vacation. I'm going back for a job. I just thought we could enjoy our travels so I planned some fun. There's a lot of things we can't figure out. We can't change the past and that's that." He was gentle in his words, but firm, "Now, calm down and please stop talking like that."

So, she did stop talking. But she couldn't stop thinking, and reflections of the last seven days began to form in her mind.

Tony had planned the trip so well. They had driven out of Los Angeles early to make good mileage at the beginning of the trip while they were fresh. He never knew exactly where they'd stop because he didn't really know how long they could go each day with little Sue Ann, so Tony didn't reserve any motel rooms. He planned to get as close to the Grand Canyon as possible the first day, and then leave US Route 66 and drive north to the south rim of the canyon to spend the whole second day there. The third day he wanted to see the Petrified Forest, those "rock trees," as he called them, and to get to a friend's house in Albuquerque for the night. This was another St. Louis buddy from high school with a wife and two kids. Claire had written to them and they answered, so they were expecting the traveling family of three. All of the fourth day was to be spent with these friends in Albuquerque. The fifth day they were to pass through Texas. Tony was looking forward to seeing cowboys and oil wells. His plan was to drive hard the sixth day through Oklahoma, where he figured there was only dust and dirt to see in that state because all the news said how bad the Dust Bowl was. Then, the last day would be a straight shot across the state of Missouri, making it an easy drive to St. Louis. He'd be on home terrain.

"We shouldn't have bought this automobile," she complained in a mumble to herself. "Don't matter that it was so cheap. If we didn't have it we would've figured out something else and not come on this trip."

Claire had known from the start Tony liked vehicles. When Tony was talking one day about Henry Ford's Model T for the unbelievably low price of $300, she hurt for him. They both knew he could only dream about having a good vehicle. He had told her how the first Model T was $950 back in 1908, and now it was a third of that price. He yearned for an automobile.

Claire remembered the day when Tony's dream had come true with the purchase of this used Packard coupe. One of the executives at the bank in California, where Tony had been night watchman, had sold it to him for $100. This executive took a bad loss in the stock market crash of 1929 and never recovered. So, one morning, this man had asked Tony if he wanted to buy the coupe. Tony bought it on the spot. Of course, this was before the bank folded, along with Tony's job. Tony had taken his savings out before it went down.

Claire was thinking that Tony was one of the lucky ones, but then she changed her mind. *No, Tony wasn't lucky when it came to money. He worked hard, saved a lot, and noticed things. He was always talking to people to learn.* He had removed his money long before his bank went down because he had seen what was happening to other banks.

We should've taken a train. Claire continued to think and remember, trying to discover exactly where they had gone wrong, trying to figure what they could have done differently to prevent the ugly, bloody death of their precious daughter. Claire started to relive the whole trip.

It had been dark when they left Los Angeles, and a little sliver of a crescent moon glimmered above. Quickly the sky began to lighten and diminish the stars, leaving two lonely morning stars, one above and the other below the moon. Claire found it fascinating that these two stars remained, and she kept pointing to them for Sue Ann to see. Finally she made two wishes and recited *Twinkle, Twinkle, Little Star* to Sue Ann.

She was always talking to Sue Ann, always reciting rhymes. Tony found driving to be a pleasure while listening to Claire's talk and Little Sue Ann babbling back to her. Tony and Claire often called the baby "Little Sue Ann" as if it was her name. Sue Ann had fine blonde curls. Her blue eyes were like those of her "MA-ma-ma" (as the baby called her mother). Often one curl fell onto the baby's forehead, and at those times, Claire would always say another poem:

> *There was a little girl who had a little curl*
> *Right in the middle of her forehead;*
> *And when she was good*
> *She was very, very good,*
> *But when she was bad she was horrid.*

With Sue Ann sleeping most of the morning, Claire dozed off and on. Tony had awakened his wife at one point so she could see the Mojave Desert and to ask for some of the coffee they had packed.

"Are you sure you want to drink it? It's got to be cold," she commented.

"Heck, I don't care if it's hot or cold…just want help to keep my eyes open."

Claire squirmed around in her seat to reach the thermos, and Tony enjoyed watching her movements out of the corner of his eye. He gave her a pat and she squealed, "Tony! Watch the road!"

"Hey, let's have lunch at the California border," he said. Claire had made a good lunch of fried chicken. Tony loved cold fried chicken.

"Sure," she answered, turning back in her seat and straightening her skirt. "Wow, there ain't nothing out here, is there? Not a tree or anything green. It's so hot for November. I just don't know how Little Sue Ann can sleep in this heat."

After a few minutes, Tony chuckled to himself when he saw Claire drop off to sleep again. He didn't wake her until they were leaving California.

Tony saw the Colorado River flowing along the border and chose a site for lunch high on a bluff overlooking the river. He put his hand on his wife's shoulder and, with a gentle shake, told her, "It's lunchtime, sweetie."

Claire rubbed her face awake as they crossed the Trails Arch Bridge, progressed to the top of the hill, and parked. "It's so hot! I don't think I've ever been this hot before. Wish you could've found some shade."

Tony smiled, knowing there was no shade for miles, "We'll just have to eat on the shady side of the Packard." Claire put a blanket down on the sandy soil, looking out over the river. Tony sat on the running board to watch as Sue Ann walked, squatted, and picked up rocks to bring to her mother. Sue Ann was enthralled by a train crossing on another nearby stone bridge. The whistle blew, and as they watched, a vulture came into view and circled above the train. The clickity-clack slowly faded and the quiet returned. They stayed an hour or so to give the baby some exercise, and then Tony playfully put her up on his shoulders and ran around. Sue Ann clung to her daddy and laughed.

"It's too hot for that, Tony, you should put her down. You just ate," Claire shouted while packing up the food. He ran toward the bluff's edge. He wouldn't stop his romping, and Sue Ann couldn't stop her giggling.

Down the highway a few miles, Tony's girls were napping again. He couldn't understand how they could sleep so much, but realized that the landscape wasn't much to look at that day.

When they drove through Topock, Claire was awake again. Tony quipped, "Man, this sure ain't Los Angeles." Laughing, they were looking at the first few structures they'd seen in a while. Grayed and weathered wooden remnants of a mine leaned against rocky slopes.

"Wonder what they used to mine?"

With a glimmer in his eyes, Tony said, "Why, gold!"

"And diamonds!" Claire added with wide eyes.

After beginning to climb in elevation, they approached the town of Kingman and a sign that told them to look back and see three states at Sitgreaves Pass. He pulled over and they turned to look at California, Arizona, and Nevada.

Claire giggled, "They all look the same to me."

Claire remembered that the trip had gone smoothly as planned, and by the end of that first day, they felt a calm pleasure when they signed into the Navajo Motel in the little town of Seligman. Before getting ready for bed, they finished the food that had been packed for the trip. Then they went to bed, anticipating the sight of the Grand Canyon the next day.

The next morning Claire put on her white dress with the three pleats that hung from the waist at one side because this was going to be a day for photographs and she wanted to look special. Tony loved her dress, or was it that he loved watching her getting dressed?

"What you looking at?" Claire had teased.

Getting up from the bed, he started toward her, "Hey, I been ready to go for a long while and didn't have anything better to do but watch you." He put his hands on her waist and pulled her close while nuzzling her neck.

"I see something in your eyes, but don't get any ideas because I'm not taking my dress off 'cuz I'm ready, too," she twittered. She turned to the mirror and slipped on her little pink linen hat that fit snugly over all her hair except for a few wisps of brown that curled around the edges. Tony liked how she looked.

Seeing the Grand Canyon had inspired them with awe. It was breathtaking and different from every angle. Claire surmised that God made the world like this to show us that he's powerful beyond our understanding. They had hiked down the trail behind the mule riders because with Sue Ann they couldn't go on a trail ride. Claire calculated that they had walked for an hour when she suggested turning around to go back up. It was too much. She and Sue Ann were exhausted. After that hike, Claire decided that seeing the Indians and getting Sue Ann's photo taken in front of a teepee with the chief in full headdress was more interesting for a small child. Tony and Sue Ann napped in the car while Claire spent time in souvenir shops. With their budget, she only browsed.

They had eaten at a little diner that was a lonely caboose lost from its train. Then they drove around a bit to explore the area, but mostly they wanted to see the canyon. The light, as the evening approached, made the rocks and bluffs change colors. They sat and gazed at the forms created from abutments. Rock arches! Tony threw down a blanket and plopped on their bellies to peer over the edge of a chasm.

"How deep do you think it is?"

"Too deep!" Tony joked while tickling Sue Ann's belly.

After a spectacular sunset, they began their search for a place to sleep. All the cabins at the canyon were filled. So they drove away with the idea to stop at the first motel they could find when they got back to US Route 66.

An hour south of the canyon, Sue Ann began to cry like she was in pain. She arched her back and stiffened so that Claire could hardly hold her. It was so sudden! Her screaming and frantic movements created an emotional frenzy in the automobile while outside a calm scene in earth tones rolled out an empty landscape, fading from view as the evening darkened. Then the baby began vomiting.

They stopped by the side of the road until Sue Ann seemed better. It was dark now, and they were in the middle of nowhere. Claire had been so worried about Sue Ann that she gave no mind to the stains on her best dress. What was important was they had water. Tony had made sure of that when planning the trip. "Can't travel with a baby without water," he had claimed. She was grateful for Tony's preparations as she changed the baby into fresh clothes and then washed the vomit out of her best dress. Sue Ann continued to get worse, though. She had a fever.

When lodging was found, they spent most the night bathing the baby to cool her. "Babies get sick a lot," they had kept saying to one another, trying to convince each other that this was a normal baby fever of the kind that frequently develop for no apparent reason. They took turns trying to comfort the child while the other tried to sleep. A little after three o'clock, the fever vanished, and little Sue Ann slept in the bed between the two of them. They had arisen late and stayed until checkout so Claire could try to wash the smell from all their clothes and the coupe. Tony played with Sue Ann, whose behavior had returned to normal.

That morning in the automobile, the conversation was of the typical baby sicknesses.

"Sure can scare you, can't it."

Off and on that day, they would go back to the same topic. "I was so scared, us out here with no doctor. No nothing!"

"All right, now we can get back on schedule and enjoy this trip like you planned," Claire announced. They passed Flagstaff, saw the big crater made by a meteor, touched Tony 's "rock trees" at the Petrified Forest, and stopped at Gallup, New Mexico, to eat. They had laughed a lot and were giddy with relief that Sue Ann was well. Two days later, arriving at their friend's house in Albuquerque, they relaxed, reminisced, and found they couldn't stop talking about the sights they had seen.

The end started on the sixth day. They had left Amarillo and had driven hard with only a few stops for gasoline and for what Tony called "nature calls" made by the side of the road.

Oklahoma was nothing but dirt and incessant sand blowing up in front of them. They were in the Dust Bowl. They traveled like in a bad dream that continues on and on, repeating the discomfort of a scene over and over so that one struggles to awaken, hoping to make it disappear, but cannot. In Claire and Tony's memory, Oklahoma would always be the scene of wind, dust, and oncoming travelers with dilapidated belongings piled high on their vehicles.

One by one, these fellow travelers materialized out of the haze in an endless parade. With such limited visibility, no one could travel at a normal speed that day, and Claire saw the scene like they were in a movie theatre playing in slow motion, with the windshield as the screen. Tumbleweed rolled across the road and the hood of their automobile. They could see every stalk and branching stem. The sandy soil swirled up and created a momentary pattern as it twisted in the air, holding its form a moment before disintegrating wherever the wind took it. Over and over they would see a lone object form ahead of them, appearing as a dark smudge and gradually shaping into a square radiator when it emerged from the dirt-filled air. It was a vehicle, closing the distance between them. Again and again tumbleweeds flew at their windshield and startled them. The wind rocked the coupe, whispering painful messages through the windows and creating eerie sounds of a dying land in agony.

"I don't want to talk because you need to concentrate so much to see where you're going, but I need to talk a little," Claire confided to Tony. "I'm so upset looking at those poor people. You would think the storm would be scaring me, but I'm scared about them. I keep wondering where they're going and what they're going to do."

Over and over Claire peered into haunting faces of tired, defeated families in old vehicles, moving slowly through the storm. Passing too close, a Model T lurched in a gust of wind, and Claire witnessed, an arm's length away, some of the ruined people looking ghostlike with dust covering their faces and clinging to their hair. Unlike the well-made, tight-windowed Packard coupe, the Okies drove older, cheaper motorcars with folding windows, broken windows, or no windows to close out the dirt. Often, bedspreads were held in place at the window openings, trying to stop the infiltration of the downfall of their lives. The dirt came in without control and covered them, like this disaster had come in and spread over every aspect of their existence. There was no stopping the dust and the sand, nor could one contain the disappearing land and vanishing lifestyles.

Three hundred thousand Okies departed from the Dustbowl and headed toward California in the early thirties. Claire and Tony had passed more than a hundred of them that day.

Tony told Claire, "I was talking with a guy at the diner this mornin' when you went to the bathroom with Sue Ann. He told me what's causing all this dust storm. He said it went way back to when settlers first came. They changed how the land used to be. You know, they made it something that it wasn't supposed to be." Tony talked on, explaining how the ancestors of many of these families had come in the late 1800s to settle in this land of natural grasses and had started its demise. For centuries before these settlers, the grasses had thrived—miles and miles of grasses. When the settlers saw the grasses, the place had seemed perfect for raising cattle. Tony was explaining, "Before the settlers, there had been years of no rain, but these grasses would protected the soil so it wouldn't blow away." The soil was sandy and in that pristine past, dried grasses fell in autumn and formed a protective covering over the land while the winds blew relentlessly.

"With all that thick layer of grass covering over the dirt, the seeds just waited until another year when the rains would finally come. Isn't that amazing?" Tony declared. "But you know what happened? This man said that it only took a few decades for the land to begin eroding after the settlers were there. You know, the cattle ate the grass down and trampled watering areas into mud, like they do. They cleared land to grow row crops for them to eat. They just didn't know they were causing this mess." Tony waved his hand in front of him. "Now we have this dust because of that." Soil in this gently rolling land was made ready for erosion by rain in good years and by wind in dry years. Now, nature's fury finally was blowing away the people.

There had been no laughter from Claire and Tony that day.

They passed Oklahoma City, then Tulsa, and were nearly at the Missouri border. At some point early in the afternoon, the wind had stopped and the day cleared. Before dark, they chose a motel sitting among cornfields. They were exhausted. They sat outside for a while to relax and to have Sue Ann walk around for some exercise. The motel had old beach chairs with frayed canvas seats, the kind with adjustable backs and a wooden frame that folded flat for storing. The motel owner offered them iced tea, and he sat a while with them to chat. It was getting cold as the sun was setting. It felt good. Cool, fresh air. They talked with the motel owner about the Okies and the problems in Oklahoma.

"Yep, times are hard for everyone across the nation."

They talked about the number of failed banks, factories going broke, the foreclosures on homes, farmers having to mortgage all their assets, and the hope in Franklin Delano Roosevelt's promises.

"I hear there are ten million people out of work," the motel owner said, "and President Hoover ain't done nothing to help. FDR says he's got solutions, but I just don't know."

"Well, I don't know if you're a Democrat or Republican," Tony began, and Claire got up, excusing herself.

"All I need after today is to hear a discussion like this," Claire whispered into Sue Ann's little ear. In her weary voice, Claire talked with her daughter about how she had seen and heard more than enough depressing events that day. Besides, she thought, the baby needed a bath and once that was finished she could relax.

It was going on six in the evening and still daylight when Sue Ann's pain, crying, and fever began again. She flailed her arms and didn't want to be touched. She became extremely hot and seemed delirious. Claire called Tony to come and help. After an hour of this, Sue Ann stopped crying simply from exhaustion. Then the vomiting began. A black vomit! They had been puzzled and tried to think what Sue Ann had eaten to make her vomit that color. One asked the other, "Could she have swallowed dirt from the air to make her vomit that color?" No, that was ridiculous. They discussed the possibility that she might have eaten something from the ground, though they knew she hadn't been out of their sight, and there was too much dark vomit. Soon they started noticing blood in her saliva, and Tony went running to the motel owner's house.

"We need a doctor! Can you tell us where to find one? Our little daughter is really sick," he shouted while pounding on the owner's door.

The owner was concerned for them. He stood in his bare feet on his porch, pointing up the road. "Old Doc Moore is up in the nearest town, more or less twenty miles east. He's got a white picket fence out front of his house and a sign saying he's a doc. He's right on Route 66. You can't miss it 'cuz it's the only house with a white picket fence," the motel owner replied. "He's a good man and knows his medicine, even though he's retired. Of course, he says he's retired, but that just means that he don't have regular office hours. I'd call to make sure that he's there, but he don't have no phone 'cuz, as he says, he don't want one of those newfangled things."

Tony and the owner had agreed on a fraction of the price of the room since they were not staying.

"If old Doc Moore fixes her up, you come on back and you can pay up the difference," the owner had assured him. So, Tony paid the bill and packed while Claire tried to calm the crying Little Sue Ann. They traveled without speaking to one another. Claire was occupied trying her best to comfort her sick child.

Without difficulty, they found the house with the white fence, passed through a gate, went up some wooden steps onto a wide porch, and approached a beautiful, though weathered, oak door with an oval etched window. Tony knocked with force against the wood and knocked more on the glass until he saw a light appear, illuminating a long hallway. Soon an elderly, stooped man stood in the open doorway with an oil lamp raised in his hand. His bushy white hair, reflecting the light from the lamp, seemed to create its own glow around his face. He had more hair sticking out from one side of his head than the other. His clothes were disheveled as if he had been napping in them, but his eyes were alert with a composed, gentle gaze that didn't change when he saw the frantic faces above the limp child.

"Our baby's sick, real sick, and we need some help," Tony pleaded.

The doctor gestured, "Please come in." When the doctor opened his door he had expected to hear a cry of desperation, but the next comment took the old man by surprise.

"It looked like she was vomiting blood." Tony's voice pierced the quiet evening, tensing the calm like a shriek from a low-flying hawk.

"Come this way." Dr. Moore turned and shuffled down the hallway past a staircase on the left and a tall grandfather clock, ticking a life away. They entered a large, paneled room with caramel-colored wood. At one end was a walnut desk in front of shelves of books and at the other end stood two white-painted metal cabinets with glass doors displaying the tools of the medical profession. Claire glanced around, hoping to see some kind of sophisticated equipment to save her child, only to focus on French doors reflecting the silhouetted form of her family—black outlines of sagging shoulders, drooping heads, and Tony's arms fidgeting nervously. The doctor motioned to an examination table with a white sheet spread across it. Claire placed Sue Ann there. No one spoke while he lit another lamp and turned to examine Sue Ann.

Claire remembered gasping upon seeing Sue Ann. Her complexion had become yellowish. Claire had noticed that the child's pallor was odd when they were driving away from the motel, but in the doctor's room it was a shock to see how much the child's skin had changed. Sue Ann began to retch again and more blackish, bloody clumps fell upon the white sheet as the doctor carefully turned the baby so she could expel it all. He opened her mouth and examined it carefully. Tony started explaining all that had happened up at the motel. Sue Ann was so hot; she was limp and oblivious to the presence of the stranger. Normally, the child feared strangers.

Doc Moore asked Claire to undress the child, and he continued his examination by pressing here and there, by looking into her mouth again, and listening to her breathing and heart with his stethoscope. This went on for a while. Now and then he'd stop the examination to go to his library behind the desk. During the first such interruption, he asked Claire to cover the baby and hold her. Another time, when the doctor stopped to read reference books again, he gave Tony a basin of water and a cloth. "Wipe the baby to cool her. And rinse it frequently to keep the cloth cool. Be sure to pass it over all of her body," he directed. Each time, he walked in a slow stooped manner toward his desk before pulling a volume from the shelves and placing wire-rimmed glasses on his nose. He read to the sound of the splashing water and Claire's weeping. The baby no longer cried.

The doctor would return to the examination table to see more and ask questions. He asked, "How long has she been like this?" Claire replied that it was a couple of hours. Tony explained further that Sue Ann had been sick earlier in the trip.

"When was that first illness exactly?" the doctor said. Then he continued, "Let's rehash exactly what you remember about the first occurrence." It seemed that Doc Moore was never satisfied with their answers, because he wanted more and more details.

Again and again he returned to his desk to read more. At one point, the doctor looked up and asked, "Where do you live? And why are you traveling?"

As Tony had related the reasons for the trip and their move to Missouri, Doc Moore listened carefully. "Back in California did you live near the ocean or a port?" the doctor asked and heard that they did not. He nodded and continued to read.

It was apparent that Sue Ann was rapidly getting worse. She barely moved.

The once calm voice of the doctor sounded beaten, "I'm frustrated and feel helpless. I've already spent too much time, so I must be candid with you. You know your daughter is very ill, but I regret to have to say that I can't help. Any ideas I consider just make no sense, and yet, as I puzzle over all her symptoms, I can see that I'm spending precious time. You must try to get to the hospital in Joplin, Missouri, where they can perform tests. I have no facilities to do the tests."

"That's so far—hours away," Tony complained, "Can't you do something to help her now?"

The doctor, looking carefully at the two anguished faces, motioned with his hand, "Come; let's sit down over by my desk." They gathered around the desk. "In all my years of doctoring, I've not seen this. Also, in all my years I haven't told my patients an idea that's so far-fetched, but your situation is dire, so I need to level with you. Now, I want you to understand that what I'm going to say is highly improbable. Nonetheless, your child has all the symptoms of a rare fever that is found in Africa …or in people who have been there."

He had stopped his explanation for a moment to clear his throat and to blow his nose on a freshly pressed handkerchief he pulled from a desk drawer. "I hesitate to mention this because it's a disease for which there is no treatment. But you need to know what you're up against. Some people survive— most do not. With the answers you have given me, it makes no sense that she has this, but she has all the symptoms and nothing else makes sense, either."

Doc Moore was a good doctor, and through the years he had read to keep abreast of new findings and ideas. "Although I can't find it this night, I'm sure that I read about a study that was done at the turn of the century to confirm that this fever could be transmitted by mosquito bites. If a person with this fever was bitten, the disease was transmitted when that mosquito bit another human. Then this second person became a carrier and could travel to another place, across even an ocean, where a different mosquito could bite him." He stopped a moment, seeing they didn't understand.

With Tony and Claire looking confused, the doctor summarized, "Although this fever originates in Africa, the mosquito didn't need to be from Africa. If a person arrived from Africa with the disease, a new mosquito could bite that infected person and transmit the disease through another bite to someone else. Of course, anyone that was bitten by that final mosquito would be infected in the new locale."

Tony and Claire insisted that they hadn't been near a port and didn't know any sailors or people who had traveled from Africa. Before, those questions had seemed so irrelevant and puzzled them. Now they made sense.

"Like I said, there is no treatment for that disease, so I don't want to ponder it more. It's possible your daughter has a different illness, but I can't find any other explanation. Please get her to the hospital. I've done all I can do." He pulled out paper and began writing a note on his letterhead. It was a message for them to give to another doctor at the hospital in Joplin. He charged them nothing and wished them well as he sent them on their way.

Within the next two hours Sue Ann had died. While she was wrapped in her pink and flowered blankets, the fever had surged, and then the baby had lapsed into silence forever. At first, Claire noticed the little whimpers had stopped, then the intense heat subsided, and, at some point, Claire had sensed that the little body seemed lifeless. Putting Sue Ann lengthwise on her legs, Claire opened the covers to see and began to sob. Tony stopped the automobile and took his little girl into his arms and walked in circles, clinging to the tiny form. He, too, wept. When Claire finally had the strength to stand, she and Tony hugged each other with the child pressed between them. Claire felt a growing pressure in her head, dark and swirling confusion that shot pain into her temples. She felt a black cobweb of threads churning and tangling in her brain, humming and circling.

"I'm dizzy and can't think. And I'm scared," she gasped. Tony sat Claire down and caressed her hair. They huddled in their vehicle.

"Are you feeling better? You know, calmer and not dizzy?"

She said she was. Tony scooted to the floor and wrapped his arms around the baby and Claire's lap. Sitting at her feet, he gazed at his motionless child with the faint light that glowed into the windows from the headlights. Finally, without words, Tony went to the driver's seat and started the coupe. They drove in silence until Tony knew it was time. He had to bury his daughter somewhere before they got to St. Louis.

"Claire, like I keep trying to explain to you, this is a private matter between you and me. We don't have money to pay any undertaker or cemetery. I don't want to arrive at my Aunt and Uncle's house with my dead daughter. This job that's waiting for me is a fresh start. We don't need to begin with a funeral. It won't do Sue Ann any harm if we choose a nice wooded place for her," Tony reiterated.

Claire had offered no complaints except to say, "Tony, I guess I understand." She wiped her nose and dabbed her eyes, "Just let me hold her as long as possible."

Tony turned off Route 66 and the Packard gave a jolt as they bumped across railroad tracks. They saw thick and sprawling woods in the headlights and a narrow country road of dirt. Tony thought this seemed like the right place. Before traveling even a mile, Tony saw a particular spot he liked.

"I'm stopping here. The town of Bourbon's not far, but there's no houses here. I think the headlights will give me the light I need by shining straight into the woods at this curve. You know, to let me see enough to dig," he stated while opening his door. His feet touched the earth, but he did not get out. With his back to his family, he reached behind and found Claire's hand. He held it and wept a bit. Finally, he knew it was time, "Claire, you sit and wait while I work."

"How can you do this?" she accused. "She's only been dead for hours and you're going to put her into a hole!"

Still seated, he pulled his legs back into the Packard and turned to Claire, pulling her close to him with his right arm. With his other hand he pressed her head to his. The blanketed baby nestled between them.

"Claire, it's not easy for me. Please understand I'm in pain, too. I keep feeling my sweet little Sue Ann on my shoulders and hearing her giggle." He stopped talking for a time. He just held his wife. Then he slipped his hand from her head and pulled the child to his chest. He took his other arm from around his wife to cradle the child. "You know, I've told you how I feel. I'm a born fire fighter. That's why it was so important to me to know I could return to St. Louis and work in the fire department again. I've fought a lot of fires, and when a buddy goes down, I don't think about anything except what needs to be done. Sometimes I don't know if he's dead or not, but I just pick him up and go. I just do what I know I need to do. That's all I'm doing now." There was only pain in his voice. He placed the bundle back into Claire's arms and stepped out the door.

After getting his shovel from the back, he started walking through the leaf-covered terrain. Inside his head he was counting his paces, and when he reached fourteen (because Sue Ann was fourteen months old), he stopped and took off his coat. The ground was moist and soft, as he had hoped. *If this had been winter, the soil would've been frozen, making it impossible to dig*, he thought. Kneeling, he brushed aside thick layers of leaves and debris with his hands until he found the dark dirt. Then he stood and picked up the shovel to begin. While he dug, he deliberated to himself about the deer and squirrels that were watching him. He knew animals were there because he had hunted in Missouri with Louie enough to know. *You look over my little girl, Louie*, he demanded in his thoughts to his friend. He dug for twenty minutes and made a hole that he hoped was deep enough. He thought about dogs and wild animals. "No, I better make it deeper," he uttered out loud and continued digging.

When he returned to the automobile and opened Claire's door, they didn't speak. He took Claire's arm to guide her to the spot. They lingered for the last time as a family of three before he removed the baby from Claire's arms. He felt the stiffening effects of rigor mortis but made no comment. Without the child's weight in her arms, Claire felt a sudden emptiness and knew what it meant. She would never hold Sue Ann again. Claire crossed her arms over her chest, clutching her own shoulders, and began to cry with deep sobs. Kneeling again, Tony placed his child on the ground and opened the blanket to kiss her good-bye. Then he carefully wrapped her tightly, not wanting the dirt to touch her face, and placed the bundle down into the gaping darkness. He pushed the dirt into place with his hands until the space was filled, and then he leaned onto the mound and pressed the dirt to compact it into the hole. When it was full, he patted it flat. Finally he placed the original leaves upon the grave's top. Now he spoke in his mind to the animals—the quail, the deer, the squirrels, and wild turkeys—to be her guardian. There had been no way to avoid getting the dirt all over him. Removing his soiled shirt and using the still-clean shirt-tail, he wiped his face and hands. He stood in his undershirt unaware of the cold. A Whip-poor-will began to sound. The mournful notes circled him, spiraled around him…*whip pooor will whip pooor will whip pooor will*…as over and over the bird sang. He pulled Claire to his side, and they gazed toward the ground that held Sue Ann. When the hymn of the night stopped, unknown to the other they each gave a silent prayer.

"I don't know what to say," he whispered and his voice cracked with emotion. "Do you?" Claire shook her head with despondency. He cleared his voice, "All I can think to say is I love you, Sue Ann." They lingered, searching for more words that never came.

Soothing the silence, the Whip-poor-will began again. Tony took Claire's hand before he went to pick up his things and held it tight as he bent down to pick up his clothes, draping his coat and shirt over his shoulder. They went a few feet to get the shovel before walking to the Packard, where he lowered Claire into her seat and then just stood there, not shutting the door, wanting to do or say something. A minute passed. Finally Claire looked up at him and he collapsed into her lap, sobbing. Her hand went to caress his hair as tears rolled down her face.

After removing a change of clothes from his luggage, he donned clean clothes. They backed up, bumped over the tracks again, and started toward St. Louis on US Route 66.

Actually, they were starting toward a strange event that would take place in a few hours and under the shadows of a lamppost at 4:25 in the morning.

CHAPTER 2

While Tony and Claire were stopped at the motel in Oklahoma where Sue Ann's final fever had started, laughter and conversation had percolated in the South St. Louis neighborhood where the Bartlett family lived.

It was an Indian summer evening, and the warmth invited everyone outdoors. Later that night, clouds would drift in and drizzle, but for now neighbors wandered outside to sit on their porches or on the concrete steps with cushions, and some families put blankets onto the grass out in their small front yards. At this time of year, it was typical for St. Louis neighbors to share their weekend evenings outside, talking as dusk changed to darkness. The rising moon elicited well-deserved exclamations and some minutes of discussion. A full autumn moon in St. Louis was a sight the residents anticipated each year, and the intensity of the big, orange display never disappointed them from one year to the next.

John Bartlett had been out turning over his garden with the help of David, who would be three years old in a few months. People began to gather. The dad had a big spade and the son a little one. The garden was located in one of the empty lots across from their flat. The first neighbor came out to the sidewalk to chat while John worked, and then a few others appeared on their front stoop. It wasn't long before many families were outside, talking across porches and from one side of the street to the other.

John Bartlett had a pharmaceutical degree from the St. Louis School of Pharmacy, and he worked at a pharmacy Monday through Friday. On the weekend, he worked around the four-family flat where he lived with his family. It was near Kingshighway, the main street on the west side of town, an area referred to as "South St. Louis." On Saturday and Sunday, John was more a farmer than a pharmacist since he was always planting and pruning in the yard, making repairs in all of the four flats, as well as working in his garden across the street. Of course, he had permission to use the empty lot because his landlord owned this and another empty lot on the other corner diagonally across the street. The repair work compensated for John's free use of the lot for his garden.

The flat was a brick building and South St. Louis had hundreds, if not thousands, of four-family flats, most of which had more or less the same interior layout. The front door opened to the living room. The main bedroom was next, and then there was a short hall, with a closet and bathroom on each side, ending at a large kitchen. After the kitchen was another small room to use as the family wished. Since the Bartletts had two children, it was a bedroom.

John's wife, Ellie, was still inside stirring some navy beans that simmered with a small slab of bacon. She turned down the heat, put down the wooden spoon, and wiped her hands on her apron as she pulled it off, catching the straps in her short brown wavy hair, which instantly bounced back into place. She went to the door that led from the kitchen and opened it, first glancing toward the back door, which led to the outside, then peering up the steps to the second-floor neighbor's flat, and finally walking out the door to look on the landing that went down to the basement. At last she caught sight of Elizabeth, her sixteen-month-old, who was playing on the landing with an older neighbor child and a kitten.

"Come now, girls. Let's go sit out in front for a bit," she coaxed while hanging the apron behind the kitchen door. As Ellie walked through the hall, she picked up a diaper and towel. Elizabeth had been walking for three months and was close behind her mother's footsteps. "Let's change that diaper before we go out," Ellie said as she knelt to spread the towel onto the carpet. She scooped Elizabeth into her arms with a "Gotcha" and buried her face in the child's tummy. The baby giggled and dropped her ball.

"Bobo, Bobo," Elizabeth exclaimed with worry while stretching her hands toward the rolling ball.

"Oh, your Bobo isn't going anywhere," Ellie chided while reaching for the ball. "Here he is." Then, Ellie took the face on the ball, turned it right-side-up, and began speaking in a squeaky cockney voice as if the ball were irritated, "Whydah drop me? That hurt! You gotta be more careful or I might just bounce out of the house and down the street to find a new little girl. Now fix me hat and give me a kiss." With that, Ellie pretended to straighten the red stocking cap on his head and give him a pat. As she kissed a rosy cheek her lips felt the slight texture of the rubber ball. There was a bump that formed a little nose and a crease for the cuff to the cap with 'BOBO' printed on it. She beamed at the ball, and then at Elizabeth, who listened wide-eyed to the sound of her mother mimicking the ball with a boy face.

"Come, come now, Bobo needs a kiss," she said to her daughter as she put the ball into the little pudgy arms. Elizabeth kissed him and began to look closely at Bobo as Ellie removed the diaper and tossed it toward the bathroom door. On went the new one with the expertise that comes with a second child.

Stepping through the front door, Ellie could hear John's discussion, which didn't interrupt one stroke of his spade. "Well, sales are fair. I can't complain. The owner asked me to start to build up a stock of items for Christmas gifts, hoping to improve the sales. You know, some toys, colognes in fancy boxes, cheap costume jewelry, and things like that. Drugstores selling simply medicines can't support two families nowadays. Got to be a little creative and..."

"Hey, Ellie," someone shouted, "didn't I say that Al Capone wouldn't stay in prison long? You did see today's *Post-Dispatch*, didn't you? It's right on the front page. There's a picture of Scarface comin' out the prison door with his hat in his hand and the biggest smile on his face. That was the shortest ten-year sentence I ever heard of.[1] When was that they sent him up for tax evasion?"

"Last May," someone called out from across the street.

Someone else wanted to know, "That's not even ten months, much less ten years! How can they do that?"

Ellie spread the towel and sat on the bottom step as she stood Elizabeth on the ground. The other little girl that had come outside with them had already departed to the vacant lot opposite the garden, where the cries and squeals of children unfurled in the air above the two-to three-foot grasses and weeds that hid them from view.

"Capone said that he was imprisoned illegally because the statute of limitations had run out in his case. I bet some lawyer probably got a big savings account overnight from good ol' Scarface."

"Did you see the column right next to Capone's picture? Right here in St. Louis, that bootlegger Grady Barnwell was arrested for 'spending too much money.'"

"What are you talking about?" asked Ellie about the confusing statement.

"Oh, they been watching Barnwell because he didn't pay his income tax for two years. When they saw him spending money that he claimed he didn't have, they moved in and arrested him. They got him with $1,927 in his pockets and a grand in the safe back at the hotel where he was staying. The *Post-Dispatch* said that when they impounded all the money from his savings and other hiding places, it was more than $12,000." Laughing, the neighbor continued, "They seized a new shiny Ford coupe, too. When the arresting detectives asked him where he got the money, he told them from his bookmaking enterprise. 'Some bootlegging, too?' they asked, and he told them 'A little.' Can you believe that?"

"He probably won't even get a month in jail. I'd like to see them get their comeuppance. These gangsters have connections and ways," someone grumbled with disgust. "They're taking over the country. The papers are filled with murders, kidnappings, bribing, swindling—just crime, crime, crime."

As the adults continued talking, there was more laughter and shouts from the neighborhood children's play. The carefree "Ollie, Ollie come home free" chant of hide-and-seek intermingled in the air with the intense discussions of their parents but didn't even diminish, much less stop, the serious and often fervent ideas that were being shared.

Interestingly, no one talked about the elections or politics. Although all the votes hadn't been counted, they knew Hoover was out. It was a sure win for FDR. With the rate of unemployment in St. Louis at 24%, people were disenchanted with politics. So the newspapers were filled with crime stories like the stories being told this quiet evening among neighbors. People knew that crime was prevalent and too close to home.

The coming changes in liquor laws dominated the conversation with some neighbors. "Hey, remember what they used to say about St. Louis? 'First in booze, first in shoes…' If we can start producing liquor again, do you think we can be the best again?" one of the neighbors inquired. "I read that on December the eighth, liquor would be legal again in the state of Washington."

For St. Louis, the home of the Anheuser Busch Brewing Company, this was good news. If Missouri were to change the prohibition laws, it would mean jobs—a lot of jobs.

Another neighbor quipped, "You forgot a part of that catchy little phrase. It goes, 'First in booze, first in shoes, and last in the American League.' Is that the status you're talking about? The Browns gave us that bad image. Now, if you mean just the shoes and booze, yeah, we should be tops in the country again."

"Yeah, remember back in '26 when the Cardinals won both the pennant and World Series? We even won over Babe Ruth! We showed those New York Yankees. Then last year we took the World Series again and the pennant the year before that. We could be first again."

The Cardinals made the St. Louis public proud—that, and the image of producing beer. They longed for those days again.

Tonight there were some people drinking a soft drink called *BEVO,* produced by Anheuser Busch. The brewery was also producing yeast in an attempt to stay afloat during these dry years—a bit embarrassing to the people of St. Louis. So the end of prohibition was of interest to the folks in this city. Soon the discussion changed to the same topic that had been discussed whenever and wherever people got together now. Not only here in St. Louis, but everywhere in the United States, at least for the last eight and one half months. Kidnapping!

Ellie saw her son David coming across the street. "Mommy, my Ha'ween cape, I want it," he demanded as he dropped his spade in front of her.

"It's in your closet," Ellie said while stuffing David's shirt into his knickers. "You can go find your cape. I'm trying to talk with the neighbors."

A friend of Ellie, living in the upstairs flat, declared, "Oh, don't even mention kidnappings. Why, ever since that poor child of the Lindberghs was snatched, it's on the front page every day, and it happened in March. They found that little babe dead in May, and it's still in the newspapers!"

"Bessie, I know what you mean," agreed the lady next door. "It hurts me so much to think about the Lindberghs. They've had so much suffering, but it isn't them alone. I read months ago that there have been over two thousand kidnappings for ransom in the last two years. Can you imagine?"

"Hogwash!" Bessie replied. "That there's the newspapers' sensationalism. They went lookin' for stories to write about kidnapping when there was no news in the Lindbergh case. Why, they probably manufactured some."

"Don't say that!" Ellie insisted. "Though it may be true, we can't assume it. We have to believe in the truth and freedom of the press. Even before the Lindbergh baby was kidnapped, didn't our own St. Louis representative, John Cockran, introduce a bill? He did it because there's too many kidnappings happening across the country. It's real. Have you read the bill?"

"Well, I don't quite remember," Bessie replied with a puzzled look.

David came out in his flowing cape. Ellie walked David and Elizabeth over to the vacant lot. David leaned down and talked to his sister in a sweet manner before running off with the other children. Elizabeth ran after him, clutching her ball and giggling.

Ellie returned to the steps. She listened awhile to her neighbors before continuing her discussion. "About Cockran's bill, the idea is, if kidnappers send the blackmail letter by U.S. mail or if they transport a kidnapped victim across a state line, they'd be committing a felony. The legislators want them to get the death penalty. I feel the papers write to let us know how serious kidnapping is," Ellie explained.

"Yeah, Ellie is right. There are too many examples for it not to be the truth about the thousands of kidnappings. It's not only children either. Did you see that Col. Raymond Robins was found today after being gone for two months? You know, he's that Prohibition crusader who was on the way to see President Hoover when he disappeared. They say he's the victim of amnesia, but it makes sense that somebody snatched him because they didn't want him crusading for Prohibition now that we are almost shuttin' it down."

"Gertrude," Ellie admonished, "there is no proof that he was kidnapped and there was never a ransom request.

Bessie lamented, "It's the kidnapped children that's so upsetting. Thank goodness they found that 11-year-old boy, Jimmie De Jute. Can you imagine being kept in a secret tunnel in that abandoned place? The police said they got a tip as to where the boy was. Those crooks are even crooks to each other."

"Obviously we mostly read about the children that are found. I wonder how many unsolved kidnapping are never put into the papers," Ellie expressed more or less to herself. She had a far-away look on her face. "Think of all those poor children that are never found or found dead."

The conversation paused. Everyone was thinking about the Lindbergh kidnapping case and their faces turned pensive.

"You know, I'm not rich or anything, but I'm scared that someone might kidnap my boy. I worry at night when I lay down to sleep," Gertrude confessed.

"I have nightmares about all this crime," Bessie confided.

Ellie had nightmares too, but she said nothing.

One of the older children approached Ellie with Elizabeth in his arms. Carefully the boy passed the baby to her, explaining that she had fallen to sleep in some of the trampled grasses so he picked her up. Ellie didn't notice that Bobo had been left behind as she cuddled her daughter. Ellie pulled out the towel on which she had been sitting and flipped it over her shoulder to cover herself as she opened the buttons down the front of her dress for Elizabeth to nurse.

It was getting late and John stopped working on his gardening and crossed the street to join the others, but the conversations were finished. The neighbors started saying their good nights and going in. John sat down on the steps and Ellie passed the baby to him. Slipping off her tiny shoes, he rubbed her little feet. Half-asleep, Elizabeth murmured, "Bye, Bye, Daddy?" That was an expected question because she always wanted to go 'bye-bye' in her daddy's auto.

John whispered into her ear, "Tomorrow, Honey, it's time for bed now. When you wake up we can go for a ride."

As John started to the vacant lot to get his son, Ellie took Elizabeth from his arms and went into the flat.

"Winkie?" the child said and Ellie knew, even though it was late, she could not skip the nightly ritual of reading the poem, *Wynken, Blynken, and Nod.* Elizabeth was a child who needed more security than other children did. The poem was part of her security. Bobo was another form of security.

Ellie quickly bathed Elizabeth and slipped on her yellow nightgown with Grandmother's hand-crocheted bodice. There was a row of pink rosebuds where the crocheted bodice met the cotton skirt. The child looked like a doll. Out came the book and before Ellie opened it she began speaking from memory:

Wynken, Blynken and Nod one night
Sailed off in a wooden shoe—
Sailed on a river of crystal light,
Into a sea of dew.

In went the thumb, and Elizabeth snuggled into her mother's bosom and closed her eyes.

"Where are you going, and what do you wish?"
The old moon asked the three.
"We have come to fish for the herring fish
That live in this beautiful sea;
Nets of silver and gold have we!"
Said Wynken,
Blynken,
And Nod.

The poem drifted into the stillness of the room and comforted the mother, too. She had become tense from the discussions outside. It was a short poem of four stanzas, but the child was asleep before the end of the first. Ellie didn't finish the poem. Carefully she placed Elizabeth into her own bed. As she passed through the kitchen she turned off the beans and heard John helping David in the bathroom so she knew she could slip into bed right away, though she didn't find the opportunity inviting. So, she sat to darn some socks.

John finished his shower and was asleep in minutes. When Ellie finally went to bed, she knew that her headwork would begin, expand, and evolve into scenes at the Lindbergh house on the night of the kidnapping. She had no control over these thoughts, which came nearly every night. She knew this happened to her because Anne had been her friend. Ellie had read everything in the newspaper and clipped many articles for her scrapbook. How annoying it was when the press referred to Anne Morrow as "Lindbergh's wife" or "the dead child's mother." They rarely used her name. Although Ellie was imagining much of the ordeal of the kidnapping and surmising what had occurred in the days that followed, the mental scenes of Anne were so vivid that Ellie felt she had been there. The pain never seemed to lessen over time; six months ago the child had been found dead and still the police had made no arrest.

"I shouldn't have talked so much tonight about all this. It makes it worse for me," she chastised herself while pulling her dark hair away from her forehead and catching it with a clip to set a wave.

On one of the Lindberghs trips to St. Louis, Ellie had met Anne Morrow in a St. Louis department store. It was in the fabric department of Stix, Baer, and Fuller, at the remnant table. Unknowingly, they each took ends of the same piece of cloth. Gradually, they began to accumulate the fabric from the jumble of material. It was like a comic scene in a silent movie as they pulled, unwound, and folded their hounds-tooth wool until they were face to face. They looked at each other and without hesitation Anne admitted to Ellie, "My! You have fine taste," and they laughed. After a few calculations they agreed there was enough for both. They paid the bill and walked out together.

"Would you like to have a bite to eat with me at the Forum Cafeteria?" Ellie asked and initiated an enduring friendship. Right away, they found excitement in conversation. Their talk wasn't of recipes or housework. Anne rambled on about flying—the thrill, the addiction, new types of planes, and record-breaking flights by women like Amy Johnson. Ellie complained of the courts, laws, and lack of interest that most women have in important topics—politics, sports, and books. With each other, they discussed topics most women didn't and expressed opinions most women wouldn't. And each loved writing her ideas on paper as well as talking. It was a fulfilling friendship.

In the early thirties Anne and Charles Lindbergh could find no privacy; the press was always in pursuit. All the pleasure of a casual time with friends vanished with the flash of press cameras. Anne had written to Ellie long before the kidnapping and told her of the 500-acre retreat that they had bought. This was where the kidnapping had occurred. It was located in Sourland Mountain near Hopewell, New Jersey, and Anne had commented that the swamps and thickly forested terrain made Charles feel secluded and safe. She wrote:

Dearest Ellie,

We are here at our estate that is called Eagle's Nest. It's a mere 90 miles from New York, but I find it to be too isolated. This place is really like living in a nest of an eagle because it's so secluded; I'm in a land of loneliness. The only access is a winding dirt road through the thickly forested hills and swamps of Sourland Mountain. (The name is appropriate because I feel stuck in a jar like a sour pickle.) But Charles is so happy here; how can I deny him some moments of peace and comfort? He plays with Buster constantly when we are here.

Mr. and Mrs. Wheatley who care for the house are so kind and try to make our weekends quiet and comfortable. I really shouldn't com-

plain. Thank you, dear friend, for listening because I have no one else
with whom I can share.
Anne

Then Anne had sketched a layout of the ten-room, two-story structure for
Ellie to picture what the house was like.

— —

While lying in bed, Ellie could see the scene of the kidnapping. Her impressions were so vivid that it seemed to be happening at that moment. In the process
of approaching sleep, Ellie's mind began to mix reality with imagination.

*It was March first of this year, 1932. Anne and the nurse, Betty Gow, were
walking with the baby to the nursery in the right wing of the house. Betty
hummed softly and rocked the baby, who was soon to be asleep. It was 7:30 on a
Tuesday evening. The baby, Charles Jr., who was called "Buster" by his father, had
a cold and had been a bit irritable. Betty bent over and gently placed the 20-
month-old baby into his crib. Outside, a dark shadow of a man was at the edge of
the woods looking up at the lit window of the nursery. The two women whispered
above the crib for a while as they peered fondly at the little sleeping child. Anne
said, "Betty, why don't you stay a while to make sure he's sound asleep?"*

*After 25 minutes, Betty rose from her chair and opened the window just a crack
for some ventilation and then turned out the light as she left the room. The wind
was howling that night and the shutter outside the window creaked because it was
warped and could not be latched properly. The man began creeping up toward the
stone estate as Betty descended the stairs to relax awhile. His progress across the
100 feet of lawn was slow because of the weight from the three ladders he carried.*

*"T'was just like theys said: the little one goes to bed rights about now, I only
needs to watch for the light to go out," he muttered to himself. He was wet from
the knees down and his shoes were heavily muddied from the trek through the
woods and swamps. The wind chilled him and after he placed his load quietly on
the ground, he rubbed his arms rapidly to warm himself. Then he pulled a ball of
twine from his pocket and began to lash the three ladders end to end, two at a
time. It was more than twenty feet up to the windowsill, and he could see now that
he had calculated a sufficient length with three ladders. The twine frequently
broke and he cursed under his breath in his native tongue.*

He had difficulties raising the wobbly ladder to a standing position…

Ellie made an adjustment in her mind and put another man into her
dream—someone to help carry the ladder to the house and, afterwards, to

carry it away when there would be an additional thirty-pound child with them. Yes, someone to steady the ladder from below, too.

This decided in her subconscious, she continued with her dream.

Now the ladder was vertical and the two men tried to ease it to the wall without a noise, but they failed with a **thump.**

Ellie's dream stopped and she sat up in bed. "I heard the *thump.* I really heard it!" she was thinking. And she was right, there had been a *thump* in her home, but she wouldn't know what had caused it or why she had heard it until morning. In her drowsiness she dismissed the sound.

"Oh, why can't I forget this kidnapping? When are all these thoughts going to stop? I keep reconstructing the crime, analyzing the facts, and for what?" she whispered aloud to herself as she turned over in bed. She tried to think of something else and drifted into a light sleep. The scene returned exactly where it had stopped with the *thump,* and like a paralyzed person trapped in a body that cannot be controlled and a mind that will not rest, she could not awaken herself though she wasn't completely asleep.

A man began to ascend and Ellie could see that these ladders were newly constructed, with each rung expertly inserted into the boards that ran vertically on the sides. He reached the top and stopped to listen, slowly pulling the shutter open and raising the window without a sound. As he lowered himself into the room he reached for the chisel in his tattered coat pocket. He was no fool. He knew he couldn't try to take this child without him crying. Also, there was the family Scotch terrier that was going to bark if even a slight sound transpired. He approached the crib, leaving muddy footprints with each step. He didn't care about that. What was important was to make no noise. He lifted his arm high to get one good blow to the skull.

Some nights Ellie would think that he wanted to knock the baby out, but tonight she knew he contrived to kill.

One good blow and no blood. Done! The skull was cracked behind the baby's ear. Grabbing the lifeless bundle and the blanket, he stopped to replace the chisel into his pocket, and he fumbled with another pocket to find the ransom note. Out of the window he climbed, placing the note on the inside windowsill, and then he carefully closed the window. Ellie could see the dark figure descending when suddenly a rung on the ladder cracked, and he fell to the ground on top of his buddy who was at the base. He did not notice the chisel falling from his pocket. Curses were exchanged between the two in whispered anger. As he picked himself up his eyes searched to the right and then left because, with the noise of the fall, he wanted to see if someone was approaching. They left the child where the fall had placed him—curled on his side with one pudgy arm flung over his muddied face. The two men lowered the ladder and silently began to unravel the twine from the wood while winding it back into a ball.

Finally one asked, "Wot took you so long?"

The other replied, "Oh, shad up!" That was the last comment before they struggled across the grounds again with the three ladders and the limp child. As they entered the wooded shadows one ordered the other, "Stash dem ladders gut. I'm going ahead mit me load."

Just then, lights began to sweep across them and they dove to the ground. They heard the motor of a vehicle approaching the house and lights passed over them, beaming out across the lawn and onto the driveway. Col. Charles Lindbergh was arriving home. Since the driveway passed on the same side of the house directly below the nursery, they could have been seen had the motorcar arrived minutes earlier. It was 8:20 PM, only 20 minutes since the nurse had put the baby to bed.

They didn't move for two minutes. Then the first man jumped up and grabbed the child. "Git outa here quick," he barked to the other as he disappeared into the darkness, going south through the woods.

"Hello Darling," Anne said to Lindy as he removed his coat and bent to kiss her. "Let's eat; I'm so famished. Mrs. Wheatley has our dinner ready."

"Sure, I just want to relax," he replied as he grabbed her hands and pulled her up to stand against him. Another kiss and she slipped under his arm with a giggle and pulled him toward the dining room. "How's Buster doing?" he asked.

"He's better," she said, picking up a small bell and creating a soft tinkling as Charles went toward the fireplace. "You were right to have us stay here a few more days and not return. This weather is horrible! The wind doesn't stop."

He poked at the fire and she continued, "There are 65 mile-an-hour gusts out there. Little Charles doesn't have a runny nose anymore and is sleeping. Come, let's eat." The door opened from the kitchen and the butler entered. "Ollie would you please serve dinner now."

"Yes, ma'am," Mr. Wheatley replied and turned toward the kitchen to tell his wife, the cook, that they were ready to eat.

They ate slowly and talked and laughed. Then both decided to read a bit by the fire in the living room. About 10:00 PM. Anne rose from the sofa to say, "Darling I'll be in our room." She walked to their bedroom on the first floor. While preparing for bed she remembered that she left the toothpaste up in Buster's room so she went upstairs. Quietly she entered the nursery without a light and picked up the toothpaste from where she had left it. She turned to leave. If I look at him he'll sense me and awaken, she imagined while she crept out silently and returned to her room.

At 10:30 PM. Betty went up to check on Little Charles. The room was dark, but the light from the open door allowed sufficient illumination to see. Peering into the empty crib she concluded that the baby must have cried and Anne, upon hearing, had taken him downstairs. But she decided to verify that idea. She arrived to see her mistress alone. "Has Col. Lindbergh taken Buster?" she asked.

A fear passed over Anne instantly. Anne's hand went to her belly as if to verify that the unborn child within was safe. And before the response of "Why, I don't know!" passed from Anne's lips, Betty had turned to run toward the room where the father was sitting. She had seen the fear in Anne's eyes. The father was alone!

"Buster's missing, sir!" The three of them were dumfounded, and their hearts began to quicken. Their faces went ashen, and the scene froze into their minds forever. Then, as Lindbergh jumped up and rushed to a closet for a rifle, Betty went to the kitchen to inform the Wheatleys. Anne returned to the bedroom to dress again and heard a cry outside. Immediately she went to the window. It seemed to come from the area of the woodpile. She shouted, "Lindy, Lindy I heard a cry!" It turned out to be nothing when Lindbergh went outside to check the area. Maybe she heard a cry of the wind or the cry from her heart because, though they didn't know, the kidnappers had left long ago.

Confusion and panic were forming a dreary grayness over the Sourland Mountain home, and it would continue to darken in the coming months.

In Ellie's dream she had watched the kidnappers as they ran quickly and silently through the moist, leaf-covered ground that muffled their footfalls.

After a mile they slowed. "Ya goin' the right way?"

"Ja," the other replied. Soon they came to a road, proceeded to a waiting vehicle, and drove away.

They traveled almost five miles farther from the home going past Hopewell, New Jersey. "This is a gut place," the one said at a deserted dark area of the road. They got out and headed toward the woods with the blanket-bundled child. They walked a few feet from the road. "You watch die road!" Then the killer lowered himself down on a knee and started to remove the child's nightclothes. He even took the pins from the diaper and left the child with only his undershirt. Carelessly wrapping him back into his little blanket, he dropped Buster face down into a ditch and kicked some dirt and debris over him. Then he stepped on top of the child and dirt to press it all down. Neither of the two even winced at this. "Ain't this too close to that road?" the other asked. "Nein," he replied while kicking some more debris on top, "let's go."

These two dark, faceless beings didn't wince, but Ellie created a low, throaty groan at the vision of him stomping on the body of her friend's first-born child. Ellie rolled into a fetal position and woke herself. Tears coursed across the ridge of her nose and dripped into the sheets. Her ardent devotion to her friend caused her insides to react. She was nauseous and her mind wouldn't stop analyzing. She questioned, *How did they know the Lindbergh family was going to stay two additional nights at their Sourland Mountain home? They had to know or why would they have come prepared with ladders for the kidnapping on a Tuesday evening when the Lindberghs usually only stayed the weekend?*

The dog always slept outside the child's door? Why was the dog in the kitchen this particular evening?

The footprints showed that the kidnappers went directly to the area below the nursery. How did they know where the child slept?

Why was the only warped shutter in the house the one on the nursery window? On such a windy night and with a sick child, why was the window opened for ventilation?

None of these questions would ever be answered, even when the police arrested a man for the kidnapping two years later, in 1934.

Ellie fell asleep again and finally slept profoundly as the dream became a surreal, nonsensical vision.

She saw Col. Charles Lindbergh searching the grounds with a rifle and slowly he transformed. His arms stretched out, and as he lifted into the air, arms became wings. His body elongated and smoothed into the shape of a gleaming metal airplane with his feet becoming an upside-down tail. His head and face remained in relief form on the silver surface and he

Sailed on a river of crystal light,
Into a sea of dew.

He glided above the trees searching for his son. The airplane was flexible while dipping and curling in and out of the woods as the father's face peered beneath the trees. It was a smooth metallic figure silently passing over the entire 550 acres of their Sourland Mountain estate. He circled completely and returned over the house that was ablaze with lights. Suddenly a large, glowing white ball rolled out the front door of the mansion. It seemed to be made of a wispy, diaphanous gauze material that billowed with each turn while it rolled around and around the house. Then Ellie saw that the ball was Anne because a face appeared as the ball turned and a trail of tears was beginning to make a creek along the woods. Anne was saying something. At first Ellie couldn't understand but then she heard, "Where's Buster? Where's Bobo? Buster, Bobo, Buster...?" On and on Anne rolled and chanted.

In Ellie's subconscious mind she suddenly realized that Bobo didn't come back with little Elizabeth when the neighbor boy brought the sleepy child from the lot. Regretfully the idea of a lost Bobo held no fears for Ellie, so she didn't awaken from her nightmare. If she had understood what had caused the *thump* and had realized the importance of finding Bobo, everything would have turned out differently.

CHAPTER 3

A little over an hour after Tony and Claire had buried their Little Sue Ann in the woods near Bourbon, Missouri, they checked into a cheap motel on Chippewa Street in St. Louis. Claire had fallen asleep during the drive and barely woke as she walked from the automobile into the stuffy room. She would have no memory of Tony undressing her and lovingly slipping her under the sheets.

After fifteen minutes of trying to sleep, Tony rose and dressed again. Grabbing his felt hat and topcoat, he peered back at his sweet wife, sleeping so soundly, and then tiptoed out the door. It wasn't cold. The air felt pleasantly crisp and smelled of the mums planted near the motel door. He gave a tug to the brim of his hat to block the bright moonlight and lit a cigarette before deciding to drive around to see his hometown. With the turn of the key, he pulled out the throttle and started the Packard. No thought was given to where he was going, so he continued down Chippewa and randomly turned left onto a sedate residential street before reaching the large thoroughfare, Kingshighway Boulevard. Unconsciously, he rolled the window closed, not to stop the wind, but to try to block the thoughts of his Sue Ann that seemed to blow in with the breeze. After several blocks, he saw two vacant lots and parked between them. He got out and looked around, noticing a garden in one lot. All was silent except for crickets and a whooshing sound made by the withered Queen Anne's lace, swaying mullein, and tall dry grasses. Shadows of the plants danced on the sidewalk. Tony walked to the passenger side of the coupe, opened the door, and collapsed onto the seat, sighing deeply as he put an elbow on each knee and let his head drop into his hands. He stared at his feet. Dead grass jutted from a crack in the sidewalk where his shoes rested. When he noticed some dirt from the gravesite on his shoes, tears rolled down his cheeks and trickled through the stubble of his beard. He passed his hand through his hair several times before standing. There was a soothing rustle coming from the grasses bending in the breeze. He went to light another cigarette and the sharp, raspy sound of the match startled the crickets into momentary silence. Smoking, Tony sauntered up to the corner.

It was 4:15 AM.

After leaning awhile on the lamppost, Tony turned to stroll back toward the coupe, and even though he was deep in thought, he heard a new sound. Glancing up, vaguely he saw discernable movements in the lot. Not at all concerned and figuring it was a field mouse, his eyes turned to watch his own shadow moving ahead of him, a bit distorted by the sidewalk cracks. He stopped his walking and thought no, that the movement seemed like it had been caused by something bigger than even a rat. Flipping his cigarette to the sidewalk, his eyes scanned the grasses in the vacant lot while using his shoe to rub out the glowing stub. Again he noticed the odors of autumn flowers and dried leaves, as well as a bitter weed smell, and he reminisced how typical a fall night in St. Louis this was, with its soft intermittent breezes and night insects. Never taking his gaze from the grasses in the lot, though his mind wandered elsewhere, he saw movement again! There was no doubt. It was definitely something progressing though the lot and heading toward his Packard.

"Might be a cat," he said under his breath just as Elizabeth stepped out onto the sidewalk, dragging one end of her blanket.

Delicate blonde curls and wide, blue eyes peered at him as she inquired, "Bye-bye?" She was a cherub. With not enough room to wad all her yellow blanket into her arms, an end was left dangling on the ground while both her hands clutched the ball, Bobo. Again she looked directly at Tony and questioned, "Dada, bye-bye?" Approaching the open door without hesitation, she put her ball and blanket onto the seat before she struggled with her nightgown to climb up with her treasures.

The scene transfixed Tony as he watched her—movement-by-movement—climbing onto the seat, turning to situate herself, picking up her blanket to place it on her lap, and finally reaching for her ball. It slipped! Bobo rolled from the seat onto the sidewalk.

Strange sensations surged through Tony as the ball bounced toward his feet. He felt heady from the whole scene, and from the thoughts of what he'd done earlier that night—both unrealistic events, perplexing his sleep-deprived mind. Though confused, he automatically reacted by bending down to stop the ball from rolling into the gutter. He handed it back to the child. To him, his movements seemed dreamlike. He found himself feeling subtly different, not the same man he was yesterday. He felt dazed.

Elizabeth placed the ball on top the blanket on her lap. "Bobo," she proclaimed as she introduced Tony to her ball. "Go, bye-bye," she commanded in definite terms.

Ten minutes earlier, Elizabeth had awakened in her bedroom with curtains blowing to create familiar shadows on the walls and ceiling. She watched the ballet upon the walls as her dimpled fingers searched her bed until she remembered that she had taken her Bobo into the lot last night. She confidently arose, carefully pulled her blanket up into her arms, so as not to stumble, and proceeded to the back door in the kitchen. Her size, of course, prevented any reach to the doorknobs, but there was a swinging dog door in the screen that she frequently used. Out she went!

"*Thump,*" went the door as she passed into the pleasant night air.

Once outside, Elizabeth scooted down the steps on her bottom, slowly and carefully, and then crossed the subdued street to the lot.

She entered the tall grasses and followed the trampled path made earlier by all the children. She knew exactly where to go to find her ball. After picking up the ball, she saw the coupe sitting with the open door. Remembering that her father had promised that she could go for a ride when she awoke, she proceeded toward the Packard. It looked much like her father's automobile. She was never shy, always outgoing and gregarious. Nor was she apprehensive of strangers. When she reached the sidewalk, she emerged into the streetlight and into Tony's view.

In the future, Claire would wonder what had occurred in Tony's mind when the child had emerged from the grasses in that lot. Were there no lights, no movement, no sounds in the neighborhood to indicate where she had come from? Did he think to go knocking on doors to find where this little girl belonged? Did he think about contacting the police to handle the situation? Or Claire would worry, Was he in such distress from the incidents of the prior twenty-four hours that he concluded that she truly was an angel sent to him to ease his pains?

Tony had told Claire as many of the details as he could remember, but she puzzled over what he could have been thinking when the child looked directly at him and said "Dada, bye-bye." Maybe, even with the lamppost, it was too dark for the child to see Tony clearly, and he looked like her father. Did Tony wonder that his coupe looked like her father's automobile? Or that a neighbor might often take her for a ride so she was used to riding in anyone's automobile? Was Tony thinking about how much she looked like Sue Ann? Did he notice that she seemed to be the same age and height? Was he thinking of me? Was he thinking of how I was in anguish with Sue Ann's death and would continue to suffer in the coming days and months? Did he conclude it was a miracle? Fate? Some greater power that was making amends for taking his little girl?

There were days when Claire would ponder other kinds of questions. She'd pick up a newspaper to read and her mind would start with the questions again. Did he realize how common it had been lately to read about abductions and kidnappings in the newspapers? Perhaps, when he read and heard how many people had been disappearing, it seemed like a normal event. Would he consider that this was not a kidnapping since the child walked of her own accord into his life and crawled into his auto? Did his mind make some kind of excuse that this was different since there was no plan for a ransom? Did he think about the fact that we had no photos of Sue Ann that were taken close enough to see that this was a different child? Did he decide that his Aunt and Uncle would accept this child as Sue Ann because they had never seen her or a photo? Did he hesitate at all?

In the future, she would want to talk to Tony about all this, but knew from experience that he'd just walk away saying, "I don't want to talk about this."

Finally Claire would ask herself if she was at fault, too? At that moment, her heart took a jump. She dropped her head back and looked up into the air while stifling a sob and realized, "Yes, I was." The pain that they had caused this other mother seemed justifiable to ease her pain. She remembered thinking, "What difference did it make for one mother or another to suffer?"

One will never know what really was going through Tony's mind when little Elizabeth began to insist on going. As the child repeated her want again and again and then began to cry, he closed the passenger door and walked around to the driver's seat. He started the engine and pulled away.

It was 4:25 AM.

Before they had passed the second block, the soft blond curls had come to rest on his thigh, her thumb had gone into her mouth, and she had passed into sleep. His heart melted with the tenderness this child gave to him, the normal father-daughter interaction. His hand touched her hair and a warm sensation passed through him.

No one will ever know if he considered everything or nothing or just reacted. He'd never explain to Claire what he had been thinking. He had told her what had happened, but not what thoughts were in his head. And Claire would accept his silence, never asking.

Actually, he wasn't worrying about his decision as he drove away. Once a decision was made to enter a flaming building, he never stood in the flames and worried why he went into the fire. No, once he decided how to progress, how to continue, he went. Somewhere in the depths of his mind he knew, "No one will ever know that I'm driving away with this little girl." And he was more or less right. No one would know for nearly two decades.

SCRAPBOOK

BY

Ellie Bartlett
1932

ST. LOUIS HERALD NEWS

ST. LOUIS, WEDNESDAY, MARCH 2, 1932

POLICE SAY NO CLEW TO WHEREABOUTS OF LINDBERGH BABY

Our Congressman Has Submitted Measures to Help Prevent Kidnapings Like the Lindbergh's

Congressman Cochran Points Out His Measures Would Aid in Hunt for Lindbergh Abductors

Staff Correspondent
WASHINGTON, March 2—With the proposed bills by Congressman John J. Cochran of St.Louis, there will be a greater penalty in hopes to prevent crimes like the Lindbergh kidnapping. In the one proposed measure it is a Federal Crime to transport a kidnapped person across state lines and the maximum penalty for this crime would be death. In the other measure, if the U.S. Postal services are used for mailing ransom notes or any material related to the incident, then the crime is considered a felony.

When questioned about his bills, Congressman Cochran pointed out that it is regretful that a crime such as the Lindbergh kidnaping happened before these bills were enacted. He hopes that it is apparent the need for laws to deter another such crime.

LOCATION OF LINDBERGH ESTATE DEEP IN SOURLAND MOUNTAINS

Private Landing Field Located Next to Home on 550-Acre Site

HOPEWELL, N.J., March 2—It is not easy to get through the muddy country roads to the Lindbergh's home deep in the Sourland Mountains of New Jersey. The seclusion of the Lindbergh Estate made it an ideal place for the undetected approach of the kidnapers. There is evidence of a ladder being used to enter the child's second story bedroom, giving police reason to suspect that the kidnapers must have driven close to the home, though no vehicles were heard.

The ransom note demanding $50,000 was left in the baby's bedroom. This note was poorly written with many misspellings and contained a special symbol that was designated to be the kidnaper's "singnature." The Lindbergh's were told in the note that only this signature would identify the real kidnapers. The drawing they called the "singnature" was two blue ovals that overlapped with red coloring in the space where they met.

LINDBERGH PAYS $50,000 RANSOM BUT IT WAS HOAX

By the Associated Press.
NEW YORK, March 4. The kidnapers made contact and said the Lindbergh baby was on a boat, but after turning over the ransom money and spending hours searching, it appears to have been a hoax.

Col. Charles Lindbergh made the decision to no longer work with the police. He asked them to leave the site of investigation at his home on Sourland Mountain. There have been many letters and telephone calls received from people claiming to have the child. Col. Lindbergh stated that he wants to make all contacts personally with the abductors. The Lindberghs appealed to anyone who may know of any detail about their baby. He weighs 30 pounds, has blond curls, blue eyes, and is two feet nine inches tall.

The Lindbergh Estate, inside and outside, has been teeming with police, detectives, and investigators of all ranks since the kidnapping occurred two days ago on March 2. Col. Lindbergh asked them to leave when he decided that he could conduct the investigation better.

LINDBERGH BABY FOUND DEAD

Over Two Months Ago the Child was Kidnaped From His Home in New Jersey

HOPEWELL, N.J., May 12, 1932
Late today a formal announcement was made by Governor A. Harry Moore of New Jersey that the body of the missing son of Col. and Mrs. Charles A. Lindbergh had been found.

A 46-year-old trucker named William Allen stopped beside the road. He was within sight of the distant Sourland Mountain home. He saw something strange in a shallow ditch near where he stood. Some accounts say he saw a child's hand, others state that he saw the skull and one newspaper quotes him to say that he saw a foot. He walked over to the place and with the toe of his shoe uncovered the child. He called the police immediately. In the two and one-half months since the abduction, the child's body had deteriorated beyond recognition. The normal ways of animals in the wild possibly had contributed to this and had uncovered the body enough to be seen by the trucker.

The father insisted on seeing his son and identified the remains mainly by the curls of the hair and the baby's teeth. At this time, it appears the child was struck on the head and killed on the night of the kidnaping.

NO CLEWS IN DISAPPEARANCE OF 16-MONTH-OLD CHILD

================

ST. LOUIS, MISSOURI, November 10, 1932
The police were notified about the disappearance of a 16-month-old child. The police are withholding the child's name for protection. No contact, as a ransom note or telephone calls, have been made by kidnapers at this time.

Detective Wm. Grant said that they have questioned everyone in the neighborhood, searched for open holes, or places where she might be stuck. Nothing was seen or heard except the mother said she heard a *thump* during the night.

The child is a sixteen months old, blonde haired, blue-eyed girl and she might have a toy ball that is a head of a little boy in a red cap with the name 'Bobo' on it.

Please call the St. Louis Police Department and ask for Detective Grant if you know of any detail about this disappearance.

AFTER 2 YEARS KIDNAPER OF LINDBERGH BABY IS CAPTURED

By the Associated Press.
NEW YORK, N.Y., September 15, 1935
Bruno Richard Hauptmann has been arrested for the kidnaping of Charles A. Lindbergh, Jr. A few weeks ago, a gas station attendant was paid with a $10 gold certificate. Since these certificates had become illegal in 1933, the gas station attendant was suspicious. He wrote down the license number of the vehicle directly onto the gold certificate and informed the police. The police identified the bill as part of the ransom money and the vehicle as one owned by a Bruno Richard Hauptmann, a German carpenter.

The police watched his home in Bronx, New York. Finally Hauptmann was stopped one day and a $20 gold note from the ransom money was on his person. Hauptmann denied everything, but $14,590 more notes were found in his garage and a phone number of the Lindbergh's contact was written on the wall of his bedroom closet.

In the attic of Hauptmann's home was a piece of wood that was microscopically identical to the wood in the ladders. Also, his carpenter's tool kit was complete except it lacked a chisel. He was a burglar in Germany and had fled as a stowaway to come to America.

Col. Charles Lindbergh Family Moves To Europe

NEW YORK, N.Y., December 15, 1935
Col. Charles A. Lindbergh and his wife, Anne, are moving from the United States to Europe. It has been over three years since the kidnapping and death of their first-born son, but they complain that still they have endless harassment by reporters.

HAUPTMANN ELECTROCUTED

By the Associated Press.
NEW YORK, N.Y., April 3, 1936
Bruno Richard Hauptmann was electrocuted for the kidnaping and death of the son of Col. Charles A. Lindbergh.

PART II

1942-1944

CHAPTER 4

1942

The wooden legs made a light scraping sound against the floor as she pushed the bed away from the wall. She stopped pushing every five inches to listen, not wanting her mother to hear. It wasn't likely that the scraping sound could be heard because her mother was working two stories below and the house was of sturdy brick construction. She kept looking toward the edge of the floor where the wallpaper with its faded paisley design was peeling from the wall, wondering what the original colors might've been. Greenish and purple, she decided. Finally, the bed exposed the particular short floorboard that, unlike all the others, had no fine dust or dirt in the cracks, only a small piece of cloth that protruded just enough for her fingers to grasp. She crouched down on all fours with the skirt of her plaid dress under her knees and carefully pulled on the protruding cloth. Up came the board with the cloth attached by a thumbtack on its underside. Decades ago the floor had been made with wide boards covered with a light, clear coat of shellac that time, dirt, and sunlight had turned dark brown. At the doorway, the floorboards were concave from wear and, although her family had only recently moved into this house, she already knew which boards were the ones that creaked wherever she was in the house. She tried not to step on them. She liked to move about the house without people knowing where she was. It was fun.

"Suzanne, when your homework's done, I want you to go to the drugstore for me," called her mother from the bottom of the stairs, two flights down.

She jumped with surprise and replied, "Okay, in about half an hour, Mom." Her homework was already done, and she wanted to play for a while.

Tony and Claire called their daughter Suzanne. If anyone in St. Louis had known Little Sue Ann, they would've wondered why such a similar name was chosen for this other child. Of course, it was chosen for that specific reason, the similarity of the sound. They had picked it carefully. Personally, Claire had hoped that a name so similar to Sue Ann's would kindle happy memories. Regretfully, saying "Suzanne" reminded her of sadness and the secrets she kept. Claire had more than one sad secret; she had a few.

Carefully Suzanne pulled a small hand painted wooden hatbox from between the space under the floorboards. It was an exquisite oval box. The lid fitted snugly over the base and was decorated with wispy yellow brushstrokes forming daffodils, a swipe of green for the long leaves, and dabs of lavender paint that created drooping clumps of lilacs. The edges had a dark green border—an elegant look. What especially fascinated Suzanne were the painted pink ballerinas, holding hands and dancing in a never-ending circle around and around. She studied the dancers—each a little different. The hatbox was small, twelve inches long and four inches at its widest part. It had been made for a child's hat or one of those small headbands of the type with feathers from the 1920s. Time, patience, and care had gone into the construction of the wood fittings. Thin pieces of wood had been soaked to form the oval shape. Age had added random patterns of thin cracks to the painted designs. Suzanne was on her belly on the floor with her chin resting on her arm as she ran her fingers over the silky paint of one of the dancers. Her mind was lost in some deep reflection because there was a slight furrow in her brow. Her thoughts changed and suddenly she sat up, brushing dust from her dress and retying the sash behind her before opening the hatbox. She smiled.

"Hi, Bobo," she whispered and kissed his cheek while the familiar rubber ball smell activated a pleasant glow inside her. "Want to put on your pretty nightgown today?" she asked as she lifted the yellow cotton gown with the pink rosebuds out of the hatbox. She gathered the gown's neckline into her left hand, placed the ball on top to make Bobo appear to be dressed in the gown, and then she played and talked with him for a while as she had done for as long as she could remember. If the other sixth graders could see her playing, she would be embarrassed, but no one would see her because the hatbox and its contents were a secret. They had to be! Ever since she was small, even before she went to school and for reasons that Suzanne could never grasp, her mother would get angry and immediately take the hatbox away when she tried to play with it. So, years ago, Suzanne learned where her mother kept it. At first, she would always return it to that same place until, one day, Suzanne took it to another hiding place and waited to see if her mother would notice. Her mother had forgotten about it. Suzanne now was extra careful to play in secret, so as to not lose her friend Bobo.

To Suzanne, it was a delightful day in April with comfortable temperatures in the seventies. A soft breeze rippled her sheer gauze curtains and fluttered the soft-shirred ruffles that bordered the edges. It was 1942. Suzanne was young, and it was too early in the war for her to know that for most of the world today wasn't too delightful. The United States had been at war only four months, and yet many St. Louis factories had been converted to munitions productions even before America had entered the war. Suzanne had classmates whose parents or family members worked in these plants. These children were more aware of the war than she. Fathers of other classmates were soldiers heading to Europe or into the Pacific, but Tony had a special classification because he had damaged his right index finger in a fire about eight years ago when he had started working for the St. Louis Fire department again. Uncle Sam didn't want him in the war without a good trigger finger. So for Suzanne's family, daily activities continued much like they had before the war—except the move to this new neighborhood.

They had bought a three story red brick home on the south side of St. Louis. It was situated on Park Avenue, only four blocks from the main thoroughfare, Grand Avenue. Suzanne knelt at the window and started to play on the sill, which was low to the floor, because her bedroom was in a converted attic room. "Look, Bobo, there's Mrs. Gebhardt walking into her bakery. I'd like to buy a coconut toast later on. Hmmm, doesn't that sound good? Mom'll say I'm spoiling my appetite, but we'll just eat one. It'll be our little secret. Wish you could really go with me. I'll save you a bite. Oh, there's that mean Billy! He's always bothering me. He tries to lift up my skirt. I hate him," she told Bobo as the boy walked under one of the sycamore trees that lined the curb. He disappeared from sight, so Suzanne turned her gaze across the street. "Look; there's those two girls that go to that Catholic school. They play hopscotch different than me. Well, they draw it different." Suzanne liked all the outdoor sidewalk games like jump rope, Mother-May-I, jacks, and hopscotch. Playing hopscotch was her favorite game, so much so that she always had an object for her place marker in her pocket. Once she had used a rusty nut and bolt, but Claire was furious with the rust stains that were left around the pocket of her dress. Now, she used a broken Coca-Cola bottle that was worn smooth from being kicked along the sidewalk and run over in the street.

"Wish I knew those two Catholics so I could learn how they play. Maybe I should go and meet them when I go outside," she whispered aloud to Bobo. Then she remembered the coconut toast and decided, "No, not today."

Living on Park Avenue was interesting to her, and she liked it. The street was busy, wide, and lined with a mix of homes, flats, and businesses. From her bedroom window, Suzanne could see the bakery across the street in the middle of the block where Mrs. Gebhardt went, and the tavern on the corner where they sold delicious roast beef sandwiches. Suzanne often went to the tavern with her dad, Tony, to get a sandwich, and he'd talk with the locals. She liked to hear the men talk, and Tony loved to go everywhere with his daughter. The other corner, across the street from her, had a vegetable store that sold the produce directly from crates sitting on the sidewalk. Though today, fewer fruits and vegetables were available since America had gone to war. There was a place where people did laundry, but Suzanne couldn't see it because it was on her side of the street—out of sight from her window view. The corner across from the tavern had a drugstore that she couldn't see either.

Her house was different from most because the first floor was built to accommodate a storefront. Claire wanted to have a confectionery. In St. Louis, a confectionery was a store that sells foodstuff like canned goods, lunchmeats, cheeses, milk, some cheap toys, candy, some sewing articles, and a few hardware items, such as can openers, hammers, and nails.

"You know, I want a store that has a little of everything," she had explained to Tony when she found the place. "I'll have all those items that a household might want from a handy corner store."

He had smiled and hugged his wife. He had always been supportive of her ideas. He loved her more with each passing year.

It was only a plan since the storefront was empty at this moment, except for a couple of showcases that were left behind after Claire had dickered with the previous owner. With the war going on, it had been easy to buy this storefront for a bargain. Good times for bargains didn't mean great times for starting a business. Rationing and shortages prevailed, but Claire was planning for the future.

Suzanne liked to go into the store area and play. She could enter, from her home, by going down the stairs leading from the kitchen. But not today! Claire had painted them yesterday and the ten steps, leading to the back of the store, were still tacky. To warn everyone, Suzanne had hung a sign with "Do Not Use" on the window of the door at the top of the stairs.

Now, Claire was busy nailing new linoleum on the stairs from the kitchen to the dining room. The living room, dining room, and master bedroom were all on the same level—four steps up from the kitchen. Unlike Tony, Claire enjoyed fixing up and repairing things. She was good with a hammer and nail. She was always busy, fixing, making, or doing something.

"You have to learn how to stop and relax, Claire," Tony admonished his wife when she'd collapse into bed, exhausted.

"I enjoy being busy," was her usual response. Keeping busy was one solution to stop her from thinking about the secrets of her past. They bothered her daily. She had changed from the Claire that had come to St. Louis. She read a lot and was interested in improving herself.

Suzanne liked how the new home was constructed. Various doors to the outside were on different levels because it was constructed on a sloping lot. There was a kitchen door to the backyard, a formal entrance into the living room on the other side of the house, and a door for customers to enter at the bottom of the hill. Each door was on a different level. This seemed intriguing to Suzanne. She considered the riddle of "the second floor" of the house. Sometimes Suzanne rationalized that the kitchen was on the second floor because if you entered the store from outside, you needed to go up steps to the kitchen. However the living room and dining room appeared to be on the second floor, too, if you came in to the kitchen from the backyard and went up the four stairs. She loved to talk about this type of mind game.

"Dad, if I told you the newspaper was on the second floor, where would you find it?" was one of her riddles.

Or she teased her great Aunt Maria, who came in through the storefront and asked where her mother was. "Oh, she's up on the second floor. Do you know what room that is?" Suzanne would say with a gleam in her eye because it could mean the kitchen or one of the three rooms up from the kitchen. Most people would play with her on these mind games. Suzanne was always thinking and analyzing. Her father loved this aspect of his daughter's character.

Claire hated it.

"Mom, I thought of…"

Claire usually stopped her before she started, "Suzanne, can't you see that I am sitting here working on our budget and can't listen to your games?"

The problem was more than Claire not having patience for childish games. Claire wasn't happy for a variety of complicated reasons.

One reason for her unhappiness was living in St. Louis. Those who had been born and raised in St. Louis could never know what Claire felt after coming from California. She found it frustrating to try to adjust to the weather, the people, and even how they spoke.

For example, when St. Louisans went to say a word with the letters, 'o' and 'r,' like *corn, horse* or *fork,* they changed the pronunciation to *carn, harse* and *fark.* On the tennis courts (and St. Louis was known for good tennis players), it was most embarrassing when someone from another area of the country would hear the score called across the court as "farty-love."

Weather in St. Louis was okay when it was spring or fall. The other two seasons were as "extreme as the North Pole and Hell," quoting Claire. She suffered each winter and summer. She remembered ten years ago when Tony had told her that they'd be moving to "the Midwest." She got some idea in her head about the term, the Midwest. "What a meaningless term!" she complained one day to Tony. "Physically, it isn't in the middle of the west, any way you try to imagine. In one way it's in the middle because it does seem as far as possible from the East Coast as the West Coast when one considers how long it takes for the new styles, new motion pictures, and new ideas to arrive here in St. Louis."

Oft times, "what's happening" on the East or West Coasts never arrived because the city had a committee that would censure some motion pictures or plays. Consequently, they'd never be scheduled to show. Frequently, books were banned in St. Louis but available elsewhere in the country.

So, was St. Louis conservative or traditional? "No," Claire claimed, "'old-fashioned' and 'vacuous' are better terms for this city. No wonder no one wants to move here." Claire was referring to the decline of St. Louis. At the turn of the century it had been the fourth largest city in America, and when they had arrived in 1932, it was the seventh after New York, Chicago, Philadelphia, Detroit, Los Angeles, and Cleveland.

Claire found her existence to be stifling, and she frequently felt unhappy. Tony expressed concern, but she couldn't explain it to him. Like most problems, there was more than one reason causing her unhappiness. And of course, there were the secrets that she suppressed by keeping busy. However, many times she didn't know what was bothering her. She only knew she was upset or sad. Often her frustration coincided with the weather. On a hot July afternoon, after she had taken her third shower of the day, trying to stay fresh, it was easy to blame St. Louis for most of her problems.

But she knew there were other reasons.

Without a doubt, her relationship with her daughter was one of the aspects of her life that troubled her. Claire wouldn't allow herself to become attached to Suzanne. She avoided holding or even touching her. Even at the beginning, when she had had an impulse to cradle and cuddle Suzanne, Claire would put the child down. At first it was unconscious. Later it became deliberate. On and on it went. Claire began projects to occupy her hands, her mind, and her hours. This gave her an excuse not to spend as much time with Suzanne as she had with Sue Ann. She became a mother who avoided the display of affection. Although she didn't understand her actions, she was protecting herself against the pain that could occur if she lost this second child.

Claire really loved Suzanne, even more than Sue Ann, if that was possible. Depriving herself of all that she and this child needed in the form of a loving mother-daughter relationship made Claire sadder. Sometimes she couldn't control how she talked and reacted to Suzanne, she just did it.

There were other factors that caused distance between Claire and her daughter. Early on, Suzanne demonstrated that she was more intelligent than her parents were. She absorbed ideas and grasped facts without being taught. She learned to read by asking questions about signs, labels, or items in the kitchen, as well as on her father's lap when he read to her. She was always developing ideas or mind games in her head like the riddle of the "second floor." Claire was proud and eager for Suzanne to learn and achieve, only she didn't express it and didn't show it. On the other side of the coin, Suzanne, since she was a thinker, could not fathom why her mother seemed cold toward her, so she came to the conclusion that her mother didn't love her.

"Why are you women so complicated?" was one of Tony's favorite comments. He made the declaration with a twinkle in his eye because he meant it in a teasing way. He had no complaints about his women. He'd say this when they were expressing problems or whining. Tony's teasing question would make Suzanne smile. Suzanne loved her father and knew that he loved her.

Suzanne put away the hatbox, returned the bed to the correct position, closed her window, and went downstairs to tell her mother, "I'm ready to go to the drugstore."

Claire got up from the kitchen table to fetch her purse, and, as she passed her daughter, noticed that she and Suzanne were eye-to-eye. Suzanne was tall for her age, which was good since she had skipped grades in school. Tony had noticed her height. He had two gals "Five foot two, eyes of blue," one a blonde, and the other a dark-haired beauty. He loved it.

"I heard that there's going to be more shortages besides the rationing that we have for meat, sugar, and gasoline. So, I want you to buy some extra things like aspirins, iodine, and…well, they're all on this list I wrote for you," Claire commented as she rummaged in her purse to find her money. "Oh, here's a five. That will be more than enough. You be careful not to lose the change. Here, take my coin purse with you."

"Can I buy some candy, too? Just some penny stuff?"

"Okay. No more than ten cents, though. Oh, that reminds me that we need a loaf of bread, so pick that up at Mrs. Gebhardt's. Have her slice it in that new slicing machine she has. I guess that's all."

"Thanks, Mom; a dime is more than enough."

Claire was reminded of the bread because it cost a dime for a loaf, and she was allowing Suzanne to spend the same amount on candy. That was spoiling her daughter since the general public earned six cents an hour, though Tony made more. Claire managed the money and held her family to a tight budget. "Suzanne'll make her candy last the whole week," she thought with a little pride.

Suzanne stuffed the coin purse into her pocket and saw her mother's project on the kitchen table. Claire did little projects to try to earn extra money.

"Oh, Mom, these are your best dolls ever!" There were a dozen paper dolls standing in their *Gone with the Wind* dresses of pinks, blues, and yellows. Claire was making them at the kitchen table. She took wooden picnic forks and, using crayons, drew a girl's face on the back of the rounded fork, then coiled yarn for hair that was glued to the tongs of the fork. She made arms with a pipe cleaner wound around the handle of the fork and slipped a paper petticoat up the fork handle. She got the "petticoats" at the drugstore soda fountains where they used cone-shaped paper for a cup of ice cream or a sundae. She decorated the doll with colored paper and crepe paper to make hats, blouses, frilly skirts, parasols, ruffles, and other creative accessories. Claire sold them as party favors, decorations for cakes, or just as a gift.

"You make the neatest stuff, Mom."

"Thank you, Suzanne. Too bad that not many people are interested in parties and presents right now. I might have to think of a new project that is more appropriate to these wartimes. Did you get your homework done?"

"Sure, Mom. I got a hundred on the arithmetic test today. Did I tell you?"

"That's good," Claire looked up at Suzanne. "Please push the glue over closer to me. Oh, and pull up your socks. Why don't you look in the mirror once in a while and try to be a little neater, Suzanne? Your dress looks dirty and you need to wash your hair tonight, too."

Claire noticed something else about Suzanne's dress, "And your dress is getting too short." She tried to remember the last time she had seen her wear it. It didn't seem small last week.

"Even if I let out the hem, the waist is getting too high. You're growing so fast," she analyzed, talking more to herself than her daughter. She turned Suzanne this way and that, while looking at the dress, "I could insert some other material and make a waist band. Yes, that's what I'll do, take off the childish sash and make it into a waistband," she decided without any eye contact with Suzanne. Then she turned back to her project.

"Will Daddy be working at the firehouse tonight, or is he coming home for supper?" Suzanne asked as she started out the door.

"Did you look at his schedule? It's right next to you on the wall. Why do you ask me that when you can see it as easy as I can? Do you want me to put down my work and get up and go look?" Claire responded with irritation.

"Sorry, Mom. I was just talking and thought you might know. Look, yes, he will. Oh, boy! Bye." And out went Suzanne without a grudge at her mother's crabby reply. She hardly noticed because the terseness was normal. Suzanne wasn't complicated. She didn't stop to worry about her mother's words or tone of voice. Suzanne was a happy person. Besides, Tony gave his daughter so much time and love that it compensated for any unusual attitude that Claire showed.

As the door to the kitchen closed, Claire shook her head and wondered why she was so irritable. "Why am I like this with Suzanne?" she mused as she worked. Claire concentrated on the design of a crepe paper parasol, not allowing herself to think about the real problems that bothered her. There was more to her unhappiness than she was willing to face. She shoved it far down, out of her consciousness, but it was there always—elusive, and malignant—filling her with guilt and impressions of worthlessness.

Claire looked in the wrong places to understand her upset. She started thinking as she worked, *It was that horrible meeting I went to at Suzanne's school. That's why I am feeling upset. The "Women's Circle" they call themselves. The "Women's Web" would be better. I didn't like that Ruth, who was bragging about her job at the ammunition plant. Ha! She showed us her muscles like she didn't want to look like a woman anymore. And she turned to me when she said something about "Don't you get tired of doing menial housework?" Humph, I did-n't give her the time of day. I do want to have my own store someday, but I'm proud of my family and home, too. I know there aren't enough men for the jobs, so women must work. Oh, this war has to end soon. "We work better than many a man," she had said. I don't know where she gets her facts. She would laugh at these little dolls that I'm making…*

Oh then, what's-her-name? Yeah, that Edna Mae started bragging about her electrical contraptions in the kitchen, telling us about all the time she's saving. She has one child, like me, and I don't know why she needs them. I guess if I had six children I would need to save time. Those things are so expensive, and I think I do a good enough job without them. Tony is proud of who I am and what I do.

The worst part of the meeting was when they brought up the agenda for next time. They want to have a sex education class for the sixth graders. Sex! How embarrassing. I don't want Suzanne in a class like that, even though I don't want to have to talk about the birds and the bees with her, either. My mother didn't tell me anything special, and I think she was right. It's so personal. Well, I never have agreed with my mother telling me that a stork brought me into the world, but I'm sure there are books at libraries now.

Claire was feeling uncomfortable even with her own thoughts. To say that sex was never discussed could be best construed by saying that the word, *sex,* was never to be said. Claire and most of the women didn't join into the discussion or say much of anything on the topic of having a sex education class. They too were embarrassed to hear the word, much less say it. Besides, sex was a private subject. Even in their homes, who talked about sex, feelings, emotions, or passions? It wasn't done.

Suzanne skipped up the street and crossed to the bakery. Obviously, the anticipated coconut toast with drizzles of white icing was first on her mind. Out she came with the loaf of bread, all sliced in exactly equal slices. She was eating her toast as she walked. It had cost two cents. Soon this bakery would use the last of their coconut, and Suzanne would have to wait until after the war to indulge in her much-liked coconut toast; of course, she couldn't know that yet. At the corner, she crossed to the drugstore and walked up to the windowed door. As she pushed on the door, she found it was locked. Then she noticed a sign hanging above her head inside the thick-glassed door. *Closed for Funeral, Open Tomorrow.* A soft "Oh" escaped from her toast-with-coconut-filled mouth as she looked up to see a woman reading the sign, too.

"We'll just have to walk up to the Bartlett Pharmacy, I guess," the stranger volunteered.

"Where's that?" muttered Suzanne with her mouth still full.

"You don't know? Well, we can walk together if you like, but you can't miss it." They started walking together.

After swallowing the last bite of toast, Suzanne introduced herself. "My name is Suzanne, and we moved here two months ago, so I don't know the whole neighborhood. My mother doesn't want me to go more than two blocks away when I'm alone, but I'm not alone with you. Right?"

The older lady laughed, "No, you're not, and I'll be returning this way, too. Shall we walk back together?"

Suzanne answered with a "Yes, that would be nice" in her formal, be-polite-to-strangers voice. They talked to get to know one another; Suzanne said that her father was a fireman and her mother wanted to open a confectionery on the corner, and so on until they arrived in front of the drugstore. The bell hanging from a string at the top of the door jingled as they entered.

Suzanne liked this place much better than the other drugstore. This one had a soda fountain and wooden display cases out in the middle of the store with greeting cards and magazines. A young man was making an ice cream soda at the fountain, and she watched as he tossed a scoop of ice cream into the air and caught it in a tall glass.

"Tommy!" someone shouted. The smile melted from his face as he plopped by hand the second scoop. With a long spoon inserted into the tall fluted glass, he placed it under a faucet and pulled on a lever where some fizzling, bubbling liquid covered the scoops of ice cream, but it didn't overflow.

"Wow, I guess you're a 'soda jerk,'" Suzanne beamed with admiration while she peered over the counter.

"Just watch this," he grinned and put his hand to the handle of the seltzer dispenser again to jerk it with the finesse of an expert. "You should see me when it's busy. I can work all the levers, pumps, and handles faster than any other soda jerk that you've ever seen, and I never spill a drop," he bragged to the wide-eyed Suzanne. The other young people, sitting at the counter, smiled and confirmed that he was the best they'd ever seen. Suzanne looked up at the list of prices and decided to plan for a cherry ice cream soda next week. For now she turned to view the rest of the drugstore.

People were standing with magazines open up by the plate glass windows that spanned the whole front, and others were casually reading the greeting cards. Dark wooden shelves lined most the walls, and a ladder was suspended from a ledge for the clerks to get to the shelves that went to the ceiling. The floor was covered in tiny white hexagon-shaped tiles except for the ten-inch border of solid black tiles that ran around the whole store. Suzanne noticed a woman tossing some sawdust onto the floor and then sweeping it up again.

Suzanne approached a counter and a man behind it asked her, "May I help you?"

Without turning to look at him, she pointed to the woman working the broom to ask, "Why is she throwing dirt on the floor only to sweep it up again?"

The man smiled with friendly amusement. As Suzanne turned to face him, he patiently began to explain, "That is sawdust, not dirt, and it's a special sawdust that has been treated with a chemical that makes it a bit oily, so sweeping doesn't raise the dust. We have all these bottles and boxes on shelves that we must clean so we try to keep down the dust."

"Oh," she responded with hesitancy because her mind was working on another question: why would anyone put oil on a tile floor? She started to ask, and in that fraction of a second before her comment was made, she noticed an unusual sensation occurring. She saw in front of her a warm, smiling older man who had the kindest face. The lines around his eyes and mouth from years of smiling had created a pattern that remained when he stopped smiling. In this way his goodness continued to show. She was attracted to this person, and he reminded her of the actor who had played Santa Claus in the motion picture *Miracle on Forty-second Street*. She thought, "If he would grow a beard, he'd look better."

Then, she blurted out her question about the oil on the tile floor, "Wouldn't that make it slippery and dangerous?"

"My, you're quite a thinker for a young lady, aren't you?" Mr. Bartlett said as he continued to explain without waiting for her to answer since his statement was more a comment than a question. "It isn't only oil, but a chemical mixture especially made for its absorbing qualities. You know, to hold the dust and dirt. It's called 'sweeping compound,' and I buy it ready-made in bulk. If that isn't a complete enough answer, I could go downstairs where I keep it and see if the exact chemical contents are printed on the side," he teased because now he noticed an embarrassment that was causing her to blush.

"Oh, no, that's good enough. I'm sorry. My dad says I ask too many questions and that I should stop and think before I speak. I forgot to do that."

Mr. Bartlett was finding this person a joy. He was thinking to himself that he'd go look for the ingredients on the sweeping compound barrel to tell her next time. He smiled and asked, "Now that we finished with the housekeeping procedures of Bartlett Pharmacy, is there something else for you, Miss?"

"Now you're teasing me," she said handing him the list. "I don't mind. I can't help that I ask questions. They just come out. I've more questions, but I'll wait until I come again, okay?" she joshed back to him.

Here they were—two personalities naturally sociable, friendly and amiable—talking together while deep inside they each knew more was transpiring. They felt it. They didn't know what it was, but they liked what they sensed, and it was fun. Mr. Bartlett returned to the counter with the items from the list and noticed that Suzanne was looking into the candy case. It was located to the right of the main counter. He leaned over the counter to see her, "Is there anything else, Miss?"

"Yes, I want some candy. How much is this?" she pointed to the strips of paper covered with colored sugar dots.

Mr. Bartlett squatted behind the candy case to see where she was pointing and told her the price. She wanted two of this, three of another, and on and on until she had spent her eight remaining cents. He filled a small paper bag with some Mary Janes, two-for-a-penny jawbreakers, three-for-a-penny gumdrops, and other sweets until Suzanne had twenty items.

"You know that you should write the prices on each box; then you wouldn't have to answer how much is this and that," she pointed out with a confident expression as if she were a world consultant on how to manage a candy case.

"Yes, but that would be a job to be done over and over because when the box is empty, we throw it out. Plus, some of the candy is in those glass jars."

Quickly she had a solution for that problem, "You need to put little cards on each box and in the glass jars. It'd save you time and trouble. You know, when you're at the end of the box or jar, you could save the card to reuse on the new box. It'd help you remember that you needed to buy more of that kind of candy if you wrote the name of the candy on the card, too."

He could hardly believe this conversation. This girl was a gem. He wondered if she was older than she looked. Otherwise, her intelligence and personality were beyond her years. He didn't want to stop the game of words they were throwing at each other by asking a personal question about her age. Instead he heard himself saying, "Oh, now that sounds like a lot of work for me, the pharmacist, who has more important things to do."

She caught the ball he threw and responded with a toss right back, "Are you offering me a job?"

And he said that he was. The game finished with a tie.

Later that night, he was sitting at his desk in the back of the store thinking about the whole scene. *She's such an interesting child.* As they settled the details of what he'd pay her to make the little cards with candy prices, he had learned that she was going into the 6th grade in September. She was to come on Saturday after she asked her father for permission. Mr. Bartlett had insisted. She was at such a lanky age. Though a child, she seemed mature. The child and young woman-to-be popped out when they were talking—first one, then the other, over and over. He smiled. Her hair was a mess. *Really dirty! Her blonde hair must be beautiful when clean*, he surmised. He sat there remembering how piercing her blue eyes were when she teased and how they turned vibrant when he bantered back. He got up with that thought and went to the sink where he had stacks of bottles, containers, and jars that he washed and reused. There was a mirror over the sink and he looked into it. He didn't want to think it, much less to say it, but he did. He saw his eyes, then hers, then his, and finally he allowed himself to face the impression he had been pushing away: *She's how Elizabeth would've looked.*

CHAPTER 5

That evening while eating their supper in the kitchen, Suzanne excitedly told her parents about her shopping trip to the other drugstore. Beaming, she asked permission to go on Saturday for three hours to do her "job," and started to explain what she'd be doing.

Before Suzanne could finish relating her whole idea, Claire became enraged. "You have disobeyed me again. This time, you went more than two blocks from home, and with a stranger, when I've said over and over and over that you're not to talk to strangers, much less go off with one! I can't believe this. Tony, can't you say something? Do you want your daughter walking around anywhere she pleases? And places that we don't know? We wouldn't be able to find her! She should have come back home when the drugstore on the corner was closed. She should have asked permission, but no, she goes off with this lady she has never seen before. I just don't know how to make Suzanne understand that she can *not* do that!" Claire pushed back her chair to stand and put her face an inch away from Suzanne's to scream, "*You can not do that!*"

Tony jumped up, gently put his hands on Claire's shoulders, and pulled her away from Suzanne. "I understand what you mean; just don't scream at her about it, Claire. You know, I don't think we've explained why it's important. She's just a kid, but she's smart, and we need to make her understand."

Claire was adamant, "I *have* tried, Tony!"

Suzanne was crying and Tony knew both his gals needed him, but he couldn't comfort both at the same time. Although his daughter was upset, his wife was distraught beyond reason. Without a doubt, Claire needed him more. "Suzanne, take your plate upstairs to the dining room to finish while I talk with your mother. Okay, honey?"

"I'm not hungry," Suzanne pouted as she got up from the table and said, "but I'll go in the dining room. I'm sorry, Mommy." As Suzanne got up, she turned and repeated, "I'm sorry, Mommy."

Poor Claire; she was sobbing now, too. She had covered her face with her apron while frustration poured from her. Her mind was irrational, filled with self-incriminating thoughts about the memories that she could not, and would not, share with Tony. Claire was especially frightened of strangers with Suzanne. She knew if she'd tell Tony about her long-kept secret—exactly what had happened—he'd understand why she got upset with Suzanne, but Claire felt he'd never forgive her. Understand, maybe, but never forgive. Or if he'd forgive her, she knew he couldn't forget and that would forever change his love for her.

Tony, for his part, assumed that Claire feared Suzanne being kidnapped. He carried a tremendous guilt because he felt his past actions were causing ongoing problems for Claire. He saw no reason to talk about the kidnapping; it was so long ago. Over the years, they seemed to have developed an unspoken agreement not to talk about it. He figured that Claire had such extreme fears and emotions about Suzanne being taken from them because she knew first-hand how easy it was to do. He was assuming that the kidnapping, as well as the death of Sue Ann, were the reasons for her hysterical emotions, and yet the real reason was a secret more horrible and ugly than either of those incidents.

While Tony sat and rocked Claire in his arms, he decided to talk more directly with Suzanne about the dangers of strangers and kidnapping. He'd never be able to speak of other things that could happen to a young woman her age. He figured it would be easier to explain that she could be killed. But he thought, "Surely she wouldn't grasp what that meant either." He decided to take her on an outing on Saturday to talk and hoped that he didn't need talk in specifics.

Suzanne finished her meal and went up to her attic bedroom to retrieve Bobo from the hatbox. She returned the hatbox beneath the floorboards and moved her bed to the right position in case one of her parents were to come up. Bobo could be tucked under the pillow quickly if need be. She was weeping and whispering to Bobo, "She doesn't love me at all. It's as if she can't stand me. Why doesn't she love me?"

Bobo peered at her with his eternal smile and she rubbed him across her lips. The texture of the cheeks and eyes protruding, just a bit, made the little bumps of pink and blue a soothing sensation on her lips. She put both hands around him and brought him to her chest, not unlike the way Claire had held Sue Ann when she was dying. It was an attempt to absorb a comfort from that which they loved—a need to make this adored ball (or child in Claire's case) a part of herself, never to be parted. The comfort and pleasure this ball had provided over the years made her secure, and Suzanne slowly became calm.

"Maybe she never wanted a child and doesn't want me. If I had a brother or sister it wouldn't be so bad. Why does she hate me so? I didn't mean to not obey. It didn't seem that it was wrong to go. Besides, what's the difference between two blocks from home and four blocks? What could happen in two more blocks for her to become so angry?" Suzanne began to run her fingers over the cap where his name was. Her fingers followed the shape of the B and then made a circle around the O, the next B, and the last O. Then she repeated the movement again and again. This ball was always there for her to talk to; he comforted her. "I love you, Bobo," she sniffed, and then kissed him and slipped him under the pillow because she knew with all the crying her eyes just wanted to close and she'd probably fall asleep.

Tony put Claire in a warm tub to soak because that always relaxed her.

Tony started thinking of what he could say to Suzanne. He decided to go see this Mr. Bartlett and introduce himself to evaluate the situation, too. Tony had no reason to prevent Suzanne from doing a little job like she described. He knew how smart she was and figured that she must have impressed the pharmacist in some way.

Neither Tony nor Claire knew that John Bartlett was the father of the child that Tony had taken. Back in 1932, they had seen the small article in the newspaper that claimed that there were "*No Clews in Disappearance of 16-month-old Child.*" Yet the article had made no mention of the family's name because that could cause more problems by letting anyone trying to make a quick buck contact the family directly. The police wanted to prevent additional problems and figured that if the child had been kidnapped, the kidnappers must know who the family was and where they lived. Therefore, why print a name and address? Tony's plan to visit the drugstore was honestly what it seemed: he needed to know where his child wanted to go, who this man was who had offered to pay his daughter for a job, and if it really was okay for her to do the job.

When Tony went up to say goodnight to Suzanne, she was wide awake. They talked a little.

"Daddy, I really want to make the candy signs at the drugstore. I want it so much," she pleaded. "It was my idea, and the druggist like it."

"I know. We'll go up together on Saturday so I can meet Mr. Bartlett." Tony believed it was her idea to make the candy signs; it sounded like some of the ideas she had. He smiled at his own thought, *She'd make a good fireman, if she were a boy. She always wants to organize everything.*

He was proud of her. Sometimes he regretted not having a son to be a fireman to continue in the same line of work. Nevertheless, with a daughter like

Suzanne, he had been able to share his world of fires as if she were his son. He smiled again thinking about all the fires they had shared over the years.

"Tell me a story, Daddy. Tell me one of your grandfather *Nónno*'s stories like you always do. You know, the ones he told you. Please, please."

"Sure, honey. Remember, *Nónno* wasn't his name; it means grandfather in Italian."

Suzanne grinned, "I know. I like to say it my way. Then I don't have to explain to people when I talk about your *Nónno*."

Tony gave her a hug. "Okay, I'm going to tell your favorite one about the Great Fire of St. Louis in 1849. Would that make you happy?"

"Oh, yes! But please talk like grandfather *Nónno*. It's more fun when you sound like him."

Tony's eyes twinkled. Yes, he couldn't have asked for more than this daughter. He stood up and bent over like an old man and affected an accent, "I will pretend to be *Nónno* who came to the states to find gold. I'll tell you just as he told me with some Italian words here and there. Are you ready?"

Suzanne sat up in bed, pulling pillows behind her back, and giggled, "Oh, boy."

"*A causa del tempo*—it one fine day in downtown St. Louis—I only eighteen years old and just arrive in the United States. I decide to walk down to the big Mississippi. From many blocks away I come, and from far away I see all these smoke stacks sticking up real high. But I don't know what they are. Some were puffing up smoke into the clear blue sky, and I not know they're stacks from steamboats 'til I get closer and see that each steamer got two stacks that go up thirty feet," he threw his arms to the ceiling, "or more! They start way up on a top deck and go to heaven. *Incredibile!* It such a sight! There lots of wind 'cuz all that dark and dirty smoke goes blowin' down the river with little sparks poppin' out of those stacks every once in a while.

"Now Suzanne, *per favore,* you got to try and see what I see that day. Close your eyes and see what I see here in my head…" He went to the window and looked out dramatically, as if he could see it all at the moment.

"Before I can even walk close to the river, I see that the levee is nothin' but confusion as far as my eye see. You know, the levee went miles all up and down the whole city and there were these wooden sidewalks. So, I start a strollin' down this long sidewalk and for fun I count the boats. Twenty-five steamers docked at the levee. I saw horses pulling wagons and mules hitched to carts. Some had wooden wheels, really big—like four feet wide. There was some fancy ones, called *carriages*, sittin' and waitin' for people to rent in case they needs to go someplace in the city.

"Some men I see, they work in leather aprons with long sleeve white shirts and vests. Some have on wide hats to shade the sun, and there are men all black with suspenders crisscrossing their sweaty backs," he turned and lifted his eyebrows before saying, "but no shirts on." Tony feigned surprise.

"The animals and people goin' this way and that. Most wagons with four-horses 'cuz they fill up with heavy stuff—barrels, crates, bales, or bundles of furs. In fact, between me and the steamers, I see rows and rows of cotton bales on the ground just waiting to be loaded onto the boats. Hundreds, no, I thinks thousands of bales. I hear a guy call those bales 'white gold' and I confused. More than that, I worry that I come for the wrong kind of gold 'til someone tell me, 'Cotton is king, and that makes those bales same as gold. So's we call them *white gold!* Whew. I sigh with relief that I don't have that wrong."

Tony wiped his brow in animation and Suzanne giggled.

"Men unloading and loading everywhere. They take things off the wagons, put them on the ground, then someone checks it all before they loads them into the steamers. I get off the sidewalk, but there was almost no space to walk between the stacks and piles of stuff. I see all different kinds of things. I pass piles of blankets held with twine, chairs tied four together—back-to-back and seat-to-seat—and then I come to barrels filled with beer. I know 'cuz one was layin' there broke, and I smell the beer that spill all over the dirt. While I am wandering through all the hustle and bustle, someone screams! I turn, just in time, as a barrel came a-rollin' at me! Jumpin' aside, two guys run fast tryin' to stop it. That barrel go twenty feet more then bump into a nice and soft bale of that *white gold*. Those two guys roll the barrel back and up a gangplank onto a steamboat.

"With all these thousands of things to put on the steamers, I thought, surely a strong young man like me find some work here. So, I ask somebody and he say, 'Okay. But, it's just for the day.' Just like that I gets a job! I takes off my jacket to start workin', and I begin the most important day in my life on that seventeen of May in the year 1849.

"One worker and I start talkin' as we carry stuff on our shoulders up to the boat. The boss man don't seem to mind that we talk and laugh a little. Soon we sweat a lot and take off our shirts. Anyways, the different guys tell me that a sickness—it called cholera—got started in St. Louis about six months before. One guy with name of Mack tell me, now a hundred people dying every day. They tell me that why they busier than usual. The problem was that official people in the city made the boats wait before anyone or anything could get off or on—they called it quarantine. So, everyone was behind schedule and stuff was sittin' on the docks longer than it should. So that's why we needs to hurry to get our steamer loaded.

"As we are walkin' to our boat, Mack points to the steamer next to ours and says, 'See the *White Cloud* over there? They're quarantined! They pulled in this morning and I heard the captain shoutin' to his men to put their mattresses in the sun to kill any cholera that might be on board. Course, nobody know what is causin' the cholera, but the newspapers say we need to be more san-a-tary. You know, wash our hands more.' We laughed about that 'cuz we were so dirty and sweaty.

"When I get my load to the steamer, some black men that take the stuff down into the boat after I bring it aboard. It sound like ten black men are deep inside the boat somewhere 'cuz they sing and sing so loud. The songs don't have no words; they only make heavy sounds that hit your chest and bump your bones. They seem sad, but strong songs that make me feel good. I work all afternoon and into the evening.

"We finish workin' at eight that night and my friend Mack and me we sit and have a beer by the water. Then I think I smell smoke, but I don't think about it too much and I keep talkin' and laughin' with Mack. He a funny man. Suddenly I hear a commotion on the boat next to ours, and I stand up to see flames coming out a door on that steamer called *White Cloud*. From one minute to the next, while I watch, it change and the fire grow fast. The steamer's all wood, and it seems to be a real dry wood, 'cuz the flames double by the time I walk around our boat and go up to get a better look. Right away when I see this fire, I know what happened 'cuz there was mattresses floatin' in the river. That was what I had smelled! I figure sparks from the stacks landed on those mattresses they had put out on deck. With the cloth burnin', it start all the wood in the decks to burn. They tossed them mattresses overboard, but I see those mattresses were still smokin' and driftin' toward other boats, and my heart jump. The *White Cloud*, it docked upriver in very first position on the levee just north of the buildings in the business district.

"Then I see a mattress hit against a steamer on our other side, and the deck burst into flames! Just like that, something happen in me. *Santo Cielo!* I never see a fire like that one before, and it was like magic to me. I was close and I could see. The flames not red like I always thought! They blue and green and orange and even purple! They just don't burn, they dance and jump and crackle and spit. The stuff that burnin' kind of magically twists and curls and moves in a slow way, then that stuff disappear into a loop of smoke. Poof it go! There's sparks and sparkles and blobs of red with blackened edges that melt and vanish with a blink. I couldn't stop lookin.' The heat started to make me back up. I don't know how long I was watchin' and thinkin' how the fire looked, but by now, half of this boat was nothing but fire and it was drifting out into the river because the ropes that held it burned through.

"Suddenly, I notice that there was a stream of fire coming at me. Then I wake up from all that dreamy fire thoughts. It was the ramps on our boat! They were on fire and coming straight to me! The fire had spread to our steamer!

Maledizione! I begin to think that, hey, those singing men are on our boat, and I run to the side that isn't burning. I have to hop in the river and climb the side of that boat and pull myself up onto the decks. You know, I still don't know exactly what I do to get inside that boat 'cuz the door I was usin' was in the fire, but I break a way in there and got down to those men. They five of them that come running out through that wall I broke. We all jump into that muddy Mississippi and swim to shore. When I drag myself out of the water, I see one of the Negroes with his head down in the river. He floatin' there so I have to go back in. He a little ways out so I can walk to him, and I pull him onto the shore and drag him up by his arms. A couple other of the guys help me, and when we turn him over he cough and cough. There's a bloody cut on his head, but he look okay.

"When I stand up I see two other steamboats all in flames. *Incredibile!* The heat felt like I was in the fire, but I wasn't. Those wooden ramps that I use two hours ago turn to cinders and everywhere I looks there's fire. As I back up to get away from the heat, one of those little sheds on the levee explode into flames. There were no fires around it, but it was so hot that it just began to burn. As I walked down the riverside, men were slappin' with empty sacks at little fires that were starting on their boat. Other steamers were trying to get out away from the levee. There were two that have steam in their engines 'cuz they making their way into the middle of the river. As I walked, more wood burst into fire, and it seemed so strange to have all those boats surrounded by water while they burn and burn. No one got any way to get that water to those boats.

"Suddenly, I think that hours must have passed because it was night. But it not night! It only dark with all the smoke covering the sky. I see men who found buckets and tried to put water on all the things on the levee. Others try to load things back on wagons to take them away. I know it is hopeless. All the steamers left were burning down by the water, blowing burning things in the air, and going to the buildings!"

Frowning, Tony sat on a chair and took a deep breath. His voice changed back to his own, and he looked at Suzanne, "I would always get such an unusual sensation inside my chest listening to my grandfather. At this point in the story I would think, 'I want to be like *Nónno.*' As a little boy I had heard this fire story and others, dozens of times. I don't know if his stories made me want to be a fire fighter or if I was just born so much like him." Tony sat quietly a moment and then jumped up to become *Nónno* again. He continued.

"As I back away from the fire, the man that hire me run away. Everyone was shouting and running in circles.

"I see fire fighters come and pull leather hoses out from hand-engine pumpers; they drag them into the river to suck up water. They started pumping—two men to a pumper—one on each side pumping up and down as fast as they can, but the water do nothing to stop the fire. I leave the riverside and walk toward the city. It startin' to burn.

"I notice my clothes are dryin' fast after that swim in the river. I dry because, in moments, the fire is everywhere and I am in the fire, but I'm not afraid. *Capisce?* No, I have no fear. I have something else. I little angry that I have nothing to fight this bully, this thing that just do what it want to do. I see how strong it is and I know it so much stronger than me, but I have something it not have. I'm a man and I can think. Why can't I think how to stop this beast that is so hungry for all it sees? I stand and turn and turn and it so hot. Now I see why. It is all around me—left and right, up and down. Warehouses and buildings were burning. I don't know why I don't burn, but I think the fire god know I am his enemy, and he scared of me because, you know what? I think of what we need to do. That's when I turn and run from the flames. I find that boss of mine, and he think me crazy, but I talk in my not so good English and blabber and use my hands to explain my idea. He's like a statue looking up at the flames behind me. I turn and see a chimney plunge to the ground. Showers of sparks float in the wind. The flames were to the heavens. *Incredible!*

"The whole area is filled with people screaming and running. Men try to load their wares into carts, but the horses don't want to stay. Some horses run away and the carts bump things and turn over to spill everything. I see people carrying money sacks and record books from offices while policemen try to make us to leave. It look like ten, no fifteen, blocks are burning and this the most important businesses in St. Louis. They all are burning!

"So I run to a policeman and tell him I have an idea to stop the fire. He don't want to talk he so busy. Then, I find men in fire fighter's clothes and I look for one who look like a boss. 'I help,' I tell him and he give me an axe from one of his men who is hurt. I watch what he do and I do the same. I work with him and we try to break into buildings from where there are no doors to let people out. We work so hard. We work and work until it is just about dawn and finally I talk to this boss. He tell me he's Captain. I ask him why he stop using water, and he tell me all the hoses burned in the fires.

Tony stopped talking; he seemed breathless. He just stood there.

Suzanne looked into her father's face and saw he was somewhere else. There was sweat glistening on his forehead from the excitement of telling of this fire. Or maybe it was the thrill of reliving his life with *Nónno*. She waited. Then, to break the spell, she asked, "Tell me again the Captain's name."

"Targee. But when he told his name, *Nónno* don't hear it too good," Tony explained as his grandfather had explained to him. "*Nónno* saw his name later under a picture in the newspaper."

"Why…" Suzanne started to ask something, but Tony was back to the story.

"Finally, I tell the Captain my idea to stop the fire. I say, 'We need to make a space with nothing to burn.' I say another way, 'To stop a fire there must be nothing to burn.' He tell me I crazy, but I say, 'We need to blow up buildings to make a space between the fire and the other good buildings. You understand? Make a space where a fire have nothing to burn.'

"Just then, it look like the Captain knows what I mean, and we start to talk how to do this. Soon a wall falls near us and we run. I don't see where the Captain go and while I lookin,' I need to help a lady and little girl carrying boxes from a burning wagon that they must leave behind. I work and work, helping people. Time pass and I think that the whole city will burn.

"Then suddenly I get knocked to the ground! Laying there, I think I hear a big explosion, then another. Nothing like I ever hear before. But, I hear many more as I work. Little by little the hungry fire stop because it got nothing more to eat."

Suzanne waited again before prompting her father, "Don't forget to tell about the Captain."

Tony knew he had been emotional, as always. He finished up the rest of the story quickly, but the accent was gone. Tony was Tony talking to his daughter.

"When Captain Thomas B. Targee left *Nónno*, he had sent word to get kegs of gunpowder from the army. He was a brave man and said that he personally was going to carry the kegs into the buildings. He tossed each keg into a window or door. They knocked down five buildings and went for a sixth; it was a music store. Captain Targee went to the door, but before he threw, the keg exploded in his hands and he died, saving St. Louis from burning down."

Tony smiled, "Let's get to sleep." He kissed Suzanne as she thanked him and snuggled into her covers.

So Saturday came and Tony walked up to Grand Avenue with his daughter and met John Bartlett. Tony liked the druggist.

Tony left as Suzanne and Mr. Bartlett started working on the candy case. A couple of hours later, when Tony returned to get Suzanne, Mr. Bartlett asked if she could work each Saturday for two hours. "I've several cases that could use some organizing, and there are a lot of things a bright person can learn. My oldest son is working one day a week, too. It's a good education for kids their age."

Tony agreed as long as it wasn't a permanent job. Suzanne loved the idea. Then they left for one of the fire stations.

"Hey, here comes *The Fireplug* with his *Poodle*," one of the guys shouted when they arrived.

"How's everything, Tony? It's been a quiet day. Want to play some gin rummy?" another one commented.

"Nah, I figure I'll walk around the station with Suzanne. She'd rather listen to me than sit and listen to you guys," Tony retorted as they walked upstairs. First, she wanted to slide down the pole. "All right everyone, turn your heads, here she comes," he shouted because her dress always billowed up. She was a kid, but she didn't want a group of old men looking at her underwear. They roamed around and he told her about the different engines and equipment like he had done dozens of times. And she asked her questions like she had with every visit. He never tired of answering.

"Tell me about you and your grandfather and his fire station," she asked like she had done so many times before. Tony had not always gone by the name Tony. He had been born Antonio Scaglione in 1901 and raised by his grandfather. The name Tony began with his California friends.

"Hey, I was born not far from here. It was an Italian neighborhood called 'Little Italy' just blocks from the Mississippi River, but it ain't here no more. It was torn down little-by-little when I was a kid." Antonio's mother had died when he was two years old, and his German-born father had died prior to his birth. His parents were never married, so he was given his mother's name of Scaglione. Antonio and Grandfather had lived in a small rented room where they slept in the same bed.

"*Nónno* would take me to the station where he worked before he retired." Tony laughed, "He was retired, but he still showed up at most fires, especially when I was with him. I remember the day when one of his buddies joked, 'So here you are with your little *Fireplug*,' and that nickname stuck. *Nónno* told me my first word was 'fire,' and he said I saw so many fires before I started school that I couldn't figure out why the other kids knew so little about them." Tony stopped his reminiscing and seemed to be reliving his youth. "You know, if I'd hear a siren, I'd run out of school to go to the fire. That drove the teacher crazy. Sometimes other kids would come with me. I just knew I'd be a fireman someday."

Just then the fire alarm went off, and Suzanne jumped. It was the end of Tony's talk. Suzanne watched with interest as the men jumped into boots, slipped into protective coats, and donned their hats. When the engines pulled out with sirens screaming, Tony and Suzanne drove right behind the hook and ladder truck down to Market Street. They parked and jumped out to see where the fire was. Tony was disappointed because it was a small kitchen fire.

"Dad, you can't be disappointed," Suzanne said. "It's good that it was a little fire. I don't want places to burn down just to see them burning."

Tony laughed at that. "You're right. Hey, there's Union Station. Let's walk over there and have an ice cream."

"Yeah, okay," she beamed.

As they turned to begin walking toward the train station, Tony noticed some gypsy bystanders who had gathered near them to see where the fire engines had gone. Their colorful, silky clothes were tattered and looked a bit dirty to him. The clothes were made out of scarves and lengths of fabric wound around their bodies or fashioned into skirts. Reds, blues, and yellow on one woman!

Suzanne was staring at the gypsy women and didn't look as she went to walk the other way. She bumped into a gypsy girl who had been standing behind her. The two girls were inches apart and froze in surprise. They seemed much the same age, with dark, dancing eyes peering into soft blue ones.

The gypsy girl's skirt was layered in different lengths and colors. She had tucked purple and yellow scarves into her skirt and a tattered red one dragged on the ground. The outfit was full and flowing like her black hair. Ends of a lavender silk scarf, rolled and tied around her head, billowed with the breeze. It looked like she had created the outfit herself. And she had. From a distance, the gypsy girl appeared as a spectacular curiosity; at arm's length, it was apparent she needed a bath.

Suzanne stood speechless—not from the beauty of the girl's face, though she was striking, and not from her pungent smell, though she reeked; the gypsy girl's blouse was nothing more than a lavender gauze fabric worn without undergarments. Two shiny plum nipples, quite apparent through the gathered blousing, startled Suzanne because she, too, had these developing breasts that were all nipples popping from a flat chest. Suzanne's were plump pink strawberries that she touched in the privacy of her room or a locked bathroom, and they were puffy, like bubbles when pushed, but her fingers had found hard disks beneath that ached from time to time. At the moment, upon seeing the gypsy's breasts, tingling sensations occurred in Suzanne's nipples. Suzanne blushed.

"I'll read your palm for a quarter," the girl wangled with a smile of arrogance.

"No thanks!" Tony took Suzanne's arm and guided her down the sidewalk. He remembered seeing the multicolored tents a couple of blocks away when they were driving down Market Street to the fire. "These gypsies come here and put up their tents every year," he brooded. "Always."

The gypsy caught her skirts with her arms and furled them in the air like an enemy flag while she skipped along by Suzanne's side. "I see danger in your future, don't you want to know?" she prodded.

"Get out of here! Come on, beat it," he insisted.

The gypsy shouted and pointed to Tony, "Well, I warned you!"

Tony grabbed Suzanne's hand and walked away. Suzanne couldn't resist a sideways glance at the retreating girl waltzing up the street with a swish and twirl; she headed toward the distant tents. Many vacant lots existed on Market Street, making a spacious open area where old buildings had been torn down. Now, tents and junk typical of the gypsy life filled the space on one side of the street.

Suzanne had been shocked by the embarrassing display of the girl's body. Was the young gypsy flaunting her body? Suzanne was curious about this young gypsy and snuck another backward look as the girl entered a tent and disappeared. There had been a flash of feelings when their eyes had linked, and it left a bond. Suzanne found her mind returning to the gypsy girl on and off for the rest of the day. She wished she knew her name. The comments of danger and the warning made Suzanne wonder about the mystical capabilities of gypsies, but it was the person, not the gypsy, that Suzanne wanted to know.

Tony realized that Suzanne had never walked in this area where gypsies lived every year, and sensing her embarrassment, he began to talk. "My *Nónno* arrived before this train station existed," he said and pointed to the regal structure in the distance. Often Suzanne had driven past the train station with her parents when they came downtown to see a parade or to go shopping in the department stores.

"It was first opened just five years before I was born. Ain't it something, honey?" She nodded in awe. It was like a castle with the spires of the clock tower rising to the clouds. "*Nónno* used to work for a beer company that stored beer in caves below the station. That was before they built the train station, of course. The caves aren't used for that now, but you can't remove a cave," he laughed and then talked a bit about his Grandfather's arrival to St. Louis.

Slowly Suzanne regained her composure.

Soon they were close enough to see all the details of the train station, and it really did resemble a castle. It appeared to have a walkway that could be lowered over a moat, if there had been a moat. Two immensely heavy chains connected the main walls of cut gray stones to the end of the suspended "draw bridge." It was actually the roof over the main entrance to the station. A uniformed man was opening an ornate door. Suzanne decided he must be a footman. It was impressive, and Suzanne felt like a princess approaching her castle.

Suddenly Suzanne noticed the sound of water and turned her gaze to the new fountain across the street from Union Station. "Oh, Daddy, look! They turned the water on in the fountain," she shouted while dodging the street traffic.

Tony ran after her. When he stepped up the curb out of the traffic, he could see Suzanne running around the large pool of water. He glanced at the fountain and remembered instantly reading about the uproar in the city over the fountain. He was embarrassed that he was here with his daughter. Water erupted around the two nude figures of a man and woman. Many smaller sculptures, surrounding the nudes, were half human and half fish.

"Oh, damn," he said under his breath, hoping that Suzanne didn't look at the nude statues. Gracefully arcing water created a mesmerizing effect with mist rising as it does on a river in the morning. The sculptor had named the fountain *Wedding of the Rivers*, seeking to honor nature's junction of two mighty waterways, the Mississippi River and the Missouri River that flows into it at the northern edge of St. Louis. Not seeing this beauty, Tony thought, *They should keep these kinds of statues in a museum, not out in the open.*

Like Tony, conservative St. Louisans were appalled by the display of nudity in the fountain. Tony didn't always agree with the uppity people in St. Louis; nevertheless, when it came to his daughter, he worried about sexual matters. Tony and Claire were always careful at home. They didn't want their daughter to see them without clothes, and here was a fountain out in the open. But there was more reason for Tony's embarrassment. The controversy was mainly caused by the name, *Wedding of the Rivers*. People couldn't abide by the implication that these figures were in a wedding, alluding to forthcoming sexual union. Tony and Claire were even more careful about doing that in their home. Even when the fountain's sculptor, Carl Mille, had explained that it was art and merely a poetic analogy of the beauty of life where the joining of two become one, such as the marriage of waters or of man, the explanation didn't help. The name had been changed to *Meeting of the Waters*.

Wanting to avoid any questions when Suzanne arrived at his side, Tony turned his back to the fountain and made a sweeping gesture with his arms.

"Look at all this place. It's really changed a lot in my lifetime. Just before I was born, they built the train station. It was all luxury, like this part of town— well, at first. I don't remember when it was beautiful 'cuz I was little. *Nónno* told me all about it." Union Station had opened in 1894, and St. Louis became the hub of national travel. Restaurants and hotels sprang up overnight around the train station. By the turn of the century, St. Louis was in its prime. "It was the best in 1904 when the World's Fair and the Olympic Games were hosted there. People from all over the world came here. Yeah, right through Union Station, where we're standing. They saw the best of St. Louis. *Nónno* said that one of the most favorite places was the Harvey Restaurant here in Union Station. Movie stars and famous people always went there. It must have been a kick to see."

"I was too young to remember ever seeing all those good years," Tony explained. "It only took ten years for downtown to get run down." Without words, Tony remembered this area all too well. Soon there was the backroom betting behind the cheap hotels. With prohibition, rough honky-tonk saloons developed with the illegal booze. By 1923, the whole area around the train station had become an unsavory neighborhood of tough people, filthy streets, and sleazy joints. The Harvey Restaurant closed with the Great Depression. Tony grew up while the city went down. Consequently, he learned how to live in tough times and he became streetwise. Finally the upstanding citizens of St. Louis had voted in a bond issue to tear down the whole area. Downtown St. Louis had been demolished the year before Tony and Claire arrived, in 1931.

"You know, like I said, when I was your age, *Nónno* and I lived around here. I'd walk right here a lot, and it wasn't nothin' like this." Tony started walking away from the fountain with Suzanne. "Well, that ain't quite true; the train station was here, but nothin' else. All the places were a bunch of fallin' down wooden buildings. It was a fire waiting to happen. Just before me and your mom came back from California, the city tore down the whole area. That's why there's so many empty lots now. You know, lots of places for gypsies to put up tents. Well, until the police run them off." He smiled really big. "Boy, this place was something when I was growin' up. Great for a boy like me!"

"What do you mean, Dad?"

"Well, you know, boys get into a lot of stuff that a nice young girl like you don't know nothin' about. There was a lot of low life stuff around here."

"Like what?" she asked again.

Trying to avoid a discussion about the nudes in the fountain, he inadvertently had started this conversation. Now he wished he hadn't.

"You know, shabby restaurants, pawnshops, and shoddy stuff like that," he gave as examples, hoping she wouldn't want any details. He didn't want to talk about the prostitutes who leaned against lampposts waiting for a john. He didn't even want to explain about the rats and filth. Trying to bribe a doorman at a speakeasy never worked, but he could walk into a honky-tonk saloon and have the time of his life. Here, there had been brothels, tattoo parlors, and cheap hotels, places he had gotten to know personally. He had grown up right here and had liked the adventure of the area. How could he tell Suzanne and still be the clean, honest father that he wanted to be to his daughter?

So here was Tony walking in 1942 with his daughter, and he found that there were aspects about his past life that he couldn't share with her. He couldn't find the courage to speak the truth, though the truth was just facts about a neighborhood. Just thinking about the real history of this place produced a cold sweat. He knew he couldn't find words to explain what he had experienced while growing up.

Tony thought, *Damn, I need to talk to her about so many things and I can't. She needs to know about personal dangers to her life. That's why I wanted to have an outing with her. But I can't even tell her how a city used to be? Why can't I figure how to say stuff to her?* Worrying, he passed his fingers through his hair.

Tony was a product of the times. Tony, like most parents, didn't talk about serious matters to children. They followed the rules "Silence is golden" and "A little knowledge is a dangerous thing." In the forties, most people reasoned it was better for children to be kept ignorant of facts that could corrupt them. Why speak openly to children about adult topics, especially in reference to sex, because a child could be led astray? Adults often didn't want to share ideas and problems with each other for the same reason; they believed that if one was kept innocent of an idea or fact, fewer problems would result. They withheld truth, opening the door to assumptions. Tony had never thought about anything like this, but Suzanne would someday. Not for years, but someday. The next generation, Suzanne and her peers, would find that they wanted the opposite—freedom of expression, tell-all relationships with those who were close to them, and a philosophy of life that could be summed up as "Truth is right."

Tony explained about the "shabby restaurants and pawnshops," but nothing more. Suzanne had no idea what was omitted. Accordingly, she couldn't react to the ugliness of how it really had been, and she couldn't ask a question about the whores and rats. She was too embarrassed to ask about the gypsies because of the sexuality that she had seen. So she continued to walk on this beautiful spring day with her father and to be happy. If he had started to talk about the low life and crime, it would've been the perfect opportunity to channel the conversation to why Claire had been so upset last night, to how children could be kidnapped, and to where there were dangers in the world. However, it was more comfortable not to talk of unpleasantness. They were happy, and that kind of talk could spoil it. Regretfully, Tony would find no other opportunity to broach the subject, and the whole day will pass without any discussion of Claire's fears.

They decided not to have an ice cream and instead went into the Harvey Restaurant, which had reopened recently with the multitude of soldiers coming and going by train.

Suzanne stopped to look at five old photos on the restaurant walls, "Look, Daddy, at these ladies in old-fashioned clothes. Oh, they were taken here in this restaurant." There was a sign below the photos:

The Renown Harvey Girls from the Turn of the Century, 1894–1915
Beautiful handpicked waitresses were trained especially to work in Union Station. Each girl wore the long black skirt, white blouse, and red tie that identified the Harvey Girls, as did their ladylike mannerisms while they
•   flowed around the tables.

Seeing so many soldiers in the station, they talked a little about the war. Tony went into a discussion of why the war had begun and who the enemies were.

"I don't want to tell anyone at the new school that I'm both Italian and German," Suzanne confided in a whisper while leaning over the table before the waitress came to take their order.

"Hey, honey, don't worry about that kind of thing. We're Americans! That's what we are. You don't know how to talk in German or Italian, do you? So you can't be the enemy, and you can't be worrying about that kind of stuff."

"Well, Daddy, it's just that someone asked the teacher about the camps that they have for the Japanese that live in California, and then she told us that they have camps for the Italians and Germans, too. So I was a little scared." Suzanne was referring to the fact that more than one million Italian, German, and Japanese immigrants had been classified as enemy aliens when United States entered the war in December of 1941.

"You know, Suzanne," Tony reassured, "everyone in this here country came from somewhere else, except the Indians. The government is looking for recent foreigners that have come here from Japan, Germany, or Italy, but our family has been here almost 100 years. We're Americans."

She reflected on that for a while, and then she remembered another question that had popped into her head from time to time because Tony and Claire had brown hair. She asked, "I'm a blonde because your dad was a German, right?"

"Yeah, honey, I guess. I've lived around Italians all my life and don't know a blonde one unless it's one with bleached hair like they do in Hollywood," he replied.

"Why don't you talk about your dad? You only talk about *Nónno*," she questioned.

"Well, I don't know much about him. You know, he died before I was born. I grew up with *Nónno*. Your Aunt Maria knows a little because she met him. Talk to her if you like." He wasn't going to get into that conversation, to have to talk about an unmarried mother and how she had had a baby. *Let good old Aunt Maria handle that one*, he thought, *but I better warn her that Suzanne finally asked about it all…and that I told Suzanne to go to her. She's going to be mad at me.*

They each ordered a club sandwich. They had been talking so much, and it felt good. Suzanne decided it was the best day she had ever spent with her father. On an impulse she asked, "How did you meet Mom?"

"Oh, now that's a story!" he said, beaming, and then sat quietly while his mind flashed back to California. "It's a good time to tell you while we wait for our food." He talked before the club sandwiches arrived, while they ate them, and for some time after they had finished eating every morsel.

"You know we met in California. I had a job at a bank as the night watchman, and I was a volunteer fireman, too. I became good friends with the guys who were volunteers like me. They worked at different jobs all over the Los Angeles area, but we got together a lot for a beer, or to see a baseball game or something. Anyways, I was single, and they were always telling me about girls. This and that one, you know, ones I should date. Most of my buddies were already married, so they wanted to fix me up with friends of their wives. After a couple of those dates, I decided I didn't need their help. The girls they picked were not for me. I wanted to pick my own. But one night when I was having dinner at my friend's place, the wife said that her friend named Claire was just perfect for me. I told her I didn't want any more duds. I was determined to find my own gal, and they seemed to get the message."

"What I didn't know was that they decided to work on Claire and get her to come over to their place one night when I was there. It turns out that she was acting like me and told them, 'No.' Well, my friend's wife talks and talks about me, trying to persuade Claire, and finally Claire agrees but only if she can see me first. Remember, I don't know about all this, right?"

"These two gals decide to come over to the bank where I work to let Claire get a look at me. Trouble was, there were more guys than me working as the night watchman. You see, one of us came to work at four in the afternoon and worked 'til midnight, and then another came on at midnight and worked 'til eight in the morning, but they didn't think about any of this."

"Over to the bank they went at six one evening and stood outside trying to see into the bank, but they can't see me. Claire says this was a dumb idea and they leave. She'd had enough."

"But, after a while, Claire gets an idea on her own how to see me. By herself, you know, on her day off or after work, she goes to the bank and asks the day guard when Tony Scaglione comes to work. She knew my name from my buddy and his wife, but the guard tells her that there was no Tony working there. So, she starts walkin' away and gets to the door when this dummy finally figures out that maybe the Antonio that works there was the Tony she was talking about. He goes after her and tells her that either me or this other guy comes on at four o'clock, but he didn't know which guy was coming. Now, he shouldn't be talking to nobody about that kind of stuff, but I guess your Mom didn't look like a bank robber to him. She writes a little note right there and then. She asks him to hand it to the guy who comes in at four. It said, 'If you are Tony, please come to the front door at 7:00 PM.'

"I did have the four o'clock shift. And this dummy gives me the note and tells me that this really good looker gave it to him for me. I complained to him that he could be in a lot of trouble doing that kind of thing. She could be a Bonnie like those Bonnie and Clyde bank robbers. Then he gets scared."

"Naturally, we had to inform our boss and the police about this. They all were concerned over the incident. He had to stay late and tell his story over and over to the detective. Then the police decided that they better be safe than sorry and called in seven cop cars to hide around the building. It got closer and closer to seven and everything was ready."

"Meanwhile, your Mom made a big sign that she folded and put into her purse. She planned to hold the sign up for me to read through the glass doors. She had written in big letters, 'ARE YOU TONY SCAGLIONE??' because she knew I wouldn't be able to open the door. She arrived a little early and figured that I wouldn't go to the door before seven so she waited at the corner out of sight. All the cops could see her, but she didn't notice them. She must have looked real suspicious. She kept looking at her watch and pacing back and forth at the corner. Of course I was watching for her inside the bank, and exactly at seven she walks up to this door that was all glass, and I saw the most beautiful woman I've ever seen. She had on a dress of pale blue that made her eyes sparkle. She looked sweet and soft. Then she opens her purse to get out this sign she made for me to read through the door. She never touches it because all the cops jump her." Tony stopped to laugh and was laughing with such zeal that Suzanne had to laugh, too.

"It wasn't funny for Claire, and I was feeling sorry for her, too, because she looked shocked and scared. I couldn't open the door and go outside. Besides, I didn't know she was the gal my friends wanted me to meet. I stood inside the bank and watched them put these handcuffs on her. They take her down to the station, and I don't know what's going on after that. I needed to finish working my shift, which lasted until midnight. All the cops left when they had her in custody."

"What happened was that they took her down to check her story, maybe to see if she had a record or was on the Wanted List. I don't know. They didn't book her because everything checked out, I guess. You know? She told them that I worked on the volunteer fire fighters with the husband of her friend. Stuff like that. Both my friend and his wife had to go to the station to give statements, too."

"Claire never got to see me. But, boy, did I see her. My buddy was waiting for me at the bank when I left a little after midnight. He lets me know what happened, and that was the first moment that I knew it was their friend. I felt like I want to die. I let him know that I found her gorgeous and I wanted to meet her. He tells me that she never wants to ever see me. That made sense, since the cops let her know that I was the person that called them. I tell my friends to let her know that I really want to see her personally to apologize, but nothing works. Then after a time I get this idea."

"I find out where she works, this office where she was a secretary. My buddy's wife helps me learn where she works, and we make sure I won't cause any problems going over there. So, I went over to this busy office and asked to see her. Remember that she never saw me before. Finally I get called into her area and shown to her desk. I don't say nothing. I pull out this sign and slowly unfold it and hold it in front of me. It stated, 'ARE YOU CLAIRE? HI, I'M TONY.' She smiled and I turned the sign over for her to read, 'I KNOW A GREAT PLACE FOR SPAGHETTI.' We went out and that was that. Ain't that a great story?"

"Yes. I can't believe I never knew this story before," Suzanne acknowledged. Throughout her life she'd think about this story and the day her father had shared it with her. It had been a unique day for the two—a father and his daughter, building memories. Then another puzzling question popped into her head, and without thinking, she asked, "Why didn't you and Mom have any more children?" As soon as the question was out of her mouth, she saw her dad's expression change and regretted having asked.

He looked sad. "I don't know." His eyes peered out into nowhere, and he was silent momentarily before he repeated, "I just don't know, because we wanted at least one more." Then, after a hesitation, he seemed to become aware of his surroundings. He looked at his daughter and brightened, "We've been at this restaurant too long. Let's go over to Forest Park for dessert, and we'll have that ice cream cone I talked about."

"Oh, Daddy, that'd be great!"

The St. Louis World's Fair of 1904 had been located in what is now called Forest Park. Little Antonio had gone there with his *Nónno* and had his first ice cream cone. It had been the first time anyone had had an ice cream cone! The fair had several new foods to show the world, ice cream cones as well as hot dogs and iced tea. He had been three years old and really didn't have his own memories of the fair. He remembered what his *Nónno* told him over and over through the years.

As Suzanne and Tony walked, he talked about the fair. "There was this unbelievable Ferris Wheel. It could hold over two thousand people!" They were strolling with their ice cream cones. "People said that it couldn't be built. Me and *Nónno* went up in it, and I'll never forget that *Nónno* told me people liked to get married on it. Isn't that something?" Suzanne nodded, licking the ice cream from her lips. They finished their ice cream while walking around a lagoon called the Great Basin in front of a palace-like structure, the present Art Museum—both remains of the Fair.

"*Nónno* used to tell me that the world was changing when I was born in 1901. They discovered the first oil in the states down in Texas that same year.

Nónno told me the birth of me and U.S. oil made the world a better place. Ha!" Tony turned with that comment and smiled, "He was always bragging 'bout me." Tony gave another little laugh and hugged Suzanne around her shoulders as they continued walking. "But he was right; there was a lot of new stuff at that time, like the telephone and telegraph. Let's see if I can remember some more. Yeah, cars—they always said 'automobile,' though, and then there were the movies: they called them 'motion pictures.' There was submarines, zeppelins, and the electric trolleys that we call 'streetcars.' All that stuff was started around the time I was born." He stopped. "*Nónno* was something special. Always telling me things. Wish you could've met him."

She grabbed her father around the waist and hugged, "It feels like I have."

It was an amazing park. It was an amazing day. Suzanne would always remember it as...her best-outing-ever with her dad.

CHAPTER 6

While Suzanne and Tony were enjoying themselves during their outing, Claire had succumbed to depression. After they had left, she had tried to busy herself by making a list of the items needed for the store and by drawing a diagram of where she'd put them. She was considering opening the confectionery soon.

After a few minutes of work, she felt overwhelmed. Sighing, she said aloud, "Oh, I really don't know where to begin with the store," and dropped her head into her arms on the table. Resting with her eyes closed, her thoughts proceeded to problems. She regretted screaming at Suzanne. She realized she was too irrational with her daughter. She knew that her dour attitude wasn't how a mother should be. Yet she knew she wasn't going to change the relationship with her daughter until she could forget this other incident and stop hating herself. She corrected her thought, "No, I hate Harry. He made me feel ashamed and dirty. But I don't want to think about him." She sat up, reached for the diagram of the store, and then put the drawing aside. "Oh, I can't concentrate on this." Jumping up from the table and grabbing the broom, she began to sweep. Still, Harry was lurking in the shadows of her mind. "I can't work either. I can't sweep the floor, much less sweep him out of my head."

She went to her bedroom and flopped on top the bed. A chill passed through her. She wrapped her arms across her chest for warmth and curled into a fetal position. In a while, the sun entered and spread across the bed, covering her in warmth. She was curled away from the window to keep the light off her face. Lying there, looking at all the nubs on the white bedspread, she began to reminisce. Her fingers fiddled with one nub, her vision blurred, and then all the white became the sunlit snow of that winter day when she had first encountered Harry. She shivered, no longer noticing or knowing that she was lying in the spring sunlight. Her mind took her back to a winter almost seven years ago.

"Hey, cutie, need a cab?" Harry asked as his cab moved slowly down the street while maintaining the speed of her walk. She had on her black galoshes with the fur around the ankles. The galoshes had the shape of her high-heeled shoes and slipped over them snugly. Her black coat with a small fur collar and darling little matching hat—angled over one side of her forehead, exposing the other—had been bought years ago with Tony's first paycheck when they had realized that she had never owned a real winter coat. She needed them to survive in St. Louis, where temperatures fell below freezing much of the season.

"No, thank you, I prefer to walk," she commented without looking because she needed to watch every step on the iced sidewalks. People had tried to shovel it clean, but the hard clumps of ice, made by yesterday's footprints that refroze during the night, just couldn't be removed.

"You look cold. I see your legs are red, and those nice gams should be warm," he continued in his crude way.

She looked at him with fire in her eyes, "I said, 'No.' I don't need a ride!"

"Hey, hey, hey, she's hot now." He took the cigar from his mouth and threw his head back, laughing. "I like 'em hot, you know," he persisted. "Where are you going? I'll give you a lift for nothin."

She tried to ignore him. She wanted to be rid of him. As she came to the corner she stepped down from the curb and pretended that she was going to cross the street. When his cab was halfway across the intersection attempting to go the same direction, she turned back and went left where he could not follow. Cars behind his cab were bumper to bumper. The drivers began to honk when he stopped to analyze what to do. After he drove out of sight, she went into a laundry shop. Just as expected, he passed in a little while. She told the lady in the store that she was trying to get away from a man that was bothering her, and the lady showed her a door out the back.

She didn't see him for a couple of weeks or a month. She had purposely avoided going down that same street although it was the most direct route to the grocery store from her home. Then one day she was stepping off a curb when he pulled directly in front of her and blocked her path.

"Hi, Sweetie, where've you been? I miss'd ya. Did you tink about me?" he chided. She could see the whiskers on his chin and brown grime from cigar smoke caked on each tooth. The corners of his eyes looked as if they hadn't been cleaned since he had awoken that morning. She found him repulsive, crude, and distasteful. It must have shown in her expression. His face changed from the confident wise guy to an expression of hurt. "What's da matter, Sweetie, you don't think I'm your type? We'll see," he said and hastily maneuvered out into the traffic.

Her heart was beating in thumps that seemed to be knocking against her stomach. She felt like she was going to throw up. He had stopped her just across the street from where she lived. It scared her. Seeing his cab disappear, she quickly crossed through the traffic and walked to her door. She unlocked the door with shaking hands and then climbed the steep staircase to her second floor apartment, which was over a tobacco store. Lifting her arms to pull the hatpin, she called, "Mrs. Stein, I'm home."

"I'm in the kitchen, Dearie, with Suzanne," answered the elderly upstairs neighbor who often watched Suzanne. "We made a batch of sugar cookies while you were out. Come have one."

Claire walked to the kitchen through their small quarters of three rooms and a bath. "Oh, how sweet of you, Mrs. Stein."

"Mommy, Mommy, I helped make them. I got to use the rolling pin and make them flat and then press the stars and circles out. Come see, come see," chanted Suzanne while pulling on her mother's arm.

"Let me get my coat and galoshes off first." Claire hung her coat on a hook next to the back door and then situated herself on the edge of a kitchen chair for the struggle to pull off the galoshes.

"I imagine you're chilled to the bone," Mrs. Stein commented. "I decided some cookies would serve two purposes—heat the house a bit and fill a little stomach." She bent down and put her finger into Suzanne's tummy. The child giggled and ran to put her head on her mother's lap. Mrs. Stein placed a small saucer with some cookies in front of Claire and then pulled her own coat from one of the hooks. "Well, I want to get my supper going before Howard gets home. Did you get to the bank okay?"

"Yes, thank you. Oh, please take some of these delicious cookies up for Howard."

"No, thanks. He's gained too much weight lately," Mrs. Stein commented as she put on her coat. She'd go across the weather-beaten wooden back porch and up the stairs to get to her apartment. Before she placed a faded red scarf over her gray hair, she slipped out a hairpin and tucked a few stray hairs into the tight bun she always wore at her nape. "Suzanne was no trouble at all to be with. Bye, sweetie." She put her hand on the soft curls and rubbed the head lovingly.

"Thank you for coming down, Mrs. Stein. Suzanne, say good-bye to Mrs. Stein."

"Bye, thank you for the cookies," the child muttered with a shy smile.

Those first years in St. Louis were frugal times for the Scaglione family. Their rooms were a bit run down from years of other careless renters, but the idea was to spend as little money as possible and save all they could. They wanted to buy a place of their own. They postponed the plan to have another child in order to save money, and Claire was being very careful about both—not getting pregnant and not buying anything they didn't need. They were halfway to the goal of $1,000. They had to save most of Tony's salary, and yet with the money Claire made from little projects she sold, they could afford a few extras like going to the picture show once in a while. Mrs. Stein was always kind enough to sit with Suzanne for those few evenings when they went out. The sweet old lady would say, "Don't embarrass me and try to pay me. Little Suzanne is the granddaughter I never had." Only five more years until they could buy a place where Claire could have a little shop. One week she'd dream of a dress shop, and the next week it was a shop with sewing accessories; she liked to use her hands to make things, and she figured that she could give classes for sewing, crochet, needlepoint. and embroidery.

She had come back from making the weekly deposit, and she slipped the bankbook away in their bedroom chest of drawers. Tony wasn't going to be home that night because he was working the night shift at the firehouse. Claire wished he were there to comfort and hug her. She wasn't sure if she could talk with him about this second encounter with the crude cabby. She had told Tony about the first meeting, and he had said that she was overreacting to what men do all the time, flirting and teasing. Tony saw it as just talk and suggested ignoring the man.

Now, with the unsettling feelings she had from this second encounter, she thought, "Tony just doesn't understand how a woman is." She didn't want Tony to know how upset and shaken she really was because he might laugh at her overreaction.

She went out on the back porch to take down the washing. The back yard of their place was unusual because the block where they lived was triangular, the result of three intersecting streets that met at acute angles. It was a small block and seemed like an island amid the traffic. There were bustling shops around all three sides facing the wide sidewalks. Families lived upstairs from the shops. Some places, like Claire and Tony's, had a front door located between two shops. The shop owners often had homes on the second and third floors, which gave them double the amount of rooms that the Scagliones had, renting only the second floor. There were some walk-up flats on the third floor, which had no front door; one could get to them only by the back entrance. There in the back, outside of every family's kitchen, was a common wooden porch—gray and weatherworn—overlooking the yard. The porch was a frequented thoroughfare bustling with activity—children playing, old folks passing time with a card game, women ironing or hanging washing—because it gave access to each neighbor's back door and the yard below. Cracked and loose wooden steps went up to each of the three levels of porches or down to the backyard of dirt where there were spaces for four or five vehicles to park.

This back area was a dangerous place for a small child because many rungs on the banisters were missing, and it would be quite a fall from the porch; down in the yard, delivery trucks for the shops came and went, entering from the street through an opening not much more than a double doorway since it was originally made to accommodate carriages and delivery carts. Obviously, the yard wasn't a place for a child to play. Suzanne knew she wasn't to go out without an adult with her.

Because Claire hadn't slipped on her coat to take in the washing, she worked quickly out on the porch. She was cold. It amazed her whenever she did the washing in the St. Louis winters. She remembered the first time she had seen Aunt Maria go outside with a basket of wet clothes up on Dago Hill, the Italian neighborhood in St. Louis. (They had lived well over a year with Aunt Maria and Uncle Vinny.) Claire had asked her what she was doing and couldn't figure out the answer. Maria had responded with a St. Louis pronunciation of the word 'wash' as well as with an Italian accent. It sounded like "goin ta hang awarsh." Finally Claire translated the word to "wash," laughed a bit, and went for her coat to help Aunt Maria. The sheets on the clotheslines were already frozen stiff. The clothes, once frozen on the line, swung like the hinged wooden sign above the tobacco store, making strange creaking sounds with the wind. To Claire it had seemed that the frozen blouses would split wide-open where they were creased, but they didn't. The wind blew and slowly, and as the clothes began to dry, they appeared malleable, then flexible, and eventually soft. The winter clothes came in softer than the summer ones. It amazed Claire. She wished her fingers were like the clothes. They cracked and bled if she forgot to dry her hands before going out to hang the wash and then to apply hand cream when she came in.

She rushed in with her arms full, quickly closed the door, put the clothes on the kitchen table, and got out her ironing board. Then she put the iron on the stove to heat. *It's good that Mrs. Stein stoked the stove to bake because I can get this ironing done, too*, she reflected. She was still rattled and trying to keep her mind off the cabby incident. Suzanne went to her room after noticing that her mother was quiet and worried. It really wasn't a room. Suzanne slept in the hallway. A tiny living room and bathroom were on one side of the hall, a bedroom and kitchen on the other side. The bathroom was ample, roughly the size of the small living room. They put a chifforobe and small cot at the end of the hall near the bathroom door. That area of the hall was wider because there was more floor space where the floor covered over the stairwell. The chifforobe had the clothes for all three of them, and more important to Suzanne, it had a space behind it where she hid Bobo. The hatbox remained in the back of a drawer in the chest of drawers where Claire had put it. Suzanne had removed Bobo from the hatbox long ago and hid him. She stretched up to slip him out. She couldn't be seen while she played on the far side of the chifforobe, and when she heard her mother approaching she could quickly slip the ball back into his dark space behind the chifforobe. A half hour passed and Claire called to Suzanne, "What are you doing? You're so quiet."

"Just playing, Mommy."

"Come in here and keep me company. I'll turn on the radio and we can listen to Amos and Andy."

"Okay, Mommy," she replied and kissed Bobo goodnight, replacing him behind the chifforobe before going into the kitchen.

Such was their lives most days in the confining St. Louis winters until the cabby discovered where she lived.

Again it had been several weeks since Claire had seen him. This time he was there when she came out of the door with Suzanne. At first she overlooked him, because he was out of the cab. There were three cabs parked at the curb, as there often were, and he was talking with the other two cabbies. Unknowingly, Claire began to walk in his direction holding her daughter's hand. Then she saw him coming toward her. Panic inside! Outwardly, no one noticed. *Why am I embarrassed? I should be angry or irritated*, Claire reprimanded herself. She really was afraid to show any emotion. *I'm trying not to frighten Suzanne*, she concluded, though not correctly. She often couldn't explain her own reactions to different situations. Even so, she knew she was too embarrassed to have anyone think that she knew this man, not only because of his usually unkempt appearance, but also because she wanted no one to think she was interested in another man.

Today he was really spiffy, clean and with carefully combed hair. He had slicked down his hair with Brillcreme—at least it smelled like that.

"Good day, ladies, how are you today?" he asked in a manner unlike the other encounters. He tipped his cabby cap and smiled at little Suzanne. Claire made no comment and went on walking. He began to walk with them. "My name is Harry. I should've introduced myself before when we met. I apologize for my not bein' polite before," he recited as if he had carefully practiced what he was going to say. She made no response. So he started to talk to Suzanne. "What's your name little girlie? You sure are a pretty sight like your mommy."

"Suzanne," she responded before Claire could prevent it.

Claire complained, "Don't talk to her!"

"Well, if you won't talk to me I feel a little funny just talkin' to the air," he defended himself, "and I want to start over and be nice. You know, friendly, that's all."

"Please leave us alone." The words came from her lips in low tones, without her looking at him.

"Why, of course, sorry to have disturbed you. At least we have been introduced now, Clara," he expressed with hesitancy. She stopped. She was shocked. He had learned her name, well, close enough. Who could have told him? She didn't like this at all and was scared. Somehow or other she decided to try to be nice and to make him understand.

Maybe with some polite reasoning he'll leave me alone, she silently hoped.

"Look, Harry, I'm normally not a rude person, but I'm a married woman and have no reason to talk with you. Please don't be offended. Please understand." Claire specifically avoided talking about his rude comments and flirting because she didn't want to irritate him. She didn't know how he'd react. Since he was trying to be decent, she wanted to try, in the same manner, to let him know that she wanted this to end.

"Why, Clara, you're mistaking my intentions I do believe. I only want to be nice to you. You're so pretty and have such a pretty little girl. I'd be proud if I could help you out sometimes and drive you somewhere when you need to go. Nothing more."

"Well, thank you, but not today. It's beautiful and sunny and we could use a little walk," she declared as she started away. She half turned and looked back, "Nice talking with you. Good-bye"

It seemed to work because, when she walked away, he stayed where he was. For a while he watched her intently, studying her movements, and then he went back to the cabs at the curb. Behind her she could hear the three cabbies talking and laughing. She worried that he was telling them about her. She wanted to die. On the return from the vegetable stand, she entered through the back yard, where he wouldn't see her, and quickly went up the wooden steps. As soon as she was in the house she went to the small bathroom window that looked out front, needing to know if he was there. He wasn't. Realizing that Tony was coming home that night, she relaxed a bit.

Thus it went for several weeks. Sometimes he'd be parked out in front and talk in the same manner as the last time, while she tried not to respond. Other days she'd go out and not see him.

Then the day arrived when she was out with Mrs. Stein and Suzanne. Both she and Mrs. Stein had their arms full of groceries and were two blocks from the triangle when he pulled up in his cab. He jumped out and approached Mrs. Stein while saying, "Hello, Clara and Suzanne, let me drop youse off at your door; I'm going that way. Here, ma'am, I'll take your bags." Deftly he took Mrs. Stein's burdens and her elbow as he led her to the cab.

"Why, this surely is appreciated. I was getting tired and not looking forward to walking those two blocks," commented Mrs. Stein as she was seated in the back seat. Harry quickly returned to the sidewalk and in a grand swoop picked up Suzanne, twirled her into the air, and whisked her to the other side, carefully placing her on the back seat before Claire could respond. Suzanne was giggling and happy with the playful gesture. Claire didn't know what she could say with Mrs. Stein there. This whole scene caught her unaware, and she didn't know what could be done. She stood transfixed on the sidewalk. He came around to the passenger side of the cab, opened the front door, and slowly took one of Claire's bags. Harry was careful not to touch her, even the slightest, as he removed the sack of groceries from her grasp.

"Have a seat, Clara," he offered.

"You mean Claire, I'm sure," corrected Mrs. Stein.

Claire stiffened with the comment. She couldn't think how to make this end.

"Oh, didn't I say Claire? Excuse me if I didn't pronounce your name right. It won't happen again." Then, he closed the passenger door, walked to the driver's seat, and slipped in. "This really was a nice convenience, wasn't it? Me going the same way, that is. You know, this here ride is free of charge. Why, Claire and Suzanne are friends of mine," he vocalized, straining awkwardly to look over his shoulder and address his words to Mrs. Stein.

"That's certainly nice, young man," began Mrs. Stein. She talked for the whole two blocks. Harry circled around the triangle to enter into the backyard to unload.

Claire's thoughts were unsettling. "It was as if he knew that Mrs. Stein lived on the third floor and only could enter her place from the back or," now Claire felt panicky, "he's showing me that he knows that I sneaked in here to avoid him that other day. He knows where I am all the time."

As they bumped up the curb into the back lot, passing through the darkened passageway, his hand quickly went under her skirt and he squeezed her thigh right below her crotch.

"Oh!" Claire screamed and grabbed at his arm. He pulled away quickly to have his move remain unknown to the others.

"That's quite a bump, ladies. Sorry, Claire, if I took it too fast and scared you," he snickered to conceal his brazen act.

By now the cab had come to a stop. Claire jumped out without all of her purchases, frantically running around to Suzanne before Harry pushed the gearshift into first and turned off the ignition.

Casually he got out, trying to distract the older lady from Claire's haste. "I'll help you, Mrs. Stein, with your groceries up to the third floor. That's a long way up all those stairs, isn't it?"

As he spoke, Claire was climbing the stairs with Suzanne while tears streamed down her cheeks. She was shaking so that she fumbled with the key in the lock, but finally got her kitchen door open. Locking herself inside, she pulled all the shades before he and Mrs. Stein had reached the second floor landing. With her back against the wall, Claire could hear Mrs. Stein and him talking as they passed her door and continued climbing up the next flight of stairs. She took Suzanne's hand, went to her bedroom, and closed the door behind her. Sitting on the bed with Suzanne in her arms, she began rocking and sobbing, "What am I going to do? What am I going to do?"

"What's wrong, Mommy?" asked Suzanne.

"Oh, sweetie, it's that man, Harry. I hate him!" Just then she heard the door rattle. She was afraid to move. Then she heard a firm hard knocking, and she held her breath. Her pulse was throbbing and she felt the pounding in her whole body.

She heard Harry saying, "I'll put your other bag of groceries here outside the door. Be seeing you later. Bye-bye." Listening, she heard his heavy footsteps retreat down the stairs. Outside, she heard an engine start and the whine of a motor slowly disappeared. She wasn't sure if it was Harry's cab, but was afraid to look. She sat there for a long, long time. Finally, Suzanne wanted to get down.

"Don't move!"

"Why, Mommy?" the child asked in a voice that finally made Claire realize that she was scaring her daughter more by remaining still.

"It's okay. You're right. Let's go in the kitchen and put the food away."

When Tony came home, Claire said nothing. Her reasoning was that she had asked him for help once and he had concluded that she was foolishly imagining things. Therefore, if she told him now, he might think that she had encouraged the man. "How can I tell my husband that this cab driver put his hand all the way up my skirt? What would Tony do? Tony'd be mad at me, I know. He'd scream at me! He might say horrible things and accuse me. Then bad words'd be said that could never be unsaid," she worried. "Or am I imagining an extreme situation?" she continued to reason. "Tony'd be frustrated that I let this become a problem where he must be involved. He'd be angry that I couldn't handle all this when it was more simple." Whatever way she envisioned it, telling Tony seemed too difficult or too upsetting, and she'd imagine the consequences as being negative. Therefore, she said nothing.

The whole situation with Harry had gotten really complicated and she knew that she *must* resolve it without Tony. She decided to ask the police for help.

It was typical for a policeman to be on one of the corners of the busy intersection outside. She often saw one and greeted him with a "Good day, officer"
when she passed. Looking from her window, hour-to-hour all day, she waited
until a policeman and Harry were both down on the sidewalk near her door.
Enough days had passed for her to think and rethink what to do. She had a plan.

The situation had to be just right. She had also decided that Harry had to
be out of his cab or he could drive away before she got downstairs. The
policeman had to be standing around and not looking as if he were about to
walk off. Suzanne needed to be napping or playing quietly. She knew it'd be
difficult to capture the right moment as she continually looked out the window and checked for a possible chance.

The day she saw her first opportunity ended with no results. The sight of
Harry heightened the beating of her heart and flushed moisture under her
arms and on her brow. She sank upon her bed and covered herself as a chill
crept over her. Fear dominated her. She cried instead of going downstairs.

At her next chance, Suzanne awoke when she started down the stairs. As
Claire walked back upstairs, she made the supposition that if she didn't do this
soon, she'd lose her nerve, or worse, Harry could make some move before she
did. She was avoiding leaving the house and had asked Mrs. Stein to get a few
groceries from the store for her. She feared a knock at the door.

Finally, one cold windy day, the situation was ready for her, and grabbing a
coat, she rushed down to the sidewalk and stopped. Looking to the right, she
saw that Harry was turned away from her and conversing with someone. She
hurried over to the officer that was standing to her left in front of the tobacco
shop and leaning on the ornamental framework of the doorway. He seemed to
be humming a tune because he was tapping his nightstick against his leg to
some rhythm. He had gray hair and a moustache, but didn't seem too old to
her, not young either. As she approached, he noticed that she was coming
toward him and straightened up.

He bent forward a bit and touched his hat with the nightstick as he greeted
her with a "Good afternoon, miss."

"Sir, I've got a problem that needs your help," she blurted while squeezing one
hand with the other. Her palms began to sweat. She wiped them on her coat.

"How can I help?" he asked.

"There is a man that has been bothering me, and I'm a married woman
with a child, and I can't make him leave me alone. I'd like you to make him
understand that he's gotta leave me alone, sir," she blurted in one breath.

"How has he been bothering you?" questioned the officer.

"Well," she began and realized that she hadn't rehearsed this part. She
absolutely could not tell him of the horrible squeeze to her thigh, yet she con-

cluded that if she didn't, what would be her complaint? It would be the same as when she told Tony. The policeman would think she was exaggerating.

"It's that cab driver over there without his cap. He bothers me and my little daughter every time we come out. He talks to me when I've asked him not to. He says things I don't like, and he won't leave me alone." She began to weep because she knew she must say more than these sniveling examples. She gathered all her nerve and said, "And he touched me when I was in his cab."

"Why, miss, I can't do much about talk, and I need to know what you mean by 'touched' because that there is Harry Schwarz, and he's a mighty friendly sort. Why, I talk to him every day and wouldn't want anyone saying something bad about him if he did something that was just an accident or not what he meant. You can see he's friendly. Look at them laughing and goin' on up there. He's always jokin' around, but he's good-hearted and always wantin' to help people. Most the time he gives people a ride without chargin' them 'cuz he don't seem to need much money. He don't have any close family. He just has his friends, and he seems to treat people good. And so, you see, I need to know more about what you mean."

"I want him to leave me alone," she declared and wiped her eyes with her handkerchief.

"Miss, my job is to help and protect people. You know? I can't solve all the grievances I hear." He was very polite. "Why don't we go and talk to Harry together? That's as much as I could do in this type of situation."

"Oh, no! I couldn't, I mean I can't…oh, please, I don't want to talk with him, I want him to leave me alone. I don't want to talk."

The policeman sensed her fear. He tried again to find whether there was some substance to her comments.

"Can you tell me any real reason why you really need my help?" he persisted.

This whole situation was becoming more and more complicated. Claire could see that the officer liked Harry. Maybe they were friends. If she told him about the hand up her skirt and Harry denied her statement, she knew the policeman wouldn't believe her. She had no proof. Mrs. Stein had been there when it occurred. *Why didn't I tell her? Now I have no witness, either*, she scolded herself. So Claire shook her head in the negative while she blew her nose trying to gain some composure.

"Look, miss, it'll be all right. Harry is a good sort of chap in his own way. He tried to join the force once, but he didn't pass all the tests. He was really disappointed that he couldn't be a policeman. This is one of the reasons that I think that he means well. I probably shouldn't be tellin' you about this. You need to keep this between you and me, about all this. I might say something to him to not bother you, if that might help. Mind you, it won't be nothin' official," he whispered in an effort to calm her and soothe her. "You let me know if there's anything else. My name is Clarence, but just call me Casey. Now you go get relaxed and calmed down."

As she retreated back to her doorway, she glanced at Harry and saw that he was looking at her and probably had seen her talking with the policeman. She turned away and opened her door, stopping and turning momentarily to look back at Harry. He had a strange look on his face. She went in.

It was obvious to her that Casey had spoken with Harry because days passed. Then it became weeks and Claire never saw Harry. Casey's words repeated over and over in her head, especially the comments, "I probably shouldn't be telling you this" and "keep it just between you and me."

What did he tell me that he shouldn't have? That he tried to join the police force? No, more likely, he meant the part about his not being accepted because he "didn't pass all the tests." It could be that they found he had a police record, she imagined. *Maybe he committed a really bad crime. A bootlegger! Yes, because Casey claimed that he didn't seem to need money. Possibly he worked or has connections with the Mob. If he didn't bootleg, maybe he did jobs for them."* She didn't want to think about the kind of jobs he could be doing for the Mob. On and on she went with this imagining about the conversation with Casey. She could not stop; her mind would begin upon awakening, whether in the morning or in the middle of the night. She wasn't sleeping well, either. She didn't relax or allow herself the pleasure of being free to come and go until more than a month had passed and he was…just gone. Even then, she realized that she'd always be wary of walking alone, though most of the intense fear was gone.

Claire was feeling good about herself. She had handled the problem. In these past years she had had opportunity to think about who she was—who a woman was and could be. Nevertheless, there was a lot of talk about women that made her feel uncomfortable. It had started in 1928–29 when the suffrage for women was passed. Claire was young back then and hadn't taken the time to think if it was important to vote or not, although she was curious enough to go with Tony when he voted for FDR. The actual act of voting didn't seem like much to her, and she definitely wasn't interested in the political discussions or in reading about the campaigns. She wondered why it seemed so important to some women. She didn't like the changes that had followed women's rights to vote. She noticed some men were critical of women who voted. These men figured that if women wanted to have men's rights that they should take the bad with the good and stop acting delicate and soft. She wondered if Casey was one of those men, but he hadn't acted as such.

Anyway, Claire was experiencing the strength and power of being a person who could take care of herself. She was thinking, *I should have the same rights*

and respect as any other person. Maybe that's what the women in the movement
for suffrage had meant for us to understand.

However, the longer she concentrated, she went in a complete circle from
optimism that gradually became only hopefulness, and slowly changed to less
certainty. Then came the doubts, and some days of depression, until she was
back to fear. She began to fear that she had been too confident and that she had
better be careful or something worse could come about.

What Claire realized was that a person couldn't control all situations. She
had hoped a person's intelligence could prevail and win, but it seemed that one
doesn't control destiny. Claire concluded, "People are just in the right place at
the right time, or like me, the wrong place at the wrong time. If I hadn't come
to live in this particular neighborhood where Harry lived and worked, I could
have avoided him. Couldn't I? Of course."

Tony left for work on the night shift when little Suzanne was sick, though
not as sick as she was going to get. It was an influenza that often developed at
the beginning of spring. After midnight, Claire went to a neighbor and asked
if their seventeen-year-old son could run for the doctor because the child was
ill with an extremely high fever. The doctor came and worked over an hour
with Suzanne until he was sure she was getting better.

"She'll be fine in the morning, but you need to get this prescription filled,"
he told Claire. "I'll stay here while you get a neighbor or someone to come be
with Suzanne so you can go for the medicine. I've another patient who is waiting for my return, or I'd stay while you go for the medicine. But I really have
been gone far too long."

Mrs. Stein came downstairs wearing a robe over her nightclothes. Her
sleepiness disappeared when she saw Suzanne.

"Do you know where you can get this medicine at this time?" the doctor
asked Claire as he put on his coat.

"Ah, yes, I'll walk over to Mr. Kauffmann's door; he has the pharmacy
downstairs and I know him. He lives right over there," Claire pointed across
the backyard porches.

After the doctor left, Claire explained to Mrs. Stein that Suzanne needed to
have a cool cloth on her forehead. Then Claire went to the chifforobe and took
out a loose housedress, deciding no stockings or shoes were needed to run
across the porch and, later, down the stairs. She'd go in her slippers, too.

She left without a coat. "It's so close," she thought and walked over to the
pharmacist's home. After waking Mr. Kauffmann and giving him the prescription, she returned to her place and informed Mrs. Stein, "He said that he'd go

downstairs to mix the medicines so I'm going down to wait." Claire looked in on Suzanne—she was so hot—and went downstairs.

The pharmacy appeared dark when she tapped on the glass window with a coin. While waiting for Mr. Kauffmann to come to the door to let her in, Claire noticed how nice the night air was, how quiet the streets seemed, and that there was a fragrance drifting from some flowers that she couldn't see.

"Hello, Mrs. Scaglione," Mr. Kauffman said as he opened the door. Stepping inside, Claire noticed a light in the back of the store. They walked toward it. "I'll be a moment longer. I just need to type the label," he explained. "Please take a seat."

"Thank you for helping me. Sorry I had to bother you so late at night."

"Oh, I'm used to this. It's a part of my job, Mrs. Scaglione. Children always get sick at night," he said, smiling with that comment, and shuffled back behind the counter. He, too, had slippers on his feet. Soon Mr. Kauffmann was starting to wrap the two items together in green paper. "Just put two drops in a glass of water every four hours for this one," he instructed, pointing to the bottle. "The directions are on it. This other one is a salve that you are to rub on her chest and back right away and again every eight hours." With deft movements of his hands, he folded the paper quickly and tied the package with a string that came from a large spool hanging above his head. She paid and he walked with Claire to the door. "She needs to drink a lot of liquids. I guess the doctor mentioned that."

"Yes, he did," Claire responded. "Thank you again and good night." Mr. Kauffmann locked the door and went to the back of the store where there were stairs up to his home.

Claire walked into the pleasant night, preoccupied with thinking about the time to give the drops to Suzanne. She didn't notice Harry parked at the curb.

Since she had talked with the policeman, she hadn't seen Harry, but Harry had been watching her place at night. Usually, he parked in front where he could see the bedroom and bathroom windows. He rarely saw more than a shadow when parked in front. On occasion he'd park on the street by the back entrance and stand in the darkened passageway to view her through the kitchen window. He'd often see her there at night when she'd forget to pull the shade. He felt especially elated at those times when she walked out on the back porch to take down the wash or talk to Mrs. Stein or another neighbor. When Tony was on the night shift, Harry came very late and tried to get the nerve to go to her door. He fantasized about being with her. This went on night after night. The infatuation he had from their encounters in the daylight hours had changed as he sat nightly thinking alone in his cab. He was obsessed.

Tonight, when he saw her come out her door, his lust was at a state that he had never before experienced. He had watched as she had entered the pharmacy and decided to confront her with his feelings. While he sat waiting he found it difficult to decide what to say. Plus, he was becoming increasingly excited as he observed her through the pharmacy door. Inasmuch as he had only seen her during the winter months, she always had been in her coat. Tonight she had no coat. Finally, he decided what to do, not say. He opened the window behind him and turned the backdoor handles in the wrong direction to remove them.

When she left the pharmacy, his body reacted instantly. Her dress was loose and the shape beneath moved as she walked. Actually, his hardness was the result of night after night of dreaming and imagining.

He waited just long enough for the pharmacist to disappear from sight before he opened the cab door. As it closed, she saw Harry coming around the back of the cab toward her. Quickly the distance between them lessened. Harry had no specific plans and no words came from his mouth. He saw the woman he desired and his heart quickened in what he could only describe as love. Claire froze, wanting to run for her door, but that would mean running toward him. She saw a look in his face that seemed elated, without a smile. She couldn't think of what to do. Everything was happening too fast. He was directly in front of her. Close, too close! His heat touched her bare arms.

"Harry, what are …" were the few words that escaped her lips before his arms encircled her in what Harry found to be a tender embrace and she took as a forceful grasp. His erection pressed against her. "*No!*" she cried out and squirmed while pushing on his chest to try to free herself. "No, no, no! Oh, please," was all she could think to say as she turned her body trying to get out of his arms.

Suddenly he could feel her breasts touching his arms, and he reacted with a rush throughout his body like he had never had with any woman. Her helplessness, her petite body, precious face, and the soft fragrant hair brushing against his face were heightening his desires. Suddenly, he stopped and released her.

She crumpled to the ground, scraping her knee against the bricks. As she was groping to stand, she wondered what had made him suddenly let go. Then she saw that the package of medicine had fallen and she picked it up. She heard a car door open, and before she could turn to look, she was lifted off the ground at her waist. His one arm held her, and he thrust her onto the backseat of the cab, slamming the door. She quickly discovered that the door handles had been removed. There was no exit. She continued to search for a way to open the door and, in panic, she thrust her shoulder against the door and pushed. Hysterically, she banged against the window. Then she stretched out her full length and pushed with her feet against the door. She screamed, "Help me!" and again beat on the windows. Harry had removed the handles for opening them, too. As Harry got into the driver's seat, started the cab, and pulled out from the curb, she cried out, "Harry, Harry, let me go! Please let me go!" She began to sob, pressing her forehead against the window that separated the driver from the backseat. Within a few minutes, the cab stopped. They were in a deserted warehouse or some large building.

Neither Claire nor Harry remembered the same details of the incident. She'd remember fighting him and his horrible smell—the bad breath of a cigar smoker, the foul body odor, and his cheap aftershave cologne. He'd remember the excitement caused by her movement against him and the extreme pleasure of touching her soft, smooth skin. While coming through the car's backdoor, his first action raised her dress and ripped off her panties. Since she was beating and pushing his head and shoulders, she didn't notice that her panties were gone until he thrust into her and she screamed in pain. Time was distorted. An eternity existed for one and a minuscule moment of an explosion's flash for the other.

A quiet followed his withdrawal. The screams, kicking of doors, and thrashing stopped, resulting in complete silence, until Harry exhaled. He rolled his body off her and hit the back of the front seats before slipping to the floor. The sound of his clothes brushing the seats and the fall of his body was magnified in the stillness. Now free, Claire quickly scooted with her hands and body into a corner away from him and away from the open door where his feet protruded. She pulled her legs up to her chest and covered her legs with the skirt of her dress. She was trembling and dropped her head to her knees.

He started to reach for her, "Claire, I…"

"Don't touch me!" Wrath swirled in her voice. "Take me home! My baby is sick and needs this medicine."

"Claire, I've such…"

"Don't talk! Just get out of here and take me home." She spoke with quiet authority, sensing that for a short interval she was in control. He swiveled on the floor space and placed his feet on the ground outside to lift himself from the cab. With his back to Claire, he buttoned his trousers and straightened his clothing before turning to close the back door of the cab. Standing there, he put both hands to his hair and smoothed it into place before walking to the driver's seat.

They drove back, and Claire calmly waited for him to walk around the cab to open her door. She waved her hand like swatting at a pesky fly to make him step away and not touch her. Wordlessly, she crossed the sidewalk to her door, inserted the key, and went in. Leaning against the closed door at the bottom of the stairs, she heard him drive away while the tears streamed down and dripped onto the dress she'd never wear again.

Mrs. Stein was sleeping soundly when Claire arrived up the steps. Suzanne was sleeping, too. Claire gently shook the older woman's shoulder to wake her, saying in a whisper, "Mrs. Stein, I have the medicine. Thank you so much. Why don't you try not to wake up too much before getting into your own bed? We can talk tomorrow."

"That's a good idea. I'll stop by tomorrow," Mrs. Stein whispered back then left for her own place.

As soon as Claire applied the salve and gave the medicine to her daughter, she went for the vinegar and prepared a douche. She bathed and douched. After trying to sleep, she got up from her bed to vomit and then bathed and douched a second time. Her body still felt dirty. Her night was spent with wide-awake nightmares of guilt and fear. If moments came to allow her to slip into a sleep, soon after she awoke, tormented by repeated visions of the rape.

If Claire presumed the worst was over, or that nothing worse could happen, she was wrong.

Two days later, when Suzanne was better, Claire went to the police station and asked what one must do to report a rape. She took Suzanne along because she was afraid to go out alone and she knew, with Suzanne on her lap, she would feel more secure talking.

After a few minutes, she was directed to the desk of a detective.

"Hello, I'm Detective Duncan. How can I help you?" he asked, offering her a chair.

Without introducing herself, Claire began, "I want to find out what someone must do to report a rape." Claire sat down and pulled Suzanne onto her lap.

"Well, that is a complex situation. Are you the person wanting to report one?" he inquired.

"I want to know what someone must do to report one," she repeated.

"Well, it's a complicated process. First, they need to come in and report the incident as soon as possible. An examination will need to be done by a medical person to determine if a physical encounter and intercourse have really taken place. If a man is to be accused, we must determine that intercourse really took place. Now, the presence of the fluid from intercourse doesn't mean a rape happened because the woman could be married or have a boyfriend. So the physical appearances of bruises, cuts, or other abrasions, you know, like a black eye, swelling, or welts on the body are important. Like I said, the victim needs to come here immediately to be examined."

Claire sat quietly thinking for a minute. "What if there are no cuts or bruises, but the woman had told a policeman that she was afraid and had asked his help beforehand?" she uttered slowly.

"That wouldn't be much of a case. You see, in court they have to prove that the woman didn't encourage or want the act to occur. You know, that she was forced. How can we show this? If she didn't want it to happen, she probably fought him and got hurt. We need to show all the results of the beating with photographs. Also, we need to prove there was a sexual relation or else it wouldn't be rape. That means an examination by a doctor and..."

"But," her voice started to crack and she took a deep breath. She covered her mouth with her hand as she waited and tried to control herself. She didn't want to cry. "It's possible without getting all bruised up. It could come about fast and a woman could be little like me and him big. All he'd need to do would be to hold her down."

The detective had already suspected that she probably had been a victim and he knew that there wasn't much to be done. It was obvious that she had no case unless the man had a record of previous rapes. He asked, "Do you know the name of the man? Or, if he has a record or history of rape?"

"No." There was a sob in her voice. She took out her handkerchief and sucked in air trying to stop. He waited without comment, and she controlled the crying again.

Although Suzanne was too young to assimilate all the conversation, she was getting upset because of her mother's emotions. The detective noticed the child's fear.

"Do you want to come back without the child?" he asked. Claire moved her head from side to side to answer in the negative while he continued, "I don't know if you said 'No' to the first question that you don't know his name or that you don't know if he has a police record."

"I know his name but not about any police records," she whispered.

"Are you the victim that you're referring to?" he needed to know.

She looked up at him and froze. The question caught her by surprise. Even if he had thought she was the victim, she didn't expect him to ask her. She was afraid, and she could smell the fear on herself. She could not move. The detective seemed to understand what was happening, and they both sat there looking into each other's eyes. Finally, her gaze dropped and she lamented in a voice that was barely audible, "I can't say."

"I'm going to be blunt with you, because I can see that you're upset." He hesitated, choosing his words carefully. "I think you're the victim that you're referring to. I also see that you have no indications of a struggle or fight." With those words Claire looked up and opened her mouth to begin to speak. He raised his hand, "Please listen for a minute and let me say some things.

"If you could name the man, and I found he had a history of rape, we might have you file a complaint. I'd need details of the incident before I could decide if you have a case. Now, if he has no record of any kind…" Again he hesitated before he continued. "I want to be completely frank with you. You would get hurt more by the whole case if you don't look like you were raped." He raised his hands to show that he knew the injustice of this. "I know, I know, it doesn't seem fair. But we can't let men get accused without proof. Let me ask you, assuming that you're the woman, do you think you have any proof?"

"No, not really, I guess."

"Listen, I'm trying to protect you against the ugliness that starts when a woman tries to prove a rape. All your family and friends will know, and the other lawyer will try to show that you encouraged the guy. They could make you out to be a person that you're not. You get the picture, right?" he said frankly.

Claire was wishing that she had never come, wishing that she could disappear without walking out of the police station. The tears were starting to roll down her cheeks, and she was angry that she had succumbed to crying again. At least they were only tears and not sobs. She dabbed her eyes and started to get up when he put his hand on her arm and restrained her.

"Sit here a minute and let me write down my name and telephone number. Call me to talk if you want. Is he gone, or do you think he might try it again?" he inquired.

Claire shrugged her shoulders and knew that she couldn't speak or she'd lose the little control that she had. She accepted the paper with his name and telephone number.

"Well, call me to talk if you need to. Maybe I could come and help," he stated in conclusion.

With that comment, her spine tingled. That comment could be taken in a way that she didn't want to hear. He had been overly nice and attentive. But was he really a kind person trying to help, or were there other connotations in his words? She was standing to leave and found herself saying, "Thank you, I must be going," while she was reprimanding herself. Why am I thanking him? He has done nothing to help me, and he may be making a pass. Why don't I tell him that he has been no help and is scaring me more? What is wrong with me?

She turned and left quickly.

This incident at the police station wasn't her final defeat. Within the week, she learned to her dismay that Tony knew Harry, too. It seemed that Harry had been stopping at the fire station for a long time. He had made friends of all the guys. He went to play cards with them and sometimes went out to see the fires.

She learned this when Harry came to their door one day. Tony was home and seemed pleased to see him, inviting him to have a beer. Finally, it was clear why Harry always showed up when Tony wasn't there. He knew when Tony was working.

Then, within a few days, Suzanne disappeared. Mrs. Stein had been watching her down in the backyard to allow the child to run around and play while Claire went to the bank. Upon her return, Claire saw Mrs. Stein without her daughter and asked where Suzanne was.

"Why, Harry came and told me you gave him permission to take her for a ride," Mrs. Stein explained. "That's all right, isn't it? He said he'd have her back in 20 minutes. Why, there he is now."

The color drained from Claire's face when she first heard what he had done. Seeing her daughter, she flushed with anger and started down the steps to rebuke him for this little game he was playing with her.

"H'lo, Claire! Suzanne and I went over to the carnival that was set up last week. We went on a ride. It was fun, wasn't it, sweetie?" he cajoled.

Seething, yet not wanting to have others hear, Claire hissed, "Stay away from my daughter. Do you hear me?" Hate and anger flew from her eyes.

"Right. Just remember that I want the mother, not the daughter." He looked at her for some seconds. If Claire hadn't been so angry, she would have noticed a starry-eyed look on Harry's face. He found pleasure in just looking at her. He continued by saying, "Be outside your front door at nine tonight. You can tell Mrs. Stein that you'll be gone an hour or so." Down deep Harry believed that Claire wanted him as much as he did her. He let himself believe that. It was his hope. He wouldn't admit it was his fantasy. To anyone watching the conversation, they were just talking; Harry had a pleasant look on his face.

"I will not!"

He smiled broadly—one of those smiles that can't be read. It was not a smile of happiness. She wondered whether it was one to hide the pain of her refusal or to show his pleasure in controlling her, as he attested. "I think you will, because you saw how easily Suzanne can disappear. Don't make me do something I don't want to do." He turned and waved to Suzanne, who had gone upstairs. Then, over his shoulder, he grinned at Claire and departed.

In a panic from his words, Claire hurried up the stairs, all the while, watching her daughter waving to him. Inside her head she screamed, *What can I do?*

Claire was still trying to think of a plan to get out of this rendezvous when at seven that evening he came to the back door. It was two hours too early. She was stunned.

"It seems you forgot to tell Mrs. Stein. But I fixed that. It's all lined up. I told her you asked me to drive you somewhere at nine. You just need to tell her where so you'll have an excuse." He hesitated for a second, wanting her to absorb his comments before continuing. "You weren't thinking of disappointing me, were ya? It'd make me feel real good if you wore that dress of yours that has buttons down the front. You know, with the blue stripes. Just the dress, nothin' else." With that he turned and took two steps at a time down the back stairs. He whistled a little tune when he got to the bottom and got into his cab.

Immediately she went to her purse and dumped it onto the kitchen table to find the note with Detective Duncan's number on it. Suzanne was playing by the chifforobe as Claire rushed downstairs to the telephone at the drugstore. Her heart was beating rapidly as she asked to use the telephone and dialed the number. In her thoughts, she planned, "We could set up a plan to catch Harry in the act with me fighting him." She feared that Duncan wouldn't be at his desk and was relieved when she recognized his voice.

"Hello, this is the lady who came in a few days ago with her little girl. Do you remember me and my problem?"

"Hi, sure I do," he affirmed. "How is everything going?"

"I was wondering if you could check on a man called Harry Schwarz for me. I...," she began, but before she could finish he had interrupted and was saying, "Hey, you have Harry helping you. He's a good guy. He does some work for the department from time to time. You know he's not a cop, I guess, but he's as close as they come. He's always there trying to help out. He sure would like to be a cop, but he had some problems. Anyway, if you were calling to check him out, take my word that you are in good hands."

Silence.

"You still there?"

Her mind froze. She looked up to see the pharmacist looking her way and she was embarrassed. "Yes, well thanks. I guess that's all. Good-bye." She hung the mouthpiece on the hook and didn't move. She couldn't breathe. Dazed.

When she returned home, she sat on the bed a while. While she appeared to be thinking, her mind was frozen. She stared out at nothing. She was defeated. Trapped. She had less than two hours before Harry would come for her, and there was no place to turn for help. All of her ideas had failed, and what was more demoralizing was that everyone found Harry to be a great guy—except her. It was as if he were two people. She had no inclination to cry. She was subdued. She was numb. She walked out to the hall and stared at her daughter.

"Why is this happening to me?" she murmured to the child. "Do other women have men that dominate their lives like this? Do they just not talk about it? No, that can't be. It's me. I don't know how to do or say the right things to stop this. No, it's not strange, I guess. He's simply threatening to do what we did to someone else."

"What, Mommy?" Suzanne asked. Claire just turned and went into the bathroom.

She bathed and dressed Suzanne for bed, cleaned the kitchen, and folded some clothes. Then she changed her clothes to the blue striped dress as he had asked. Soon Mrs. Stein was there, and Claire mentioned that she was going to drop by Aunt Maria's. It was nine by then, and she went downstairs without a display of emotion.

Claire was determined to not speak to Harry, and he made no effort to speak, either. Claire sat in his car wondering how she got into this situation, pondering why other people liked Harry so much and speculating about who he really was. As he drove, he was occupied with his cigar and humming a tune so quietly that she could not discern what it was. Harry was driving to his place. Claire would find his place to be another confusing aspect of Harry. He lived by himself on Hawthorne Avenue, an exclusive neighborhood of the wealthy. Harry pulled his cab into the driveway, and they walked to the front door. To her amazement, the house was decorated like a rich man's home. She only saw the foyer and a bedroom, but nevertheless, from quick glances as she passed other rooms, she knew the rest must be of the same elaborate style. The foyer had wainscoted walls and draperies of silk and wool damask in a sub-dued yet rich pattern of deep red. They climbed the spacious staircase to a bed-room, and Harry continued to hum. He went to the windows and opened the transoms behind the valance at the top of the windows and then pulled the draperies closed. As he flicked on a lamp, Claire saw the walls were light green with moldings a shade darker. The draperies matched the mauve bedspread, which had a fringe below a border of rose, green, and mauve. She felt the balmy out-of-doors drift into the room from the transoms.

"Whose home is this?" she asked without thinking as he walked toward her.

"Mine," he said as he began unbuttoning the top of her dress. He knelt on the floor with one knee as he carefully unbuttoned the bottom ones, leaving the dress hanging closed. Then he stood and draped each of the unbuttoned sides over her shoulders, exposing her luscious softness. No other conversation or comments passed between them that night. When Harry returned Claire to her home, again they made the drive in silence.

Over several months, the event was repeated about once a week. At those times, she wouldn't speak to him and only listened when he spoke. Over time she learned more about him. He had inherited the house with an income from his mother's sister. When his aunt died, he had been left with no other family. He expressed to Claire how much he loved her. He said that no other woman had meant anything like this to him. He confessed that he knew that he wasn't good enough for her, but that he needed her unlike he had needed anyone. He asked her what he could do to make her like him, and still she wouldn't answer. She remained without emotions and accepted all as her fate. To give in to anger, hate, fear, and loathing would hurt her more by creating a daily anguish for her. She was helpless, like a prisoner who must be accepting because there is no alternative. For reasons twisted and tangled in confusion, she rationalized, *This is just how it is.* Never once could she unravel the whole situation and reach a logical interpretation.

Then suddenly, after almost a year, Harry disappeared with no explanation. He was gone! Regretfully, Claire didn't feel as relieved as she would have imagined because she didn't know where he had gone. She feared he'd appear at any moment, and more importantly, she knew the experience couldn't be erased. Claire was forever changed.

Claire heard Tony and Suzanne when they came home from their outing, and she rose from the bed to go down to the kitchen. She was so glad they were home. She felt especially grateful that she had Tony and Suzanne.

"How was your day?" Claire asked as she swept Suzanne's hat from her head and gave an uncommon hug to her daughter. It was a hug with her head buried into her daughter's shoulder, with her nose touching Suzanne's neck.

"Mom, your nose is tickling me," Suzanne said as she giggled and squirmed. Since the family didn't display much affection, none in the presence of others, Suzanne reacted with discomfort. In later years, Suzanne had no memory of either parent ever kissing her.

"I'll show you what a tickle is," Claire said and wriggled her fingers into Suzanne's belly.

"Help me, Dad," Suzanne cried.

"I'd rather help your Mom," he hissed with a spooky voice as he began tickling Suzanne, too.

When Suzanne finally collapsed to the floor to get away from them, it ended.

"To answer your question, we had a great day. Wish you had been with us," he told Claire as he gave her a big hug and rocked her in his arms. He liked seeing Claire happy like this.

"Yeah, Mom, I found out how you and Dad met. What a story!"

Tony felt great as his two girls started to talk. He retreated down to the empty store to work on a shelf that Claire had asked him to fix. He started to sing the song about his gals.

Five foot two, eyes of blue
Could she, could she, could she 'coo,'
Has anybody seen my gal?
Turned up nose, turned down toes
Dum de dum dum, goodness knows
Has anybody seen my gal?

He couldn't remember all the words, but that didn't seem to matter to him. What a day this had been.

If you should run into, a five foot two
Covered with pearls,
Diamond rings and all those things
Bet your life it isn't her.
Five foot two, eyes...

CHAPTER 7

Each Saturday working at the Bartlett Pharmacy became an adventure for Suzanne. It was an adventure for John Bartlett, too. He had come to adore this child. She brightened the whole day, even though she worked only three hours. They decided she could come from nine until noon or after lunch from one to four o'clock.

One Saturday, she came into the store and saw a large sign on the counter of the soda fountain. It stated,

"Soda Fountain Is Closed Until Victory Day

Bartlett Pharmacy is doing its share to

Make things better for our fighting boys

We hope everyone tries to use less

So more supplies can be sent to the front for our boys."

"Where's Tommy?" she asked upon noticing the soda fountain sign. After learning that he had been accepted into the Air Force and wouldn't be back, she exclaimed, "Oh, no! I wanted to learn how to make all the soda fountain stuff and, especially, how to catch ice cream balls in cups like he could." Turning, she saw the disapproving look on Mr. Bartlett's face and stammered, "I thought..." and then changed her tactics, relenting with, "I mean...I realize it was a frivolous ambition."

In the spring of 1942, to many people who were not touched directly, the war wasn't real. The United States had declared war a few months earlier on December 8, 1941. Sure, there were the rationing coupons, rapidly dwindling goods, and young men disappearing from daily activities, and yet if a family didn't have someone from their home gone or leaving for overseas, the dread or fears were not there. It was too soon for news of those lost in battle, or the knowledge of the horrors of war, to begin to filter into everyone's personal lives.

The Bartlett family was more affected by the war than the Scagliones were, though neither of the men had been called to serve. John had started his own pharmacy a few years ago and knew that some pharmacists had been selected to remain on the home front. He thought the size of his family—four children and one on the way—might've been a factor for this. He had no guilt for remaining home and showed his support in many ways. He listened with interest to the progress of the war, leaving the radio tuned to the news all day in their home as well as on his desk in the back of the drugstore. He had had a vegetable garden before the war, but now he had one in his yard with the flag flying in the tomato patch; it was called *The Victory Garden.* He showed his sons how to take the flag down at the end of the day in the proper manner. When they wanted a bugle, John made it clear that first they must became experts with the flag folding. He also had several nephews and friends who were called to serve. The Bartlett family had moved, soon after he started his own drugstore, to a large home on Hawthorne Boulevard, and they opened their doors to men in uniform—family, friends, or strangers—as a place to drop in and relax while away from home. At times, a visitor would bring a gift to show thanks, like an ashtray with a war slogan. War objects began to accumulate in their home. A couple of times, Ellie had organized a dance with neighborhood girls. The servicemen were grateful for the dance, and to show their appreciation before shipping out, they gave the Bartletts a lamp made from the casing of a torpedo shell. The torpedo lamp stood five feet high with the lampshade. Ellie graciously accepted it but found it atrocious. The four Bartlett boys loved it. And the boys loved the uniformed visitors telling about the weapons of war, maneuvers, battles, and any other details.

The Bartletts were trying to make a difference. Simply by being at the drugstore with the Bartletts and hearing of these activities, Suzanne began to learn about the war as much as the pharmacy business.

On her third Saturday of work, she was working on organizing the toy case. "It'd be best if I separate the toys for boys and girls because it'd be easier for people to find what they want," she decided. "Should I make cards with the prices like the candy case, or do prices change because of inflation or something?"

John had to strain to keep from laughing, "No, we retain a mark-up of 33% over the cost on most items. We don't adjust the prices once we put them into the case to be sold." He had already talked with her last week about mark-ups and wholesale prices versus retail prices. "Only if the item is really slow moving and expensive do we mark it to the current increase."

"Okay," Suzanne says.

"I do see a problem with your plan though. What if the toy could be used for either a girl or a boy?" he commented.

"Oh, that's a good point. Shall I make three categories and put the toys in the middle that could be for both?" she asked.

"Hey, that sounds good!" he replied. "I'm going to work in the back for a while. Come on back if you have any question. Later on today, I want to give you a lesson on making change to prepare you for handling the sales in the candy and toy cases."

John went on back to continue with the preparation he had started for the paregoric. In a few minutes Suzanne was watching and asking a lot of questions.

"Why are you filling so many bottles of this stuff?"

John explained that he sold a lot of paregoric. "People use this medicine for their babies—to relieve the pain of teething. But they've got to be careful because it's habit-forming."

"What does that mean?"

With his usual patience, John explained, "If taken too often, the baby could become addicted. So, they are to use just a little. I show the customer how to use it by tilting the bottle and letting only a drop of liquid spill on their finger. Then they rub it on the baby's gum and relief occurs in seconds." John stopped his work, and raising his eyebrows, he emphasized, "It should give instant relief. It's made with opium. Do you know what that is?"

"Kind of," Suzanne said. "I've seen movies and it's something bad."

"Only when people misuse it. Watch me mix up a batch." John told what he was doing as he added 4 grams of powdered opium to 4 grams of benzoic acid, 4 grams of camphor, and 4 ccs of oil of anise. He commented on each step. "The use of opium in a drug is controlled by law, of course. So people have to sign a book when they purchase it. They only can have 2 ounces per day." Finally, John added 40 ccs of glycerin and 950 ccs of diluted alcohol. "I have to let the mixture soak for some twenty minutes before filling more bottles. While I wait, I'm going to put the labels on." With a sponge he moistened the back of a label marked "PAREGORIC" and adhered it to the outside of a glass bottle.

Suzanne saw that the lesson was over, "Okay, I'm going to finish the toy case."

After John came out to the front of the store to put the paregoric on the shelf, he walked over to the toy case. He noted that she had also organized the toys by price. The left side of the case had toys for boys while the right displayed toys for girls. The bottom shelves had the cheapest items and the top the most expensive. It looked good.

"Nice job, Suzanne. Finish up and let's get that lesson on making change." He started the lesson as they walked toward the cash register. "It's important to make sure the customer sees and agrees right on the spot that you have given them the correct change. This will avoid a complaint later on." He stopped and turned to face her. "If they get home and can't find the five dollar bill from their change, they should be reminded, 'Oh yeah, I remember that the little girl gave me the right change, so what did I do afterwards to lose it?' The customer will not think that you gave them the wrong change if you make a point to count and call their attention to what you're doing. I want everyone who works here to give change in the same manner, and, in that way, if there is a problem, I can say to the customer exactly what my clerks do. Do you understand?"

"Yes," Suzanne responded. She liked the idea of having a procedure for how to return a customer's change. She thought as he did.

John continued with some comments about drugstore etiquette, "Always be polite and courteous, and remember that you are here to serve the customer." John opened the cash register with a key and got a handful of coins. "Let's go to my desk in the back so we won't be interrupted."

The walls of the back room were lined with wooden drawers, cubbyholes, and differently shaped compartments with brass knobs. Herbs, chemicals, drugs, and other such products in powder, liquid, or some solid form were stored here. In the center of the room was a desk butted up against a glass-covered counter where the pharmacist prepared the prescriptions and other drugs. A balancing scale with shiny brass weights neatly lined up beside it caught Suzanne's attention. She'd like to learn how to work that!

John demonstrated a couple times how the change was to be given to a customer, "Do you see that you're counting backwards to the total money they gave you?"

"Yes, I get it. If they spent 20 cents and gave me a fifty-cent piece, I'd say this. 'You have 20 cents of candy, 25 (she put a nickel into John's hand), and 50 cents (as a quarter was dropped).'"

They practiced a bit more and John reminded her, "Of course, you can't work the cash register yet. That will be for later. You are only to help people at the candy or toy case and then come to me and I'll ring the sale and give you the change. I will stand by you when you give the change back until I know you really can do it yourself."

"Oh, that's great," she sounded excited. Then, with a slight hesitancy she looked up at Mr. Bartlett and asked, "Can I show you a puzzle that I invented with numbers? It's not anything to do with the drugstore, but while we were counting change I remembered about it. I invented it one day when I was thinking about numbers."

"I'm interested; show me."

"Well, have you ever noticed that we have numbers for one to nine if we count on our fingers?" Without waiting for an answer she went on talking. "And then the tenth finger doesn't get a new number because we use a one and a zero to mean ten. That seemed strange to me. Well, I made a system that has a number for every finger," Suzanne said and then began to count. She held up each finger as she progressed with each number; "One, two, three, four, five, six, seven, eight, nine, and the last one I call 'Bobo.' Do you get it?"

John's heart skipped a beat. He hadn't heard the name in years. The face of the ball was vivid in his memory, as were the feelings attached to that memory. He was sure his face showed the pain of the past and was confusing Suzanne, so he answered her question, "Yes, I understand." Then, because he couldn't resist asking, "But why did you make this system?"

"I think it makes more sense to have a number name for all our fingers. Not to start repeating the one and zero until we run out of fingers. Don't you? Besides, I can teach someone like you, and we have our own secret code of numbers that no one else can figure out. Isn't that a neat idea?"

He forced a laugh and thought, *She made no mention of the ball. It was just a coincidence. Nothing more."*

Every Sunday during breakfast, John would tell Ellie about the antics of Suzanne, but he didn't mention the counting system with the tenth finger named Bobo. Ellie was pregnant and he didn't want to do anything that might upset her. It was just a coincidence, anyway. "When you need to work on the books again, why don't you come when Suzanne is working?" John suggested. "I'd like you to get to know her."

Ellie, like John, didn't have much experience being with a young girl; they had four boys—David, 12; William, 8; Johnny Jr., 6; and James, who was 3 years old. With Ellie being pregnant again, they both were hoping for a girl.

So Ellie arrived with John one Saturday and began her work at the back counter. People went to the back counter if they had prescriptions to be filled or a monthly social security check to cash. So it wasn't as busy as the front counter. Ellie worked on the books and helped only if someone came up to her.

Suzanne arrived to work and stopped at the front counter while shouting back to Mr. Bartlett, "I'm here. I want to write down a new idea to give to you. I've got a new mind game for you to figure out. It'll only take a minute." She ripped off some of the brown paper used to wrap the purchases. She took the pencil that was always tied next to the cash register and began to make a hop-scotch drawing. There were no customers. As she drew, she talked and talked, "I was walking here and saw a hopscotch on the sidewalk near where I turn on Grand. You know where the sidewalk gets wider? Anyway, these kids had made it neater than I usually do, and as I walked, I saw the numbers made columns. Well, sort of. Anyway, I started to add."

Mr. Bartlett noticed that she talked a mile a minute when describing her "little mind games." She was so elated.

She continued, "I always like to add numbers or multiply them to see if there is an interesting relationship or something. It's fun. Well, anyway I started rearranging the numbers in my head, and I got this idea for a new mind game for you. Want to see it?" She started walking toward Mr. Bartlett. She had drawn the numbers without the hopscotch squares.

9		10
	8	
	7	
5		6
3		4
1		2

Totals	18	15	22

"Oh," Suzanne exclaimed when Ellie came into view, "I didn't know some-one else was here. Are you taking Tommy's place?"

"No, she's not. She failed the ice-cream-toss test," Mr. Bartlett teased, "but she passed the best bookkeeper and mother-of-my-children test. Suzanne, this is my wife."

"Oh, nice to meet you, Mrs. Bartlett," Suzanne responded pleasantly.

"It's a pleasure to meet you, Suzanne. I would've preferred a job tossing ice cream, actually. My work is a bit boring, I'm afraid. How old are you?"

"I'm going into sixth grade," she answered.

"No, I meant what's your age," Ellie corrected.

Suzanne smiled and answered, "We women don't tell our ages. Your age shouldn't matter, my mother says," and she snickered a bit. Actually, Suzanne didn't want people to know how young she was. She was always embarrassed about it. Especially with other children—they made fun of little kids. She was glad to be in a new neighborhood where no one knew she really was just a younger kid who skipped grades.

"*Touché*," replied Ellie, "You're right; I'd rather not tell you my age, either."

"Gosh, if you're a bookkeeper, you must like numbers. Like me! You might be interested in my new mind game. Want to see it?" She showed them her drawing of the hopscotch pattern and explained that the problem is to change the positions of the numbers in the first and last columns so they total to equal amounts. "The trick is that I want the numbers to remain in an order that'd still let me play hopscotch with the numbers in order. Do you get it?"

Ellie didn't feel she had time to play and said, "I really need to get back to work right now," and turned back to work on her books.

"Yes, I think I get it," confirmed Mr. Bartlett, "and after I finish this prescrip-tion I'll work on it. Meanwhile, your job today is to restock the candy case. I know you remember how. Here are all the cards from the boxes we emptied. A candy order came in late yesterday and is stacked over there on the floor. Remember to check the stockroom for any other candy you could fit into the case."

Suzanne busied herself, working and humming. The store began to have customers.

Mrs. Bartlett was interrupted from her bookkeeping and Suzanne overheard the conversion she was having with a woman customer. They seemed to know each other well.

"When is the baby due, Ellie?" the lady asked.

"Sometime within the month, and I'm getting excited. I always like having a little one. My boys have reached an age when they're pretty independent. So I have time for a baby."

"I'll keep my fingers crossed for a girl." The customer lifted her hand to show crossed fingers.

"Thanks, but I keep telling myself that having a healthy baby is all that's important. What can I get for you today?"

"Doctor told me to take some Geritol for a month or so, I must have 'iron poor blood,'" she quipped like the advertisement on the radio. "Have you ever tried it?"

"No, I haven't, but then, I'm always pregnant and John won't let me take even an aspirin while I'm pregnant. We have a pharmacy full of medicines, and it seems kind of silly that he doesn't want me to take anything. He says that the experts don't know enough about the effects on a baby inside the mother. So, I listen to my personal expert. I listen to him and every one of the boys came out healthy." They laughed while she finished the sale and then Ellie cried out, "Oh, feel this: the baby is dancing inside me today." Ellie took her friend's hand and put it on her belly as they quietly smiled. They exchanged a few more words and said good-bye.

Suzanne was puzzled by the overheard conversation. She looked up at Ellie and their eyes met.

The store was empty for the moment so Ellie motioned for Suzanne to come over and said, "You want to feel, too? She—I hope she's a she—is always moving around. Here, quick give me your hand."

Suzanne stood up from the candy case and came forward. Ellie placed Suzanne's hand carefully and they both became motionless. Ellie waited with upturned eyes.

"There, did you feel that? And that! Give me your other hand. Wow, she *is* dancing isn't she? That's a pirouette and an entrechat! Those are ballet steps that I learned in my younger days," Ellie teased with a tilt of her head and a smile.

Suzanne stammered, "You have a live baby in you?" with such serious innocence that John, who had been listening, stifled a laugh.

Ellie tried to maintain her composure. She was surprised that Suzanne didn't know about babies. Her boys had a lot of pets, the family had a farm with animals, and she was always pregnant, so her children were well informed. "Yes, but I'm hoping not for too much longer. I can hardly walk because she's getting so big. It is time, any day, for her to be born."

"So you're fat because you have a baby in you?" Suzanne didn't wait for an answer because her mind jumped to the next puzzling aspect of this new discovery. "But how does she get out?"

Ellie began her answer as the drugstore door jingled so she had to make it a quick one. "Yes, I hope to be a lot thinner when the baby comes out. It's a special place down here," she gestured below her enormous belly. Ellie changed to a whisper as the customer came closer. "That special place stretches open especially for the baby; afterwards it returns to normal." Then she walked over to help the customer.

John had overheard most of the conversation while he was working on the hopscotch problem. "I solved your mind puzzle. Come look," John called to Suzanne. She wandered to the back of the store.

"See, I found various solutions," he proclaimed as he pushed a paper toward her. "All I needed to do was change the positions of two numbers in any row. Of course, this change must be done in two rows. See, in this one I changed the top row and the bottom one. I could have changed the two middle ones. They'd always make a total of 20, and you could play the hopscotch as easily as the original way. Right?"

"Right," she smiled, but not with her usual enthusiasm because she was still thinking about babies. Looking into his eyes, she commented, "You're good at my mind games. My parents aren't as good." She hesitated with a frown and then asked, "Could I ask you some questions that are really confusing me?"

"Well, I've some time. I'll try," he answered, knowing that the questions probably had to do with his pregnant wife.

"Why does your wife keep having children and my mother doesn't?"

"Suzanne, that is a personal question that only your mother and father can answer," he responded as unemotionally as possible. "Sometimes people really want to have children and they can't. Even the doctors have not discovered all the reasons why they can't. It's one of the mysteries of medicine that we hope to learn someday." He wanted to answer any question Suzanne had, but nevertheless, he knew that it wasn't wise to interfere in another family's ways. He couldn't fathom why people were overly closed to discussing natural topics. Yet he knew that his education and training had informed him more than others.

He realized there were many parents who had never learned in sufficient detail about their own bodies to find words to describe the ideas to a child. "I'll see if I can find some reading material and then I'll ask your Dad to give it to you. He might want to read it first. You know, sometimes parents can't answer questions because they don't know the answers."

"Yeah, that's possible with mine. Sometimes I can't believe how different we are." Making that comment, she sounded like an adult.

"You know, you should come to the drugstore with your mother one day. I'd like to meet her. Don't be hard on your parents. You may be smart, but you're too young to understand about their personal matters. You don't know all the facts of their lives. I want you to remember to never assume. If you really investigate and gather all the information, you can then make a decision. Not before! Remember just a few weeks ago, you told me you learned how your parents met. You have a lot to learn about your parents before you can assume why they do things…or don't do things. Ask more questions and don't assume until you learn as much as you can."

This short conversation made more of an impression on Suzanne than the knowledge she had gained about birth and babies. Never assume without all the facts. She found this idea was logical. It suited her logical mind.

On their drive home that evening, John and Ellie talked about Suzanne. Ellie agreed that she was an unusual child and enjoyable to be with. They laughed over her clever little mind games and hoped her parents wouldn't get upset over the discussions about babies.

Even without talking about their daughter Elizabeth, it was impossible for them to not think about her at this time. They had had so many years without her that it wasn't as if they thought every day about the unsolved disappearance. Still, both of them entertained the idea that this is how Elizabeth would look if she were alive.

"Did she tell you about her counting system?" Ellie asked. She knew by asking they would be reminded of Elizabeth, and it was a topic they usually avoided.

"Yes." John knew where this was going.

After a few moments of silence, Ellie realized he wasn't going to say anything more unless she did. She decided not to hold back her thoughts. "Well, I was impressed with her intelligence; nevertheless the name for the tenth finger took my breath away. Wasn't that unusual?"

"You mean the name?" he asked and then answered himself, "Bobo?"

"Yes. I asked her why she called the new number 'Bobo,' and she let me know that it could have been 'boo' or 'dada,' but she liked the sound of 'Bobo,'" Ellie said. Then after a hesitation, Ellie ended the comment with, "I don't!"

Without looking at his wife he questioned, "You don't what?" His gaze was straight ahead as he drove. He was avoiding the issue.

"Come on John, you know what I mean. That was the name of Elizabeth's ball. She had it the night she disappeared," she complained and her impatience was apparent. "It was her favorite toy! It was left outside that night and I did-n't notice. Remember now?" She was exasperated with him, knowing he just didn't want to broach the subject, but she went on talking. "Do I need to remind you that I finally concluded that Elizabeth had gotten up and went out to find that ball? Remember, I heard the door *thump!*" She sighed, "Anyway, I don't like the sound of the new number for those reasons." She took a deep breath to calm herself.

John put his hand on Ellie's knee as he drove. He understood her upset, but wanted her to know he didn't think there was any reason to dwell on it. "Oh, I must admit that I reacted to the name, too, but then realized that it's just a coincidence."

"Yes, I'm sure it is," she sighed again and purposely changed the subject. "I have some leftover stew in the fridge at home, if you're still hungry."

Deliberately, neither wanted to discuss that Suzanne looked the age Elizabeth would be and that she looked like Elizabeth would look. They were realistic and knew that there were hundreds of blonde-haired, blue-eyed little girls in this city filled with German ancestry. They had decided years ago that it was best not to talk too much about Elizabeth or to dwell on their loss. It was more important to dedicate their energy and emotions to their other children and to each other. They didn't cling to problems from the past. Just these few comments had upset Ellie. *And for what?* she complained to herself. It was over and they could never change anything that had happened. She knew that they both would like to know what really had happened when Elizabeth disap-peared, but she felt they never would.

John's thoughts were going in a different direction. His eyes smiled as he thought about the natural rapport he had with this child. It had occurred right away that first day at the candy case. He knew how much he liked children and liked being with children, but this was something different. He just wasn't sure what made it different.

John Bartlett's Saturdays with Suzanne came and went. Ellie gave birth to a lit-tle girl and named her Rebecca. The Bartletts had their son David working on Saturday, too. If Suzanne worked the morning three hours, David worked the afternoon and vice versa so they didn't meet. The weeks passed into months.

The Bartlett and Scaglione parents did meet. They spent only five or ten minutes together during the first encounters, but it was enough time to start a relationship. From time to time, Tony found himself walking up to Grand Avenue just to talk with John. He'd tell John about one of the fires or ask about something that needed fixing at the house. Ellie often stopped by Claire's with the baby and they'd share a recipe or work together on one of Claire's new projects. Claire didn't think about going over to the Bartlett house since she had many interests at her own place. She was a homebody. Besides, impromptu visits were not a part of Claire's personality. Ellie was the one who liked to go out and socialize. Ellie drove and Claire did not. Ellie didn't like housework and Claire did. Ellie was spontaneously social and Claire was not. Ellie enjoyed getting out of her own house and into the quiet at Claire's. Most of the time, Ellie came to visit while her older boys were in school; little James and Rebecca came along. So Claire got to know those two Bartlett children, whom she called Jimmy and Becky, but Suzanne didn't know them because Ellie came during school hours.

Workdays at the drugstore meant a lot to both Suzanne and David. John Bartlett had a lot to give to children, but he left for work when his own children were at school and he returned after the store was closed when they were in bed. So at the drugstore, he gave time to his oldest son David. His other boys would have the same experience in the future when they turned twelve and came to work with him. Including Suzanne, he was a teacher with two eager pupils. They were constantly learning John's philosophies besides the concepts of business and running a store. Like the idea to never assume without all the facts. It was his nature to talk about philosophical ideas or morals. Some incident would occur and he'd talk with them about integrity. Or he'd see an article in the newspaper and he'd speak about intuition or prejudice. He also had much to say about communication, but his most frequent commentary was about truth. John was consistent and calm, with a firm work ethic and love of all mankind. He gave a lot to these two special young people and filled their three hours with ideas. Over the months, his time with them implanted impressions they would use throughout their lives.

One Saturday after Suzanne had been working approximately a year at the drugstore, she complained to Mr. Bartlett that she hadn't met any of his children. "My Mom knows Becky and Jimmy, but I don't," she whined.

Trying to sound professional, Mr. Bartlett informed her that this was a business and employees don't necessarily meet the families of co-workers. "In fact," he pointed out, "it isn't normal to socialize with a co-worker's family unless working for a large company that has special occasions, like a company picnic, where families are asked to come."

"But..." she started to complain some more, but John just continued.

"You met my wife because she works here. You sound like you're pouting about this. Why? Is it important to you?" he inquired, making note of her first display of a child-like characteristic suited to her age. He had enough children to know how they act at different ages, and she had always seemed too mature. Girls act differently than boys, he noted with amusement on seeing her protruding lower lip.

"Now that you explain it that way, I guess it isn't important. Gee, it's just that I don't have any brothers and sisters and I was curious to see your children. I'd like to see the baby and play with her. I've never been with a baby."

He laughed out loud, "All they do is cry, eat, and sleep at this age! At least that's a man's impression. I've got an idea. When you finish work and you're eating lunch at home, why don't you ask your parents if you could go home with my son, David? That'd be at four o'clock when he finishes working. It's an easy trip on the streetcar on Grand Avenue. You go for a ten-minute ride and then there's only a walk for half a block. If you like the idea, I'll call Ellie right now and see if it's possible." John would've called Claire and Tony, but they didn't have a telephone. "If you can stay for supper at our house, I'll go home at six. That would be a treat for me since I usually just eat here at the drugstore. Tell your parents that I'm working late and could bring you back at seven-thirty or eight o'clock tonight. What do you say?"

Suzanne said, "Yes," and her parents did as well. Tony was glad to see that Claire was finally relaxing in the new neighborhood and allowing Suzanne to go more places. He was sure that Ellie's visits helped.

Suzanne decided that this was an occasion that required a bath, washed hair, and her blue-dotted Swiss dress. After the bath, she asked her mom to tie a blue ribbon in the soft waves of her loose-hanging hair. Claire knew Suzanne was getting too dressed up, but said nothing. She figured that any of her suggestions might spoil the anticipation. Besides, she hadn't seen Suzanne this excited in a while. What difference did it make if she looked like she was going to a party? At least the dress fit. Most of her dresses were ready to give away because she had outgrown them. As Suzanne was putting on her clothes, Claire noticed that Suzanne was starting to show developing breasts, but the surprise was short-lived because Claire was laughing to herself about the baby, Becky. Suzanne had no idea what babies did, and Claire imagined her coming back home with spit up all over the dotted Swiss dress. *It'll be a new experience for Suzanne, no matter what*, she mused.

Tony walked up to the drugstore on Grand Avenue with Suzanne.

At the drugstore Tony went directly to the back walk-through to talk with John while Suzanne stopped at the front cash register where a boy stood with his back to her as he dusted the shelves just above the cigarettes. Looking at the back of his head, she decided that this was David because she knew everyone else who worked at the pharmacy. He was cleaning off the men's shaving articles: shaving cups, the round soap to drop into the cup, razors, lotions to use afterwards, some powder, and camphor sticks for the cuts. *Oh, he's tall,* she thought. She knew he was almost 14 years old and going into high school because she had asked Mr. Bartlett. He had the same blonde hair that she did except it had more waves. *Shorter hair, like her Dad's, waves,* she surmised.

Thinking she was a customer, he turned to wait on her. Seeing him face to face, she was pleased and something tingled inside her body. It was a new sensation, and she was surprised that she blushed for some reason.

"I said, may I help you?" he repeated.

She hadn't heard him say it earlier. "No, thanks. I'm Suzanne."

"Oh! It's four o'clock already? Holy cow! I never can believe how fast the time goes when I come down here to work with Dad. Are you ready to go? I've a lot of stuff to do at home and want to get going."

"Sure," she agreed.

"Let's go say *adieu*. Do you have money for the streetcar? I only brought enough for me."

"Yes," she replied as she came around to walk behind the counter toward the back of the store.

There was a quick introduction between Tony and David, and they left. They walked up to Grand Avenue and ran across the street as a streetcar approached. "That was luck that we didn't have to wait," David beamed as he climbed up the stairs. She followed and they slid into a seat right in front.

She liked him and knew it. He had wide shoulders, fuzz on his chin already, and seemed confident though in casual, easy-going kind of way. He was talking about his stamp collection, and she noticed that she kept not hearing him because her mind wandered. She liked how he acted as if he had known her for always. He didn't behave like the boys in her class. Either they spent time bothering girls with stupid remarks or ignoring them. David acted like she was just one of the boys or a longtime friend.

David started showing her some stamps. "See, Dad gave me some today. These are the ones he got in the drugstore's mail this week. Aren't they neat? I want to mount them as soon as I get home. I asked you if you had a stamp collection; do you?" A puzzled look was on his face. He couldn't figure out why he had to keep repeating his questions to her.

"No, I don't. What do you do with a stamp collection exactly?" she asked.

"Do you mean, what are the procedures, or why do I like to collect?" He looked straight at her by turning in his seat to see who this person was. He wasn't sure if it was a dumb question or a meaningful one. He needed to see the expression on her face. He decided it was a dumb one.

Oh, oh, she thought, feeling panicky, *I asked a stupid question.* She could read his expression immediately and didn't want him to have a bad impression of her. Mr. Bartlett had told her once that it's best to be honest and be your normal self. She decided to give it a try instead of trying to think of something clever and deceiving. "You must think I'm stupid, but I don't know anything about stamp collecting. I'd like to hear whatever you want to tell me, though. Maybe I'd enjoy doing it, too."

David responded as most people do when asked to talk about their interests or themselves: he was happy to accommodate. He began talking and they almost missed the stop. Since the tracks of the streetcar ran down the middle of the street, they jumped down into traffic and had to wait while cars passed all around them. As before, they ran quickly across Grand Avenue when they saw a break between vehicles. There was no stop sign on this corner.

Safely up on the curb, he continued the interrupted conversation, "So why don't I show you when we get home? You can come on up to the study where I've got my stuff and you can help…that is if you're careful."

They were walking down a street unlike any place Suzanne had walked. It was beautiful, with tree branches entwined across the street and well-groomed yards with deep lawns and driveways. The homes were large and luxurious. No two were alike or made of the same materials. Some were brick, and others stone; there were English Tudors and ones that looked like miniature castles with rounded turrets and spires. David was oblivious to her amazement. She was astounded that he made no comment about the place.

"This is it," he indicated with a bob of his head. They were approaching a big stone house. The door was double, actually two doors with one side only decorative and permanently closed. They were heavy doors made from oak with inlaid moldings and a wrought iron knocker. The door handle was of the identical black metal.

"The handles are huge!" she noticed with amazement. "Have you lived here all your life?" she asked.

"No, we lived in a four-family flat off Kingshighway Boulevard until I was about five. I don't remember it too much, but Mom drove by one day to show me." They walked in. "Mom, we're home!" David called out.

Ellie came out with the baby propped on her hip. After giving Suzanne a welcoming hug with her free arm, the baby was quickly and casually passed into Suzanne's hands. "Babies are pretty sturdy. Just don't drop her. Other than that, don't worry about her. Becky enjoys being with people. You could probably carry her upside-down and she'd be okay. Come meet the wild bunch."

Ellie turned and walked a couple of steps and then changed her mind. "Actually, the boys are all over the place. Why don't you meet them as they appear? If they don't show up before supper, you can meet them then. I'm sure you prefer to be with Becky, anyway."

Suzanne was trying to find a way to hold Becky. Upon receiving the child she had tried to cradle Becky like a baby doll, but Becky squirmed and wanted to be upright to see things. Then Suzanne tried to remember how Mrs. Bartlett had been holding the baby with an arm around its belly and a hand grasping a thigh while its bottom rested against the mother's hips. Suzanne tried the same hold and the baby started slipping, but she kept working at it while David spoke with his mother.

"I was going to show Suzanne my collections, Mom. Okay? Becky can come, too. Could you give us a blanket to put her down if we want?"

"This diaper'll do." Ellie removed the diaper from her shoulder and handed it to Suzanne, who was still trying to arrange Becky in her arms. Suzanne was glad that Ellie had emphasized that any position was okay as she settled for a face-to-face bear hug.

"She's so cute, Mrs. Bartlett. Oh, look at her little cheeks." Becky smiled with that. "Oh, she smiled!"

"Mom said you never held a baby; it sure is obvious. Come on, you can coo over Becky up in the study," David teased as he started up the staircase.

"Supper at six. Call me if she needs a change, David. Suzanne doesn't need to worry about that. Or you can change her, David, if you would."

"Okay, Mom. This way, Suzanne." He turned to the right at the top of the stairs. "She's a nice little baby. My brother James was a pain. He cried constantly. He's almost four, and we can't get him to stop going in his pants. He's older, but hasn't really changed 'cuz he's still a pain."

They got to the door of the study and a boy rushed out. "Hey, what are you doing in there? You know it's off limits to you clowns," David complained.

"Shhh," he whispered. "I'm playing hide-and-seek. Be quiet or you'll give me away."

"That's Johnny. Johnny, this is Suzanne," David whispered with a smile on his face and a shake of his head to indicate that his little brother could neither be controlled nor told what to do.

"Hi, got to get out of here. Nice to meet you," Johnny whispered back and disappeared down a hall.

"He's, ah, seven, I think." David strained to remember the ages that were always changing.

Then they entered the study. A swath of light coming from the chandelier at the top of the staircase showed a large, high-ceiling room with thick burgundy carpeting. David flipped on the light switch.

Suzanne had never imagined such a place could be someone's home. It was a museum! Bookcases from the floor to the ceiling lined one wall, which had a wooden ladder to reach the higher shelves. Suzanne gazed to the adjacent wall, where a stuffed head of a bear sneered, an elk regally displayed a huge rack of antlers, and a white mountain goat silently fixed its gaze on a graceful swan hanging from the open wooden beams across the ceiling. Turning again she looked to a wall of four foot high glass cases that displayed insects and, on the top shelves, butterflies. Then she saw the coins mounted in collector books—stacks and stacks of them. She turned some pages, seeing United States coins that she never knew existed. Not stopping to read any dates, she figured they were old.

Seeing this one room made Suzanne realize that there was a lot more to know about Mr. Bartlett and his family. Though she was young, she knew that she truly wanted to be like this family and learn about a lot of different things. Looking back into the cases, on the lower shelves she saw broken pieces of pottery. She wondered about them, but didn't ask because she had too many questions. Then she stopped at the arrowheads and other Indian artifacts.

David told her, "We dug all of those up at my Grampa's farm. He's my Dad's dad. When he's going to plow a field he lets us know and we go on the weekend. Look at this tomahawk. My Dad found that when he was my age."

"Golly," was all Suzanne could say.

"Would you like an arrowhead?" he asked. "We have a lot of little ones that are alike and a little broken. Here you can have this one and here is another. They're made from flint, you know, because the Indians could chip them carefully to shape a sharp point."

"Golly," she exclaimed again as she studied the first arrowheads she had ever touched and then slipped them into the pocket of her dress.

"Here's my stamps." David motioned for her to come to see where he was working at an old oak desk.

"But all this," she stammered, twirling in a circle while pointing to all the wonders on the walls, "where did all these stuffed heads come from?"

"Oh, Dad, likes to hunt. Likes it a lot. Those are all his," And then pointing to a ten-point mule deer above the desk where he sat, David boasted, "That's one I got last year. Dad and I took a trip and I shot him."

She started to respond and then found she was without words.

"Come on, can I show you how to do the stamps? We could get it done before we have to go down to supper," he said, looking for a way to show her about himself without bragging. He was ashamed that he had boasted about the deer head. "Dad is the real collector. I'm just learning. I like it because I learn a lot."

The two youngsters spent the next hour or so working on soaking the envelopes to remove the stamps, talking about all the different collections, playing with Becky, and mainly just being together. A whole new way of living was opened to Suzanne. She had had no idea that a family could be completely different than her family. Were all families as different, she wondered, or were the Bartletts special? She experienced, on this single visit, impressions and ideas that began to mold her. After this day she frequently found herself puzzling, *In the past why have I wasted efforts crying or being lazy when there were so many interesting hobbies?* She began to think about what was important to her. This was a new direction of thought. After one visit of a few hours, suddenly she knew that she controlled who she wanted to be and where she wanted to go. *Look at all the interesting things that I didn't know about before,* she professed. *I want to learn about all of them.*

That night in her bedroom with the thrill of the day turning in her head, she got Bobo out of the hatbox and told him all about it. She slipped the three arrowheads into the hatbox for safekeeping as she told Bobo many details she hadn't told her parents. Claire and Tony were down in the kitchen still talking about her adventure, too. To Bobo, she confided her strange and new sensations "of some kind of goofy feelings toward David," she whispered. She didn't know much about hormones changing her feelings. She knew less about having a crush. The older girls at school were always talking about one of them having a crush on one of the boys. She sort of knew what they meant, but they had never talked about how it felt. She had heard or read of people who experienced meeting someone and feeling something "click" in their relationship. These people felt that they had known the person forever and that they were alike in important ways that allowed them to think the same. She decided, whatever was going on, she couldn't define it. "Working on his collections made me feel close because he really seemed to like to show me all about them," she continued to think as she explained to her old friend, the ball. She knew that she and David had something special.

David and Suzanne may have had more reasons than most friends to feel close and alike, but Suzanne wasn't looking for reasons. She was feeling a new kind of happiness and told Bobo, "I think I love him…and I want to marry him." She whispered this into the ear of the ball, and then giggled.

She was in love with the whole Bartlett family. Without any effort, they had made her welcome in their home. It was easy to belong with so many other kids running around.

It was September of 1943, and she was entering the eighth grade. David was going into his freshman year of high school. She wished that she could go to his school. Later she found it didn't matter because his family, and he, invited her into their home all the time. Claire and Tony allowed Suzanne to go over to visit the Bartletts and work on her homework because they found David to be a fine young man—a gentleman. David usually came to the Scaglione's house for lunch on Saturdays before his three-hour shift at the drugstore. The two families were growing closer.

"Hi, Mrs. Bartlett," Suzanne chirped as the screen door slammed behind her, "Oh, Becky, look at you. You're a mess! I think that there's more food *on* you than *in* you."

Ellie was sitting at the kitchen table working on one of her scrapbooks. She stopped cutting an article and turned to say, "Hi, Suzanne." Looking at her baby, Ellie shook her head, "You're right about Becky. She is a messy one. After I feed her and make sure she has enough in her belly, I let her try to feed herself. As you see, very little gets into her mouth, but it keeps her happy and lets me get some work done in the kitchen. See, I got some cookies baked, and now I'm catching up on my scrapbook. Grab a cookie before you go upstairs. David's probably in his usual place—the study. Actually, I think I hear the radio; maybe he's in the living room."

As Suzanne passed through the dining room, she could hear The Kingfish from the *Amos and Andy* show. She went to sit on the floor next to David as Andy was berating Amos. The show never seemed to change. It was ending and she was glad because her love of it had ended years ago. It seemed like such a silly program to her. It was long ago when she used to listen with her mother. A certain nostalgic memory returned upon hearing the voices, but she preferred to listen to the newer programs.

"How could it be on the radio? I heard they were going off the air." she asked David.

"Yeah, but they're going to start again next month for a thirty-minute broadcast instead of the fifteen minute. This was a special to announce the new show," he informed her.

"I prefer to hear *Inner Sanctum Mysteries* or *Mr. and Mrs. North*. Golly, did you hear *Inner Sanctum* last night? It was so scary! That Peter Lorre was on. His voice makes me want to wet my pants," she giggled. "I'm so mad; they're changing to a later time on a school night next month. My mom was glad. It will be too late for me to stay up. She thinks it's too scary for girls anyway. At least she doesn't mind *Mr. and Mrs. North*," she sighed.

"Nah, *Amos 'n' Andy* is the best. They're classic. All these other programs…Oh, I don't know," David groaned. Then, he made the point, "Suzanne, that *Mr. and Mrs. North* is for girls. They're always going on with that *lovey-dovey* stuff."

She didn't think that that was true; it seemed like a good mystery program to her. It didn't matter that David had a different opinion. It was one of the aspects of the friendship that she enjoyed. She learned many new things listening to him talk about his ideas. Being younger seemed to make no difference. The friendship was on an equal footing with no regard to age.

"Do you think you don't like *Mr. and Mrs. North* because they're married or something like that?"

"Nope." He was disinterested in this talk and ended it. "Hey, come see the new stamps. They're from Europe."

Suzanne concluded that boys don't have the romantic ideas that girls do. David didn't spend his time with thoughts of love or girls. His mind was on his collections, going somewhere with dad, playing basketball, looking up an answer to an idea in a book, and stuff like that.

When David had been asked by his mother and father what he thought of having a friend who was a girl, he had thought for awhile and just said, "She's okay for a girl." If they had pressed him to explain more, he might've said that she would've been a great sister because she was interested in the stuff he liked. He had had that thought. He liked that she learned fast and went on to investigate more at the public library. He had often noticed that she was as knowledgeable in school subjects as he was…well, almost. He liked her humor and ideas, too. It was easy to talk to her about anything that came up.

They both had their own friends for school and sports, but they remained close. Together they shared their weirdest thoughts and wildest dreams. Neither would develop any other closer friend during this period in their lives because there was no need to have this kind of relationship with someone else. This wasn't only a friendship based on doing activities together; this was a bond of the mind and inner spirit. David would come home after a basketball game, do his homework and get ready for bed, and then think of an idea that he wanted to share. Many times he wished she had a telephone so he could call her. When he saw Suzanne next, he'd tell her. They talked of what they'd be when they grew up. He was sure he'd go into science, and she talked of mathematics. They shared ideas and activities that other kids would think were screwy or too serious. They shared like a brother and sister.

If these two families, the Bartletts and the Scagliones, had known that there was a link from the past that bound them—the abduction of Elizabeth—they would've realized that David and Suzanne's ignorance of the abduction put them on a disastrous path. The Bartletts had tried not to talk about Elizabeth through the years, wanting to go on with their lives without the pain. Since Elizabeth wasn't discussed, David didn't know of her because he had been too young to retain memories of her. He was a year and a half older than Elizabeth was—too young to remember. Any photographs of Elizabeth had been put away, family and friends were too polite to talk about the loss, and the Bartletts had moved to a new home soon afterwards. So the four-family flat where David and Elizabeth had played, cried, and laughed had disappeared from David's mind.

His other memories were kept active as he grew by hearing his family retell the stories of past outings or special holidays. What he heard was sometimes reinforced through photographs or by seeing the place over and over where a particular incident had occurred. David didn't know in his conscious mind that he had had a sister before Rebecca. If he were to ask about Elizabeth, his parents would've talked with him, but he couldn't ask because he had no memories of Elizabeth. John and Ellie weren't trying to keep it a secret; they just didn't talk about her. The name of Elizabeth should elicit some response from his subconscious, but it was his mother's name, too. He couldn't ask to learn what he didn't remember. John and Ellie had planned to discuss the whole situation of Elizabeth when he was older, when all the children were older. They didn't want to worry the children, to build a fear in them that they could be kidnapped. While John Bartlett knew and preached that truth was important, that communication was a key factor in good relationships, he made an exception with the story of Elizabeth because he assumed that it wasn't important for David to know. Oh, how he'd regret all this in the years to come. One should never assume without all the facts. John knew that he lacked that one horrible fact: who had taken Elizabeth?

CHAPTER 8

Winter worked quietly one night, delivering a silent delight. The white stillness woke Suzanne. Before opening her eyes, she saw that the light of the morning was brighter than usual. In this exceptional quiet, she knew a noiseless blanket of snow had fallen.

She thought, *I don't hear any cars; that means it's deep. I can't hear any people either so no one has shoveled yet. Oh, it's probably going to be perfect—with no footprints or tire tracks!* Suzanne leaped from her bed and went to the window. "Wow, look at it," she said in a soft voice. She opened her window and some of the snow that had piled on the windowsill fell into her room. She picked it up and pressed it into a snowball and then threw it at the lamppost. It stuck! "It's great for a snowman. Oh, boy!"

Quickly she started dressing, turning to peer out the open window to admire the crisp air, silence, and beauty. Every limb on every tree had a stack of snow a couple inches high. Every lamppost and telephone pole was topped with a winter hat like the knitted cap she pulled on her head. Any object that had the slightest jutting surface was edged with white. It was such a wet snow that the sides of the trees had snow sticking to them. Some parked cars seemed like dunes on a white sandy beach because they were completely hidden by drifts.

Finally, she closed the window and went downstairs to her parent's bedroom. Entering quietly, she knelt and gently touched her Mother's arm, waiting. Claire peeped from sleepy eyes and Suzanne asked, "Mom, can I go over to David's to make a snowman? We planned to do it on the first snowfall, and Mrs. Bartlett said it was okay."

It was a Sunday and that meant an Italian meal for the Scagliones at Aunt Maria's restaurant on Dago Hill where Tony had lived after his grandfather died. "What about eating with Aunt Maria?" Claire muttered. With the war, Aunt Maria was having a difficult time finding all the ingredients needed for a varied menu at the restaurant. Even with a limited selection, the trip on Sundays was still a treat. Besides, it had become a family tradition.

"Can I ask David to come and eat with us? We both could be here by noon on the streetcar. I'm sure they're running on Grand Avenue. The streetcars go all night and I'm sure that they kept the snow clear from the tracks. Hey, that's an idea! If I go now, I'll be able to tell you if it's possible for all of us to go to Aunt Maria's place by streetcar. I don't think we could drive. It's really a deep snow." She went on relentlessly, looking for excuses to help her mother say it was okay. "I'll ask if buses are running on the Arsenal line, too." Suzanne made some good arguments, and Claire liked the idea of having a private Sunday morning in the house with Tony.

As Claire listened to Suzanne clamoring down the stairs into the kitchen she realized, *I certainly have relaxed in this neighborhood. I let Suzanne do things I wouldn't have allowed a year ago. I think it has a lot to do with my friendship with Ellie and John. Yeah, also I have a safe feeling from all the wonderful people in the neighborhood who love Suzanne. They're looking out for all the children.* She snuggled against Tony and put her arm around him.

On went Suzanne's corduroy leggings under her dress and then the galoshes over the shoes. She put the woolen gloves into the pocket of her winter coat for an extra pair and slipped on her mittens. Going out the door, she knew this was going to be a day for dreams to come true. She and David had talked and dreamed of making this unusual snowman.

Her solitary tracks were evidence that she was the first person on the streets. It was hard to walk with snowdrifts up to her knees in some places, but it was like having the world to herself. It was prettier than any picture of snow on any Christmas card, she decided.

By the time she boarded the streetcar, her cheeks were chaffed from the wind and the piercing cold.

"What you doing out this early?" asked the conductor.

"This is a snowman day. Don't you think?" she answered with a smile that made her teeth hurt—tingling teeth like icicles. She quickly pursed her lips over her teeth to warm them.

At the Bartlett house, Suzanne got the hidden key and let herself into the back door. It was as quiet inside as outside. No one was awake. She walked up the stairs to David's bedroom and found him pulling on his v-necked sweater over his shirt.

"I knew you'd come," he whispered. "Isn't this a great snow?"

They spent hours building the snowman of their dreams. They had talked about how to build him many days ago. He wasn't a snowman at all. He was the shape of a huge rabbit! The face had bulging cheeks, the eyes were two blue jawbreakers that Suzanne had been saving, and the rabbit had a real carrot from the Bartlett refrigerator in one hand. They made two protruding front teeth that were oversized and comical. Even eyelashes were applied with the needles from a pine tree in the yard. Sticks were stuck into the top of his head in preparation for his long ears. When David went to get a kitchen chair to be able to make the rabbit ears, the younger Bartlett boys were told to come out and see.

"We made a snow rabbit! Come watch me make the ears. Hey, ya want to help?" David had an idea. "You could roll a ball of snow for a fluffy-looking tail, and we need to rub him all over to make him hard and shiny. The more hands to rub, the better. I think he'll last longer if he's really hard." David had made sure the snow rabbit ended up being a thrill for them all.

Ellie called and called to get the snow rabbit team in for breakfast. Excitement followed the group into the kitchen table. "Dad! Mom! Come out to see!" Johnny insisted.

Ellie and John ventured out without coats and marveled at the rabbit. During that late Sunday breakfast, Suzanne and David relived the building of the rabbit with all the details.

At two o'clock they were seated in Aunt Maria's restaurant and told about the snow rabbit again with a bit more excitement than the first time. David hadn't met Aunt Maria until this day. He knew who she was and could see the matriarchal role she held. Aunt Maria was like a grandmother to Suzanne and was the sole mother figure that Tony had ever known. For Claire, who often needed a shoulder to cry on and a woman to relax with, she was as close as a big sister. Aunt Maria was seventy-two and not getting any younger—only feistier with each year that passed.

She told David, "My own children, they move away and only call when they need something from me like money, a recipe, or me to come visit to baby-sit. Never do they come 'cuz they miss me," she complained. "Tony always comes. He stops and says, 'I wuz just in the neighborhood,' but I know he wasn't. He drove here to see me and ask if I need something."

"Now, Aunt Maria, you know that isn't exactly true. All your kids love you and miss you," said Tony.

"Well, look. Even little Suzanne bring her friend to meet me. *Grazie*, Suzanne. You think I ever meet any friends of my grandchildren? Well, I tell you. No, I never, not one. It is nice that you come, David. You come anytime. Now I stop my complaints and we talk about what is most important in life. You know what that is, David?"

He became pensive with a twinkle in his eye and knew he'd miss the point trying to guess. "I think you're going to teach me what that is."

"Oh, listen. He's like Tony when he's this age. No shy, quiet boy who doesn't talk to old peoples. That is what I like. Yes, you're right, I tell you. Most important in life is Italian food. We can't have life without food, right? You die without food so everyone agrees that food is important to life. But I tell you if you're going to have food make it the most important food—Italian," she preached.

"Now, David," Tony began to tease, "she has stopped and is waiting for me to tell you that more important than Italian food is Aunt Maria's Italian food." He held his arms up to cover his head. "You got a tomato that you're going to throw or can I put my hands down?"

They laughed and Aunt Maria told how it was when Tony came to live with her after his *Nònno* died. "I waste more tomatoes. I never hit him! He catch them."

"See, she admits that she was this horrible woman who threw tomatoes at a little kid," Tony joshed. Then, the stories started to fill the restaurant.

"Mio Padre, he so stubborn to not let you live with us all those years, Antonio," Aunt Maria complained, knowing it would have been hard to feed another mouth back in 1903 when her sister died. "See, Antonio—I mean Tony, it so hard for me to call him this nickname—he a good boy and I see that *mio padre* teached him to be clean and neat. Tony come to live with me when he eleven, and he know I proud of him like he mine." Aunt Maria turned to Tony. "You even picked a good friend in Louis, he a good boy, too." Now Aunt Maria had to clarify, "Louis, Louie—you know who I mean."

"Antonio met Louis his first day at school when he had come to live in Dago Hill with me. After that, they always together. He at the house for dinner, or he there before school for breakfast. 'Hello, Louis, how's your mother feeling today,' I say everyday."

Maria was a small plump woman who was always singing. She had been naturally happy back then as she was now. She and her husband accepted Antonio into their lives as if he had always been there. Antonio learned to help in the restaurant, even cut, prepare, and cook. By the time he was thirteen, he had to work like all their children did in the summer when there was no school. He didn't want to go to the brick factory where his Uncle Vinny and his older cousins worked, so he chose to go downtown near the river where he and *Nònno* had lived. He had found work there, although never steady jobs. He had worked in the market, loading or unloading steamers as they came in. He'd go to the train station and help people with their baggage, whatever. He was neat and clean and likeable. St. Louis was "first in booze, first in shoes…" which created a flow of beer and shoes on the transportation systems going out of the city. People came to know him and would let him know when there was work.

"Tony not work with my husband but he always find work. Someone tell him, 'Antonio, the Steamer *Quiet Waters* come in on Thursday and I want you to work with the unloading.' Or, someone else let him know that the Brown Shoe Company plan a big shipment to New York and they want help loading boxcars."

"Louis went with him and learn about places and people in the city that he not know exist. Antonio learn the city from the adventures with his *Nònno* and he teach Louis. They a real sight. They look so different. Short, wavy-haired Antonio and tall, blonde, stringy-haired Louis walking down the street."

Tony interrupted his aunt. "I told him, 'Louie, if you gonna stick around me, *The Fireplug*, I think I'm gonna haf ta call you *The Hose*,'" Antonio quipped. "Louie liked the idea and he was long enough to be a hose, too, 'cuz he was so tall. I would tell Louie, '*The Fireplug* and *The Hose*, here we come!'" People had agreed that Antonio's nickname was correct because from a distance, as he walked— knickers billowing out from waist to knees and stocky solid shoulders held in a rigid stance—he had looked just like a fire hydrant. The nickname, *The Fireplug*, suited him. His cap even looked like a hydrant top with the cap's indented wrinkles shaped like the grooves in the fluted hydrant top.

Aunt Maria took over the story again, "Of course there a reason that Antonio want to have no steady job; he love fire fighting. He think I not know, but I know that he go to lot of fires in the city. After work or when he was looking for job, he went to be with his grandfather's friends at the firehouses. Other times, the sirens in the downtown area tell him about the fires. Since everything was close, he sneak a ride on the back of a passing truck bed or just run to the fire. I not complain to him because he give me all of his money from his jobs and then he work with me into the night in the restaurant, too. When he help me in the restaurant, sometimes he would tease me and I throw a few tomatoes at him. Ha! Like I tell you before, he usually catch them. We would laugh and run around the kitchen." Aunt Maria stopped talking for a minute; she loved him so. He had a spirit that her boys never showed. Her sons were more like their Dad—reserved and serious. Then another memory popped into her head.

"Back then Tony is such a crazy kid. *Incredibile!* He go and buys this old good-for-nothing truck. It hardly run! One day he come by with it full of…what the word for the shits of cows?"

Tony told her, "Manure." He knew what was coming.

"Oh, yeah, that truck was smelly and full of manure. I tell him he going to ruin my restaurant business with all that smell drowning out the good smells of Italian sauces."

"Wait a minute! It wasn't full. It was empty. You always nagged me over my truck and here you're still complaining years later. It wasn't the best looking thing, but that's how I made money." Tony, to defend himself, had turned toward David and Suzanne, who were sitting side-by-side, "I bought this ol' truck for five dollars and kept working on it until I got it runnin'. I did a lot of different kinds of jobs with it. I used to empty people's ash pits. They'd pay me 50 cents. I could clean out 20 ash pits in one day and only have to pay the dump a quarter to get rid of it all. But that manure job was the best business idea. I would clean out the stables in Forest Park where the police kept all their horses. Isn't that great? The cops paid me to clean it out. Then, I'd mix the manure with some dirt from construction sites to sell it all to rich people for fertilizer. And, I got paid again. I'd put the manure on those people's lawns and flowerbeds. Got paid $20 for each home.

"See, that wasn't crazy. I used that ol' truck for years and I sold it for $25, or was it $45?" Turning back to his Aunt Maria, he wanted to set her straight about that truck, "I came here to wash the truck. It was empty 'cuz I had already put all the fertilizer on everybody's lawns. Well, there was a little stickin' to the truck bed."

"Well, it stink. *Santo Cielo!* You made a mess!" Aunt Maria reverted to Italian mannerisms, with her arms flying up in disgust.

"I did not!" He turned to Suzanne and David to defend himself again. "She had nothin' but dirt between the sidewalk and the street out in front. Nothin' would grow. So I decide to clean out the truck here. You know, I hosed it down, and with the little manure left in it, I figured I'd fertilize her yard. Then, I even planted daffodils. Remember? They still come up every year. That maple tree out front that is big now and has the beautiful yellow leaves every fall. I planted that for you, too."

"*Si, capisco.*" She lovingly smiled at her nephew. "I think you gave me all the money you earn that day, too. Those were good days. I liked it better when you went to the icehouse down on Vandeventer and buy ice to sell. He fill the truck with blocks of ice and go sell it all over the city to people. It was lots of ice. How much, Tony?"

"Oh, I think they were 300-pound blocks. The iceman up the street told me I could make some money selling ice. I went and there was a ramp where they'd slide those blocks into the truck from the storage 'cuz I couldn't lift them. I'd drive around and break the ice up with a pick. Taverns would buy it for two bits or four bits for chilling the beer, other people for the iceboxes in their homes and I'd give a lot to kids on the street to eat. You know, *Nònno* told me that he saw them cut ice from the Mississippi the year I was born. It was for the whole city. Millions of pounds of ice to use in the summer." Tony stopped his talking. With the mention of his grandfather, *Nònno*, Tony remembered the old man who had raised him. Although *Nònno* had died when Tony was eleven, he missed him still.

Aunt Maria patted Tony's hands and changed the mood with, "Now, who wants some antipasto that I make with my own hands for my special family?" Aunt Maria signaled the waiter and spoke in Italian to him, "*Questo non é pulito.*" She handed him a plate that she had observed wasn't clean. Soon two large platters arrived. "*Buon appetito!*" A meal was family time and an opportunity to talk. Aunt Maria used the opportunity and continued talking with her loved ones as they ate.

"With this stupid war I can get nothing from Italy. Why Italy join with that Hitler make no sense. It is luck that I have two large barrels of olive oil. That is what is most important to make Italian food. I close the restaurant every day but Sunday now," she told her nephew. "I no need to have it open 'cuz my kitchen workers go to factories that make munitions or airplanes. This will be extra job for them on Sundays. All of them like my idea."

"You won't have financial problems?" Tony asked with concern.

"No, I fine. You not worry. I promise to tell you if I have problems." Aunt Maria patted his hand because she could see an honest worry in his face.

Suzanne asked, "Aunt Maria, if you were born here in the states, why do you speak with such an accent?"

Aunt Maria laughed, "Oh, we only live in places in the city that is for Italian people. My mother and father always speak Italian with us. All the people speak Italian, so I speak Italian." Again her hands flew out, adding expression to her words. Then she chuckled, "We supposed to go to school, but the laws were not like now. I don't go until much later, and that's why I have this accent. It is good for my restaurant business. People like to hear me talk, I think. *Non so perché.*"

"You lived downtown in Little Italy where I lived with *Nónno*, right?" Tony wanted to verify.

"*Si*, that right. I move when I marry and come to this other Italian place, here on Dago Hill. So, I talk even more Italian here."

Suzanne remembered, "Oh, Aunt Maria, I wanted to know more about my Grandfather and Grandmother. When I asked Dad, he didn't know much and said I should talk to you. Could you tell me something?"

"Your Grandmother was my little sister, Isabela. Ah, *mia sorella*. Beautiful: she look a little like Claire. Both were small and pretty, but Isabela was foolish. She see this German right when he come to St. Louis. He speak no English. I mean nothing. I don't know how they talk. That was the problem. They don't talk too much. And, soon she going to have a baby." Aunt Maria turned to Suzanne to explain, "She only seventeen when your father was born. Oh, I had my first boy when I was seventeen, too, but I marry Vinny before I pregnant. Isabela not married. It was a sad."

"Why didn't they marry?" Suzanne asked.

"Oh, my father not like this German. You know, we don't even know his name. Your *Nónno* not want her to see him, but that not work. *Capisce?* Isabela sneak out to be with him, and soon she pregnant. She not tell *mio padre* until one day there is an accident and the German dies. Then she must tell him she going to have a baby."

Suzanne leaned on the table, absorbed in the story, and asked, "What happened to him? How did he look?"

"Well, you have hair his color and eyes, too. He very, very tall. More than six feet! I see him only once or twice since I was married and not living with my sister. I think, yes, he worked in the breweries. One day there was an accident and he was crushed between two of those train cars. I don't know how it happen. Isabela went to his work and found out. After that, she not want to live. She always sad even after the baby come. Your *Nónno* try to make her understand that it possible to love two people like he did with his first wife, and then my mother. She not want to listen."

"What do you mean?" expressed Tony with surprise. "*Nónno* had two wives?"

"Sure, *mio padre* no marry my mother until he was, I guess, fifty. You think he not have a wife until then? *Scusi!* His first wife had no children and died after they married twenty or twenty-five years. I don't know much about her. Of course, my mother never want him to talk about the first one, that's why he don't. He love her a lot, I think. She wasn't Italian, I know," remembered Aunt Maria.

"*Nónno* never told me about her," Tony conveyed a puzzled look and passed his fingers through his wavy hair. "That seems strange since he told me about everything else."

"It not strange. *Naturalmente,* he tell you about things a little boy likes. He talk fires to you and fishing. You not want to hear about loving a woman who wasn't your Grandmother," she admonished. "Besides, it was many years before you were born."

Tony was thinking he'd talk again in private with his Aunt because it was possible she knew more than she was telling. "Hey, I'm hungry! I think we've talked enough 'cuz we've forgotten our meal. And we've learned more about my *Nónno* than my father, but I didn't think we knew much about him. What's the main course, Aunt Maria?"

"Now we must eat. *Cosa prende?*" Lovingly she looked to Tony and smiled before turning to the others to say, "We make three delicious meals today. There's Linguini in tomato sauce with oregano, garlic, and both green and black olives. It's good if you want a red sauce. Then there is Pasta Tuscany that is made with capellini pasta in cheese sauce with garlic, oregano, peas, mushrooms, with just a little cut tomatoes and lots of chunks of chicken. If you like chicken and cheese you're going to like the Pasta Tuscany. The last choice is Pasta Pisilla. It has rigatoni noodles with peas, fresh mushrooms, bacon, and meat in a cheese sauce." She paused, "Any questions? I say again if you like, but they all delicious."

"I don't know much about Italian food. Would you order for me?" David asked Aunt Maria.

With the served food at the table they continued their meal. The conversation continued, too, while they ate. David asked if Aunt Maria had family in the war.

"Not right now, David. My boys are older than Tony and not been called. All the grandchildren who are boys are sixteen years or younger. So, at the moment they don't go either. There is one that will join on his birthday when he turns eighteen, I know. I hope it ends before that day. A lot of my workers are soldiers now, too," she informed. "Do you have family in uniform?"

"Yes, some of my cousins and a lot of friends," he answered. "One of my cousins from Ohio died last month. I had met him once when I was little, but Mom and Dad knew him well and were pretty upset."

"Oh, *sono spiacente!* I sorry to hear that," Aunt Maria said as the restaurant door opened and some people left. "My, it must be getting colder. Look, that man almost fell! I guess the sidewalks are turning to ice."

Tony got up and went to look out the front door. Icicles had formed where the melting snow had dripped and a mix of ice, and rain was coming down. Coming back to their table, he commented, "If the temperature is dropping, it's going to be really dangerous to move outside. We should start home earlier than usual. I've got to go to work tonight. David, your house is on the way, right?" Tony didn't know exactly where David lived. Except for Suzanne, the Scagliones had never been to the Bartlett home.

"Yes, sir. I'll get off the streetcar before you do," David informed him.

Aunt Maria began to talk and eat again. "I know this weather is bad, but it not as bad as when I was young. The Mississippi River froze all the way across. People go out there and walk on it, but I never like to do such a thing. And once I go down to the levee to see all the steamboats destroyed by a freeze on the river. The boats were crunched like a giant had played with them and squeezed them in his hands."

Actually that freeze had taken place in 1865, and her father, Tony's *Nónno*, had told her the story so often that she seemed to remember that she had seen it. He had always been a storyteller. Aunt Maria had been born in 1875. Age melts one's memories into waters that ebb and flow in the mind; past events blend, like joining rivers, never to be separately distinguished again.

CHAPTER 9

When Tony got to the fire station that night, he arrived with several plates of the Pasta Tuscany and Linguini for the other firemen to enjoy. Since the weather had turned for the worse, Aunt Maria had decided to close early. She packed up the remaining food for Tony to take with him.

"You smell like you been cooking all day," said one of his buddies.

"Him cook? It wouldn't smell like that," someone else replied. "This smells like I'm going to overeat and love it."

As the firemen sat to chow down, the talk turned to the weather. The storm continued to get worse. Rain turned to sleet. Whenever St. Louis had these winter storms, it was equally dangerous and ethereal. Not only were the trees iced, but also, the bushes, every blade of grass, statues, and park benches. The world looked glasslike and fragile. The men got up to look outside. The little park across the street was beautiful.

By the time they finished cleaning up the dishes and were ready to head upstairs to their bunks, they had hopes of sleeping late this Monday morning, like the rest of St. Louis. The thermometer was still dropping. It looked like the city was going to be iced in.

The alarm sounded at 4:08 AM. As the men rolled out of their bunks, they stepped into their fire-fighting pants, which had been arranged on the floor before going to bed, and slipped the suspenders into place onto their shoulders in one fast movement. There was no time for belts, which needed time-consuming hand and finger dexterity. They twirled down the pole. The man on duty at the Joker Stand watched a thin paper tape roll out with coding to show which firebox had been activated. He hurried to pull a running card from the files to learn the firebox location. On his way to tell the fire fighters, he punched a key, confirming that the information had been received, and ran to the shed, where all the vehicles were humming and ready to pull out. Men were tugging on their boots, which were stored on their assigned engine. The boots went all the way up their legs. Finally, they each lifted their heavy rubber coat from a hook on the engine and slipped it on. It went down to their knees and over the boots.

"It's on Compton off Olive Street," the operator shouted as the pumper truck with five men began to move out fast. The hook and ladder careened out next with six more guys. The men were still clicking the clasps closed on their rubber coats. Once out, the engines slowed. There was to be no speedy traveling in this weather. Tony rode the hook and ladder out into the frozen night. It'd be his job to go to the upper floors, if necessary. Then the hose wagon with one man followed. They knew it was a multi-alarm fire, but didn't know if it was a three-, four-, or five-alarm fire.

No other cars were on the streets. The ice was treacherous. Some places with inclines had cinders where city night crews were working the streets in preparation for the morning. As the men turned a corner, the fire came into view. Even from a distance, it was obvious that it was a multi-alarm fire; there was a glow in the night sky and flames were visible. Someone must have seen the fire from afar because the firebox that had sent the message, at Compton near Olive Street, wasn't where the fire was. They turned left and headed toward the burning three-story warehouse. Half the place was in flames. Suddenly there was an explosion and an eruption of flames from the center of the building. The men on the engines watched as they approached. It looked like chemicals or highly flammable materials in there.

Upon arrival they saw another fire company already on the scene. That company had evaluated the fire and, at the firebox, alerted the department how bad it was. Word spread among the men that the Battalion Chief was on his way from his home. The Deputy Chief was already working. A call had even been made to the top man, the Chief of the St. Louis Fire Department. Those men only came to the worst fires. And this fire was to be infamous. It was a five-alarm fire—the first five-alarm fire in the history of the St. Louis Fire Department!

Fire fighters were pulling and attaching woven cloth hoses to the hydrants. Three more pumpers arrived within minutes. Firemen streamed off these engines ready to go. On the pumpers, the drivers do the water hook-ups, and when they need more waterpower, up to four hydrants can be attached to each pumper. The firemen were searching for more hydrants on the north side of the building. The first company on the scene had started ventilating the building so no backdrafts would occur. They used axes to open the building in any way possible. No one needed to wait for the hydrant hook-ups because the pumpers carried 400 gallons to be used right away. Men were running swiftly with the four-inch diameter cloth mesh hoses, holding the nozzles and pulling to the maximum length of 100 feet. They began to douse the fire.

As the hose wagon arrived from Tony's firehouse, the Deputy Chief ran up and jumped on the running board. There's only one man on the hose wagon, the driver. That one fireman operates high-powered equipment to shoot the water great distances with a three-inch hose attached to a deck pipe, which is an extra large nozzle permanently fixed to a platform on the engine. The Chief was telling the driver what needed to be done. Tony watched the hose wagon turn the corner and disappear from sight as it went to the other side of the building. Tony knew it was getting situated so it could spray into the center of the building, where the fire was the strongest. Tony knew from that explosion they had seen.

Tony and the others quickly evaluated what they were up against. The building was brick with wooden beams; it had walls and windows of wood; and, of course, the main problem was the burning chemicals they had seen. The fire fighters had begun to observe the fire as soon as they could see it, and before the engines stopped, they knew a lot. Their first concern was the preservation of human life, and their eyes scanned the building for evidence of people. After that, they tried to locate areas of danger.

Every man tightened their leather helmets to their heads and grabbed axes or pike poles before jumping off the pumpers and heading toward the fire. The hook and ladder was being positioned to lift the ladders. Fire blazed on the upper floors. The hook and ladder held water like the pumpers, but not as much, 200 gallons. Only five minutes had passed since they left the station.

The driver maneuvered the ladder into position. Tony yanked the strap on his helmet again, making it tight. The helmet's wide brim dipped low to cover his neck, leaving no space for hot falling objects to slip down his back. His hands grasped the pike pole—six feet of steel with a hook at the end—used to poke, gouge, and pull debris. Before a ceiling could fall on him, Tony would pull it down where he wanted it to go.

As the ladder swung against the building, Tony was all the way up and anxiously poised to enter through the window while thinking, *There's no evidence of any people—no parked cars—but a clean-up crew could be here. People who came on a bus.* With his pole, he broke the window and knocked off the jagged glass edges. Looking around, he crept onto the window ledge and into the room. Two others, Hank and Joe, followed him with their axes. Inasmuch as they were going in where there appeared to be no major burning, they could work their way into the building without smoke, which would have limited their vision. They dropped into the room. They stood quietly for a few seconds to listen for cries or voices. There were none. The room had three desks and chairs. They approached the closed door, and Tony stood back while Hank cracked it with his axe to check for backdrafts. Nothing happened; Tony opened the door. They stepped into a wide, deserted hallway and stopped to listen again before splitting up, two going right and Tony going left, hacking and opening each door as they proceeded down the hall. Tony was aware that he was going toward the area of the explosion because, when they were approaching the building, he had noted the general area.

He kept listening for shouting or cries for help. It was hard to hear; noise came from everywhere: shrieking sirens from police cars, ambulances, and more engines arriving; shouting and cries of confusion from the fire fighters yelling to each other; clanging tools on hydrants; and gushing water thudding as it smacked brick walls. But the loudest noise was a roar ahead of him—the fire.

A fire is not a quiet affair. Noises from a cozy winter fire in the living room fireplace are consoling sounds. The crackles and snaps seem to relax and sooth the soul. Sitting on the couch with the warm glow thrown across one's legs, like a cover against the winter outside, one enjoys the sounds of a fire spitting sparkles.

Now increase the size of that comforting fire by over a thousand-fold and the noise can be deafening. With the increase of size, fire fighters know there's loss of control. Without control, they are left with the unknown. Unknowns are always on the fireman's mind. Fighting a fire is a battle against an enemy who can always surprise you.

Tony was at war as much as those soldiers on the front in Europe. He knew his enemy was there. He just didn't know where. Unknown to him, the fire was lurking around some corner, waiting above him or hiding below. He didn't know for sure. He took each step with caution, as he expected an attack from out of nowhere, at any second. The fire could shoot out in an instant. Plus, Tony didn't know what weapon would hit him—destruction from the impact of backdrafts, an explosion from combustible material, or suffocation from a smoke-filled area. Would the fire ambush him from all sides, leaving no path out? Would the fire lash out and hit him with heat that would batter him like the firing from a machinegun until he exploded into flames? The ceiling could fall and painfully set him ablaze or mercifully crush him to an instant death. The possibilities of death were infinite, so Tony reasoned that it did no good to worry about how he could die. Instead, he filled his mind with how to bring down the enemy that lurked ahead and how to save any others who were less aware of the ways of this war.

The hallway was wide, ten feet across, and it appeared that the hall turned at the end and continued. Tony was wrong. When he came to the end and turned right, there was a door. It was a double door, and, he thought, it appeared that it might be to a meeting room or an executive office. He gashed a hole into it. No backdraft. He opened it. Hell unfurled into his face.

At that instant, Tony's mind flashed with a memory. When you face death, you think of someone you love. Nevertheless Tony didn't visualize only the face of Claire; he remembered a whole scene—the room, the time of day, the polka-dot blouse she had removed and placed on a chair, and how her hair had tickled his cheek. He was seeing the moment when she had asked, "What's it like to open a door and face a fire?"

He'd told her, "It's like someone throwing a pan filled with hot, just-off-the-burner grease into your face. It feels like welts are going to instantly bubble out from your skin." They were in bed after making love, and he had been smoking a cigarette as she cuddled into his shoulders. He had been talking about his day and what he does best.

Now here he was, living his answer to her.

With the heat in his face he reacted. His hand was on the knob and he closed the door enough to buffer the heat from his face while he tried to see again what he had seen in that fraction of an instant while the opening burned into his brain. People—six or so! He leaned back and shouted to the two others. "Down here! Get the hell down here! There's people!"

Then, leaving the door open ten inches, he stepped in front of the other closed door to angle his vision into the room. He had to embed the pike pole into the floor and wedge it against the door to prevent it from blowing open. He stepped to the left. "Oh, my God!" he gasped. A baker's dozen of pleading eyes peered back. Thirteen eyes because there was an injured woman with half her face gone. The group of seven huddled behind metal cabinets and desks. It was a room with one corner of the walls remaining and holding up the floor. They were protected from the heat and fire, for the moment, by two-thirds of a brick wall behind them and metal furniture that they were hiding behind. "This is from the blast we heard earlier," he imagined aloud. There was a gap in the floor of four feet between him and the people as they crouched in front of the inferno. He could see a room below the gap that wasn't in flames yet. He kept recalling what he had seen when he opened the door; the fire had seemed to be to the left and behind the people. An orange glow and dancing shadows flowed from the cracked door.

The other two firemen ran up to Tony, and he began to talk loudly above the noise as he explained, "There's a partial brick wall that faces us—you know, opposite us—and the floor is attached to that brick wall, but it only extends halfway across. There're seven people. It looks like that blast blew away most of the other walls on the right and left. Go ahead and look. There's a corner supporting them. It comes this way off the right-hand brick wall and that's why they haven't fallen, but it's got to go at any sec. One of you guys go back to the closest door down the hall and tell them to get some hoses into the windows to get some water in here." Joe dashed away. "Did you see anything that we could lay across that four-foot gap in the floor and get to those people?" Tony asked.

"Hell, our problem is the heat from the fire!" shouted Hank. "They can't move 'til we get water to cool it down. If they walk away from the brick wall or those cabinets, they'll burst into flames."

"I know, I know," Tony insisted, "but we got to be ready when the water gets here. Did you see anything we could use in any of the rooms? I can't remember seeing anything in the ones I looked in."

Hank looked through the cracked door to evaluate the size of the gap they needed to fill while Tony continued to talk.

"The worst of the fire seems to be behind that brick wall that's holding up their floor. Man, their little island can't have long before the volcano erupts and blows it away!" Tony shouted to his companion. "Let's move!"

"I did see something that might work!" Hank bellowed.

They ran back down the hall, and Hank opened a door to a small storage closet. There was a ladder. A wooden ladder!

"Hey, I know it's wood, but I didn't see anything else. If we pull a door off a metal cabinet we could put it under the ladder to stop some of the heat temporarily. That is, if there's water."

As they turned, they saw Joe coming at a run. "Two minutes and they'll be here," Joe shouted.

"Where did you see metal cabinets?" Tony asked Hank.

"Over here." Hank pulled open another door.

"Good, there are two doors on it. Let's take the whole cabinet. Empty it with me!" They opened both doors and pushed it over. It fell to the floor with a thud. Like a planned action they had done many times, they worked as a team. Hank was at one end lifting while Tony raised his side. They awkwardly carried it and their tools out into the hall.

Joe arrived to help. "What's the plan?"

"This is our bridge." Hank shouted. "Grab the ladder over there, too."

They trudged down the hall, and two other fire fighters with a hose nearly collided with them. "Where're we goin'? Chief wants to know how many, too."

"There's seven and one needs a doctor quick. Half her face is gone. Tell them to move the power wagon onto the east side and aim into that area," he pointed in that direction. "That's all I know for now." Joe ran back to the window with the message and the rest of them headed toward the double doors.

"Okay, listen up, this is what I figure." Tony screamed his ideas as fast as he could while they were setting their loads on the floor in front of the double doors.

"We use this whole cabinet as a bridge. Those people can't walk a ladder. This cabinet is empty, and the air space inside will give us some time. We can't drop it across the gap because the force might break more of the floor off. So, I'll put my pike pole across and connect over the gape. Then, we slide the cabinet on the pole to reach the other side. Then, I pull out my pole. Hank, you hold the ladder up for them to grab and steady themselves while they walk across. Now, the hoses have to douse the left side when we open these doors. Spray an arc from seven o'clock up to eleven and back. Then I'll put the pole down while you guys keep the water goin' wherever you think it necessary. One more thing: I go across to the other side as soon as I've got my pole in my hand."

"Wait a minute, Tony; what for?"

"There's a lady down and I need to get those other six moved out of there. I don't want anyone running out before they should. Let's go!" He nodded to Hank and they pulled open both doors as the hose unleashed the waters.

Two were needed to hold the hose as a thousand gallons a minute poured onto the fire. They aimed the hose and sprayed an arc once, and then again. Tony stepped out and bent to extend his pike pole over the gap in the floor. Hank and Joe were sliding the cabinet as Tony's hand held the pole in place. They worked with precision again. Done. They had a bridge! While Hank and Joe lifted, Tony pulled out his pole, stood, and cautiously put his left foot onto the cabinet. It seemed firmly in place. Hank held out his hand and Tony took it as he stepped up onto the cabinet. Then, in a blink, he was across. The hoses continued to work as Tony pulled a man to his feet and pushed him toward the cabinet. The man crossed in two strides without grabbing the ladder. Joe rushed that first man out of the hall toward the window. "Follow the hose. There are men waiting for you over there." As Joe turned back, his next charge was jumping from the cabinet and he directed him, like the first.

The next man did use the ladder for hand support and was slower to cross; fear showed in his face. Three rescued, three more to cross, and then Tony with the injured woman. Joe noticed that there were two women and a young man left. He knew that each person had been chosen by Tony and not randomly sent across the bridge.

Tony had chosen who would go first for a reason. He had grabbed a man who appeared to be anxious to get out and noticed that they all had on the same kind of uniform. Tony knew that if the others saw someone cross with success, they'd have more courage. The second had been a young person just as eager as the first. He had flown to the hall and out the building as Tony had hoped. Then Tony needed to get rid of a fearful man and leave a young man to help with the woman if it was necessary. He could have been criticized for not sending the women first, but he also knew that a woman could sometimes balk. That would've jeopardized the lives of eight people. These women looked scared. With three people out, it would be obvious that the idea was working and a woman would be less likely to balk. He was right. He chose the oldest woman, who looked to be 50 years old. Holding her hand, Tony directed her to climb onto the cabinet.

It shifted!

She screamed and stepped back down. Tony took no time to talk. He grabbed the cabinet and changed the position until it was firm again. Taking her hand firmly as she tried to pull away, he stepped up and pulled her behind him. He grabbed the ladder and passed it to her. "Hold on tight Ma'am. Both hands." Then he turned and shouted, "Pull her, Hank—carefully!"

Hank did. She stumbled into Joe's arms, and he decided to carry her to the window.

Tony went back to the other woman. She was terrified and he grabbed her hand before she could protest. At the same time, he commanded the remaining young man, "Follow us and cross as soon as she's down." The flames behind the broken brick wall were starting to come into this area. Something else worried him more. Before, when Tony had bent to secure the cabinet, he had seen bigger trouble. The fire had arrived to the room below. However, it was what he saw in that room that made his heart jump. Barrels! Not one or two—it was a storeroom full of barrels. He knew the fire posed a great danger if the barrels he saw in that room had anything combustible in them. He had no idea what kind of business this was, but even if he took the time to ask these people about the barrels, they might not even know; they looked like the housekeeping crew in those uniforms. It wasn't worth the chance of losing even a second. He figured that maybe they had been cleaning the offices and had stopped to have their midnight lunch break in the executive conference room. The fire must have been going on the other side of the building, unbeknownst to them until the explosion occurred.

Tony guessed that whatever had exploded before might be in those barrels. He had to let the other fire fighters know.

After he pushed the woman into position up on the cabinet and she traveled forward, he pushed the young man onto the cabinet. "Go!" Then, before turning back to get the injured woman, he let his comrades know.

Pointing down he shouted, "Barrels below! Get out of here! All of you!"

They ran! No one questioned his words. Why would they? Six of the seven people were out. They had been ready to bolt with the seventh, but Tony would get himself out without any of them. They knew Tony would've said if he needed their help. They also knew that it would be his decision to leave or go for the injured woman. Tony was admired for his sixth sense or natural instinct of fires. Tony was one of the best when it came to reading fires. He seemed to always know what was going to happen.

Not this time.

As Tony grabbed the woman's arm and rolled her over his shoulders into the fireman's carry, they both flew into the air and disappeared in a *BOOM*. So powerful was the explosion that they heard and saw nothing. The force was so great that it ripped the strap from his chin and flung his helmet to a far corner before the flames touched them. They went upward—the arms of the flames reaching out and encircling them—and disintegrated.

Before the blast, Hank had been the last person to head for the other room across the hall. When he got to the window, he looked back for Tony and saw there was no one in the room but him. Instantly, the boom blew him against the window frame, cutting through his thick rubber coat, and laying open his arm. The impact of the sound arrived before the fire. Bleeding, he scrambled out as flames roared through the crumbling doorway of that room. Frantically he lunged from the window ledge onto the ladder while screaming, "Pull out! Pull out!" Tony wasn't going to be coming.

Within the next hour, they had the blaze under control. It had taken five hook and ladders, fifteen pumpers, and three hose wagons. With the heat of the fire diminishing, the fire fighters continued to spray until men could enter and confirm there was no danger. The firemen began to feel the subzero temperatures returning and a strange transformation began spreading over the building. A light, frosty glaze began to freeze on the wet bricks. Where the water was dripping, icicles began to form. Every ledge of every window had cascades of icicles decorating them in a fairyland manner. Some dripped until they were three feet long. Crystal designs began appearing on all the glass windowpanes, whether broken pieces in the frames or fragments on the ground. Unique shapes, like snowflake crystals seen in a microscope, formed for the naked eye to see. White. All was white. Sidewalks became sheets of ice with tiny icicles over the curbs like frills hanging from a satin altar cover. Silence dominated the place. No one spoke or wanted to speak as they prepared the hoses and equipment to leave. They had lost one of their own. A water tower loomed above like the belfry of this white cathedral, demanding silence and prayers.

Claire and Suzanne were aroused at seven that morning with the news of Tony's death. Hank and Joe came with the Battalion Chief and Deputy Chief. After an explanation of Tony's heroic actions, the men divulged that there was no body. Only his charred helmet had been found in the building. Claire sobbed and couldn't suppress a desire to see the place of his death. She asked to go to the burned-out building site. She needed a concrete scene to accept that he was really gone forever.

Suzanne covered herself with a shroud of silence.

The trip to the site was a wonderland of iced trees, shimmering shrubs, ice-cubed mailboxes, and glazed lampposts. The telephone lines that overhung the streets looked sugar coated and glistened in the sunlight. Suzanne looked wide-eyed out the car window while listening to the talk of her father's death. Finally the tears came and she was scared. Nothing she saw and heard seemed real.

Suzanne was amazed when she saw the ice-covered structure—a huge white cathedral sparkling with the light of dawn. Unbelievable! What she saw was as unreal to her as his death.

She sat on the car seat, gazing out at this shocking sight, not able to move. *Only in those silly fairy tales do scenes like this exist,* she thought, *and I never believed those stories even when I was little.* Now she wondered. And now, she broke down and felt hopelessly like a little child again. Regressing to childlike feelings, she was comforted in this moment of mourning. She imagined that maybe her father was under some spell and had temporarily vanished. *Yes, I could bring him back if I could just find the frog to kiss or know the magic words,* she daydreamed. She scooted out from the car and stepped delicately on the iced sidewalk, looking up at the iced building. With a running nose and sobs, she whispered, "Daddy, what do I need to do? Are there magic words to make you appear? I'll be really good and kind. I'll never lie. Please come back, Daddy."

They all walked around the building close to the area of the explosions. They could see the charred and blackened place inside and looking up at the remains of jutting floors and partial walls, Hank and Joe softly told the tale of the fire, pointing here and there. Suzanne saw her father in her mind's eye and heard her father's voice with the words they told her. When the story ended, they all stood silently. Suzanne kept looking to the exact spot where they said he had vanished. Poof! She gazed at that empty space to see a clue of what she might do. *Ala Kazam* and *Open Sesame* came to mind. She listened and heard ice cracking and crackling in the morning sun. She listened, hoping that some spirit in this White Cathedral would whisper the secret to her.

CHAPTER 10

Two days later, the afternoon before the funeral, John Bartlett arrived at the front door of the Scagliones and knocked three firm raps on the wood. Suzanne opened it.

"Mr. Bartlett! Please come in. Do you want to talk with Mom?" she asked.

"Yes, if you please. How're you doing?" he inquired with a sad face.

"Okay, I guess. It's funny. It's like my body only has one cup of tears a day, and when I use that up I don't need to cry anymore until the next day." She paused and they both just stood there, not knowing what to say. Finally, Suzanne said, "Please sit down. I'll get my mom." She turned and walked down the hall to her mother's bedroom and knocked softly.

After Claire greeted John, he gave his condolences and apologized that he couldn't go to the funeral. "Ellie and David will be going." Then he addressed a matter that had been worrying him. "I wanted to talk with you personally because I'm worried about you and Suzanne." John noticed that the door to Claire's bedroom moved a bit. Suzanne was listening to the conversation and he decided it was best. "I want you to know that I want to help in anyway that I can. Ellie feels the same. I want you to know how much we love you and Suzanne. We want to help you and your daughter if we can."

"Thank you, John," Claire said with a strange look. John couldn't guess why she had this look.

"Maybe this isn't the right moment since it's just before the funeral. Then again, speaking now might offer you some solace and help you get through this," he said. Claire just shook her head that she understood and blew her nose into her hankie. He continued, "I'm especially concerned about your financial position and we'd like to help. I know a fireman's pension can't be enough to cover a mortgage and college and things like that, so we..."

"No, John, I don't need help," she interrupted and cleared her throat. "However, the thought and offer will always mean more than any financial help." They stood motionless while John tried to absorb what she meant. "I see you're puzzled. I guess that I should clarify my situation since you and Ellie are my closest friends. I've never told anyone else about this before, but I inherited a lot of money over five years ago. It's enough to take care of Suzanne and me." Again she stopped, letting John absorb her words. "There's no mortgage. This place, the confectionery and home, is all paid for, and I have no debts. With Tony's pension and this inheritance, I'm secure. Plus, for Suzanne's college education, I inherited a trust fund of over $20,000. She can't touch the money until she starts college, and after she's 26 years old, whatever she has not used will be given to her."

John's quiet amazement elicited a little smile from Claire, though her eyes continued to hold her sadness.

She summarized, "So, we are fine in the money area."

"Claire, I'm a bit embarrassed that I pried into your finances. I didn't mean to have you tell me all this, although I'm relieved to know that you're without that kind of worry. I think that..."

"John there's something you can help with. You know how much I want to have a confectionery. For years, I've wanted to have my own store, and I need some help to begin. Of course it isn't the best time with the war, but I think it's the best time for me. I don't want to sit around and feel sorry for myself. I'm not sure if there are enough products and food items available to start a store, but I want to try. I could use some advice and, you know, step one, two, and three on how to begin," she contemplated. "Too bad I couldn't start tomorrow. It'd occupy my mind."

"There you are, we can start right away. Before you open your doors, you need to learn about the business from a store that is functioning. You can come help at the drugstore. Since Tommie went into the Air Force, I haven't found anyone to replace him. Ellie helped until she had Becky, so now I'm short-handed again. If you'd come and work, we could teach you about sales, bookkeeping, ordering, and all those things. It'd be perfect for you, and Suzanne, too! You could work during her school hours, finishing before she gets home at three-thirty. How does that sound?"

"Oh, Mommy, say yes." Suzanne emerged from the hall to come and sit by Claire. She hugged her mother, hoping she wouldn't be balled out for eavesdropping. "It's just you and me, Mom, and we need to share and be a family. This is a good idea. Please say you will," Suzanne begged. "You could always stop if you wanted."

John interrupted, "No, she can't! A commitment is important. I need a clerk and I'll be depending on your mother if she accepts. You both can talk and let me know as soon as you can. I'll be leaving now. Remember that Ellie and I are here for both of you. Oh, Ellie said to insist that you get a telephone. We were going to offer to pay for it, but now..." He stopped and asked, "Claire, why don't you have a telephone?"

"It's difficult to explain, John. Tell Ellie that I agreed to get a telephone." The three went to the door and gave hugs as they said their goodbyes.

Suzanne asked, "Can I walk up to the drugstore with Mr. Bartlett? I'll come right back." Her mother knew that it was a good idea to let her get out and talk.

Claire turned and leaned against the closed door. "There, it's told," she sighed. It was such a simple reason why she had no telephone. She didn't want Tony to know that they could afford one. It had been one of the little ways she pretended to save money. They ate simply and bought carefully so Tony would see that they were saving money. In that way, he wouldn't doubt that they finally had enough money to buy their own place. She had hid many facts of their lives from Tony, she admitted to herself. Finally, she had shared her financial situation with someone, and it was a relief. Tony had never known. She could never decide how to tell Tony. She had dreaded the time when Suzanne was to start college because she would have to tell him. If the fire hadn't killed Tony, the knowledge of how she had obtained all this money would've. As Claire started to stand away from the door, her elbow hit the wood with a loud knock. Waiting for the pain to subside, she flopped on the couch and put her head back. Her mind swept to the day she learned about all this money. It was six or seven years ago this spring. At that time, she hadn't seen Harry for at least four months. With the sound from the knock of her elbow, the scene came to mind.

Knock, knock, knock, came three firm hits on the door of her first home on that triangular block in St. Louis. Claire went to the bedroom window above the front door and leaned out to see who was there. Two gentlemen in felt hats and gray topcoats stood waiting below.

"Hello," she called down to them, "how can I help you?"

"We want to speak with Mrs. Claire Scaglione."

"That's me. What is it you want?" Her voice changed and she had a foreboding feeling about those two standing at her door.

"Well, it's important business that should not be shouted on the street. May we come in?"

"Can't you tell me why you're here?" she said. She couldn't imagine why these men needed to speak with her.

"I have some financial matters that can only be discussed in private, ma'am."

"All right, I'll meet you at the diner over near the corner." She leaned out the window and pointed. "I'll need a few minutes to dress my little girl."

"Please get someone to stay with her and come alone. The topic is not for a child's ears, if you please. Also, you must bring some documents that show that you really are Claire Scaglione. A birth certificate, marriage license, passport, or bankbook, and some envelopes with your name and address, would be good."

"Oh, what is this about?" she said to herself. She was scared. She looked for the papers she needed and then left to take Suzanne upstairs.

"What would I do without you, Mrs. Stein?" she said, waving as she retreated back down the stairs from the third floor. She changed into a better dress, put on a light coat, and picked up all the documents. "They're certainly over dressed in their topcoats on a day like this," she murmured, trying to keep her mind busy. She was trying not to guess what they wanted with her.

The diner was filled with intermingling odors and noise. Claire noticed the sound of sizzling bacon, the clatter of dishes, and lots of talk as she closed the door. Someone laughed. Claire passed a waitress wiping a table, and the rank smell of the soured cloth momentarily drifted into her nostrils and quickly disappeared under the delicious smell of coffee. She enjoyed smelling coffee more than drinking it. The regulars were dressed in clothes that reflected their work—paint-stained pants, blue overalls, and cabbie hats. Claire easily found her two mysterious visitors, conspicuous in their tweed suits. The walls were shiny white tiles. The seating choices were stools at the counter or booths along the window. They had taken a booth and sat together on one side, leaving the other for Claire to face them. She slid into her seat and sat back with folded hands in her lap.

"Good day. I'm Mr. Connelly from the law firm of Hauptmann and Hirsh, and this is Mr. Weinberger from Prudential Life Insurance Company." He tapped his finger on two cards that were already on the tabletop and continued, "I'm here representing the estate of Harry J. Schwarz. I was his lawyer, as I had been to his Aunt before him, and with his death…"

"What do you mean, his death?" she cried out. Inadvertently she had said it louder than anticipated. Her hand went up to her face in nervous embarrassment.

"Why Mr. Schwarz was killed in an auto accident December last. Excuse my thoughtlessness. I thought you were aware of his passing."

"What happened? I hadn't seen him, but I had no idea."

"He was driving his cab and ran into a large tree. It seems that he was killed instantly. He was having one of his epileptic seizures at the moment of impact. They said he really hit the tree hard. You know, going very fast. His body probably stiffened, causing his foot to push on the accelerator. Witnesses say that the cab began to swerve and increased in speed before he hit the tree. Luckily no one else was hit or hurt."

"An epileptic!"

"Yes. You look surprised. Didn't you know he had been epileptic all his life?" he asked.

"No, I really didn't know much about Harry." Claire sat quietly for a moment and then inquired with impatience, "Why are you telling me all this?"

"Mr. Schwarz has named you his beneficiary," he commented and noticed her puzzled look, but continued. "His heir, you know. He has named you and your daughter, Suzanne, to inherit most everything he had. His cab is one exception. It goes to some friend, and, well…. I'm getting ahead of myself."

"There must be some mistake. I'm not related to Harry," she insisted.

"No, I realize that. Harry had no living relatives. Let me rephrase everything, in a better way, and include some details of Harry's history. When Harry's aunt died, her home and monies went to Harry as her only relative. She had married a wealthy man and survived him. Harry's mother, her sister, had married a poor man. Both of Harry's parents died when he was a teenager. He was on his own. I've no idea where he slept or how he ate. He was sixteen and legally an adult. I don't know if his aunt offered any help or not, but I don't believe so. When she was making her last will and testament, I would meet her at her home, and she mentioned Harry from time to time. She said things to me to make me think that she had not been in contact with Harry while her husband had been alive. Her husband, I believe, forbade her association with her nephew. Well, anyway that is neither here or there, is it? He finished his high school and tried to become a policeman. He went through most of the training before they discovered that he had epilepsy. He was refused for this reason. He shouldn't have been allowed to drive, either. However, I imagine he refused to share his medical problems with the licensing people. So he did whatever kind of labor he could find until he realized that he could help the police department as an investigator; you know, like a private eye. He began working on his own and helped the police on special cases all the time. He had worked in this capacity for the last fifteen years. It seems he was very good at his work"

Claire nodded in agreement, "Yes, he certainly was." Now Claire realized how Harry had learned so much about her and why he had always been where she was. It was his specialty.

"So, at some point, he bought that cab and created a front for himself to go and learn more about whatever case he was working on. According to the officers I've spoken to, he was well respected. They indicated that Harry was good at appearing to be someone he wasn't, to get information that was needed for the police." He took a breath and asked. "Have I explained enough of the background?"

"Yes, I guess. I didn't know any of this, other than that he had an aunt who gave him his house."

"Well, yes, to continue, Harry has left you that house, and last year he came to me to set up a trust fund for your daughter, Suzanne. The trust is set aside until she starts college and is to be used for her education, books, housing, living expenses—everything for her to live while she goes to college. Our firm will administer the funds. That is part of the stipulation of the will. After she graduates or when she's 26 years old, whichever comes first, whatever amount of the twenty thousand dollars that is left will be transferred to your daughter. Now…"

"You said twenty thousand dollars? There must be a mistake. This can't be. It's not true."

"Yes, it is quite a sum, is it not? Actually it's more, since it'll be accumulating interest until Suzanne begins to use it. I need you to come to our offices to read all the documents and officially sign papers. Then we can legally transfer the house and finalize all the other details."

"I don't want that house," she stated firmly.

"Well, legally it's to be yours. I can't change that."

"Can't it be sold?" Claire asked.

"Oh, yes, of course. You can do what you want after all the papers are signed."

"No, I want you to sell it for me. I don't want anything to do with the house. Couldn't your firm handle the sale or find a way to sell it and pay your fees from the sale? Or, something like that?" she seemed to plead.

"Yes, you're right. We could help you with that. It isn't usual that we do that, but I'm sure it could be arranged. It'll be more costly than if you sold it yourself. However, if that is what you wish, we can make arrangements when you come to the office. Now we need to give Mr. Weinberger some time to speak."

Both turned to look at the mousy and anemic-looking Mr. Weinberger. His voice fit his appearance. It squeaked. At least he spoke quickly and concisely to let Claire know that Harry had taken out a life insurance policy for the sum of $25,000 to be paid to her upon his death.

"I needed to meet you and verify that you are Claire Scaglione. May I see some of the documents that I noticed you brought with you?" He paused to look at the papers. "This is a normal procedure for an accidental death in a policy that has a double-indemnity clause," he continued in his high-pitched voice.

Claire was feeling lightheaded. She was having such mixed emotions about Harry at this moment. He wasn't the man she had known at all. A new person was forming with the accumulation of words piled on words. Her imagination envisioned the words, moving slowly in a spiral, forming two legs, and then more words swirling into a torso, and up and up until a face appeared on top. Since she had arrived at the diner, each mention of his name had produced an image from the first time she had seen him, biting a cigar between grimy teeth, with dirty hair speckled in dandruff and a day's growth on his chin. She remembered how he had changed, and it had puzzled her. In the end he had been groomed, and she remembered seeing love in his eyes before and after he had been intimate with her. He had never talked about himself. Never! Was she wrong not to ask? No! He was wrong to control her and force her and scare her. He was a bad person to threaten her. At least the mystery of why everyone liked him finally had some substance; she had never known this other Harry.

At the meeting in the offices of Hauptmann and Hirsh, Claire timidly sat and listened to the reading of the Last Will and Testament of Harry Schwarz: Harry Schwarz, a single man with no known living relatives, paternal or maternal, being of sound mind does declare this to be his Last Will and Testament...

But she didn't listen too intently. She wanted it to end quickly. Tony knew nothing, and she was only worrying about his possible discovery of this whole matter. By sneaking out to this meeting Claire found that guilt festered in her conscience. It was like spending time with Harry again. Now with Harry's money, would this whole episode ever end? How could she keep this secret from Tony?

The reading of the will ended, and Claire brought her mind back to the matter at hand. She composed herself sufficiently.

Within weeks all was settled and a new savings account held the fated funds that came to her for being in the wrong place at the wrong time. Years would pass before she touched any of the money, and then she began to transfer small amounts to their house savings account to speed the purchase of her dream home with a storefront. Tony had always left the finances in her hands because he was inept with handling money. He never knew if they had too much or not enough. Tony was grateful she could manage without him. He wasn't a man of wants besides his family and his work. He figured that if there was enough food on the table, they were doing all right. He was proud that Claire was resourceful at saving and at earning extra money with her little projects.

Claire came out of her daydream thinking, *I hadn't planned to be drawn into these memories right before the funeral. How confused I am, with the shame of Harry and the sadness for Tony.* She pondered to herself. *Or is it shame of Tony's crime and sadness for not knowing Harry? I don't know.*

Late that night, after the drugstore had closed at eleven, John Bartlett drove into his driveway and stopped abruptly. With the headlights shining into the front yard, he saw to his disappointment that the snow rabbit was gone. In its place was an indiscernible mass of melted snow and the footprints the children had made—some iced over, forming an exact foot shape, and others melted down, showing matted grass. It looked a mess. John's heart ached to think that David and Suzanne had built the snow rabbit only the day before yesterday, and like Tony, it suddenly was no more. Along with the melted rabbit, much of the enthusiasm and happiness inside those two kids had dissolved in the last couple of days, too. They had planned for months for this snow and had worked hard to reach their goal.

It was late and the funeral had ended only hours ago, so with this sight and his mood John had a thought apropos about David and Suzanne, *Many dreams built in the morning sun are like snowmen...too soon they melt and are gone.*

SCRAPBOOK

BY

Ellie Bartlett
1944–45

ST. LOUIS HERALD NEWS | Final Edition

ST. LOUIS, THURSDAY, April 12, 1945

FDR DIES IN THIRD TERM

By the Associated Press.
WASHINGTON DC, APRIL 13, 1945 Yesterday President Franklin Delano Roosevelt died from a cerebral hemorrhage, during his fourth term in the Office of President of United States. The Vice President, Harry S. Truman will become President.

V-E DAY

- - - - - - - - - - - - - -

GERMANS SURRENDER

- - - - - - - - - - -

By the Associated Press.
WASHINGTON DC, MAY 8, 1945
During the first week of May, 1945 the Germans surrendered one by one in all areas of Europe. May 8th has been named V-E Day for the Victory in Europe.

TEENAGE GIRLS OBLIVIOUS TO WAR

In 1944 there were 6,000,000 teenage girls in the United States. In interviews with several hundred, it became apparent they were unusual not for their pompadour hairdos or the idolization of Frank Sinatra, but because they existed in a blissful society basically untouched by the war. Only if their fathers or other family members were overseas, were they interested enough to learn facts about the war.

ATOMIC BOMB USED AGAIN

- - - - - - - - - - -

By the Associated Press.
WASHINGTON DC, AUGUST 10, 1945
Four days ago, on August 6th, the President of United States, Harry S. Truman, executed the decision to use the atomic bomb on Hiroshima, Japan. Yesterday, an atomic bomb was dropped on Nagasaki, Japan. An atomic bomb has never been used in war before.
These two cities had not been bombed previously. The government said that about 120,000 people were killed.

- - - - - - - - - - -

JAPAN SURRENDER ON BATTLESHIP MISSOURI

By the Associated Press.
WASHINGTON DC,
SEPTEMBER 3,1945
On August 14, 1945 the Japanese surrendered after the atomic bomb was used on two cities, Hiroshima and Nagasaki. They signed the official papers yesterday on September 2 at a meeting on the Battleship Missouri in the Pacific Ocean.

Statistics about WWII:

- 61 countries took part in the war
- It has been estimated that more than 55,000,000 died in 30 countries.
About 20 million from the military
More than 30 million civilians
    (other than the Holocaust)
And 6 million in the Holocaust.
-   The total military and civilian losses for the U.S.A. were estimated at 410,000
-   The cost of the war was estimated to be $1 trillion as follows:
    U.S.A. $ 341 billion
    Germany $ 272 billion
    USSR $ 192 billion
    Britain $ 120 billion
    Italy $ 94 billion
    Japan $ 56 billion

NEW YORK, N.Y.,
SEPTEMBER 22, 1945
Television broadcasting that was begun on April 30, 1939 and discontinued with the advent of WWII, will soon be resumed.

PART III

1949–1950

CHAPTER II

1949

Saddle oxfords and bobby socks were in style. Penny-loafers and ballerina slip-ons were, too, but girls wore them without socks, and Suzanne was told, by her mother and Mr. Bartlett, that saddles and socks were best for the health of her feet so she wore saddles and socks. Invariably when her mother would lecture on the subject, Suzanne would be shown her mother's feet for the umpteenth time.

Claire would comment, "Look! My feet were deformed from wearing the wrong kind of shoes. I wore shoes without socks and shoes that squeezed my toes, like high-heels with pointy toes." Claire's big toes permanently slanted toward the other four toes with a large, oversized joint at the base. Suzanne was not allowed to wear high heels.

"I know, Mom," Suzanne said in an irritated tone as she furrowed her brow and bit her tongue against saying more. She had no boyfriends and decided that no boy wanted to go out with her because of how she dressed. She wasn't allowed to wear any make-up either. She had never been on a date.

"Just a little lipstick, Mom, that's all," she'd complain.

"Your lips are beautiful and full of color just the way they are, Suzanne," Claire said over and over.

Another irritation to Suzanne was the rule: nothing black! Any article of clothing that was black wasn't allowed.

"Suzanne, black is for an adult woman, not you. Black is for a funeral or for an evening dress. You'll be able to wear it soon enough, so enjoy the colors that are meant for the young," Claire berated her.

Suzanne complained to herself in her room, "Who establishes these rules? Do parents stop to think of the reason for their restrictions?" In her history class she had heard how the people of St. Louis had protested against the name for the Mille fountain in front of Union Station. She learned it was changed from being called *Wedding of the Rivers* to *Meeting of the Waters*. "My mom is just like all the stuffy, close-minded old fogies in St. Louis. Mom is probably relieved that I have no boyfriend because then she would have to talk with me about the "birds and the bees," as she would say."

Suzanne was a senior in high school this year, and although she knew that she was younger than the other seniors, she would've liked to think it was a time that she could start to make her own decisions, at least about her clothes. Still, Suzanne didn't want to argue with her mother. She had watched her mother work hard every day in the confectionery and be alone every night since her father died. She didn't want her mother's life to be made worse by arguments. Besides, Suzanne wondered if boys would notice her anyway. Aside from her unfashionable appearance, she had the idea that her brains and good grades probably threatened the boys. Finally she had concluded that learning was more important and more interesting. She was hoping to be valedictorian of her class.

This year she was President of the Girls' Athletic Association, called GAA (she lettered in field hockey and swimming), Vice-President of the Math Club, in the Latin Club, on the Student Council, and on the school newspaper staff. She didn't really have time to date. She worked at Bartlett's Pharmacy as well as at the confectionery with her mother. Suzanne enjoyed sewing her own clothes, too. Also, she wrote poems, especially when she needed to express her feelings.

Going in Circles
I seek a man to love and hold me,
While wanting time to learn and mold me.
I need a family, kids and home,
A job with meaning, time to roam.
I fear a life I'll always loathe,
For I know I can't have both.

Suzanne liked high school, but her best friend had just moved away. She knew a lot of other girls because of her involvement in many activities, but she felt alone. She remembered how it felt when she and David had grown apart. After being close friends for over a year, David and Suzanne had both started getting into their own high school activities and soon had no time together. They attended different high schools so it was logical that their paths didn't cross. David had even stopped working at the drugstore, and Mr. Bartlett had started William, the next in line. So at the pharmacy, David and Suzanne didn't see each other either. Without her best girlfriend around to talk to about David, Suzanne had begun to daydream about him. She knew her fantasies of marrying him seemed like childish wishes, but she couldn't stop thinking about him. "Is this puppy-love that I feel for David?" she'd wonder.

While Suzanne had never had a date in high school, David was one of the more popular guys at his high school. He could have dated any girl he wished. He usually did. He had gone steady a couple of times and had learned that going steady meant more than just giving a girl your class ring to wear. As he had explained to his mom, "Going steady takes too much time and money; besides I prefer to be free to date any girl I want."

With his good grades and his tennis ability, Washington University in St. Louis had offered David a scholarship. He had been accepted to other universities but had decided to take the scholarship and give his father a financial break; there were four more Bartlett kids to put through college after David. As long as David played for the tennis team and maintained good grades, his scholarship would pay for tuition, fees, books, and the other necessities, except room and board. So he lived at home and drove the family's 1941 Studebaker Champion to classes. His major line of studies was Pre-Med to prepare to become a doctor.

Suzanne and David were two wholesome young adults, studious and full of interests, but completely unaware of the power of love. In fact, they lacked the most basic information about sexual matters. Suzanne was unaware of the power of sexual drives, though she had completely read on her own about reproduction and the anatomy of the human body. On the other hand, David was familiar with hormonal explosions and secret yearnings that he'd never discuss, such as mentally undressing girls as he passed them on the street. And he was familiar with the shame he felt from masturbating to satisfy the lust that stemmed from just looking at some girls. Unlike what he had told his mom, sexually he couldn't tolerate going steady. The relationships always reached the point when he worried that he wouldn't be able to stop before he forced himself upon his steady girl. What was clear to him was that he had a strong sexual drive and feared the loss of sexual control. He had trepidations about getting the wrong girl pregnant. It was better to date around and not ever reach that point of intimacy that happens when going steady. Of course, he had the always-present Trojan in his wallet, waiting to be used. He really wanted to do it. Sometimes he'd asked this or that girl to go out when he had heard in the locker room that someone else had gotten into her pants. His guilt was overwhelming at those times, and he'd never found the right moment on those dates to do it.

John and Ellie had talked about discussing sex with their children.

Ellie had proclaimed, "John, since you're the father, you're the one to talk to the boys. It isn't the place for the mother to tell her boys about life."

John had decided Ellie was right and had talked to the two oldest boys. David had a Trojan prophylactic in his wallet to "take care of that moment when he may find himself in a compromising situation," as his dad had put it. John had gotten out a textbook he had from college to show graphically what restraint could avoid. He had shown them photos of syphilis. The boys were sufficiently appalled by the gore. John was sure that he'd done a good job teaching his boys how to maintain themselves in situations that were "getting out of control."

Other than that, the boys had learned from the other boys. They knew as long as you "pull it out before you come" that everything would be okay. They also knew that "girls want it so they can get pregnant to marry you." That was why they needed to "pull it out before you come."

Suzanne worked two weekday evenings seven to eleven and four hours on Saturdays as well. She really enjoyed the work. Her sole disappointment in the drugstore had occurred soon after the war ended when Mr. Bartlett had had the soda fountain removed and an all-glass display case for cosmetics installed in the same location. While the soda fountain had been there she had hoped that one day it would be open again. She had complained to Mr. Bartlett.

He had shaken his head and looked forlorn, "I'd hope you'd aspire to be something more than a soda jerk."

Suzanne had laughed at his corny joking around.

Upon entering high school, Suzanne had taken Latin after Mr. Bartlett had suggested it. He emphasized that Latin was a language used everywhere in science. When she had realized how much Latin helped her in English classes as well as science, she had planned to take three years of it. Mr. Bartlett let her put the Latin to use in the drugstore by reading the prescriptions. The prescriptions had to be translated twice. First, the hieroglyphics of each doctor—their penmanship was atrocious. Second, they had to make a translation from Latin to English to fill the prescription and to type the directions in for the patient.

Suzanne asked Mr. Bartlett one evening at the drugstore how David was doing in his first year at the university, "He must be almost finished. Don't his classes end before mine at the high school?"

Mr. Bartlett answered as he worked on a prescription, "David says that he's doing fine. Yes, he'll be out of class next week." The response came in a faraway voice since he was in deep thought, trying to decipher a doctor's handwriting. "By the way, look at this prescription and see if you can help me, Suzanne. It's that Dr. Schmidt, and I can't read it. I'd rather not call him if you could figure it out for me." He passed the paper to her as he removed his new glasses. He couldn't get used to those things on his nose. He rubbed his nose.

She stopped filling little jars with an *unguentum acidi borici*, Boric Acid Ointment, used for burns and abrasions. "Wow, you're right!" she exclaimed as she took the prescription. "These doctors must take a class in how to write sloppy." They laughed, but she read the prescription for him.

"I'll finish filling these jars and start to check out the cash register. It's almost ten o'clock and we should start the restocking right away. I've a paper to finish for tomorrow. Are the restocking lists ready?" she asked.

"They sure are. I knew I had to be ready or you might scold me," he teased. They used a system for restocking that she had perfected a few years back, another of her organizing ideas. John had learned through the years that she knew how to make even the most complicated job more efficient.

Within fifteen minutes the front door was locked, and they proceeded to the back office where the stairs went into the basement. The stairs were unfinished, worn wooden steps that might never have known the touch of a broom. As they proceeded down with the familiar creaks, a bare bulb lit their shadows ahead of them, and John knocked down a spider web above his head.

Suzanne pulled a cord connecting to another bare bulb that lit a large, open room filled with cartons, cases, boxes, and more cartons, cases, and boxes. Mr. Bartlett purchased in volume to get a better price. There were boxes of Bayer aspirins, Hadacol (because they "Had-to-call it something"), Johnson's mustard plasters, Milk of Magnesia, Park and Davis Alcohol, and on and on.

"Here are the restocking lists, Suzanne. I'll put away that delivery that came today," Mr. Bartlett said as he walked toward the far right side. He pulled another cord and lit another area where he was going to work on the order from St. Louis Wholesale Company that had come into the basement through the metal doors that opened from the street. He and Suzanne talked from opposite ends of the basement as they worked.

"How is Mrs. Bartlett feeling?" Suzanne asked as she tossed ten boxes of Johnson's Corn Remover into a cardboard box to take upstairs.

"Not too good. The doctor is still testing her. We should have some results soon, I should think," he answered in reference to some problems that his wife was having. "I'll let you know when we know. How are you doing with school? All set for graduation?"

"Sure. Had some bad news, though. I'm not the top of the class. I'm number two. Guess I'll live, though." Something else was bothering her more. "And no one's asked me to the graduation dance at the Chase Park Plaza. That's where our class is going after the graduation. I sewed this beautiful and sophisticated white sheath dress with a scoop neck. I want to go, but we have to have a date…and, like I said, I don't. I bought high heels. Mom doesn't know about them. She might get mad when she sees the pointy toes and four inch heels," Suzanne giggled. "Want to take me, Mr. Bartlett?"

"Sure would! But I think I'd be out of place. My dance is the Charleston. Do you know that one?" he inquired.

"Actually, I *do* know how to Charleston. The band may play one...but only one, if we're lucky." They chuckled at her joke.

"Why don't you ask David to take you? I think he'd love to go."

"Oh, I don't know. I'd hate to put someone on the spot. If I ask him, he'd feel committed to saying that he'd take me. Besides, I would've enjoyed having one real date while I was still in high school. You know, someone to ask me to go."

John thought a minute and decided to say something that he had often wanted to say, but hadn't said, because he didn't want to embarrass Suzanne. He decided that today was the day. "Dates in high school don't mean too much. The boys there don't know a good date from a bad one. They're learning about girls and are often too scared to ask a real winner. You, Suzanne, are a real winner. I'm not talking about your grades. Though you know that I think that they're most important, of course. I'm saying that you're a beautiful and wonderful person. I think you're going to find that, once you're at the university, you'll have to beat the boys away from your door. Well, they'll be men. You'll have to beat the men away. You'll see."

He claimed all this with such authority that Suzanne found herself blushing. She had never had anyone tell her such things. It was quite a moment. He spoke so matter-of-factly as if he had merely told her "your eyes are blue." He had said she was *beautiful!*

She felt light-headed with the bare bulb above her head casting a strong light, making one side of the stacks of cartons and boxes bright while the other side dissolved into the blackened shadows. The bulb swung slowly from its cord, shifting the shadows back and forth. Her thoughts swayed, too, denying the possibility of her beauty and then wondering if it was true. Yet, down deep, she knew she was beautiful. It's just that no one had ever seemed to notice. At least, no one had ever avowed it. She found herself saying, "Why do you say that I'm beautiful?"

"You are! That's why. You're too beautiful for those high school boys. They're still boys and can't handle it. It takes a man to see beauty in a woman. Now, back to what I was saying about David; I'll mention the dance to him and let you know. I won't embarrass you, I promise." Then he asked Suzanne to be sure to get tickets to her graduation for him and his wife Ellie. She already had them.

They finished the work and left the drugstore. He walked with her down to her house as he always did when she worked the evenings. During the walk

Suzanne wanted to tell Mr. Bartlett how much he meant to her and how he was like a dad to her, especially since her dad was gone. She could not find a way to start. That was strange. She had been able to talk with him, say anything that came to her mind, since the first day she looked into his eyes. *For some reason, I'm embarrassed to say those things,* she thought. *Yes, I feel so much, but I can't say it. That seems so strange.*

When they got to her kitchen door, they said goodnight. Without thinking, she spontaneously hugged him and ran inside the door. She quickly closed it and ran upstairs. As she plopped on the bed she whispered to herself, "Wish I could tell him how much I love him."

Love. This is not something a man admits to having thoughts about, but John was having some thoughts as he walked back to his car. Normally, he'd only allow thoughts that were analytical and intellectual. But this night he allowed himself to think about it, though not for too long. *What is it I feel for this young person Suzanne? I know that love takes many forms. There is the love of my children and a different love for my wife. And Ellie has told me that she loves each of her children equally. Humph, my mother told me once that she loved us all in different ways, but not one more or less than the other.* John decided they were both trying to say the same thing.

Then John turned a corner and his mind took a turn, too. *There seem to be many degrees and types of love. Definitely there is a Platonic love as opposed to a love with passion…or maybe not. Possibly passion isn't love at all. People might think passion is love because it's such an intense feeling that occurs with carnal knowledge or the desire to have sexual fulfillment. Both could be confused with love. Love is not easy to explain,* he concluded as he drove home to Ellie.

On the other hand, a young girl thinks of love a lot. Suzanne was no exception. She had often wondered, "What is love?" Tonight, as she was all snuggled in bed, she started thinking about David, as she often did. Just hearing David's name in the conversation tonight had given her butterflies in her stomach. *I wish I could tell if I really love David or if it's just a crush. I don't even know how people know when love is real!* Suzanne knew that no one could tell her what love is. She looked in the dictionary and Webster said that love is profoundly tender or passionate affection for a person. Even with her lack of experience she thought, *Come on, what can a dictionary begin to say?* She realized people must feel love in many different ways—starting with a gentle tenderness and growing to a sexual passion. She had no experience to differentiate between love and passion so they were somehow connected, except that passion seemed wrong for some reason. She listened to songs and heard phrases. *Love makes the world go round. Love is eternal. Love moves the sun and stars.* She was sure love was important since it was always in the movies and books. She fell asleep to those thoughts.

David knew that all of those little ditties were actually talking about sex. He argued with some friends one night, "Go ahead! Replace the word *love* with the word *sex* in any of those songs or some other expressions you can think up. All of those expressions are wrong! Love is private, personal, and usually between two people, not the world."

David and Suzanne would soon see why love was hard to define. Love is as unique an experience as birth, when we entered the world and screamed out, "Look at me! I'm alive." Being in love is returning to a childlike exuberance— enjoying life at its simplest, like splashing in puddles, counting the stars, and watching an ant carry a crumb from here to there. Love is closer to a delectable, endless happiness than sex. Love is exciting, like having an ice cream cone every day in any flavor you desire—new flavors you never imagined, with nuts or extra chocolate. And sometimes it drips.

Sex is the drip of your ice cream cone. Not all love starts with a drip.

David was glad to take his friend Suzanne to her high school graduation dance. He called her and asked her if he might. She agreed and was pleased. She would've been thrilled if Mr. Bartlett hadn't initiated the date, but that didn't matter. Her excitement at knowing that she was going with David was stimulating. No one would know that David was prompted by his father to ask her. Besides, it made sense that David and she were going because they were friends, two people who really were fond of each other. *It'll be fun to be together again and talk. We always liked talking,* she remembered.

"Right, we've got a lot we can talk about. I'll tell you what it's like at the university. Hey, where should I go to meet you?" David asked

"Listen, just come to my house about 9:30 that night after the graduation. I don't have a ticket for you anyway. I only have three because of limited seating in the auditorium. I plan to turn in my cap and gown and come right home with Mom. Gee, it will seem strange to end high school. But I think I will feel free! You don't feel like you'd want to go to the graduation anyway, I'm sure. It'd be boring for you, the same as your graduation was," Suzanne laughed.

"Good point, sure. So I'll see you at your house about 9:30 on Friday."

Suzanne was glad all the plans were working out. Before leaving with David, she was going to spend time at home with Aunt Maria, Mrs. Stein, the Bartletts, and others. Claire was preparing some finger foods and a punch.

David arrived while Suzanne was upstairs dressing for the dance. She was flush from the excitement of the date, giving a rosy blush to her cheeks. Her freshly washed hair was sparkling. She was applying mascara and lipstick and felt clumsy. "I was better at doing this than when I was playing dress-up as a seven year old," she giggled. Suzanne was wearing a strapless bra that went to her waist, the type that cinches the waistline to a size as small as possible, and she had on her Sunday girdle, not the one she wore daily to school. She finished her makeup and put on silk stockings, high heels, and her white sheath dress with the scoop neckline. Actually it was a low-cut scoop in the front and a deep-cut scoop in the back, held up with spaghetti straps. The strapless bra and the girdle made the close fitting dress with the snug waistline appear smooth. Even with all the under-armor, her curves were showing. She worried that David would feel the stiff stays, hard boning, and thick elastic when they danced.

When she was ready and stood to see her own reflection, she found that she couldn't believe it. "That's me?" It was as if the words of Mr. Bartlett saying she was beautiful had truly transformed her. Walking downstairs she might've been embarrassed, knowing the reaction she was creating, but she wasn't. She knew that she was finally able to show people who she was. She felt unlike ever before. She felt like a woman.

This particular night in every home of a graduate, whether male or female, congratulations were being offered on scholastic accomplishments as well as on appearances. Each graduate dressed for the event in a special way. It would be normal for Aunt Maria, or anyone, to say to Suzanne how lovely she looked.

In fact, no one said anything to Suzanne.

As she walked through the living room toward the dining room greeting people, the impact of her beauty left people without words. The sight of Suzanne as a woman for the first time, a woman with poise and grace, a young lady with composure and radiance, stunned them. Suzanne could see this in people's faces. John Bartlett saw his beautiful prediction walking in his direction and knew that the pause of quiet that lingered in the room was soon to become embarrassing. He broke the silence with a raised glass.

"Let's drink to the graduate. May she set the world alive."

Everyone relaxed and broke into words of congratulations—all except David. He was overcome. He drank to the toast and then carefully he set his glass on the table, unaware of his actions, while he watched her speaking with the others. She gradually came toward him. He swallowed. She was hugging Aunt Maria and receiving a small gift and then she continued in his direction. She smiled at him from across the dining room table, and then turned to greet Mrs. Stein and to speak a few words with her elderly old friend. Suzanne's back was all he saw, and it was bare almost to her waist. He swallowed again and then reached for his glass. His throat was dry. His palms were moist. He picked up a napkin to wipe them. Her back was smooth with fine hairs that glistened in the light. He wanted to touch it. Would it be as soft as it looked?

As Suzanne came around the edge of the table coming directly to him, he thought his heartbeats were surely showing through the black suit coat. All sounds of the room were not registering when he noticed that she was speaking to him.

"What?" he blurted.

I said, 'Good evening, David,'" Suzanne repeated.

He fumbled a bit as he picked up the corsage he had brought and extended it to her with some meaningless sounds.

"Oh, thank you," she gushed, as she pulled on his lapel to bend him close enough for a small kiss to the cheek. Wisely, Suzanne turned to leave him to handle his reaction to the little peck. She smiled and said, "I'll be right back." She went to her mother to ask for help with two final details for the night—a necklace that Aunt Maria had brought for her to wear and the pinning of the flowers to her waist. The top of the dress had those thin straps that weren't wide enough for any pins.

"Suzanne, I…" began Claire with her usual look in the eye about make-up.

Suzanne quickly interrupted, wanting to avoid the all-too-familiar subject about clothes and make-up. "I know, Mommy. Didn't the dress come out beautiful? With all white in my dress and shoes, the red flowers are the touch my outfit needed. And, look at the necklace Aunt Maria gave me! It's red, too. She said that it was her mother's and it's called *The Gypsy's Teardrop*."

"My goodness, it looks expensive!" Claire lifted the necklace from the blue, velvet-lined box and clasped it on her daughter's neck. "It looks old, too."

Claire finished pinning the corsage and stood facing her daughter. No words came. Suzanne hugged her mother and whispered, "I love you, Mommy…wish Daddy was here."

The grand ballroom was a perfect fairytale setting to begin a love, with lights sparkling from chandeliers and dim corners where lovers could pursue a forbidden kiss out of sight from the chaperones. Everyone was in his or her finest. Gowns that rustled or shimmered. A terrace and moonlight. The first drink passed from a flask that's quickly slipped back into a coat pocket. The endless hours unhindered by a curfew, for it was the night that would last until dawn. The music encircled and wrapped them in sounds, carrying them of its own accord around the dance floor. When it was a fast dance, the rhythm and happiness let them dance to exhaustion. Laughter was floating to their table from somewhere and everywhere. When friends separated Suzanne and David, while dance partners were switched, they were made aware of how much they wanted to be with each other. Together they found this to be a new experience, a touching experience—pleasure with arms embracing the other in a dance, excitement from the touch of a hand, exhilaration while sitting knee to knee in the car and talking until the sunrise appeared, not wanting the night to end.

That night became the beginning. It was as if they had not known each other before. They discovered emotions and feelings with a childlike giddiness. David would say to himself how much he loved her. Suzanne would confirm that she had more than a crush or puppy love for David. She knew he was the man to be the love of her life. Though it was the beginning of their romance, they'd not kiss this night. At the door, shuffling his feet, David tried to do what he wanted, yet couldn't. A kiss was too much to ask. They simply planned to meet again.

The next day in the late afternoon, the phone rang and Suzanne found herself being asked by a classmate, who had been the captain of the football team, to go to the movies. She accepted. He couldn't help saying how he was amazed that he had never noticed her at school. Suzanne smiled at his comment. It was interesting how coyness and a bit of flirting seemed to come natural to her. All of a sudden, Suzanne, walking down the street, turned heads.

Do I walk different than before? Probably not. It started with Mr. Bartlett telling me I was beautiful. How can those words change things? she thought. But she had changed. She became confident and carried herself differently as she walked. She had poise and instinctively knew how to give a guy a flirting look and talk with her eyes. She found self-assurance that was growing and being reinforced with each feminine action and male response.

The summer after her graduation was filled with dates, though she knew in her heart that she only wanted David. It was simply that she was getting asked to go out by others, and David hadn't asked her to go steady. Also she realized that she had no experience with dating and possibly what she felt for David would be the same with other guys. *After all, what is love? How do I know if I really am in love with David?* she thought.

She refused a second date with most of the guys for a variety of reasons. She learned about kisses quickly—kisses and groping hands. She learned about her own bodily reactions to this necking and was surprised about her own desires for guys who meant nothing to her. The promises they made while necking were often humorous. In a steamed up car one night, she was on a second date with a boy who pleaded, "Come on, let me! I'll marry you if we need to."

Suzanne pushed him away and pulled the car door handle. "'No,' I said!"

As the door opened, he was irritated and retorted, "You can walk yourself to your front door. I don't think I need to see you again."

"Jerk!" she shouted with a grimace as she slammed the car door. But running to the house, she giggled at how stupid he was. In the house, Suzanne went to the bathroom and smiled in the mirror, repeating softly this time, "He's such a jerk to think all I want is to marry him."

David and she seemed to have at least one date a week. David was aware that there were others vying for Suzanne's time and this made him insecure. *Suzanne probably is only going out with me because we're friends,"* he lamented while trying to figure out how she felt about him. With his insecurity, he didn't attempt a kiss all summer, with worries in his head like a roller coaster— anticipations filled with agony as they climbed slowly upward, peaking with hope only to fall rapidly back into doubts. He wanted to be with her all the time. In his imagination, he took her to bed every night. He showered with her while masturbating. His lusting mind created sexual encounters that made him embarrassed when he'd meet her in person. He began to worry whether he'd be able to study when classes began. He was miserable.

She was happy, happier than she had ever thought possible. Her life had changed. When September came and it was time to start college, she awoke everyday with excitement. She could have gone to a prestigious Ivy League college back East, but her reason to go to Washington University in St. Louis obviously was to be with David. To David the reason she was going to the same university wasn't apparent, and in his misery, all he had was the hope to be with her as much as possible.

It was apparent to Mr. Bartlett. He knew she chose Washington University because David was there. He may have been more aware of what they meant to each other than they were. Mr. Bartlett had told her that she should stop working at the drugstore and use the time for her studies, knowing she'd be reluctant to approach him to say she needed to quit working. He was also aware that her trust fund was going to provide a lot of money and the amount earned at the drugstore wouldn't be needed.

The trust fund and college changed her relationship with her mother. Suzanne was more relaxed because she felt she was an adult. Every day was a new and carefree adventure because she was in control. Not having to ask her mother for money and not having to wonder if she might be straining her mother's budget made her feel free. Having her own money made her realize that she had always been careful and prudent about spending. Suzanne had never known how her mother was set financially. She had overheard the conversation about money with Mr. Bartlett on the day of her dad's funeral, but it wasn't clear to a ten-year-old what that meant. Suzanne remembered thinking that it sounded like most of the money was going to be for her college education. So all these years Suzanne had wondered and was cautious not to strain her mother's budget. She didn't feel she could ask since it wasn't proper to discuss the finances of a parent. Now it didn't matter. Suzanne was independent.

She made decisions to wear make-up and to don black skirts and pointy shoes. And to go where she wanted. Whenever she wanted. She completely controlled her own life, for the first time. She truly felt grown up.

One day, David suggested, "Want to ride to Wash U. with me? All last year, I went down Grand Avenue to get there. To get you it would be only four blocks down Park Avenue to the confectionery and back."

"Sure, that'd be great!" she answered, relieved that he had finally asked before she had to suggest the arrangement to him.

Since they rode to the university together, David and Suzanne saw each other every school day. Eventually he started going to Aunt Maria's restaurant on Sundays with Claire and Suzanne as he had done years ago. He remembered Aunt Maria and where she lived in the Italian neighborhood called The Hill. The two young people found they were comfortable together, and their lives seemed to become one. Although they shared no classes, they'd meet for lunch or to study in the library. While the fall days were warm and sunny they might choose a grassy place to sit on the tree-filled campus and help the other study. David had many lessons in Pre-Med that were purely memorization. Suzanne would help him by quizzing him about the names of the organs or muscles. She'd joke that she was learning to be a doctor without going to the classes.

Late one sunny afternoon, David recited the bones of the body to Suzanne on the campus lawn. They had been studying over an hour and were getting restless. She slipped off her shoes and with her toes began to fiddle with the grass. "That was right. Now spell it for me," she prompted him.

"H-U-M-O-R-U-S," he said as he watched her bare foot, this *naked* part of Suzanne. With each wiggle of a toe his penis grew. His mind pictured her toes in his mouth and that was it for learning bones; he had his own to worry about.

"David," she reproached, "that's wrong! It has an E, not an O. You said it right the first time I quizzed you."

"Gosh, I'm hungry. I'll work on my studies later. Let's go to Aunt Maria's a little early," he said to end his torment.

"Okay. I'm starving, too," Suzanne said as they gathered their books.

Aunt Maria wasn't always in the restaurant if they'd arrive late at night after a movie. So they made it a point to call her and plan a meal. She was still spry, though growing thinner as the years passed. They listened to her stories of young Antonio, *Nónno*, or Vinny, when The Hill had been called "Dago Hill." "Funny how we can't use a word that years ago we always use. *Dago* not a Italian word so who we going to offend?" Aunt Maria said. "Now it a nasty word. I don't understand all this stuff."

David tried to explain, which led to laughter from Suzanne as she watched David struggle. "I looked it up and the word *Dago* was coined by someone who thought the Italians were Spanish and referred to them by the common Spanish name of 'Diego.' You know…"

Aunt Maria didn't seem to understand, and there was no explaining to an aging Italian woman who had always used the name *Dago Hill*. "It not a bad name. I always like it. No, it not wrong that people call my neighborhood 'Dago Hill.' Why? When the government came to take census they call my place 'Dago Hill.' It's a good name since always. We use *Dago Hill* when my Papa was here," she insisted.

"But people say *Dago* when they're thinking badly about Italians," David declared again.

"All these ideas are new stuff that people makes up. It make no sense and I'm not interested," Aunt Maria insisted and ended the discussion. Then she said with mischief in her eyes, "Besides it's time to eat. Time to eat some of my Dago Hill food.

They ate and laughed through the meal as the daylight started to wane.

"Suzanne, he say that he don't know bocce ball!" Aunt Maria exclaimed as she got up to open a window to the evening air. "*Santo Cielo!* You must take him over to play and teach him good." Turning to David, she chortled, "It's fun. She used to play with her father and her father with his *Nónno*. It a good game. Then you meet some good Italians that are my friends, too."

"We should do that, David," Suzanne implored. "You teach me tennis and I'll teach you Bocce ball. Let's go tonight! Fridays are more fun because there are a lot of Italian speaking people playing and it makes me feel like being in Italy. Come on, it's fun. Actually they talk in half English and, well, more than half Italian. What do ya think?"

"Why not? I could use some exercise," he quipped, knowing that it wasn't at all strenuous.

"Should we go over to the Bocce Ball Club on Marconi and Bischoff, Aunt Maria?"

"No, that one always too busy. Why not drive around and see another place," she said. "Try the one on Marconi and Wilson first. It called Milo's Bocce Garden and I think you like it better."

David always enjoyed the drive on The Hill where the restaurants and stores displayed Italian names—Viviano Grocery Store, Gitto's Deli, Oldani Brothers, Favazza's Tavern, and Giovanni's Restaurant. Homes were intermingled with the business establishments. As they drove they noticed that Mama Campisi's Restaurant looked like it was going out of business. On Daggett Street they passed one after another of the "shotgun" houses that were unique to The Hill. They were long, narrow houses. "They can't be even ten feet wide," David said. "How do they fit any furniture in them? I would like to see one of them on the inside."

"My Dad told me that Uncle Vinny and Aunt Maria bought one of these "shotgun" houses. He said a lot of *Nónno's* Italian friends had bought them in the late 1800s. They were small, but affordable for the Italians. That's how they got out of the slums downtown," Suzanne commented as they drove. Simple but colorful flowers surrounded the houses, lawns were well groomed, and the whole neighborhood was clean, displaying the pride that had existed over the decades since the Italians had come in the late 1800s.

Many people were out and about as they parked and walked toward Milo's Bocce Garden. The place was teeming with talk; bocce ball is a social activity. Seeing the thick cigarette and cigar smoke billowing out into the night air and hearing the hearty conversations and raised voices in disagreement, David concluded that bocce ball actually was strenuous—in a social sort of way.

"It's not a complicated game, David," Suzanne insisted as she began to explain the rules. A couple of older men, short and sturdy Italians, agreed to play a round with them. "Here, take this little heavy ball. See, it fits perfectly in your hand. Now watch Mr. Gitto taking his bowl. He's trying to get his ball as close as he can to that white one out there on the green." They stood watching Mr. Gitto's ball roll across the grass. "Oh, look how close he is! Each of us takes one bowl until everyone has had a bowl, and then we get another try. The person with the ball closest to the white one gets a point. Go ahead, it's your turn."

David's toss rolled ten inches farther than Mr. Gitto's ball. Not too good.

Mr. Gitto's partner rolled even closer to the white ball.

"Oh, you're so good, Mr. Biani. My turn!" Suzanne sighed, "I don't think I can get closer than your bowl, but I'll try." Her hand dropped and, swinging her arm forward, she released the ball, excitedly jumping up and down like a child. Disappointment followed as the roll went farther than anyone else's.

At the finish of that game, they switched partners, got a glass of beer, and started another round. It was a delightful evening as it cooled down and the moon came up. David stood there gazing around, listening. Almost everyone at the court was from the neighborhood, and most conversations were in Italian. He smiled, feeling as if he was under a European moon. Mr. Gitto asked David what he did, and they talked about Washington University until it was David's turn to bowl. Like someone who bowls every weekend, David played his ball, watched the roll, and then turned to continue his conversation with Mr. Gitto.

David wasn't looking when Suzanne walked over to make her toss. With his back to her back, he stepped over to reach for his beer, unknowingly moving toward her just as she finished her bowl and pivoted to say something to him. They collided! She fell into David's chest. His arms flew out to balance himself then he grabbed her shoulders as he started to fall. They teetered! He reached around more and clutched her. Her arms grasped at his waist to steady herself.

Finally they stopped, still standing, but belly-to-belly and clinging; their eyes met, their gaze locked. Heat and sensations occurred. This was it! The first kiss was coming. Like a child on a playground swing, David went weightless, looking into Suzanne's eyes he soared to the top of the arch. He balanced for an instant in that uncanny hesitation of the swing, where the thrill is the highest, before beginning a swoop downward. A surge of exciting pleasure took his breath as he descended to her lips. Silky hair brushed his cheeks as he felt the whoosh of the ride.

One of the old men called out, "Are you going to play or not?"

The lovers lingered an instant before stepping apart, not a bit embarrassed. The fervor of the kiss had given them a rush and left a flush that prickled their cheeks.

As kisses go, it was not that great—too tightlipped. Yet for the two of them this intimate experience—click—turned off their senses to the rest of the world. The sounds of the game, the talk and laughter, even the buzzing locusts, droning into the night, all became silent. Glaring light bulbs, smelly cigars, perspiration, and the humid air were no longer seen, smelled, or felt. They finished their game with no words passing between them, simply looks and smiles. They found it impossible not to smile and, during the drive home, impossible to stop kissing.

In the coming days they were inseparable. Their hearts laughed with love. Events that were silly or foolish had meaning. One night they watched raindrops, and then walked barefoot in the warm puddles. On a picnic by a stream, they stacked pebbles and giggled when they fell. At the park, they skipped stones and flew kites. During the picture show, the romantic scenes made them tingle when they heard phrases such as, "Nothing could ever change how I feel for you." And, it didn't matter what they said to each other because nothing needed to be said. Everything important was touched, smelled, tasted, or seen.

CHAPTER 12

With that kiss came an unspoken and natural development, not only with the relationship of David and Suzanne, but with the Bartlett and the Scaglione families, as well. Since the two lovers had become inseparable, the homes of their families always had an additional person. All through the school year, studying was usually done at the university or at the Bartlett home; eating, at either home or Aunt Maria's place; and necking, in the car, unless a stolen kiss was quickly and accurately placed while no one was looking. They both helped at the drugstore and the confectionery for holidays or when another clerk was sick, if and only if they were allowed to go together. Their love was seen by their looks to each other, the glow of their spirits, and the rapport of their conversation. Their happiness spilled over and left a trail for others to follow. Being in their presence made everyone want to smile. It was infectious. In fact, Claire caught it.

Through the fall, Claire enjoyed being with the two young people and found herself happier than she had allowed herself to be for years. Tony had died roughly six years earlier, and she had worn the black of a widow for years in her heart if not always on her back. Harry had died about fourteen years ago, and she finally no longer thought about that episode, nor carried the guilt that had haunted her when Tony lived. She felt good and found herself talking more and wanting to be with people.

"David, since you're having lunch with us tomorrow, why not have your father come down and eat, too? With your mother in the hospital, he may not be getting any good meals. I made a delicious stew. Tell him I'll put some biscuits in the oven if he comes. He must tire of eating sandwiches, or if what Suzanne says is true, he goes without a lunch many days," explained Claire. In this way, a new relationship began that had not existed. The glow of the young lovers naturally passed to the two older people. Claire's lunch on the weekends with David and Suzanne evolved into a lunch during the week as well, with

John and the young couple, and then it became a few lunches during the week, without the two young lovers.

The conversation during those lunches was often about Ellie, who had fallen ill with tuberculosis. "Ellie must be lonely. It doesn't seem right that the sanitarium only allows one visitor a week. That must be hard on her. Does she say anything about that?" Claire asked one Tuesday while they ate.

"Well, she's despondent about everything right now. The doctor says that it's normal at the beginning in tuberculosis cases. They have no energy and must remain completely at rest. It's difficult," John replied.

"How long does the doctor expect it to last, this depression?" Claire wanted to know.

"I don't know. I'm sure it depends completely on the individual. Let's see: she has been there over four months, and we know that it could go on for six months more or even a year."

"How are the children doing without their mother?" Claire asked.

"Well, there's an older woman, Mrs. Mueller, coming to the house at three to be there when school ends. She cleans the house, irons, and prepares the evening meal. Other than that, the children handle all other matters. Billy and Johnny are old enough, at 15 and 13, to do the laundry. There's a lot, but they do it on the weekends. Jimmy's only 10, but he's in charge of putting the dry clothes away and does a good enough job. Matching socks is his biggest problem. Each child must make his own bed and prepare a lunch for school with my supervision in the morning. Becky must set the table each day and do the dishes with one of the boys on the weekend when Mrs. Mueller doesn't come. It works out. They're on their own a lot, but the neighbors volunteered to help if the boys have an emergency. David is there most evenings."

"Yes, well, I guess I meant how they were doing emotionally with the absence of their mother. Probably it's hardest on Rebecca," Claire wondered.

"Actually, I think that the strong relationships of the brothers, together and with their sister, have made it work. They have a lot of hobbies and interests that they share. They're all too young to understand how sick their mother really is. She doesn't look sick, and I've answered their fears about her dying. She's going to get well since we found the TB early, but only with complete rest. The doctor prescribed this rest home. The kids know they'll need to continue to help around the house to keep her well when she can come home."

Claire was curious about the disease and continued to ask questions, "How did Ellie get TB? Can the children or you or me get it?"

With those questions John surmised that Claire had apprehensions that it was contagious. While he was aware that she needed to know more than his children were told, he didn't want to get too technical, thus he began a simplified explanation, "Most people don't realize that twenty-five percent of the population carry the infectious bacilli even though we don't get sick. When the body's resistance is down, the disease can become active. For example, if hunger or extreme stress weakens us, these bacilli could activate. That's why tuberculosis is more prevalent in impoverished places.

"Ellie had been feeling tired a lot, so she went in for a check-up, and since there had been a few cases here in St. Louis, the doctor checked her saliva. He found the tubercle bacilli present. It's transmitted to others by a sneeze or cough."

"Have you and the children been tested? Should I go get tested?" she asked with concern.

"The doctor and I aren't too worried, although he'll give them a test when he sees each one for annual shots. We're all healthy and strong. Ellie had been dieting for a long time and she wasn't taking her vitamins; I insist they all take one every day. She started smoking, and I must admit, the kids do create a lot of work and stress for her. Concerning you, if you're worried, get tested. If it'd give you peace of mind to know, do it. Thank heavens streptomycin was developed a few years ago. Before 1944, there were no drugs to treat tuberculosis effectively, so Ellie is fortunate, but she must rest to get strong."

To say the lunches began in all innocence would not be the truth. Nevertheless, one would have to say that John and Claire never planned to have an affair. It was a subconscious elation with the love she saw in David and Suzanne that infected Claire and created a happiness in her that allowed her to begin to think about John. He was an attractive man, and she remained the same energetic, good-looking woman as years ago. Claire could pass as Suzanne's older sister. Claire told herself that she was simply concerned with serving a good lunch to this man whose wife was in the rest home for who knows how long. And that was the truth, but she was also attracted to him. Not that she thought those thoughts. Heavens, no! She could not let anyone, much less herself, think that she was attracted to him. Claire would leave the confectionery open and jump up to wait on the customers during their lunches to prove to everyone (actually, to prove to herself) that nothing clandestine could be occurring during those lunches. Yet things were. A natural fervor was starting to cook between them. Place a mature man with no wife at home with a delectable woman who had been without a man for many years, sauté over a low heat, and appetites grow. In other words, it hadn't begun in total innocence. In fact, it may have begun with a hope and a hunger.

One day their knees touched beneath the table, and they moved quickly away. The next time it happened, after they each had thought about that accidental touch, they didn't move away. They didn't acknowledge the touch to one another nor the subsequent sensations either. They both daydreamed about each other after that. Claire found herself taking more time to dress and do her hair. John often took a small box of chocolates (wrapped in the drug-store's brown paper to hide the contents) to the lunch. He wouldn't give them directly to Claire as a gift. He called the candy "some dessert."

The knee incidents occurred over and over, and conversations changed to avoid discussion of Ellie. They talked about the weather, the kids, the stores, the neighborhood, or anything, avoiding talk about themselves or Ellie.

Then Claire thought of little situations for John to help her, situations that required closeness.

"Could you help me take these jars down to the cellar?" Claire held the door. "That box is a heavy one," she said as they brushed against each other going through the doorway.

"Would you mind getting down the mixer from that top shelf so I don't have to get the ladder?" And their hands would touch as John passed the mixer to her.

Simple incidents were suggested where they would have to squeeze around the other in a hallway, touch the other's arms, or brush against each other. All this "cat and mouse" seemed unreal, and yet one must remember that they were two people who never wanted to harm a loved one. They also wanted to do the right thing and to be good people. Yet, they were both lonely. They were people with grown children and could barely remember how it was to court or to be courted. Besides, they would never admit that there was any courting going on here. They were just friends, two lonely friends. In the culture of these times, emotions were not openly displayed between a husband and wife, so one wouldn't expect these two to openly display any of the feelings that were developing. They avoided the obvious thoughts. To themselves, they denied having any feelings, even as they were enjoying their time together.

Suzanne noticed. Though she did not know exactly what was going on, she could see the attraction between Mr. Bartlett and her mother. She saw changes in their mannerisms. Her mother seemed giddy at times. Mr. Bartlett couldn't seem to stop smiling and looking at her mother. David was oblivious to it all. Suzanne said nothing to David because she was a bit embarrassed over their actions.

As the middle of November approached, Claire realized that she couldn't offer to have only John and David to her home for the Thanksgiving meal, and knowing that her house would be too crowded with all the children, she decid-ed to offer to make the meal at their house.

"You know, John, I'd love to have you all for Thanksgiving, but I was think-ing it might be best if I cook and serve the meal at your house. That way the children would have all their things and could be occupied before and after the meal. If they were here, I don't know what they'd do with themselves. Besides,

I've never been to your home, and I'd love to see it. Would you like that? I know David and Suzanne would."

"That's a wonderful idea," John answered. "I was trying to decide what we could do. I could never cook a turkey for the occasion." Then, giving the offer some thought, he allowed his feelings to surface for the first time and suggested, "You know, maybe you should come to the house beforehand to see if we have all the dishes and things you'll need for the meal. It would be good for you to see where the pots and pans, you know, where all the things are. Why wait until Thanksgiving Day arrives? Although the children will help with anything you ask. We could drive over there next week during lunchtime when the house is empty and look at everything in the kitchen and dining room. If we went when the kids were there, it'd be distracting. You wouldn't be able to concentrate, I think. Well, it's up to you."

"I think it might be good to see the kitchen," she commented with some hesitancy, knowing and yet not really knowing that this might mean something else. "Suzanne says that you have an interesting study. I'd love to see that as well."

The scene was set—the opportunity for them to touch accidentally, at the right moment that would lead to a kiss. *Maybe under the stuffed elk head*, he fantasized. *One thing could lead to another. My bedroom's directly across from the study and...who knows?"*

In the days before Claire was to go for that kitchen inspection and tour of the study, he would walk into the study and kind of plan what he'd be saying and where they could be. Then his mind would go a bit further and he'd imagine undressing her and how her body would look. Needless to say, he was excited with merely the thought of that coming day. He placed a Trojan in his bathroom cabinet.

Claire fantasized, too. She'd lie in bed at night and do the same thing. She'd plan what would be said and how the conversation would progress. Then she would think of herself in his arms and they'd be kissing passionately like one sees in the movies.

When the day arrived and John went to pick her up, he parked around the corner, a couple of blocks away, and walked to her house. He had this elaborate plan and explained that he'd leave her house first. She was to walk to the car by heading in a different direction because, he said, "We don't want anyone to get the wrong impression."

Claire agreed.

When Claire got into the car she told him, "I packed a little lunch of ham sandwiches and potato salad that we can eat after I look over the kitchen and after we tour the study," continuing to pretend. They were nervous and silent on the short drive down Grand Avenue.

As John pulled into Hawthorne Drive, Claire had déjà vu. She instantly got a sick sensation in her stomach, exactly like she had gotten when Harry drove her down this street. The number of times she had traveled this route she didn't know, but she knew it by heart. Nothing looked changed. The trees were the same, overhanging into the street until the branches from one side brushed those from the other side, and the houses she knew well because she had memorized each one as she'd try to occupy her mind, riding with Harry. Suddenly, she realized that John and she were getting closer and closer to Harry's house. She hadn't seen it since the last time she went with Harry.

Her mind was panicking. Silently, she told herself, "I thought I was over this nightmare!" Then, John began to pull into the driveway.

Her mind screamed, *He lives in Harry's house!* Her body went rigid, and her vision pulsated white and then black. The bedroom of the house flashed into her mind. She saw the ceiling and the cornice at the top of the draperies where she used to focus to forget her body. Harry's smell was in her nostrils just as the taste of his mouth and the feel of his touch. It was smothering her.

"Stop," she cried and pulled on the door handle. She scrambled out and shut the door. Outside the car she calmed a bit and realized the confusion that she had created. She was standing there facing the car and breathing rapidly, before she finally saw that John had pulled into the driveway of the house next door to Harry's. Deep inside she made a little cryptic laugh at her mistake. Next door! John lives next door. Trying to gather her thoughts to explain why she acted that way, she smoothed her skirt, and took a deep breath. John pulled on the hand brake and stepped out of the car. He looked at her from over the car as she blurted, "I have to go. I forgot I have a doctor's appointment that I must keep." She turned, clutching her purse, and ran down the sidewalk.

"I'll drive you," he shouted after her.

"No, I'm fine, it's close, a short walk. You go have your lunch. I left it on the car seat," she called back to him after a slight stop. Quickly she pivoted on her tiny feet, causing her light coat to flip open and her silky pleated skirt to flair as she hastened away. He found the sight of her delightful as he watched with dismay and complete amazement.

What happened? he thought as he saw her reach the corner. She turned north and vanished from his sight. He replayed the minutes before she bolted from the car and could think of nothing to cause her reaction. He began to think that she didn't really want him. *She must have realized what I had been thinking. What have I done?* he thought as he returned to the driver's seat. Slowly he drove into the driveway and pulled behind the house. He sat in the car thinking. Squirrels played in the two pin oak trees above him, chattering and leaping from branch to branch. His expression jumped quickly from disappointed sadness to guilty shame.

The next time they met the atmosphere was different than it had been during the prior months of lunches. David and Suzanne were there, which helped ease the discomfort. After a few strained seconds, Claire found a moment to apologize and let him know that she was sure she could make Thanksgiving a successful and delicious holiday without a preliminary viewing of the house. Though she knew it would take an effort to travel that street again, she needed to do it. On Thanksgiving Day, she planned to go with David and Suzanne around to the back of the house to enter through the kitchen door, not the front where she could see Harry's house. If she could concentrate exclusively on their house, not looking at Harry's place, and if she thought about cooking and completing the meal, then she could overcome her sickening fears.

She worried she might be nervous, so she told John, "I'll prepare most things here in my kitchen and we'll simply need to warm them at your house. That way it'll be easier. David said he'd come over on Thanksgiving morning and help carry the turkey. I plan to get a twenty-five pound bird, and it'll be difficult to carry. Is about 11:30 okay?"

It worked. She closed her eyes on the drive down Hawthorne until the car was stopped and David opened her door. The whole meal was completely served and eaten before she had to venture out of the kitchen and dining room area where there might be windows to see Harry's. The passage of time through the meal and listening to the Bartlett children relaxed her.

"Later on, I want to show you my doll collection," Becky, the seven-year-old, mentioned. "I have three Madame Alexander dolls that are my favorites. My most favorite is a fairy princess."

"Dad told me that Mrs. Scaglione wants to see the study, not your doll collection. The study is more interesting to an adult," Johnny, the fourteen-year-old, said with the sincere belief that he was saving this pretty lady from a boring time in his little sister's room. "I'll show you around the study and explain everything."

This wasn't the usual behavior of his son to volunteer to be with an adult. John turned to look at Johnny and realized that his son probably saw in Claire, who looked like a young girl, exactly what he saw in Claire. Johnny was ready for a talk, the father concluded.

"May I see both the study and the doll collection? If I could, that'd be great," Claire had noticed Johnny's interest, too. She found it sweet.

"Sure," Johnny said.

It was a pleasure to be with these young people. The casual talk and laughter, the bickering and teasing, the noise and energy that occurred during the meal were entertaining and different from the quiet meals that she and Suzanne had together.

"If no one wants another helping of pumpkin pie, let's go for the tour. We can clean up the table afterwards." Claire found all of her clean-up crew in agreement to postpone the work.

The staircase was beautiful even with children's objects cluttering the steps. *If I never, ever look out the window in the direction of Harry's, I'll be fine,* she thought. The children had the habit of placing their books for school on different steps, along with clean clothes to go up to their rooms and other objects destined for the upstairs. Claire climbed the staircase to see the study with no problems. It was an enjoyable day for all.

John watched the group traipse up the staircase. *Claire's such a good friend…a platonic friend. How could I have allowed myself to imagine and fantasize things that would've affected the lives of all these people?* He was a bit ashamed that he had had adulterous thoughts. *Thank Heavens no one knew.*

A month later, the same dinner was organized again for Christmas, when Ellie was allowed to come home for two days for the holiday season. Ellie saw the changes in the relationship of her son and Suzanne. Nothing was apparent to her about Claire and her husband. However, she did notice one strange thing the first night as she was taking the toothpaste from the bathroom cabinet. She found a prophylactic! They never had used them.

"What's this?" Ellie asked John.

"Please, dear!" For an instant he felt guilty while thinking of a way out. "You know it's time for me to talk with Johnny about such things."

"Oh, I'm sorry, darling." Ellie was feeling foolish and turned red. Then she wondered what ideas her husband imparted to these innocent young boys. *What does John do with the prophylactic? Surely no demonstration. Would he give it to Johnny at his age? Well, I guess they must learn the ways of life,* she pondered to herself.

John watched his wife come from the bathroom. Though her gown was long and modest, her full breasts and well-rounded hips reminded him of his first attraction to her. Ellie was a woman who embodied everything a man wanted in a woman, he thought. How he loved her childbearing shape. Her soft flesh and ample endowments made him want to bury his head into all her warm, dark places. He pulled her into a bear hug and squeezed her tightly.

"John, do you think we should?" Ellie asked, "The doctor said I was to rest and take it easy on this first visit."

John took his face out of her bosom to say, "If your doctor didn't think it was all right, he wouldn't have let you stay the night." With a boyish grin he went on. "That makes sense, doesn't it?"

"Yes, I guess so," she giggled.

He sat up and pulled her legs toward him. Memories of mysterious and magical smells wafted into his mind, and he became that small boy who one day had opened the attic trunk that held so many secrets and surprises. He had looked into it and could hardly contain the pleasure that the memory of musty odors and newfound wonders gave him. His head went down into his treasure box while his arms explored for what exciting secrets could be discovered this time.

Suzanne and David were discovering the secret ways of men and women, too, during the two-week winter holiday from the university. Actually they were learning about the deprivation and longing associated with lack of sex. Suzanne refused to give in to her desires. After all those years of hearing how wrong it was, she knew she should not do it before marriage. She had been told how bad a person she'd be and she knew that David would lose respect for her. But she loved him and wanted him so much that her body often screamed to have him. More of a concern to her was the physical pain that David seemed to have because she said no.

She asked him one evening after they steamed the car, necking and tormenting each other until desire became unbearable, "Are you in pain? You know, physically, are you hurting?"

He looked at the steamed windows and saw all his condensed sweat starting to roll downward, drip, drip, dripping and disappearing onto the car floor. "I don't know. Listen! Must we talk about this, Suzanne? Yes, it hurts to think about it and talk about it. Can we change the subject?" he replied a bit irritated.

"Well, I've thought a lot about this and if you're really hurting, I guess we could do it. That could be our holiday present to each other," she murmured with her mouth one inch from his mouth. He was so happy. Her words, "I guess we could do it," were floating, just hanging, in the air in front of his nose. He smiled and—pop!—they were gone. They kissed and she continued, "On one condition: I will not do it in a car. You promised that everything would be all right if you used one of those rubber things. So, I guess, if we were in a real bed…" She stopped trying to find the words. "I want this to be a beautiful experience for both of us." She rambled on and on, nervously trying to find the right way to say what she wanted to say. She was still a bit unsure, and she was scared. "I've read that it can be very painful for a woman and I'll bleed. Did you know that?" she asked. There was no answer other than his embrace of her and another passionate kiss.

He was happy. She talked on while he was thinking, *Now how can I get a bed?*

That turned out to be easy. His mother was back at the rest home, his father worked late, especially on nights when there was restocking to do, his brothers and sister went to bed at 9:30, and they all slept far from his father's bedroom, which would be empty. There was the whole plan.

Suzanne had to decide what she would wear. She worried for a day or two before getting an idea. *A silky slip! I can wear my full-length slip with lace at the top.* Pajamas were the only kind of bed attire that she had, and her pj's would never work. First of all, she wanted to look pretty, and she didn't want to buy some luxurious nightgown because then she'd have to pack the gown into a bag. Besides, someone at the Bartlett house might wonder why she had a bag to come to study. *It has to be something I can wear that would sufficiently cover my body*, she thought since she knew she could not be undressed in front of David. *I can't be naked! Never! A slip would be perfect.*

On the chosen night after they arrived at his house, David called the drugstore a few minutes before it was to close at ten. He wanted to confirm that his father would be restocking that night. The conversation went like this.

"Oh, hi, Dad. I wanted to ask you to bring some toothpaste home."

"I brought three boxes home on Sunday, David. Are you sure that we need it?" his father questioned.

"Oh, I guess I didn't notice that we had some. Sorry. Listen, are you going to restock tonight?" David continued nervously.

"Yes, I always restock on Tuesday. Why?" his father asked.

"Oh, I was just wondering. I guess that's all, Dad. See you when you get here, or maybe I'll be driving Suzanne home about the time you come."

"That's good. You can pick me up and save me taking the streetcar. They don't run too frequent that late. Great! See you at eleven tonight," his dad said and hung up.

David was disappointed. "That only leaves forty-five minutes to do it, and the trouble is, I don't know how long it will take," David worried.

Suzanne was up washing and undressing while he was on the phone. She had removed everything but her slip when she got into the bed.

David arrived in his parent's room thinking, *No reason to tell Suzanne that we must leave by 10:45; that'd make her more nervous.* He went to the bathroom and realized that he hadn't shaved. He didn't want to scratch her. Her face always got all red when they were necking when he hadn't shaved. *She'd be embarrassed having a rash so I better shave quickly*, he mumbled to himself. Of course he cut himself more than he thought possible because of the situation.

With little pieces of toilet paper on various cuts and while wearing his underwear, he went toward the bed.

"What's wrong with your face?" she asked.

"I'm okay, I just cut myself—a little."

"Did you put on the rubber thing?" she inquired.

"I can't do that now! I have to be hard," he complained with exasperation caused from his frustrations.

"Oh," was all she could think to reply as he was getting under the covers.

He touched the silky slip with his hands, felt the firm, bare body beneath, and was ready for the Trojan, but he had already forgotten about that detail. As the passion levels rose, nature took its course, and he found himself within her. Sweat, heat, heaving breath—the boulder began to roll slowly while gaining speed. It reached the precipice and then with an exploding force bounded over the edge and fell crashing into exhaustion.

To her it happened a bit differently. He slid toward her, and as his hands touched her slip, she sensed a love that was all encompassing. Her mouth could not kiss him enough or open enough. His hands brushed her breasts and she experienced a flash of heat as her legs surrounded him. She pulled him as close as possible with her arms around his shoulders and legs around his hips. Her head kept thinking how much she loved him, that she wanted his baby, and that she loved him more than life itself. She could hardly breathe, and low guttural sounds came from her throat. Feelings that she had never thought possible came from within her body, and her head told her that this was why one lives. Then a rush of intense warmth passed over her feet, legs, and arms, swirling everywhere within her body.

As soon as she got her breath, she proclaimed, "They lied to us. They lied!"

He found that he didn't have the energy to talk, but managed a brief and puzzled, "Who lied about what?"

"They said it was wrong and bad. Anything this wonderful *is right*! They lied to us! This is how we should be." And she snuggled into his chest and hugged him. "This was the most marvelous experience I've ever had. I love you, David."

"Me, too," he responded.

"Do you think it's like this with everyone? Am I being naive?" She worried that her inexperience in sexual matters might be giving her false feelings. "I love you so much, David. You know how we often feel what the other feels, without telling? It's like hearing your thoughts. I do feel we are one. Am I being silly?

He shushed her and pulled her closer into the hollow of his shoulder, placing his cheek on her hair. "No, you're not being silly." With this experience of lovemaking, coupled with the love he felt for Suzanne, he knew they were having sensations that were more marvelous than most have had. He just didn't know how to say all that to her. How many people could really claim to have a totally true love like they had? He felt that they loved with their minds, their souls, and now their bodies. "What you're saying isn't silly, it's profound," he told her.

In her heart she knew she had found that one special person who is her other half. Rising on her elbow, she smiled and kissed him.

Suddenly he jumped up. "Where's my watch? Oh, yeah, it's in the bathroom." He went and saw that they had plenty of time, but suddenly realized that he forgot to use the Trojan. "Oh, no!" He said quietly and sat on the toilet seat to lament. Finally he took a deep breath, walked back to the bedside, and told Suzanne.

"Doesn't that mean that I'm pregnant?" she said with wide eyes.

David feigned a laugh. "No, it's not likely the first time. Don't worry; I'm sure you're not." Then, changing the subject, he explained to Suzanne about the phone conversation with his father. "It might be best that we get up and straighten things before we go."

She rose and saw that she had bloodied Mr. Bartlett's sheets. "What'll we do? Oh, if I wash it out, it'll be wet when he gets into bed. David, what are we going to do?" she worried.

"We'll change them to some clean ones. Just rinse the stain out as much as you can, and I'll put them downstairs with the laundry. My Dad won't notice."

He did notice. When John was in his pajamas, he stopped, looked with a puzzled expression at the sheets, and said out loud, though quietly, to himself, "Those are different sheets than last night." He climbed into bed and couldn't sleep. "Who could have changed the sheets? The kids change the beds on Saturday before they do the washing." Then, after lying there for several minutes, he remembered the phone call and realized what had taken place in his bed. He also knew why the sheets had to be changed, and he didn't know what he should do.

He did nothing. Nothing! What could he do, he thought? He wouldn't know how to begin to handle this topic. He believed the personal, sexual relationships between people were private. It was something never to be discussed with someone else. He hoped that David had used a prophylactic.

Sleep didn't come quickly for he thought about his first time and about Ellie. He missed her. He loved her. He prayed that she'd get well soon.

Now that the lovemaking had begun, it was an addiction. They couldn't love each other enough. Life was giving them more than they ever thought possible. They sat and talked for hours about nothing and came to enjoy the simplest event, for example, looking closely at eyelashes or freckles. Then poems flowed from Suzanne to David.

My Favorite Freckle
Just a dot—
A little spot—
But, where and whose is what
Makes that brownish fleck upon your eye
A mark upon my heart.

They talked about their lives together and laughed a lot. Their studies came easier because there was no tension in their relationship. In the coming months, Suzanne thought they were one, a force in the same direction. They wanted to learn about the other and to spend time telling of their pasts, exploring every inch of their bodies, and talking about any thought that came to mind.

After seeing a movie one day, as they walked to the car, David mentioned, "Boy, your dad really looked like Gene Kelly."

"No he didn't!"

They argued back and forth a while.

David finally said, "Why are you so adamant about a simple comment?"

Suzanne explained, "I know what you think. They have the same body build and dark wavy hair, and they both seemed to be really happy people, but I don't think of my dad when I see Gene Kelly."

"Well, I do," answered David. "Golly, it was just a comment."

They reached the car and got in. Suzanne snuggled against him, "David, I'm teasing you. We had never argued, and I decided that I'd disagree with you for once and see how it went. You aren't mad are you? Wasn't it fun to kind of have our first argument?

"Suzanne, you are crazy!"

"No, I'm not! I don't care if we laugh or argue. Nothing is important except being with you. You know what I'm trying to say?"

"Yes, I do, but don't do that again." They kissed and drove away to David's house to make love.

Suzanne gave him a little poem to apologize the next time she was with David.

To share
A pair
Where?
Don't care!
Just…Together
Two share.

The funeral of Aunt Maria came during this time in their love. One cold February night, she died in her sleep with no ailment or reason other than old age. At 75 years, Aunt Maria had lived eleven years longer than the average woman. Suzanne was thankful that David had known Aunt Maria so well. Suzanne wanted David to know everything.

"Oh, David, I just remembered someone who's been very, very dear to me that you have not met!" she exclaimed one spring day. "Come, let's go to my house and you can meet him. He was the love of my life before you. He's sweet. You better love him, too." Suzanne continued her prattle on the drive to Park Avenue to meet Bobo. "If you want to know everything about me, if we are committed to love forever and ever, you must know about Bobo." On the drive she talked about her ball and how she used to play with him. How she had to hide him from her mother although she never understood why.

"Did you ever ask her?" he questioned. "Maybe she'd tell you now that you're grown."

"I haven't thought about that puzzle for years. I can't remember the last time I got him out of his hiding place. He better be there."

He was.

As Suzanne pushed aside her bed and lifted the loose board, there was the little hatbox. David reached down, took it from between the floorboards and placed it on her bed. She picked it up, "Needs some cleaning, I think." After she wiped it with the edge of her skirt, she hesitated briefly and smiled before she raised the lid to reveal her precious past. First the ball, and then the nightgown was shown to David. She laughed and talked about Bobo, explaining how much he had meant to her when she was little and showing him how to hold the gown with the ball at the neckline for a head. "Isn't his face sweet. See how his eyes, nose, and name on the cap are raised and make little bumps? I always was comforted feeling the texture of the ball." She began describing the different hiding places in the old house when David picked up the hatbox and grinned. He saw those three arrowheads he had given her years ago. But then he removed the newspaper that had always been at the bottom.

"What's this?" he asked.

"Just some paper at the bottom." Suzanne had noticed the newspaper wedged at the bottom of the hatbox and hadn't thought it to be anything except a liner on the bottom, nothing more.

"Hey, look," he said as he unfolded it. "It's from 1932. Wow, it's old!" They spread it open on the bed and began to read the news from November of 1932. David commented on an article about Al Capone. There was some information about the election counts for Hoover and FDR that they found interesting. "This is when prohibition was ending and the states were voting if they wanted to legalize liquor. How interesting," David said.

"Oh no, David, read this!" Suzanne pointed to a small article at the bottom of the front page, *No Clews in Disappearance of 16-Month-old Child.*

"Oh, "clews" is just how they used to spell "clues," years ago."

A little irritated, "No, I'm talking about the article. Read it!" There was a description of a blonde haired, blue-eyed little girl who had a toy ball with the name of Bobo on its red cap. It went on to say that the she was in yellow night-clothes. "What is this, David?" she gasped with panic in her eyes.

He saw that she was breathing heavily. "Let's not get excited," he demanded with his hands on her arms. "Let's think through what we're seeing here."

"David, I've been telling you for the last hour that I've had this ball always. I remember Bobo with me in my first memories. You know I'm a blonde, blue-eyed girl. There could be more than one of these balls in the world, but not with a yellow nightgown," she blurted while her distorted face was inches from his. "I am this child that disappeared. What else could it mean?"

"Look, Suzanne, you may be right, but don't jump to any conclusions. I'm simply saying that we need to calm ourselves and try to think what this means."

"The thing that doesn't make any sense is that I wasn't born yet in November 1932," Suzanne pondered.

"Hey, have you lied to me about your age? Are you an older woman and didn't want to tell me?" He was grinning and trying to brighten the situation.

"Be serious, David! I'm upset! Do you know what that means?" Suzanne's mind was grasping more possibilities with each second. "Oh, my God!"

"Suzanne, please calm down," David implored as he took her shoulders with both his hands. The look on her face was frightening, and he was beginning to sense the fear that she was exuding.

She pulled from his grasp with a look of disdain toward him. "Don't you see how serious this is? How can you be telling me to be calm? Mom never mentioned that I disappeared when I was sixteen months old. Dad would've loved to tell me a story of how I wandered away and how they found me. It wasn't me that disappeared. David, it wasn't me! Me, Suzanne! It was some other little girl. Do you see?" Tears started to fill her eyes.

"Suzanne, come on. Sit here by me and we can talk," he coaxed as he began to try and cuddle her.

"That's it! Everything makes sense. I never felt my age, the age my parents told me. You know, I could read when I was three or something, so they told me. Then, when I went to school, I skipped grades because I was advanced in reading and math. They always had me take exams during the year with the kids in the next grade up to prove I could do the work, and then I'd skip that grade. I was always with older kids and I adjusted to them. Always! So, think! If my Mom and Dad lied to me about how old I was, why would they do that?"

David didn't respond immediately, hence she repeated, "Tell me why would they never tell me the story of my disappearance? It was in the newspaper! What an interesting story it would've been to tell me. Why would they try to hide my age? Why, David? And why did my mother always try to hide Bobo and this hatbox from me?"

"Suzanne, please," he pleaded in desperation while turning toward her and taking her head in both his hands. He put their foreheads together and began to whisper although she could see that he was upset, too. "There's probably some simple…" Suzanne gave him a look that told him not to condescend to her, so he changed course, "or complicated answer to all this. You're making me upset and I want to stay calm and try to understand what we're seeing. Suzanne, can you please calm yourself, and we can look at this logically? Please," he was whispering. He stopped and they didn't move. Then he tenderly kissed her. They hugged.

"Oh, David, I'm scared. Thanks for being here, but help me. Please help me."

"Suzanne, whatever this all means, it's from the past, and it'll not change who you are now. You're all that's important to me. This, whatever it is, will not change us. Please try to relax," he pleaded.

She kissed him and opened a drawer for a handkerchief to blow her nose before they said anything more.

"Let's handle this as a great mystery and we're the detectives," he cajoled while trying to lighten the air. "First tell me what you've already assumed." He grinned because they both had had enough lessons from his Dad on "never assuming before you have all the facts." She knew what he was saying and gave him a little punch.

"Okay, young Mr. Bartlett. You're right, I've assumed that my parents kidnapped me and made me their little girl, whom they called 'Suzanne.'"

"Do you hear how ridiculous that sounds when said that precisely?" he asked as he smoothed her hair and hugged her again.

"Yes, it sounds ridiculous to say, but I keep thinking of things that make it seem true. It'd make sense why Mom never had any more children if she never could have any to begin with and that would be the reason why they took a child."

"Please, talk quietly. Don't start getting excited again. Just say all you want to say. In fact, we should make this a real investigative project and begin to write all these facts. More importantly, we need to list what other facts are missing that we need to answer. Do you agree?" he questioned.

Suzanne didn't seem to hear. Her mind seemed to be elsewhere, and she started talking about the memory of her best-outing-ever with her father.

"Because I would've liked to have a brother or sister, I asked my Dad once why they never had any more kids. You know what he said?"

"Tell me," he stated patiently, though he was a little exasperated because she wasn't trying to handle all this in a logical manner.

"Well, my Dad's head went down. It hung there and he looked real sad. Then, he sighed, 'I don't know' and repeated it again 'I don't know.'"

"So, Suzanne, what does that prove?" David entreated.

She looked at him out of the corner of her eyes, threw back her head, and sighed, "Nothing, I guess." She gave him another little punch in the ribs. "You're right, I need to calm down," she resolved and finally smiled.

David made Suzanne promise not to say anything to her mother. If it were true that she was kidnapped, they couldn't simply walk up and ask that. He explained, "You don't want to corner someone and let a lie be told. They may have planned a pat answer. You know, years ago they may have decided what to say and your mother may be ready with an explanation. Don't forget we must remember that the two men, Uncle Vinny and your Dad, are dead, and it was probably one of them that really did the kidnapping. We don't want to start some problems before we have more information."

Suzanne wondered whether Aunt Maria had known about all this. The women, Aunt Maria and her mother, may not have known all the facts, she thought.

"If I wasn't this kidnapped child and I started asking questions, I'd look pretty foolish. More importantly, all this would really upset my mother," she worried aloud as if talking to herself. She agreed that they needed more facts before asking questions directly.

Then they did what David had suggested and began a plan for investigating. It became a master list of things to investigate. As David wrote the first item, Suzanne gasped. On the paper he had written:

<u>**Things to Investigate**</u>

Find Her Birth Certificate or go to the Bureau of Vital Records.

"David, I have seen my birth certificate. When I went to get my driver's license I needed to have it to prove that I was sixteen. Mom said that it was different than a normal certificate because I was born at home and not in the presence of a doctor. She said that she applied for a certificate when I was older. I don't know how old," Suzanne explained as they both fixed their gaze into the other's eyes and didn't move. "I remember that Aunt Maria had signed the back, but I don't know why she did that. I didn't ask Mom any questions about it."

Slowly David turned toward the paper, "Well, I'll rephrase that item because we need to know more about your type of birth certificate. I'll scratch the *or* and put *and*. Don't try to figure this out until we have time to learn more.

Okay?" he insisted as he pulled her close and put his face into her hair. Oh, how he loved her smell.

When they finished the following were listed:

Things to Investigate
Find Her Birth Certificate and go to the Bureau of Vital Records
Look for photos of her as a baby, before 16 months old
Baptism Records, if any?
Did she have a doctor as a baby? If yes, go see records
Go to Grade School for First Records
Talk with Dad's cousins (Aunt Maria's boys)
Question Newspaper people about this Article
Ask Police about the Disappearance of this 16-Month-Old Girl

That night in bed, she started thinking about her past and worrying about how to learn the truth. She knew that she'd worry every night until they started to resolve this. She knew that she needed to do things in a logical manner, but she kept thinking about the kinds of evidence that were purely emotional. She was remembering how sometimes she felt that her mother didn't love her. Suzanne didn't have any concrete examples because it was just a feeling she had had. Maybe her father had taken that little girl because he wanted a child and her mother had never wanted one. On the other hand, maybe her mother had wanted a child, too. Suzanne whispered to herself, "but never realized that I could have such a different personality. That could be why we don't feel real close. When you have your own child, it must come naturally."

She remembered the anger her mother had shown when she had tried to play with Bobo. It made sense that she got angry if these articles were evidence of the kidnapping that they wanted to hide. "Why didn't they just throw them away?"

From now on, her nights were filled with searching thoughts. In bed each night she journeyed back and relived incidents from long ago while pursuing any memory that might give her a hint how to solve this.

One night, as she tried and tried to remember something new, she remembered being left with Mrs. Stein a lot. She remembered her mother crying a lot. She remembered the anger her mother had displayed before her dad took her on that best-outing-ever to the train station and Forest Park. She drew no conclusions from those memories, but instead found herself remembering the whole day of that outing. She loved her father so. She still missed him. Tears came as she remembered his tale of meeting her mother.

Another time she had thoughts that her parents must have told her half-truths or lied by omission. This made her angry to think that she had grown up with this type of deception. *But how can I be angry when I don't even know if they really deceived me?* She couldn't remember them talking about her birth or when she first walked. She realized that she was making herself upset thinking about what they did or didn't tell her. Her mind wouldn't stop searching her memories for clues.

Sleep came slowly every night. It was hard to resolve many things on that list, and she found herself frustrated at how long it took to answer one item. Nothing was easy. Finally she found a way to help the sleep to come. As she became drowsy she tried concentrating on thoughts of David. *At least I have David to be with me through all this. I love him so. He's wonderful.* Then, just before sleep came, she'd smiled, remembering when David had talked of their marriage.

CHAPTER 13

On Sundays and Thursday evenings, Suzanne had offered to help Jimmy with his math since he was failing and there was still time before the school year ended to help him. Normally she enjoyed going to the Bartlett house whatever the reason, and, since mathematics was a part of her, she usually loved talking about it with anyone. She was changing. Her every moment, day or night, was consumed with the mystery of the kidnapping. The more she and David talked, the more they agreed that they must learn the truth on their own. Asking Claire a direct question might open the opportunity for a deception and that was to be avoided. They knew they needed some facts before questions were asked. David and Suzanne knew that if her parents had been willing to talk about the kidnapping, they would've done it years ago. With these thoughts replaying over and over in her mind, she arrived at the Bartlett home and went around to the backdoor.

"Mrs. Bartlett!" Suzanne exclaimed, coming into the kitchen. "It's good to see you home. Everybody missed you so much. How are you feeling?"

"Oh, Suzanne, good to see you, too. I'm fine. I think that I could have come home a month earlier. It's good to do the things I used to complain about. We never appreciate what we have until it is gone. Right?" Ellie talked while stirring something in a large bowl that rested upon her left hip with her arm encircling it. Before Suzanne could reply, Ellie commented, "Since David isn't home yet it means that you're here to give some lessons to James. Right?"

"That's right," Suzanne answered with less than her usual perky voice. "Is he upstairs? I hear the piano in the living room, and I can tell that it's Becky playing. None of the boys have mastered a touch like she has."

"Yes, I think he's up there somewhere. Someone else is upstairs practicing on the other piano. You'll hear when you get halfway up the stairs."

"I'll go and find him," Suzanne stated as she left through the swinging door between the kitchen and dining room. It swooshed as she passed through. The piano music became clearer, and Suzanne recognized Beethoven's *Fur Elise*. She quietly passed and started up the staircase while noticing that Mrs. Bartlett was correct that the delicate sounds of Beethoven began to fade in the middle of her ascent and another piano with the sound of scales came to her ears. It was a monotonous and brash sound that made her nervous. Not only the piano, but also the radio was on somewhere in the house. So much noise! She wondered how Ellie could tolerate all of it.

She stopped and stepped down so she could hear the upstairs and down-stairs pianos as well as the radio. *What a mess! This sounds like my life.* "Sounds *of Suzanne's Concerto-Confusions of her Life in B Flat,*" she thought, *I was so happy. David and I were so happy! Now with the discovery of that kidnapping…I'm a nervous wreck.*

Earlier, she had taken a moment to write some of her impressions on paper in the form of a poem.

There, there,
I say
It will work out
Though pouring from this pen's fine tip
Is all the pain I feel,
Flowing on this page
A past, that cannot heal.
Don't think things
That only hurt!
Can't stop!
They're there.

She wasn't sure she believed her own words. All day long she vacillated between negative thoughts about her past to optimistic sentiments about her future with David. Of course their parents hadn't been told about their talk of marriage. It was too soon, and the problem of the kidnapping dominated his and her thoughts anyway. First, she had to resolve this problem.

As she reached the top of the stairs, she found James on the floor in front of the radio. The landing at the top of the staircase was spacious, with the radio, a table, and chairs, as well as a small sofa. With this many children, the Bartletts needed a lot of work areas for homework and other projects. Two pianos were needed to have sufficient practice time for the four who took lessons. They had three radios—one large model in the living room that stood four feet high, this one at the top of the stairs, and a small one in the kitchen for Ellie. Yet three radios were not enough to prevent arguments when a fourth or fifth person wanted to listen to something else. Mr. Bartlett used this problem as a reason not to buy a television, and he wasn't going to buy more than one at the price of that "contraption." He decided that they wasted too much time listening to the radio as it was.

James was listening to the *Red Skelton Show*, and "Freddie the Freeloader" was up to his usual antics. James was laughing out loud and doubled over. Suzanne found herself laughing with James. It was contagious watching the children laugh.

"Hi, Suzanne," he said.

Looking at her watch as she slipped off her navy blue blazer, she answered, "Hi, Jimmy." She saw that it was a few minutes until nine when the program ended. They had thirty minutes before he had to get ready for bed. It'd work out just right. He had a short attention span for numbers, and she knew better than try to make this eleven-year-old work too long. He'd hate the subject more.

She loved all of the Bartlett boys and had a good time whenever she came. As she put her worksheets out on the small table, the jingle for Tide Detergent came on the air. "*Tide's in, Dirt's out!*" they sang. Jimmy turned the large button, and the noise of the radio stopped, leaving only the piano scales. Before getting up from the floor, he refolded the left cuff of his blue jeans. He wore the typical white dress shirt—two sizes too big, unbuttoned except for the bottom two, and tucked into his blue jeans so that it was smooth around his waist in the front and flared with pleats in back. He had no belt on his blue jeans that slipped low down his hips and were pressed with a sharp crease. He did the ironing job himself to make that crease just as he wanted. He was cool.

The piano scales stopped and Suzanne relaxed. She sat down and started putting some worksheets in order, using her toes to slip off her shoes. Suddenly, she noticed the delicious smells of snickerdoodle cookies drifting up the stairs. "Hey, it smells like you'll get cookies and milk before bed tonight," she said to Jimmy.

"Yeah," he grinned.

Suzanne thought, *How these kids must love having their mother back home.* She was right.

As Jimmy started to sit down, "Gee-man-etley! Suzanne, you have new shoes. Penny loafers! They're cool! Dad won't let me wear them. Hey, let me get a couple of pennies to put into the slots for you." With that comment he ran to his bedroom and returned with two pennies. He sunk to the rug with his legs Indian style and inserted a penny into the space at the top of the left shoe then the right shoe.

"Thanks, Jimmy. Yeah, I love my penny loafers. These are my first ones. When I was your age, my mom wouldn't let me wear them either. She would say, 'They don't support a growing foot.' Know what I mean?"

"Yeah, Dad says those exact words whenever I ask for them. I'd really like to have some."

"I used that x-ray machine that the shoe stores have to see if the shoes fit right. Have you seen those machines? They look the same as a drugstore scale. You step up like you're going to weigh yourself except there are two slots to stick your feet into and a screen to see the bones and an outline of your foot in the shoe. It's so cool!" Suzanne tried to talk his language to make him think she wasn't too much of an adult. It made math lessons easier. She was glad he started talking about her shoes. She knew it was important to build a rapport using topics he liked before starting the math.

He shook his head in the affirmative. "Yeah, I know. My shoe store has one, too."

"Okay, let's get to the books," Suzanne told Jimmy.

David arrived a couple of minutes before the thirty-minute session was complete. Suzanne slipped back on her penny loafers and started gathering the papers they had created. "Well, that's enough for tonight, Jimmy. I'm going to let you go a little early since you worked hard." As she followed David into the study, she realized how anxious she was to hear what David had learned from his visit to the Bureau of Vital Records, where he had gone to ask about the birth certificate for home births. They had decided to pick separate items from their list. Suzanne had worked on trying to find old photographs of herself as a baby.

"How'd it go? Did you learn anything about the birth certificate?" she asked.

"Very informative, but not too helpful for validating your birth. It was and still is pretty easy to claim you had a baby at home without a doctor. You need to write to the Department of Vital Statistics, Health Service Division in Jefferson City. Get this! They mail the papers to be filled out. In the mail! The form asks for the name of the mother and father as well as the child's name and birth date. Home births won't have a footprint or a weight on them like the hospital birth certificate does. If we knew the kidnapped kid's name, and if that kid had a certificate made in the hospital with a footprint on it, then we could try to see if your foot matches. I don't really know if it's like fingerprint identification or not. But, if it worked the same, that'd be proof that you're the kidnapped kid."

David stopped and took a breath before continuing about his day. "I was surprised at what I learned. The authorities never have to see the baby. Someone can get a birth certificate easily. Rule one: It must be done before the child is twelve years old. Twelve! You were right that you could be older than your birth certificate says. Let's suppose that your mom or dad kidnapped you; then, when you were really a six-year old, they went to register your birth and said that you were four. Rule two: A parent or some other person can fill out the forms and then a witness must make a sworn affidavit that the facts are true. You know what I mean? The witness puts their signature on the back, and by signing the certificate, swears that the facts that a baby girl was born on this date are true. Your Aunt Maria was chosen by your parents to be the witness to sign the back of your certificate. That's all there is to it! No other rules, just a step one and two and you can get a birth certificate." David was shaking his head and showed that he was surprised that the system of birth certificates really does not verify a birth. "Do you think Aunt Maria would swear on an affidavit even if she didn't see you born? No, that's right, she didn't need to see the birth. I think I understood correctly that her sworn statement means that she only claims the facts to be true. Would she swear the facts to be true even if she really didn't know they were?"

"Sure! She would've believed anything my father said," Suzanne blurted. She stopped speaking to think and reflected, "It's possible that she didn't read the details on the Birth Certificate before she signed it." David looked at her and frowned. "Okay! Maybe they lied to her about when and where I was born. Yes, that's it! This was when they were moving from California. That'd be why she never saw me as a baby and could accept whatever age they told her. Obviously, it was years after I was born that they registered my birth. Of course, the day we went to get my driver's license, I never looked to see when the birth certificate was issued. I'll find it and see what the date of issue was. Aunt Maria and everyone accepted that I learned to do things early because they didn't know I was really an older child. If my parents claimed I was eight, but I was really ten, I don't think that my Aunt Maria would've noticed. Yeah, she would've signed it."

They both sat silently in the study for several minutes. Each was lost in thoughts. All these facts didn't prove that she was the kidnapped child, nor did they prove that she was not. David realized that this information could be depressing to Suzanne and he asked, "How did you do? Did you go through the photographs that you found at Aunt Maria's when she died?"

"Yes, and that was a waste of time. There were none of a towheaded child, only kids with dark eyes and dark hair." She shook her head and continued, "The photographs I found at my house don't have any dates on the back. I can't tell how old I was by looking at them. There were some with me walking or at least standing. Actually, it looked like I could walk. There were no photographs of a baby in my Mother's arms, and I know that doesn't prove that I did or didn't exist because I couldn't find many of my parents either." She sighed and explained the reason for this. "Since times were hard back then, I imagine that they didn't spend their money on photographs. They didn't seem to have a camera until I was older. Also, the photographs are so tiny that I can't be sure I'm the baby or not. I've never seen any professional one except of my parents. Here it is, and it's the only one I found. I think it's a photograph when they got married because she has some flowers in her hands." Suzanne sighed and pulled the photo of the wedding out from one of her books. "Do you want to see? Here are five other photographs with a little girl that looks like it could be me. I don't know. I guess they never showed me photos because there were not many to show. Then again, it seems that Dad would've shown me the ones that they had of me. If I think about it, it would be just like my Dad not to know where they kept the photographs. I had never seen this professional one, either. I've concluded that they just never took the time to show any photographs. I can't remember if I ever asked to see any, either.

"Oh, there was one interesting item. I found Aunt Maria's Bible among the things we took when she died. Inside there are dates of births and deaths. No, don't get excited, my birth isn't there. Let's look at it when you're at my house. Actually, I think it was her parent's Bible because it goes back before the 1880s. There are people I don't know. Anyway, what is interesting is my Dad's birth. It has his mother as 'Isabela' and where the name of the father should be, it says, 'Unknown.' I guess that they really didn't know his name.

"The other day I was thinking that Aunt Maria and Dad made up the story that I had a German grandfather. You know that is the only thing that explains why I have blonde hair and blue eyes. We still don't know if it's true, but this Bible is old, and it seems that they really didn't know the name of my Dad's dad. After finding this Bible, I looked around to try and find my Dad's birth certificate. I didn't find it. I was hoping that Isabela had put the father's name on it. I figured that she might've written the name on the official birth certificate even if her parents didn't want to recognize him. Do you think we should investigate that?"

David pulled the list out. "I don't know. It wouldn't give us any real proof of anything unless we could find out about his family. The Bible clarifies the stories that you have heard about your unknown grandfather. It seems that no one was telling a lie. That is good to know. If we find out that he's really from Europe," David shrugged his shoulders and shook his head, "we'd need to go there. We're not going to do that! If you think about it, there's nothing we'd learn that would help." He jotted a note on the list and began to scrutinize the next topic they needed to investigate.

"Oh, another thing," Suzanne stated with a hesitancy that showed she was about to explain something that David might dislike hearing. "I asked my Mother a couple of questions and…" She stopped talking when she saw David was beginning to disapprove. "Now wait until you hear what I have to say."

"Okay, okay."

"I didn't know if I knew where all photos might be, and then there was this thing on the list about baptism. I told Mom that I was looking into joining a sorority at the University and they wanted a photo of me when I was a baby. I said that they wanted it for a game to guess which baby is which grown girl. I know, I know! It was a pretty lame idea. Don't worry! I don't think she suspected anything. She just answered that she didn't have any. I ask her if I was ever baptized in case there were photos of that event. We never went to church, and it had never came up before. I know she didn't think that it was a strange question." Suzanne stopped a minute in her explanation and got a faraway look in her eyes.

"What? What happened?" David could see something had occurred.

"Oh, Mom was upset about my not being baptized. She started all this explanation about how she had wanted to get me baptized. She explained that it wasn't important to Dad. She started to explain to me that she used to be religious. Then she stopped. She seemed to become sad and didn't want to talk anymore. I guess she was thinking about Dad. I felt badly about bringing all that out to worry her."

David decided to proceed and not let their hopes be dashed with no results. "Okay, let's not dwell on any of this. We have completed the first three items and haven't learned much of anything. We researched everything we could. If you stop to analyze what that means, we must conclude that there's nothing more to learn. Don't you agree?"

"Yes," she giggled. "Wow, that comment showed that you'll make a great doctor. The patient feels sick, but you can't find anything wrong, so we must conclude that there's nothing more to learn. Thank you, Dr. Bartlett! It was a bit confusing, and I don't know exactly what you tried to say, but I think I agree."

David laughed, too. He felt good seeing Suzanne laugh.

"Dr. Bartlett, what's next?" Suzanne asked.

"Listen, I've a lot of studying to do. I don't think I can spare anymore time this week. Could you work on the records from your kindergarten or the doctor when you were a baby?"

Suzanne got a frown on her face and commented, "What are the grade school records going to prove? I can't see that there is any reason for seeing them. I was five years old when I started kindergarten. That is a long time after the kidnapping. My Mother would've shown the school the same birth certificate that we used for my driving test if she had to show one. They may not have wanted to see one. Let me see when it was issued first. If it was issued before I was five, then we don't need to go there. Right?"

"You're right," David said. "I jotted that list in a hurry, trying to think of what to research. The doctor may have some value if he saw you at an early age. He might know something. I'll think more about the school records, but don't do anything with the school. I think you're correct. I was trying to think of any possibilities on that night I wrote this list."

"Good! I had an idea about how to find out about the doctor. I know where we lived before we moved to Park Avenue. There is this older lady…yeah, you met her. Do you remember Mrs. Stein from my graduation party? She lives in the same place where I used to live. She used to watch me and was a friend to my Mother. I could go visit her and ask about the doctor. What do you think?"

David liked the idea. "Then, this weekend we'll go to the newspaper office together. The newspaper and the police are the places where we are going to learn the most. I hope. At least they should have the name of the parents of this little girl who was kidnapped. Then we could talk to them."

Suzanne had an apprehension. "David, you're talking about meeting my real parents…" She added the words, "if I'm the kidnapped child. No! I am! What other explanation could there be?"

"Suzanne, don't do this."

"Don't do what. I can't stop thinking about this. I think about this situation every moment. The more I think, the more evident it is that I am that little girl. You're the one who seems to be upset. I know what you're thinking, that it doesn't matter because I'll always be this person that I am. Yesterday can't be changed."

"No, Suzanne, the point is deeper than that. I mean that you can't casually be saying that you're that little girl. We are going to be exposing information about a kidnapping that could cause problems for many people other than you."

"Oh, you're right." She stopped and thought about that idea. "If my Mother did have something to do with this, then I guess she could go to jail if it were known."

David continued, "If we do discover who the child's parents are then we must proceed carefully. We could cause them much pain, too. This could change the lives of many people, and not necessarily for the better. We've got to plan before we go to the newspaper office. We mustn't let them know what we suspect. Think how they'd love to have such a story. There'd be no quieting the press."

When Suzanne looked at the birth certificate, it had been issued in October of 1937 and stated her birth as May 29, 1933. It was hard to read in some areas because it was a copy and a rubber-stamped note at the top stated, "Original remains in Jefferson City." She knew that she had started school in January of 1938. She remembered that her parents had told her she was reading words when she was a three-year-old as well as writing her name. "If I never was that precocious child of three but actually the kidnapped five-year-old, they may have lied about my age on the certificate because people might have been looking for an older child. That'd explain why they wanted me tested to skip grades because I would've started school late. They would've wanted me to move up to where I really should be," she said to herself while looking at the birth certificate

Suzanne stopped by Mrs. Stein's third floor rooms on Friday. She told her that she was in the neighborhood as they went to the kitchen to sit. Suzanne used the same story about the sorority wanting a baby photo of her and asked Mrs. Stein if she had any.

"Oh, darling, I sure don't. I only have some photos that people have given me. We never had a camera," Mrs. Stein said with regret.

"Here are the photos that I found at our house. Would you want to see them?"

As Mrs. Stein went for her reading glasses, Suzanne went to the kitchen window and looked out into the back. Nothing had changed. The backyard scene looked like a black-and-white movie with the unpainted back stairs in weather-beaten gray, black earth down in the yard, and the ubiquitous white sheets and underwear on clotheslines. She remembered playing on the walkways under the sheets as if it were last week.

"Let's see those photographs, sweetie. It's so good to see you. My, how you've become a lady!" Taking a look at the first photo, Mrs. Stein held it in her left hand, and with her other hand touching her soft drooping cheek, babbled on, "My, oh my, just look at the little Suzanne here in the photograph. Why, that's just how I remember you. Why, I even remember the little dress that you're wearing in this photograph. Oh, you were so sweet. I just loved being with you and your sweet mother. It was hard for me when you moved, though I know it was best for your family. Oh, let me see another."

With each of the five photos there were exclamations of "my, oh my" and some comments.

Suzanne began her planned progression of questions. "Could you tell me some of your memories of me? I'd love to hear any stories that you have to tell about me when I was little. Mom and Dad never talked too much about living here."

"Well, I don't know, honey. Let me think of what I could tell you. You know I just don't know what to tell you at the moment. Let me think some about it," she began in embarrassment.

Suzanne thought she might help spark her memory with some questions. "You used to take care of me for Mom. Was I a baby that cried a lot or was I quiet?"

"Oh, you were never a baby here. When your family moved in you were walking. You and your family had lived with your Aunt Maria for your first years. My, my! When you came here you must have been about the age of these photos. Oh, I don't remember exactly, I think about two years old. Oh, yes, that's right. See, if we talk a bit I'll remember. That is how I met you and your mother. Some months after you came, it was your birthday and you were turning three. She made you a cake with candles that I saw through the kitchen window when I was walking up the stairs. I came back down with a little present. Hmm, I can't remember what it was. That was long ago. I do know I came back to give you a little something. There were four candles on the little cake, and your mother said that there was one for each year and one to grow on. Oh, you were so shy and so sweet. Even though you were so shy, we soon were friends." Mrs. Stein picked up another photo to look at it, but went on talking about the birthday party.

Suzanne sat quietly with her mind swimming in thoughts. She hadn't known that she had lived with Aunt Maria for her first years. *How could I not have known? Why didn't anyone ever talk about that? I was never close to Aunt Maria's children because they were really Dad's older cousins and had moved away from St. Louis. I think I saw them from time to time on holidays, and you'd think that someone would've made some comment over the years. I must try to call them. This is similar to that outing with Dad when I asked him how he met Mom. If you don't ask, people never tell you. What else do I not know about myself? Or…*She stopped and her heart skipped a beat. Had she discovered a piece to the puzzle? *Or did Mom tell Mrs. Stein that I lived with Aunt Maria for the first two years of my life because I was living with my real parents. Without Aunt Maria here to clarify this, I'll have to ask Dad's cousins.*

Mrs. Stein concluded her talk about the birthday, "Then your father came home and I met him, too."

"Mrs. Stein, do you remember if I was sick as a baby or child?"

"Well, my, my, of course all children are sick from time to time. I did come down to stay with you when your Mother needed to go to the bank or get some groceries. I think Harry the cab driver may have driven you and your mother to the doctor once. Yes, of course, you were sick. I don't think anything unusual. Why do you ask?"

"Oh, I was wondering if you knew who my doctor was?" As soon as the question was asked, Suzanne realized that she hadn't phrased it as she had planned. She was going to let Mrs. Stein tell of a sickness and then casually ask if a doctor had come. She hadn't wanted to ask directly for a name of the doctor. Quickly, she had to think of a reason for wanting to know that detail. She professed, "I need to know all the vaccinations that I had when I was a child. You know, the University wants to know all kinds of historical things."

"No, I surely don't remember the doctor's name. I'm so sorry. I'm sure your dear mother will remember. Have you asked her?"

Deception was uncomfortable to Suzanne. She saw that she had made a slight mistake in how she worded a question, which caused the logic of her questions to become dubious. She decided to stop before she was in deeper. This sweet older woman was noticing that the visit wasn't a normal one.

"Yes, I'll ask Mother. It seems I'm thinking of things at random. I really need to be going. I enjoyed seeing you. I'm sorry that I don't stop by more often."

When Suzanne left she realized that again she had failed to learn much of anything. She detested this type of secrecy and deceitfulness. *I'm not good at this type of work*, she complained in her thoughts as she rushed down the three flights. *I must let David handle the talking to the newspaper. Who knows what I might say? I'd ruin it.* "At this point, I don't care to know who the doctor was. He'd see that I was fishing for information. I'm tired of doing all this!" She reached the bottom of the stairs and realized that she had said that last sentence aloud. She stopped her one-way discussion and walked to find a bus to get home.

Later as they talked on the telephone, David laughed when she recounted the scene with Mrs. Stein. She loved his laugh. He could have been angry and instead he laughed. The laugh made her relax and she laughed at herself. This was one of the many reasons that she loved him. Her affection was calm and yet inside she felt like she could explode with her love for him. She wondered how he was doing because, since Ellie had come home last week, they had not been able to use his Dad and Mom's bed. The convenience of going to David's house for their sexual encounters was gone. A couple of times they had sneaked to Suzanne's bedroom when Claire was busy in the confectionery. With Suzanne's bedroom being the only room on the third floor, she had promised David that her Mom wasn't going to come up. *I guess that is going to be the place from now on*, she thought and giggled.

"What was that giggle about?" he asked since he had finished the laughing about her episode with Mrs. Stein and was discussing the next move.

Though her bedroom was on the third floor and private, at the moment she was talking on the telephone in the kitchen. Her mother appeared and Suzanne's conversation became stilted.

"Oh, nothing. It was a silly thought. That's all. What were you saying about this weekend?"

David repeated his comments, "I was saying that we need to take some time to plan what we'll say to the newspaper people. Let's talk about it at my house on Friday. Mom invited you for supper, and then we can work up in the study or go for a drive and have some privacy. What do you say?"

"Sure! Listen, I must study. I'll see you tomorrow when you pick me up. Okay?"

David replied, "Okay and bye," and disconnected.

Claire asked how David was and Suzanne let her mother know that she'd be having supper with the Bartletts on Friday.

"I hardly see you anymore since you started the University. And with the death of Aunt Maria we aren't eating together on Sunday. Let's have David over on Sundays, and I'll prepare some Italian food. We don't want to lose the tradition. What do you think, Suzanne?"

"Oh, I don't know, Mom. Let me ask David and see. When we have this much studying to do, we often go over to the University and get a bite to eat at a hamburger place on Sundays. We kind of enjoy our time alone, but I'll ask him."

Claire had noticed that she and Suzanne seemed to be growing apart, and she didn't know if this was natural or if there was a problem. Yet, she didn't say anything more. She worried in silence and hoped it was because of Suzanne's studies and having a boyfriend.

A jingle of bells sounded from the confectionery. "Oh, Suzanne, by the way, I put some items that we needed from the confectionery into the bathroom. Would you put them away?" Replacing the lid on the soup she had been stirring, Claire started for the door to the confectionery, "I'm planning on us eating in about one hour."

As her mother turned from sight in the doorway and hurried down the stairs, Suzanne was sure that her mother meant that she had put some Kotex in the bathroom. If it had been shampoo her mother would've said "shampoo" and not "some items." Just in case, Suzanne went to check the bathroom because she knew she'd need the Kotex for her period that was coming up. Abruptly, she stopped at the door to the bathroom and returned to the kitchen to see the calendar.

She stared at it and thought, *No, I'm wrong. My period should have started the week before last. Hmm, it's always on time! Guess I didn't think about it because of all this kidnapping stuff going on. I've heard that an emotional upset can change the cycle. That's probably why it's late.* In the bathroom, she found the new box of the Kotex pads and put them away. She wouldn't allow herself to think much about the other reasons why her menstrual cycle might be late.

Later, when she was ready for bed, she removed the hatbox from the floorboards. She took out Bobo and the yellow gown with the pink crocheted flowers before sitting on the side of her bed. Her fingers caressed the ball as she had done when she was young. She touched the little hat and eyes. She kissed him and stared at the ball. "Goodnight, little friend," she whispered and returned him to his hiding place.

In bed, the complexity of her life, with all the unsolved problems, made it difficult to breathe. The room was stuffy. She got up from bed to let in some fresh air. After opening the window, she took a deep breath, smelling the spring breeze with the scent of blossoms. Unexpectedly, she had a tingle in her breasts. She remembered having felt the same kind of tingle earlier that day and had given it no thought. Now she gave it a lot of thought. This was a new sensation. Also, she sensed differences in other ways. She couldn't explain them to herself, but she had noticed sensations inside that were indescribable. From the back of her mind, the awareness of these changes in her body connected with the knowledge of her late period. Then, she remembered the two times that David hadn't used those rubber things. Her heart began to throb in her chest.

Sleep came slowly that night.

Within the next few days, as her period never came, she became more and more sure that she was pregnant. She told no one, not even David. She wanted to be positive before she let him know anything.

CHAPTER 14

There were three major newspapers in St. Louis: the *Globe Democrat*, the *St. Louis Post-Dispatch*, and the *Star-Times*. The article that David and Suzanne had found pressed into the bottom of the hatbox was from a newspaper called *The Star* because back in 1932 it had not yet merged with *The Times*. They discovered that all the newspapers had offices in the same area downtown. In fact, the *Globe* and *Post-Dispatch* had offices in the same building at 700 12th Street. *The Star* was across the street. That seemed strange to them until they discovered that the newspapers used the same presses to print. At least it made the investigation job easier. They went to 12th Street and Franklin. They were going to be able to visit all three newspapers.

"So, you want to know who wrote this article," said the only reporter available at the *Star-Times*. He took the yellowed newspaper and read for a moment. "Wow, that's almost twenty years ago!" he exclaimed. While it was obvious that he was too young to have been working here in 1932, they were glad that he took the time to read the short article. He commented, "Do you see that there is no name of the reporter on this article? That means it was general information and probably given to the newspapers by the police. The cops probably even wrote up what they wanted to have printed. Did you check to see if this article was in the *Post* and *Globe*? I'm sure it was, but you could go to the morgue to look and see. If it was, then what I'm saying is a sure thing. Listen, I need to get back to work. I'd like to help you more, but I think that is what happened."

"What's the morgue?"

"Wow, you two are lost. Listen, the morgue is what we call the library where we keep all the back issues of the newspaper. If you want my advice, go use the one over at the Terminal Railroad Building where the *Globe* and *Post* are located."

They headed out and crossed the street. The architecture of the building they were approaching was impressive. "Is this art deco?" Suzanne asked. The building's construction date, 1931, was cut into the massive white stone slabs above the entrance. The date sat atop a tiered pyramid relief surrounding the three main doors with zigzag designs patterned into the pyramid. There were many figures and symbols above the pyramid. An open-winged, eagle-like thunderbird was at the top with human figures below the bird. Flowers and leaves entwined in different areas while vines snaked across the building, creating an image that conveyed mysterious and exotic impressions.

"I don't know," commented David. "It looks Egyptian with those bird figures on the top of those two staffs." Two staffs were carved on each side of the pyramid, and each one was three stories tall. The building exuded the idea of great things, and they felt humility upon opening the main door and entering. A vast hall of marble awaited them inside. The walls were adorned with large brass gratings that had similar entwining plant-like patterns pressed into the metal in relief as had been seen on the outside. A bustle of life was coming and going as the click, clomp, tap, and plop of footsteps echoed off the floors and walls. They made a few inquires to find their way to the morgue. It was an elevator ride down to a lower level. David whispered on the descent, "Wonder which pharaoh is buried in this Egyptian tomb?" There were other people in the elevator so Suzanne punched his side and put her finger to her lips to quiet him.

Soon they approached a wooden counter. There was a library atmosphere, and a stern-looking woman approached them from the other side of the counter. People sat at large tables reading newspapers. Only the rustle of turning pages was heard, and in the quiet, it seemed loud. David lowered his voice and said, "May we see a copy of the *Globe* and *Post* from this same date in 1932." He produced the copy of the *Star* that he had taken from the hatbox. "Or can we see several copies from this date and for a week afterwards?"

"Yes, I can find what you request. Please take a seat. It'll be just a few minutes." The woman stated her words very concisely and then departed to complete her task. Ten minutes later she returned with a stack of newspapers and motioned to them.

Suzanne went up to the counter with David and asked the woman, "Do you have any cross-referencing capabilities? You know: if one article has a follow-up article at a later time? Or a way to know if they found a person who committed a crime?"

"No, we don't." They took the pile of papers to a table.

Within minutes they found and read the same article in both the *Globe* and *Post-Dispatch* papers that *The Star* had written. Same title, too: *No Clews in Disappearance of 16-Month-Old Child*. It seemed obvious that the reporter at the *Star-Times* was correct that the article had been written and given to each of the papers to print without changing a word. They divided the stack of papers and spent the next couple of hours looking though hundreds of pages in search of more information about the same incident. David and Claire found nothing more. At first they talked about some of the advertisements that showed the styles of the times and laughed at some of the cartoons. They even took time to discuss articles of interest.

"We should get going." They really didn't have time to leisurely enjoy reading and sharing the pleasures of yesteryear. They needed to work on discovering whether this kidnapping had been resolved or not.

"Yeah, there's nothing more here about the disappearance of this 16-month-old child. Look at all the kidnappings going on. Can you believe all these other articles about kidnappings? And court trials that were going on about kidnappings. This is futile. With so many cases, it could have taken a month or a year to solve. We can't look through all the newspapers." David sighed and continued on with his disappointing conclusions. "We've learned enough by looking through newspapers. Let's go ask this woman some questions to see if she knows of anyone who may have been around at that time."

Returning to the counter with the old newspapers, David nodded to the woman to indicate that he wanted to speak with her. "I was wondering if there is anyone with whom we could speak that might've worked here around the year nineteen thirty-two."

"I was working here for the *Globe Democrat* in 1932," she replied.

"Oh, well, we're trying to find some information about a kidnapping that is referred to in this article," David said to her while pointing to the *No Clews in Disappearance of 16-Month-Old Child* article. The woman picked up the paper and read the short commentary.

She looked up with exasperation and shook her head, "Do you realize during that period in United States there were thousands of kidnappings every year?"

"Surely not in St. Louis!" Suzanne blurted. "There must have been just a few. It'd seem that someone working as a reporter back then might remember this particular case."

"Yes, maybe so. I was never a reporter. I've worked in the organization as a secretary and then here with historical back issues." Her hand went to the top button at her neckline, and she began to twirl it while she replied, "There is a retired gentleman that comes in after lunch. He volunteers his time to help here in the morgue. You might stop back after lunch at about two o'clock. His name is Mr. Dudley."

"Do we need and appointment?"

"No, no, simply stop back here and you can speak with him. I wouldn't get your hopes up, though I do know that he did work with reporters and was active in the news stories."

David and Suzanne went up to the corner to the Dunne Restaurant, a kosher deli. They joined a line of people and took a tray to serve themselves. After paying, they selected a table for two and sat quietly eating while trying not to show the disappointment they were feeling. Suzanne made some comments about not liking detective work. David agreed, "We don't seem to be good at it. That's probably why we don't like it." They became quiet again.

They sat at a table by the windows and Suzanne was gazing out at the passing people. Some shoppers were scurrying along the sidewalks with paper-wrapped, string-tied bundles, while others leisurely strolled, looking in the storefronts, doing some window-shopping. The sidewalks were wide in front of a traditional three-story brick building that faced the newspaper's exotic Egyptian facade. This one brick building extended the whole block and had shops on the street level with canvas shades that rolled up or down from above the window displays. Tall lampposts with a single lamp lined the sidewalk, and some older ones had double lamps jutting from the post. Businessmen passed with suits, ties, and hats. Every man and most women wore a hat. The clothes were the somber, dark colors of the winter clothing. Spring could still bring a snowfall so the winter wools were not put into mothballs until May came to St. Louis.

Then in the distance approached three colorfully dressed gypsy women. They wove in and out of the people on the crowded sidewalk, speaking to many. Suzanne stared at them, watching carefully how they worked the men more than the women. They'd reach out and take someone's hand and then begin to talk. Some people jerked their hand back, away from the gypsy's grasp, and hurried away. Others quickly tried to find a coin to be rid of them. As the trio came closer, Suzanne tried not to gawk, but she found them intriguing. Suzanne remembered her first encounter with gypsies many years ago when she had been so close to the young girl. Just as back then, she wondered about them—their lifestyle, where they came from, how they lived. Why did they live this way? As far as Suzanne could see, actually they were begging even though they claimed to be telling your fortune. Suzanne wondered if it was true that they stole from the customers. She had heard that they were expert pickpockets.

"Suzanne," David whispered in disgust and startled her from her thoughts. As Suzanne turned to David to see why he had called her, she saw a young gypsy studying her as deeply as Suzanne had been studying the others. The two girls locked eyes, only separated by the glass of the deli at a distance of three feet.

"I know you," mimed the young gypsy girl, pointing a finger to her chest on the word *I* and then pointing to Suzanne on the word *you*. "I know you," she repeated. The gypsy continued to stare intently at Suzanne.

Suzanne recognized her, too. The gypsy was dressed less flamboyantly than the last time Suzanne had seen her many years ago. A long-sleeved blue satin blouse was tucked into her straight black skirt. If she hadn't been wearing beads of every color on her neck, large hoop earrings, and bangles tangling from both wrists, she wouldn't have looked like a gypsy.

"What's going on, Suzanne?" David asked. Suzanne had no time to respond before the gypsy bent closer toward Suzanne and mimed another sentence.

She mimed with a definite clarity, though no words could be heard, "Your dad is gone. Right?"

David and Suzanne understood the mouthed words. They didn't need to hear. David looked over to Suzanne and then back to the gypsy girl. He saw a panic appear on Suzanne's face. No, terror! As he turned to see why Suzanne was terrified, the girl repeated, "Your dad is gone." Then she motioned with a wave of her hand for Suzanne to come outside.

"Where are you going?" David exclaimed in disbelief as Suzanne rose from the table, picked up her jacket, and started toward the door.

"I'll be back," was all Suzanne said.

"No, I'm not letting you go out there alone! What's going on? Suzanne, please say something. Who is she and why are you going out there? What did she say about your Dad? Did I understand that she was talking about your Dad?"

Suzanne related the incident as she walked across the restaurant to the door, "Years ago when I was with my Dad I bumped into her on the street when we went to see a fire. She was dressed obnoxiously, and Dad wanted her to go away. She wanted to read our palms or tell our fortune or something. It was that best-outing-ever with my Dad that I've told you about. Anyway, as we walked away from her she shouted, 'I'm warning you' or something." Suzanne didn't know why she wasn't telling David the haunting warning. Suzanne remembered it well. *I see danger in your future. Don't you want to know?*

"And that is why you're going out to talk with her?"

Suzanne stopped, turned around to face David, and confessed with a puzzled expression to her voice, "I don't know. I guess I'm curious about these people. Years ago it seemed to me that my Dad was rude. How he acted was uncalled for. I don't know. I just want to talk with her." Then Suzanne turned and continued toward the door.

At first David didn't move. All this seemed unlike Suzanne. He shook his head in disbelief and huffed. "Wait up," he called.

As David approached, the two girls were standing face-to-face, seemingly studying each other in a relaxed rapport. Their size and shapes were similar, probably their ages, too.

Suzanne broke their silent swirl of memories and asked, "You were saying something about my dad when you talked through the window just now."

"I'm sorry about your dad."

"What do you mean? What are you sorry about?"

The gypsy's confident expression faded as she looked around as if to see where her two companions had gone. "I'm sorry that your dad died is all I wanted to say."

"How do you know this?"

"Listen, I've got to go. Could you give me a coin? I'm going to get into trouble if I don't have some money."

"David, do you have a quarter?"

"What? Suzanne, what is going on?" David gasped in disbelief.

"Just a quarter, David; it isn't a big deal. Please!" Suzanne responded.

As the quarter was passed, the gypsy mentioned, "We're down on Broadway this time—you can't miss us—if you want to talk. My name is Valerie. Ask for Valerie. Anyone can tell you where I am." She turned and hurried to catch the others.

"Suzanne, what was that all about? Are you out of your mind? Those people easily steal from you." Quickly he reached to his hip to check his wallet. He removed it to see if all his cash was still there. It was. He looked at Suzanne's hand to see if her class ring was there. It was. "I don't know why you want to have anything to do with gypsies."

"Don't worry so, David. Nothing happened."

"You aren't going to see her, I hope. Why put yourself in danger? She guessed that your father was dead. Big deal! What does that prove? She may have seen it in the newspaper. It was in the paper wasn't it?" David was making his point. He sounded like a good detective.

"I know, David. Please don't worry. You've made a good point."

David was unaware of what had occurred when Suzanne first saw the gypsy years ago. That warning the young gypsy had given to her Dad before he died had come to Suzanne's mind several times over the years. *I see danger in your future. Don't you want to know?* Of course, as she began to think about it, a warning could mean anything. The gypsy had never claimed that her Dad was going to die. Realistically Suzanne had to admit that all that fortune telling and palm reading was a hoax, and yet the ways of gypsies intrigued Suzanne. She thought, *I really know nothing about them. I'm intrigued about the unknown and what I imagine.* She told herself that it was just a coincidence what Valerie had said about her Dad. *And I'm just curious about gypsies.*

Suzanne wanted to end this subject so she blurted, "Let's get back to the morgue and talk to that Mr. Dudley. I want to finish this. I'm tired of all this detective work that goes nowhere."

"Like I said before, yeah, me too." David sighed. He was tired of endless puzzling occurrences, too. He could see that Suzanne wasn't going to explain about this gypsy thing. It was ridiculous.

They returned to the newspaper morgue and heard the expected disappointing comments. Mr. Dudley was a skinny little stooped man who shuffled over to the table to sit with David and Suzanne. He confirmed all they had learned before, but nothing more. As the reporter from the *Star-Times* had said, it was an article given to the papers by the police and only the police knew any of the details.

Mr. Dudley liked to talk, "You know it was all friendships, favors, and connections between the newspapermen and the police that determined whether we heard the results of any of the police work. I watched a lot of the reporters spend time and their own money buying a beer or a drink after hours for a cop to establish a relationship. You know what I mean? Your little story would not have had any interest to the reporters unless there was an incident or side to it that was appealing to the public." He sighed, "I remember all the kidnappings. It was crazy back then. People made a living not only kidnapping, but also claiming that they did the kidnapping and getting ransom money. You know what I mean? The public is strange about what they want to read. They drive the newspapers. Since people wanted to read about all those kidnappings, it was a popular topic in the news. My theory is that the more people that read about it, the more that got ideas to try it. It was hard times back in the twenties and thirties. Crime was prevalent with the Mob and bootlegging and such. This was easy money to some people. Kidnapping was discussed frequently in the newspapers. Every day! And there was barely any punishment for those who were caught. It was an everyday thing. You know what I mean?"

Mr. Dudley continued rambling in this fashion while Suzanne squirmed in her chair trying to catch a pause where she could get back to their problem.

"If I remember right," Mr. Dudley continued, hardly taking a breath, "this here little article of yours was about the time of the infamous Lindbergh kidnapping. That was news! You know what I mean? Every day for probably a year it was front-page news. The reporters drove those two parents crazy, I understand. Why, it was sensational! Now, if it was the time of the Lindbergh baby's death and such, it could have gotten lost among the other articles. You know, I guess that St. Louis was especially interested in the Lindberghs. His plane was the *Spirit of St. Louis* because…"

Suzanne could stand it no more. "Mr. Dudley, please excuse me. I have a question. I was wondering if you know anyone from back in 1932 in the police department or one of these reporters that had connections with the police. It'd help us if we knew someone to contact in the police department. I imagine it'll not be easy for us since it was eighteen years ago."

"No, it won't be easy. Let me think." Mr. Dudley rubbed his chin and looked down at the floor while he thought. "You know, I might need some time to look in my papers and talk to others to see if I can come up with a person for you. I can't promise anything. I don't want to get your hopes up. Did you know this little girl or the family? Is that why you're concerned?"

David answered carefully so as to not give Mr. Dudley anything to talk about. "This is a private situation, Mr. Dudley. When we can get some connection or learn more information, we'll be able to talk freely about the situation. I'm sure you understand that to protect the innocent, and all that kind of stuff, we need to be secretive. If you could help us, I'd enjoy sharing with you what this is about at a later date. I can't just now. I hope you know what I mean." Suzanne kicked David as he mimicked the little man with the "you know what I mean" comment.

David's guise worked well enough. Mr. Dudley began to whisper and moved his head closer to David as he spoke to prevent anyone from overhearing the conversation. "Yes, yes, I know what you mean. I'll do my best to find a connection to the police department. Someone who might know something from this time in the thirties."

Suzanne stood up. She wanted to get out of this dead end street. David was writing his phone number on a piece of paper and asked, "Now, please don't say anything if someone other than me answers the telephone. Let's have a code. I'll write it here. If you learn a name of someone that could help us connect with the police, call and say, 'Call Dudley at the University.' If you find nothing, say, 'The library has no information for me.' How does that sound? I cannot let my family know about this. Do you know what I mean?"

"Oh, yes! I'll be able to keep this quiet for you. Now, don't you worry. This is all very interesting and…"

Suzanne interrupted, "Excuse me," and turned to David to say, "We're late and don't want people to wonder where we are." She was trying to keep the idea of intrigue going in the mind of this little old man. She then turned to Mr. Dudley and continued, "Thank you for your time and help. We must be going."

They shook hands and said the farewells quickly. David and Suzanne smiled coyly to each other as they walked quickly out of the room and to the elevator. When they got to the first floor, they rushed from the building for fear that Mr. Dudley might follow with more comments to tell them.

"Wow! So did you have fun with that little cloak and dagger intrigue?" Suzanne teased David.

David just laughed.

"He sure was talkative. Don't you agree?" Suzanne said.

"Holy cow! He couldn't stop. I admit that he had some interesting things to say, but he didn't know when to slow down and let us talk. We really are having a hard time getting any facts on this kidnapping. I need to study for my classes and here we are listening to this old man recount the history of 1932," David lamented. "I really need to go study. Do you have studying?"

"Of course, but I'm having a difficult time concentrating when I do study. My mind continually wanders, thinking about all this. I wish we could just stop for a while. Well, at least for a few days."

"Right!" David agreed. He was frustrated and welcomed a break from the investigation of the kidnapping, too. "Let's do that."

A different kind of break came that night. Actually it was at 2:17 AM when Suzanne sat up in bed wide-awake. *The money!* Before going to bed she had written herself a reminder to go to the bank for her monthly allowance. While she slept, her mind had made a connection to the idea that the money that was left as an inheritance could be the ransom money from the kidnapping.

For the next four hours in the dark, ideas tumbled from her head. *They could have collected the ransom money and kept the child. That'd explain how we got all this money. Mom had always called it an inheritance. I heard her say that to Mr. Bartlett. She never would tell me who left the money to us. Mom said once, "It's not important, Suzanne. Besides you don't know the person."*

We always lived frugally until after Dad died so possibly it was my father who was afraid to use the money. Or they could have decided to wait ten years before using it and then...*Yes,* that's it! They bought the confectionery with the money. When Dad died she needed it. I bet Mom decided to put some aside for my college." Suzanne could hardly wait to tell David. It was a new item for the list.

Although they knew that they should be studying for the exams, they were both excited with this new idea. They went to the bank right away. Suzanne asked the teller if she could speak with someone about her trust fund, and they were shown to the office of a vice president. It was a small neighborhood bank and all the workers seemed friendly.

"Good morning, Miss Scaglione, and..."

"This is my fiancé, Mr. Bartlett," Suzanne proclaimed with a beaming smile on her face. David and she had decided that the simplest explanation was for them to be looking into her trust fund because of the pending marriage.

"So nice to meet you both. How may I help you today?"

Suzanne began, "I was hoping that you could give me more details on my trust fund. Since we're getting married I thought I should know more about it. I really don't know how much it is in total. I was wondering if there are any restrictions. Will the marriage affect it? I want to have all the details clearly stated."

"All right, I have your file right here. Let's see, it's managed by a firm called Hauptmann and Hirsh. They're located at 570 Washington. We don't have any of the details because our responsibility is only to pay you. They deposit the funds and manage the trust. Our job is to receive the deposit and make it available for you. We do no more than that. You need to speak to them about the specific details. There is a handwritten note in the margin that we worked with a Mr. Connelly at that firm."

"I see," said Suzanne. This added another failure to the list. They didn't learn much. She and David shook hands with the vice president and left the bank.

They went directly downtown to Hauptmann and Hirsh and were received with a slight frown by the gray-haired receptionist.

"You really should have called for an appointment. Mr. Connelly no longer is working here, and everyone is quite busy. Please be seated while I try to find someone to assist you. This is not my job. People usually come in with an appointment." At this point she seemed satisfied that she had reprimanded these two youngsters sufficiently. "It may take a few minutes or you may have to come back. I'll start to call each secretary to see whether someone can speak with you. It was about a trust fund in your name, you said?"

David and Suzanne waited twenty minutes and finally were shown into the office of a Mr. Nuss.

After introductions, Suzanne began what they had planned for her to say. "We want to have our financial situation clear before the wedding. Could you tell us all the details of my trust fund? I think it ends when I'm 26 years old, and I know what I get every month. I don't know if there are more details. Can I know who set it up or is that a secret? When was it done? I'm curious if you can tell me. Can I know the whole value? Anything that you can tell me."

Mr. Nuss had listened without moving, waiting for the comments to end until he opened the folder and began to explain. "Mr. Connelly, who was with us for twenty-five years, has since retired. I understand that he moved to Florida. He was the administrator of your particular fund. I tried to read this file before you came in. Possibly I'd need to study it more thoroughly than I have. Let me tell you what I've learned and then if you need more information, you could return on another day when I can schedule time with you. How does that sound?"

"Fine, I think. Thank you," Suzanne replied.

"Your trust fund was established in 1935 with our firm. The monies were $20,000 at that time and were to be distributed to you when you started college, not before. Today you have $31,092. Hauptmann and Hirsh take a small annual fee of $20 for administrating your fund. However, it stipulates that you're to receive all original funds and the accrued interest on your 26th birthday whether you have finished college or not. As you most likely know, you began to receive the allowances last year in August when you started at…" Mr. Nuss stopped and placed his glasses to his eyes to read. "Yes, here in St. Louis at Washington University. Is that correct?"

"Yes, it is. Who set up this fund? Can you tell me?" Suzanne inquired.

"Why a Mr. Harry J. Schwarz."

Puzzled, Suzanne asked, "Who is this Harry J. Schwarz?" She had expected to hear her mother or father's name.

"Why, Miss Scaglione, what do you mean? We don't keep a history of the people that come to do business with us. If you don't know who he is, possibly your parents can tell you. This file has an address for Mr. Schwarz and a telephone number, nothing more."

"May I have them?" Suzanne asked.

"I don't believe that they're valid since Mr. Schwarz died many years ago."

David spoke up and asked, "Do you know where Mr. Schwarz worked?"

"As I said, I don't have a history of this man. Why don't we continue another day? Mr. Connelly may have known more and I can look in his other files." Mr. Nuss stopped to wait for the response to his suggestion.

"May we have a minute alone? I'd like to clarify something with my fiancé," Suzanne asked.

"If it truly is only a minute. I have an appointment in ten minutes. I can give you all the time you need on another day—an hour or two, if necessary. You could call and make an appointment at your convenience."

Suzanne repeated, "Just a minute or two. Thank you. Shall we go out or…"

"No, no." Mr. Nuss seemed embarrassed that they thought him rude. "I shall give you a moment here in my office while I speak with my secretary right outside the door. I shall leave it open. You may call me when you're ready."

When he had left, Suzanne explained. "I think this Harry Schwarz is a person that I knew as a child. Mrs. Stein mentioned Harry the cab driver when I was talking with her the other day."

"A cab driver, Suzanne?"

"I know. It makes no sense. I think we need to go and think about all this and hope that Mr. Nuss can find some information about Harry Schwarz for us. Let's not make an appointment today. We should wait. What do you think?"

"Okay. I'm confused and tired."

In the car Suzanne recalled, "I seem to remember going for rides in taxicabs. I remember the black and white paint job like the cabs used to have. But I don't remember anything else. I don't remember this Harry Schwarz."

Then she started guessing, "Don't you see? Mom and Dad had to find some-one to help hide the money. They paid this cab driver to come and set up a trust fund to have some of the money put aside for me and my future."

David was exasperated, "Suzanne, please. You're guessing. Making up stuff. Let me think." They rode in quiet for a while. As they arrived at her home, he commented, "You remember that Dad asked us to work three hours tonight at the drugstore? Right?"

Suzanne was cuddled close to him and nodded with a "Uh-huh" sound.

"Then I'll see you at the drugstore about eight o'clock tonight. I look for-ward to a few hours with Dad at the drugstore. It always relaxes me to work and talk with the customers."

"Me, too!" Suzanne admitted. "It isn't the same at the confectionery. I guess your Dad makes the drugstore interesting for us. Do you think?"

David agreed.

Nonetheless tonight it would be a different experience.

CHAPTER 15

It started as a typical Saturday night at the drugstore—busy! A lot of people came in to buy cigarettes, candy, magazines, and money orders to pay bills. Then there was the usual number of customers for liniments, aspirins, bandages, vitamins, and such sundries. One customer looking for a birthday gift for his wife bought a big box of candy and a bottle of cologne. Between 8:00 and 9:45 in the evening, the flow of customers didn't let up long enough for them to take a bathroom break. David and Suzanne were working the front of the store, and Mr. Bartlett was busy all evening filling prescriptions in the back. He'd come to the front of the store solely to hand the medicine to the customer and ring up the sale in the cash register. It was an NCR cash register.

The drugstore had two registers from National Cash Register Company. One in the front of the store that had four drawers; each clerk used a different drawer and was responsible for counting and balancing their money at the end of their shift.

The other cash register was at the back of the store for the cash from money order sales. This one, old enough to be an antique, had just one drawer of two in working condition. The broken drawer was open at all times, never used for money. If someone pushed it closed it could not be opened again without Mr. Bartlett getting a long wire and climbing on a chair to look with a flashlight into this little hole to see where the wire needed to go to release a spring mechanism. So, they just stored black grease marking pens, paperclips, and tacks in this drawer. It was also the lost and found for small articles: keys, rings, a lucky rabbit foot, and that kind of junk.

Out in the middle of the drugstore, where customers could walk around, were the magazine racks, display cases for greeting cards, a couple of chest freezers with Pevely Ice Cream in pints and quarts, Popsicles, Drumsticks, Brown Cows, and Dixie Cups. All other items were behind the counters so customers had to ask for what they wanted.

David and Suzanne were kept busy running from one side of the drugstore to the other. For example, a customer came in and asked Suzanne for some Prid salve, and she went to the back near the antique cash register. Another person wanted a package of Johnson Mustard Plasters, and Suzanne crossed to the opposite side of the store behind the jewelry case. If someone was buying a whole carton of Pall Mall cigarettes—that was easy—she just reached to the shelves under the counter by the front cash register.

"Dad, where's the Pazo Ointment?" David asked, and his Dad stepped out from the prescription-filling area to show him the drawer behind the candy case where the hemorrhoid medicines were kept.

Mr. Bartlett handed the item to David, pointing and saying, "There are three drawers with those medications."

"Dad, how do you go to the exact drawer? Look there are hundreds of drawers—five down and 40 across—and you casually walk up to the right one and open it."

Suzanne squeezed between them to pass and commented, "And he probably knows how many of each item is in every one of the drawers, too." She giggled and continued on her way to get a box of Kleenex tissues.

Mr. Bartlett was busy and didn't have any time to chat that night. This was the night that the doctor in the upstairs offices had evening hours, so a lot of sick people came down to the drugstore with their prescriptions. People seemed to get sick on the weekends. Years ago, Mr. Bartlett had talked with David and Suzanne about his theory on this. He surmised that people were probably getting sick during the week but wouldn't let their body put them in bed because they'd miss work. As a result, when they had a day off, the sickness developed. Mr. Bartlett felt that people had more control over their body than they realized. As with most of Mr. Bartlett's theories, Suzanne thought it was logical—an interesting idea. She had wanted to keep records about herself to see if it were true but hadn't gotten around to it.

The doctor saw his last patient at 9:30 and had gone home by 10:00. Finally the traffic in the drugstore started to quiet down. The store closes at 11:00 on weekends. Suzanne went to the back to help Mr. Bartlett put away the bottles of medicines that he had used to mix prescriptions. She knew where most items belonged. David never wanted to be involved with making prescriptions; that was Suzanne's interest. Consequently, he couldn't help. He had no idea where anything went.

David asked, "Suzanne, could you hand me the broom from back there? I'll sweep the floor between any customers that come in. Dad, is there anything else that you want me to do?"

"Just straighten up out there, David. A good sweeping is needed tonight. I saw a lot of trash on the floor." John turned to Suzanne, who had gone for the broom. "Hand him the box of sweeping compound, too, Suzanne."

Before starting on the floor, David straightened the magazines and filled the greeting card displays if there was an empty space. Customers were coming in one at a time, allowing him to straighten up things. He had to call to Suzanne just once when a second customer came in. Between 10:30 and 10:45, it slowed down even more, with only one customer. David was getting the sweeping done. At 10:50, ten minutes before closing, three men entered the store.

David looked up from the sweeping and guessed that these guys were trouble. The drugstore was in a homey neighborhood with middle-class families that had conservative standards of dress and living. These three were dressed in blue jeans and short leather jackets. Their hair was slicked back into the style called a "DA" for "duck's ass." A respectable young man in his early twenties wouldn't dress like this. David wore khaki pants and a dress shirt.

The three came in and spread out into different areas of the drugstore. David leaned his broom against the ice cream freezer and started moving behind the back counter to signal his Dad. Too late! The first gun came out. The guy was directly behind him.

"Just move slow and no one gets hurt, buddy," this one growled. The other two hoodlums went behind the counter and into the back. "Let's go up to the cash register in the front and empty it. Move!" He gave David a push as they were passing the back antique cash register and he fell against the broken drawer. It closed with a click. "Come on, move it!"

When David was up front and opening the first drawer, he could see his Dad and the others coming out from the back. One went with Suzanne to the back antique register. The other, with Mr. Bartlett, came toward David to the safe that was next to the candy case. David and Mr. Bartlett were just three feet from each other.

Mr. Bartlett had rules for all his clerks to follow during a holdup:

1. Give them anything they want.
2. Do not talk to them, if possible
3. Do not take any risks

Mr. Bartlett knelt on one knee, opened the safe, and removed several packets of money. The safe was a guise. It always had $200—in ones, fives, and tens—mixed and in several stacks, each held with a rubber band. Nothing else of value was in the safe. Any large quantities of money were hidden behind drawers or secret sliding panels. The idea was to give a robber these thick stacks of bills, knowing they would not take the time to count the money, and then hope they would leave the store.

David opened all four drawers of the cash register. Only three of them had money, and he dumped it all—coins and bills, but not the pennies—into a heavy cloth bag imprinted with "Tower Grove Bank, Corner of Grand and Hartford Street" that was for holding rolled coins from the bank. The fourth drawer was empty because only three people were working that night. Mr. Bartlett told all the clerks to leave cloth bank bags under the cash register for just this reason and to never give them the pennies; robbers get mad. The robbers in this neighborhood weren't professional and didn't plan too well. They often came in with nothing to hold the money, and it was best to have something ready for them. They easily got angry. Over the years, the holdups and robberies became more frequent. Now the drugstore averaged two a year. This was the first one this year.

Mr. Bartlett was thinking, *So far so good. They're calm and everything is running smoothly. They didn't want anything but money; that was good.*

Then things changed. From the back he heard a gruff loud voice of one of the hoodlums complaining, "Just open it! Damn it! Don't give me any lip!"

David looked to his Dad, standing a few feet away, and gasped, "Oh, Dad, earlier tonight, I pushed the broken drawer closed by accident."

The hold-up guy grabbed David's arm and forcefully jerked him against the cosmetic case, saying, "Shut-up! Didn't I tell you not to talk?" David got shoved again and knocked to the floor. The guy turned from David and hollered to the back of the store, "Hell, Jimmy! What's going on back there?"

Mr. Bartlett didn't react or move. He saw David wasn't hurt. What concerned him more was the argument coming from the back. Suzanne was out of his sight behind the large old NCR cash register. The man holding the gun stuck it into his ribs and said with annoyance, "All right, Mr. Drugstore Man, let's go see what's the problem back there. Move it!" Mr. Bartlett calmly walked to the back antique cash register.

As they came around the corner, Suzanne was being held by her hair with a gun at her throat. Her face was distorted in fear. "I can't open it because it's broken. Honest, there's only junk in it," she pleaded.

Mr. Bartlett was ten inches from an alarm button located beneath the old cash register. He knew he couldn't push it with guns pointed at each of them. He began to speak calmly, "She's telling the truth. It's broken. Do you see the hole where there should be a button to push for drawer number one?" Mr. Bartlett didn't move his hands to point, knowing that any movement could scare them. He tilted his head in the direction of the missing button.

While the robbers peered up and saw a "2" on one button and above it a shaft for the missing button, Mr. Bartlett warned, "Look, I think I better tell you that an alarm will sound at 11:00 if the doors are not closed and locked. My watch shows that there are seconds until that happens. What she says is true: only pens and junk are in that drawer because it's broken. It's not used for cash. The police try to pass here at closing to check out things. I don't want to tell you what to do. However, I don't want more trouble and you can get away now. But not in thirty seconds!" Mr. Bartlett hesitated momentarily before he continued, "You can believe me or wait and see. Why take that chance when you already have so much money in your hands?"

Those two holdup men looked at each other and decided to leave. "Ah shit! Let's go!" As soon as Mr. Bartlett saw the three passing through the front door, he pushed the alarm to have them think what he had told them was true.

He eased Suzanne to the floor in case they turned to shoot and demanded, "Stay on the floor! I'm going up the back aisle to the front door to see if I can get a look at their car." He started quickly up the aisle, shouting out, "David, stay down!"

From a window away from the door, Mr. Bartlett saw the three running up Park Avenue. Ducking behind the magazine rack, he went across the drugstore so he could see at a better angle. Hearing slamming car doors, the revving of a motor, and then a screeching of tires, Mr. Bartlett ran to the door to look. To help himself remember, he said aloud, "It's a late model Chevrolet, royal blue, four doors, and with a Missouri license plate, starting with 'SL-8.'"

Needless to say, the next hour and a half was spent with the police in the drugstore. Suzanne had regained her composure. On Mr. Bartlett's suggestion, one of the policemen had gone down to the confectionery and returned with Claire, giving Suzanne the security of having her mother by her side. David was doting over Suzanne. He was in anguish, knowing that his elbow had closed the broken drawer and caused the whole incident. He kept thinking, *She could have been shot.* It turned out that the robber had roughed her up, slapping her several times before grabbing her by her hair. Her scalp was sore and she held an ice bag against the bruise on her cheek.

Besides a couple of policemen, a detective was on the scene. Detective Frank Wharton had introduced himself to everyone before asking any questions. Suzanne told the detective all the details she could remember and commented, "He was sure that *that* was the drawer with lots of money. He said that it wasn't possible that I'd made so little, just a few hundred. He insisted that he saw how busy we had been all evening."

Detective Wharton interrupted Suzanne. "No, I want you to tell me the exact words he said, not a summary in your words." The detective turned to Claire and David, "Excuse us, I need to speak with Suzanne alone. She'll be fine. Why don't the two of you sit over on those nice ice cream parlor chairs while I finish with Suzanne? Thank you." He watched until the two were seat-ed, and then turned to face Suzanne again. "Okay. Now, Suzanne, can you remember how he said those things to you?"

"Well, he used a lot of curse words that I left out," she admitted with a grin to the detective.

He nodded his head and made a Clark Gable type of smile with raise of an eyebrow and glint in his eye. "I figured that! You can't talk like he did with your mother standing here."

Suzanne liked him.

The detective took out a pencil and extended it to Suzanne with the com-ment, "Listen, I don't want to get blamed that I corrupted you—you know, turned you into a person who uses foul language. Here's a pencil. Bet you could write them down even if you can't say them. Don't worry if you misspell any, I'll probably know what you mean." He took out his cigar and gave off a robust laugh.

Suzanne blushed and smiled back.

Claire and David stopped their conversation to turn and look at the hearty laughter. Claire looked long at the man. Detective Frank Wharton looked about 45 years old. He was tall, and Claire could see at a distance that he held himself erect and confident. His face was chiseled like a statue except with scars that one never sees on a work of art. He had a slight belly that went with his age and the beer he drank every night. He hadn't taken off his felt hat, and a thick mass of wavy blonde hair in need of a cut was protruding down to his collar. What Claire couldn't see was that there was a receding hairline almost back to his ears hidden under that hat. He detested any references to being bald or balding. He accepted the terminology of "deep receding hairline" if a refer-ence had to be made. The top of his head was his weak spot, his Achilles heel. He was a tough cop and known for his results. His buddies had learned to never joke about his pate. He knew his job and how to handle people. He was doing just fine in relaxing this young girl to get all the information he needed. Suzanne concentrated for a few moments before she wrote down five lines on the paper and handed it back to the detective. Claire stopped watching and turned back to talk with David again. Claire liked the man.

Out came his laugh again after reading, and making that special playful glint in his eyes again, he acknowledged, "Okay, I can understand your reluc-tance to say these things. If you'd tell me again what he said and just point with your finger, when you come to these precious little expressions. Try to say the exact words he said." He stuck his cigar back into his mouth and grinned real big. He held a list with the words as follows: *bitch, fucking, Goddamn,* another *bitch,* and a *shit.*

Suzanne began the dialog that she remembered. "After the two robbers came into the back room where Mr. Bartlett and I were working, mine pulled me by the arm to put me in front of him and muttered, 'Let's go, _____,'" Suzanne hid a smile with one hand while pointing with the other to the first word, *bitch*. "When we got to the back cash register he said, 'Now let's have all the _____ money and make it fast, sweetie.' I removed the cloth sack we have next to the register, opened the drawer, filled it, and tried to hand it to him. He grumbled, '_____ the other drawer, too.' That's when I explained that I couldn't open it and it only had junk in it. He slapped me and started shouting, 'You little _____! I was watchin' the place and saw all those people comin' and goin.' You only put two hundred and some in the bag. There's gotta be more!' Then he grabbed my hair and wrenched my head back and shouted at me, '_____, we have a long drive and I'm tired of this!' That's when Mr. Bartlett came around the corner and my robber didn't talk again."

Detective Wharton had been writing notes in a small spiral book. "Good, that's good! Actually much better than before." Obviously he was pleased. "I think it's time we all call it a night. I'll need to have you come down to the station sometime tomorrow. Let's see now, I can call you at this number?" He turned the little notebook for her to verify the telephone number. "You said your mother would be there to take a message at any time." They were walking toward David as he talked.

Suzanne nodded to indicate he had it all correct. David put his arm around her shoulders and they started toward the front door. Mr. Bartlett and Claire were standing up in the front of the drugstore talking with another officer, waiting to leave and lock the door for the night. The three were concerned how the neighborhood seemed to be changing and that the changes were not for the better.

Mr. Bartlett and David drove Suzanne and Claire home after they had asked Detective Wharton if the two young people could make the trip together to the police department tomorrow. It was arranged that way.

At three in the afternoon, Suzanne and David arrived at the main police station on Twelfth and Clark in downtown St. Louis. They were sent upstairs and greeted on the second floor by Detective Wharton at his desk. Without any preliminaries, he explained, "We're going to have you view a lineup. You each must do it alone. That's the rules." He looked tired and disheveled, like he might have been up all night. He definitely hadn't shaved. His shirt was excessively wrinkled, with rolled-up dirty cuffs, and his tie was loosened, hanging lopsided at his neck. He motioned for them to follow him into another area on the same floor as he continued to talk. He was so tall, leaning over as he spoke, that he gave a good view of the smooth top of his head. "I'll go with both of you into the lineup area, but one at a time. You'll be behind a window that protects you from being seen by the men in the lineup. They'll have bright lights shining on them and you'll be in the dark. Understand?"

David asked, "Why are we to view a lineup? Do you think you have those guys already?"

"Listen, David," the detective declared as he stopped and turned to explain. "The ones we don't get right away, we usually never get. We've learned that we got to work on each case immediately. If we wait until morning, our leads are old and the clues are cold. Hmm, that has a clever little ring to it, doesn't it?" He had hoped to relax the two. They gave him a smile. "Yeah, so we worked last night. I haven't been home yet. Don't I look it?" He ran his hand across his stubby beard. "Come on, let's see how we did."

It was the same guys! David identified his man and then Suzanne did the same. She was astounded to see her holdup guy standing in the lineup. She told Detective Wharton, "This is amazing! How did you find them?"

The detective explained, "Well, Mr. Bartlett was very helpful. Right after the holdup he rushed out of the drugstore to see the getaway car. He saw the type and color of the car besides the first three numbers and letters of the plate. That was the best lead. He also noticed the use of a name Jimmy, when one of them called to the other robber in the back with Suzanne. Then you, Suzanne, told me that your guy said they had a long drive. That's why we put men on all the roads out of St. Louis. You know, Routes 66 and 40, as well as the bridges. We sent officers and cars out. Got 'em right away. So that's that. Let's go to my desk. I'll need you to sign statements—one from last night and also today's."

David was shaking his head and commented, "Wish we could work like you. Detective Wharton, could we ask you a favor? I know you're busy, but we have this problem. Well, actually it's a mystery."

"All you can do is ask and if I can't help then I'll tell you. Give it a try."

"Actually it's complicated and we don't want to get anyone into trouble…" David stopped and sighed. "Can we confidentially tell you something; you know, not wanting you to arrest someone, if you discovered facts about a crime? It could involve someone we don't want you to arrest. I shouldn't have started talking about this. I know I'm not making much sense."

Suzanne spoke up and protested, "David, this was a good idea! It may be our last chance to learn something. Detective Wharton is just what we need. I think we should ask him."

"Hey, hey, hey! That ain't polite. You don't talk about someone when they're right here. You need to tell me what this is all about 'cuz it sounds like you may have big trouble here." They finished their walk and arrived at his desk again.

The detective plopped into his chair, indicated seats for them, and leaning on his elbows, waited for some response. "Come on now. What's this all about?"

"Well," Suzanne took the initiative and began, "we found this old newspaper in my home from 1932 and…"

She told it all. If she forgot to mention a point, David took over to fill in the detail. When they finished, the whole story was known. Detective Wharton hardly moved except to chew on his cigar while she explained all her feelings and doubts about her parents since she was young. "I don't want anything to harm my mother, but I must know. I can't live without knowing. Do you think you could help us find out about this 1932 kidnapping?"

"Whew! You kids have a complicated situation here. Man alive! Yeah, I'll do my best. Let's see, that's eighteen or more years ago. I don't know who was around then. I wasn't. I was in Chicago back then. I came here about ten years ago, so I know the ropes and a lot of the old timers. I'll do my best. I can't promise anything. Just don't make me give you a time frame. Let me work on this nice and easy. Since we are concerned about the involvement of your mother in this case, I don't want to open a can of worms, if you know what I mean. I'll give it a nice and slow try."

"Oh, thank you, Detective Wharton," Suzanne beamed.

"No thanks yet. Nothing's been done, and I may never have anything for you. I'll call as soon as I find something or when I give up. Have patience. I will call."

They left experiencing an excitement that they finally had done something to get to the bottom of the kidnapping. This was the last item on their list and they had had no idea how to begin with the police. It seemed to be working out.

David said, "If nothing comes from this, Suzanne, I think you're going to have to make a decision. There are two choices: the first is to try and forget all about this, and the second is to talk to your mother."

"Yes, I know. I don't have to think about that just yet, and I don't want to. Detective Wharton might find information about the parents of the kidnapped child. Oh, I can't keep saying 'the kidnapped child' because I know it's me. I want to hear who my parents really are!"

David didn't want to say anything. He was annoyed with all this intrigue and drama. He was uncomfortable with the idea of Claire kidnapping a child. No, he found the idea difficult to accept and to learn the truth might make them need to face this fact. He really didn't know what they would or should do if that were the case. He could anticipate the inevitable problems coming toward them. He was learning that Suzanne was different from him. She didn't evaluate what the results would be if one did this or that. She wasn't evaluating the possible consequences of her actions. He needed to talk with her again about that.

More than two weeks passed before they heard anything from Detective Wharton. During that time, Suzanne was trying to locate Aunt Maria's children. Also, during these weeks Suzanne never started her menstrual cycle and her breasts were definitely getting larger. She knew she was pregnant. And morning sickness occurred daily. She didn't care. She realized that she was content to be pregnant with David's child and didn't care about the nausea or vomiting. She knew that she needed to tell David soon, but she wanted the time to be right. He'd be happy, too. She was sure. After all, he had already proposed.

The little mechanical phonebook that Claire had by the telephone was the only way that Suzanne could think to begin to find her father's cousins. It was a flat tin box painted green with gold trim around the edges and the alphabet listed down the right-hand side. A sliding lever, with a metal flange that slipped below cards and pointed with an arrow to a letter of the alphabet, passed the 'A,' 'B,' and 'C' as she zipped down to 'G' for Gianelli and then pressed a square button. The metal top sprang open, lifting the cards 'A' to 'F.' With those cards being held out-of-sight by the metal finger, Suzanne viewed the 'G' list.

There on the first line of this 'G' card was the name 'Aunt Maria—Prospect 8673.' Three crossed lines were drawn through the information. It hurt to see that. She wanted to glue a paper over her Aunt to properly cover the death. It seemed cruel to 'X' out the name and telephone number. "I'll do that later," she murmured.

At the bottom of the 'G' card there was a neat list of three phone numbers written under the name of GIANELLI. Beside each number was written a name and a city as follows:

Angelo—Albuquerque, N.Mex.
Lenny—Whittier, California
Paul—Cuba, Missouri

It was obvious to Suzanne that her mother had gotten these telephone numbers at the funeral of Aunt Maria. They all appeared to have been written at the same time—same color ink, same handwriting. She thought, "Should be correct numbers if they're recent." Suzanne couldn't put a face with any of these three names. She knew the names were Aunt Maria's boys, and she had talked with them briefly during the funeral, but only to give her condolences. They were strangers to her. Growing up, she had heard her father and Aunt Maria talk together about these second cousins, but she couldn't remember them coming to

St. Louis to visit, so they were people she didn't know. And, she knew Aunt Maria had grandchildren, but none of them had come to the funeral.

Not knowing how she'd explain to her mother about making long distance calls and not worrying about that future problem, Suzanne dialed '0' for Operator. "I want to place a call to Albuquerque," she said and then gave the number. No one answered. "I have another call for Whittier, California," Suzanne told the operator. She gave the number and waited.

"Hello?"

"Hello, I'm trying to reach Lenny Gianelli, my second cousin."

"This is Lenny and who are you?" He asked in a pleasant voice. He laughed upon hearing that it was Tony's daughter. "Never expected to pick up the telephone and get a call from you. What can I do for you?"

"Listen, I don't mean to bother you, and this is an expensive call, so I'll quickly ask my question. I was wondering if you have any photos of me as a little girl when I lived with your mother, Aunt Maria. Or, if you could tell me any memory that you have of me during that time."

"Ah, memory lane. Well, I sure do. You danced at my wedding."

Surprised, she exclaimed, "What? I don't understand."

"When I got married here in California my mom, your Aunt Maria, was disappointed that we married without her seeing the wedding. I had been a bachelor a long time. Being older than most are when they marry, I didn't want any big ceremony. Mom was happy, when she heard I got married, but kind of mad at me. 'How will I ever meet the bride?' she wanted to know. We came to St. Louis and got married again for her. You were there!"

Suzanne was confused. "I was too little to dance. Was I walking? When was this?"

He laughed because he knew he was teasing her. "Well, I danced with Tony's little girl called 'Susie.' That's what I called you. That was the first week in December. I don't remember the date because our real wedding was on 20th of November 1932. It was about two weeks later. I know that it was December. You were walking all over the dance floor doing your own little dance. It was cute. I picked you up and danced around the reception hall with you. You were laughing and loving it. I think I could find a picture of you with our photographs. I'll send one if I do. I got your address from your mother at the funeral parlor. Guess it's the same place. Right?"

"Yes, it is. You said that it was in December of 1932? Are you sure?"

"My wife never lets me forget. Eighteen years we'll be married in November. Our oldest is going to be seventeen so I think my arithmetic is correct." He laughed again.

"Did you ever see me again?"

"No, not until Mom died. We made our life here and never got back to St. Louis. It's a long trip, you know."

Suzanne was elated with the conversation. Finally she had a success and some proof. "Well, I better end this before I spend too much. I really, really thank you for talking with me. I'll look for a photograph in the mail. Goodbye."

"Nice talking with you, cousin. Goodbye."

Later Suzanne related the experience to David. "When I called this Paul in Cuba, Missouri, he sounded drunk. He was the opposite of his brother—extremely irritated that I had called. He claimed he didn't know me and started talking about how his mother had loved my father more than her own sons. I ended that conversation as fast as I could. He did tell me that he was the only one that still lives in Missouri and that he didn't move far enough away. It wasn't a nice talk with him."

David was frowning, "If Lenny really knew you in 1932, I can't think of any other explanation except you would have to be the kidnapped child. If you were walking, you couldn't have been born in 1933 as your birth certificate states. Let's wait to see the wedding photographs with you in them though. Wait a minute!"

"What, David?"

"In December of 1932, you had just been kidnapped. How could these people accept the appearance of this little girl who never existed before?"

"You heard how much my family stays in touch. I doubt if Dad ever wrote to Aunt Maria. She wrote to him and told him that he could get his job back at the Fire Department. He told me that he never answered, just came. Well, he sent a telegram to the Fire Department. If he did call, when she saw me she would've been mad at him because he didn't tell her anything about a baby, but you saw how easily he talked to her when she was mad at him. There was no baby to tell her about so maybe he said that he wanted to surprise her. To use your words, 'I'm guessing.' There are a lot of possibilities. We could guess all day. All I know is that Lenny Gianelli danced with me. Had me in his arms—Little Susie."

A week after the call to California a note card with two photographs arrived. A bride stooping in front of a blonde-haired little girl and giving her a flower was one. In the other, Tony and Claire were standing beside the groom who was holding the same child in his arms. Written on the back of both was the date 'Dec. 1932' and the writing looked old. A note was enclosed and signed by Lenny's wife with the following message:

Dear Suzanne,
You were the star of my reception. We wanted a daughter just like you.

Please enjoy the photographs. I saved a couple for myself, which were about the same.

Love from your cousin Hettie.

P.S. If you ever come to California, please plan to stay with us.

David finally conceded that they had tangible proof of her identity. Their investigations had found some facts.

Suzanne remembered that her mother had wanted to have David over to eat Italian food on Sundays, as they had when Aunt Maria was alive. Suzanne asked David to come one Sunday, planning to ask her mother a question while David was there, but she kept her plan a secret.

The meal had been enjoyable and was nearing the end when Suzanne started talking about her childhood memories. David held his breath. He knew that Suzanne was up to something. He hoped she'd not say the wrong thing. What could she be doing?

"I was telling David the other day that I can remember a lot of little things that happened before I was five years old. He doesn't believe me. Didn't you have some fur-trimmed galoshes when we lived in the other place?"

Claire laughed, "Yes, I did. I haven't used them for many years, but you saw them a lot until you were eight years old."

"Oh," Suzanne responded and went to the next subject. "Well, didn't we go a lot in a taxi cab? I seem to remember the cab driver." Claire was startled. Without hesitating in her dialogue and trying to sound nonchalant, Suzanne pushed on, "Wasn't he called 'Harry'?"

Claire went white. "Yes, how can you remember that?"

"I think he took me to my first carnival. That made an impression on me. What was his complete name?"

In a daze, Claire responded, "Harry Schwarz."

Suzanne thought, *Bingo!*

David saw the pain in Claire's face and nudged Suzanne under the table. He ended the subject by saying, "Okay, Suzanne, I believe you. You win. I can't remember events before I was five so you get the prize for the best memory. Now, let me help clear the table, and then I must go study. Didn't you say that you needed to study, too?"

It was near the end of the semester at the University when Detective Wharton finally called David. He let David know that he had found some results and that he didn't want to talk on the telephone. The detective suggested that they come to the police station and talk. Suzanne and David went that afternoon.

As usual, Detective Wharton didn't beat around the bush. "Once I learned who the parents were, I did additional research to confirm several facts. Before I could tell the two of you the results, I needed to know I had all the correct facts. I do. I want to prepare the two of you. You're not going to like the results. It was a shock to me, and it'll be worse for you."

David and Suzanne thought they knew what he was going to say, but they sat and waited.

"So, the kidnapped child's name was Elizabeth Rose. Does that mean anything to you, David?"

Quickly David answered, "No! Why?"

The detective continued, "Okay. Her complete name was Elizabeth Rose Bartlett. Does that mean anything to you?"

"No, I'm confused. My mother is Elizabeth Mary Bartlett. Is there a connection?" David asked.

"Yes, there is." The detective took a puff on his cigar and continued. "A John and Elizabeth Bartlett reported that their daughter was kidnapped in November of 1932. The case was never closed. That means that the case was never solved. This John and Elizabeth Bartlett lived on Parker Street. Did you ever live on Parker, David?"

"Yes, until I was four or five years old. I'm not following. My parents reported a kidnapped child?"

Suzanne sat transfixed, uncomprehending.

"That's right." Detective Wharton continued, "When I learned this, I went to check it out. There was a birth certificate issued for a baby girl born at St. Mary's Hospital on July 21, 1931 and named Elizabeth Rose Bartlett. Her parents are your parents."

"What does this mean?" David asked in disbelief.

"What do you think it means?" Detective Wharton shook his head. "I'm sorry to have to tell you this, but these are the facts. I also went to find Suzanne's birth certificate at the same time and…"

Suzanne threw her arms into the air in exasperation and exclaimed, "We know! We know that mine was a home birth with no doctor present, and the witness is my Aunt Maria who is dead."

A moment passed, both David and Suzanne sat with their thoughts. Suddenly David blurted, "Suzanne is my sister?"

"Listen, I didn't say that. Even though it looks that way since she has that ball called Bobo and the yellow gown…"

Before the detective could continue, Suzanne finally allowed her body to respond to what she was hearing and her hands went to her mouth. It was apparent that she was going to retch. Detective Wharton rushed her to a small bathroom a few feet away. She vomited.

When she returned Detective Wharton apologized. "Sorry about that filthy bathroom. No one ever cleans here, and it's us men that use it. Sorry. Listen, I think you should take her home, David. The two of you have a lot to talk about, and you need to talk to your mother. Officially, I'm not going to say anything about any of this. What for? I want to know more of the facts for my own peace of mind, if you ever learn more." The detective pondered for a minute and furrowed his brow. "Tell me, David, you don't remember a sister?"

"No, absolutely not. And, how could that be?" David implored, hoping the detective could make more sense of all this than he could.

"When were you born David?"

"December 19, 1929"

"That means that you were younger than two when she was born. You hadn't even turned three when she disappeared. Just a little kid," Detective Wharton reasoned. "It makes sense that you don't remember."

Did it make sense? Suzanne was numb, and nothing was making sense to her. She couldn't grasp how she could have been happy and feeling so wonderful five minutes ago. She had David, the love of her life, and was to be married. A few words passed someone's lips and her existence was destroyed. The knowledge of those few words changed her whole future. This morning the mirror had showed all her happiness, but now it slipped from her grasp and shattered into sharp jagged pieces. She felt frantic. No, she felt insane. Why would this happen? How could so much be so wrong? I'm David's sister, Mr. Bartlett's daughter, Becky is the sister that I always wanted, and little Jimmy is my little brother. I'm also the mother-to-be of my brother's child. Her arms flew up to cover her face, "Oh, my God!" Suzanne uncovered her face and looked with fear into the eyes of Detective Wharton. She couldn't look at David.

"David, take her home. It'd be best right now." The detective got up with them and came around his desk to help with Suzanne. He took one elbow and David the other as they coaxed Suzanne to stand.

David was still trying to absorb the implications of what they had learned. The three of them progressed down a corridor where people rushed to and fro, oblivious to the crisis they faced. No words were said as Detective Wharton held the door for them to leave, but he stood for a long time watching the two young people. He was a tough cop, but this moved him more than he would have thought possible.

After they were across the street from the Police Station, Suzanne started spouting, "Take me home; it would be best, he says! There is nothing that is best!" Anger and frustration mixed and made her feel crazed. Suddenly she was near tears, "My god, I want to die!" She leaned into David and clung to his arm.

David's was still groping to find the positive aspect of all this. He struggled to be optimistic. It might not be true. There could be another John and Elizabeth Bartlett. Then he realized the chances of another couple with that same name were remote. He kept trying to find another answer.

In the parking lot, they got into his car. He pulled her to him and squeezed. He, too, was beginning to succumb to the emotional impact. He couldn't find any other explanation. There was tightness in his chest. Men don't cry he thought as he began to cry. He sobbed into her shoulder, "Oh, Suzanne, I love you so much. I can't seem to think straight. I can't believe what we heard. How could this be true? How could I have a sister who is not a part of my memory?"

Her tears flowed silently. She remained silent and really wasn't listening to David. All she could think about was her baby. She had been happy to be with David's child, thinking and planning much of their future. She had begun to think of possible names. She loved this little person inside of her, but now things were changed. She was scared.

Suzanne remembered first hearing about incest when she had been playing dress-up with some little girls. A boy, older with dark hair and brilliant blue eyes, came rushing into the room, looking for the other boys. "Where'd they go? Did you see the other boys?" he asked. No one answered him. He was there just a minute then ran out. One of the little girls said that she was going to marry him. Suzanne could still hear the sassy little voice of the other little girl saying, "Well, I can marry him, but you can't. Not you, 'cuz you're his cousin. Your babies would be born funny!"

Suzanne remembered all this so clearly. The concept had made such an impression on her, scaring her, making her wonder if it was true and what it really meant. And, after all these years, she thought, *I still don't understand. Is it a fact or only a probability that the babies are affected? And, just how is the child affected? Are there laws to prevent these marriages?*

Half dazed in her thoughts, she said aloud, "I really don't know."

"What?" asked David?

"Nothing," she answered and went on thinking. She took out a hankie and blew her nose. She was planning to do some research to learn exactly what it meant for a brother and sister to have a child. Surely, the University would have information on this or the public library downtown. It calmed her to have a plan to learn more before she had to tell David about the pregnancy. She felt strongly that this wasn't the time to tell him because she really hadn't thought about all the implications and was sure that he hadn't, either.

David was planning to verify it was his sister who was kidnapped. He told Suzanne, "I'll find some evidence in the house. There must be photographs! At home you should see how many photographs there are of me—tons as a baby and more of me as a little kid. With so many photographs of me, there must be photographs of Elizabeth, too. I won't believe any of this until I see some real evidence." Suzanne listened, but wasn't hopeful.

CHAPTER 16

In less than twenty minutes, David found old photographs of Elizabeth from 1931–1932 and a scrapbook filled with newspaper clippings. Flipping through the scrapbook, he saw the same article that had started this whole mystery— *No Clews in Disappearance of 16-Month-Old Child*! All of this had been hidden in the back of his mother's chest of drawers where she kept her under things, a place not even Becky would have had the gall to look.

He didn't care what rules he was breaking or whose privacy he was invading. He took everything to his room and sat on the bed. There were two cigar boxes filled with photographs. He saw the evidence of a sister that he couldn't remember. He tossed one photograph onto his bed: David posed on a tricycle with Elizabeth standing behind and holding on to him, a second with Elizabeth on the same tricycle with her feet dangling above the pedals, and another of David sitting on the front steps with Elizabeth in her mother's arms. There was one with Elizabeth lifted on top of her daddy's shoulders and David standing with his arms wrapped around his father's leg. On and on he flung the photographs onto his bed, and each verified to David that he had had a sister named Elizabeth. A sister he tried to remember, but couldn't. Then, there were the photographs with Bobo. Rummaging through the two cigar boxes, he found one, looked a moment, and then tossed it on the bed. Back to the boxes—another and a toss. Then another, and another. Some were not clear because the ball was the size of a baseball, but he knew what was in Elizabeth's little pudgy hands. He knew the feel of the ball and how much it meant to his sister. Only when he found one with Bobo's face showing clearly, did he stop his fevered search for photographs. In the foreground, on a blanket spread on the grass, was Bobo, during a picnic with his family of four, in some park he couldn't remember and in a life he never knew existed. David fell back on the bed and up billowed the small black and white photographs around his face, between his arms and one fluttered onto his belly. He picked it up and ran his fingers around the rippled edge of the border, staring at Elizabeth laughing at her big brother. The photo was creased and bent as if he had looked at it dozens of times, loving the image, crushing the edges with his little hands. "Or did she bend the photographs?" he wondered. He wondered about a lot of things, straining to remember, but the memories never came.

"Everything Detective Wharton said is true. Here's my sister, Elizabeth, but I'm looking at Suzanne! A little Suzanne! It's evident in all these photographs. Here I am, here she is, here we are, and there are my parents with us—one beautiful little family. Shit!"

After he put the photographs back into the two cigar boxes and slammed the scrapbook closed, he remained seated on his bed, staring. He couldn't move. What could he do now? He wished he could go back in time. He gazed out into a nothingness filled with darkness and remembered the moment when he first saw the old newspaper about the 1932 kidnapping. Remembering, he saw Suzanne's frantic realization that she was the kidnapped child. He recalled the struggle to investigate and how they had gotten closer and closer to the impending truth. He wished he had never picked up that old newspaper and read it.

Without calling, he left to go over to Suzanne's with the photos. He hoped she had slept well and was feeling better. At Grand and Park he changed his mind. He headed for Washington University. He had one more final exam and needed to study. Besides, he reasoned these photos would only make it worse for her.

Suzanne was already at the University. She had gone earlier that afternoon after David had taken her home from the police station. She was thinking how she had been upset for months after they had discovered the article about the 1932 kidnapping, and yet there was no comparison to the internal panic she was experiencing now. Before, her concern had been for Claire as a possible kidnapper and for herself as a possible child of other parents. The frenzy in her mind now was for the health of her child. She was determined to learn about babies born from a brother and sister. On the bus ride to Washington University, she realized that her prior worries were minuscule compared to those she now had. Nevertheless, she concluded that she had worried excessively before knowing the real facts. *That wasted a lot of my energy.* She was determined to learn what it meant to have an offspring that was the result of a mating between a sister and brother. *I must remain calm and analytical,* she told herself. *I'm overly sensitive and must concentrate on trying to be intelligent and logical.* In this way she hoped to keep herself calm.

In the library she requested to see books on heredity, genetics, incest, and inbreeding. Suzanne learned heredity and genetics were new areas to the scientific world. Darwin's Theory of Natural Selection, first proposed in 1859, had started people thinking, but his ideas lacked a workable concept of heredity. Later Darwin alluded to the idea that an individual's personal characteristics came from information stored in his father's sperm and mother's egg. Many thinkers of the time questioned Darwin's ideas. Suzanne finished that book about Darwin's ideas and took another. A monk named Gregor Mendel had discovered that plants carry hidden, recessive characteristics. Mendel's Laws of Inheritance explained that each parent has a pair of traits for each characteristic with one of the pair being passed to its offspring; either the dominant or the recessive characteristic could be passed.

The next books took her to events at the turn of the century. It wasn't until 1906 that William Bateson coined the term *genetics*. Suzanne was seeing that nearly all awareness of heredity and genetics had begun in the twentieth century.

Suzanne thought, *I'm reading about what's happening right now in my body.* She found delight in knowing, *My baby has two genes for each chromosome, one from David and one from me.*

But Suzanne wasn't finding much about her problem, and the books were old. She walked up to the desk to see if the librarian had found any references to inbreeding or incest. At the moment, the lady had two, and both were desk copies. Looking at the date of printing, Suzanne asked, "All this information is old. Have you any recent information?"

"Well, we close in twenty minutes. If you could come in tomorrow, I'll help you in the morning."

Suzanne agreed that she would come and took these last two books to her table. She shook her head as she read the publication date, 1923. She barely began reading, and it was time to go, but it didn't matter. The books were dense and referred only to animals and plants, not humans. She returned them to the counter and, standing with sagging shoulders and a frown, thanked the librarian. "I'll be back in the morning."

At home Claire was in bed, and Suzanne wanted to get to sleep, too. Undressing, she thought, *What a drag. I think I blush just asking to see books on inbreeding and incest.* She'd gone to the dictionary for the specific definition of the word "incest" and learned that it means sexual relations between two persons so closely related that marriage is forbidden. "I really didn't want to see that definition," she whispered and slipped into bed. With effort, she reviewed the facts she had learned that night and then her mind turned to David. She had a pang of love and wanted him to be there with her. Since it was late she hadn't called him. She had avoided him tonight, and maybe he was avoiding her. There was no note downstairs to indicate he had called her. *He probably needed some time away from our problems.*

Dreaming and hoping, she reasoned they could marry if no one else knew they were brother and sister. Except for the definition of incest, Suzanne did not know what all this meant in respect to their plans for marriage. "Only three people—David, Detective Wharton, and I—know about this," she whispered to herself and then wondered if they'd be breaking the law to marry. She still didn't have answers as to why incest was forbidden. She wondered what was going through David's head.

Their love was being tested.

In the morning Suzanne called the Bartlett house and found it uncomfortable to talk to Mrs. Bartlett. *This is my mother!* It was an incredible thought—an embarrassing feeling. Suzanne had a hard time listening. Her mind kept wandering.

David had told his mother that he was studying for his exam and he'd call Suzanne at suppertime. His exam was scheduled for tomorrow, Monday. Not wanting to meet up with him at the university, Suzanne thought it was good that he'd be in the Medical Library and she'd be across campus. She'd have all day to continue her investigations.

But it didn't take all day at the University Library. The librarian found two more books and one technical journal that was complicated and confusing. At least the journal was recent, from 1945. The authors, Beadle and Tatum, were new to her. These men were the first to give some clues as to how the chromosomes and genes were copied exactly from cell to cell. Suzanne disregarded it as too scientific and not too pertinent to her situation.

In one of the books she saw a comment that she copied verbatim in her notebook. She wrote:

> *Many rare diseases are caused by recessive genes and few by dominant genes. If a double recessive is passed to an offspring then the likelihood of a rare disorder surfacing is more likely.*[2]

In this same book she read and wrote another comment:

> The susceptibility to various diseases is genetic. Some examples are:
> Schizophrenia
> Malaria
> Several types of cancers (types not named)

Migraine headaches
High blood pressure

She wondered if these were facts or someone's hypothesis, if these books were up to date, or if there were later results. She wondered if this related to her situation. *Without a doubt David and I could have passed the same recessive gene or the same dominant gene to the baby. If it was a good characteristic, that's great. If not…"* She didn't know how to finish the thought.

The last book was about mutations. She didn't know what that meant and began to read:

> *Mutations are usually recessive. The harmful effects are not expressed unless two of them are brought together. This would most likely occur as a result of inbreeding; the mating of closely related individuals that may have inherited the same recessive mutant gene. For this reason, inherited diseases are more common among children whose parents are cousins than they are in the human population as a whole.*

Finally, she was learning about the negative effects of having a baby with her brother, but the book had no real specific examples of what the mutation could be.

She decided to go downtown to the main public library. She thought, *It's a gigantic place and must have more information. I must find out exactly what could happen to my baby.*

At the main library the information was old as well, but she finally had some books in her hands on the results of inbreeding and incest. She took them to a quiet area and sat down to read. She found more facts than she cared to see.

In the first book were case histories of six families who had practiced incest for several generations. The families were characterized with problems of stupidity, lack of ambition, and records of crime. Suzanne reasoned that these were simply six families who might have been socially poor and lacking good education. There was no proof of problems that could affect her child.

Then she read another book. The wording seemed stilted, but example after example left her feeling faint. It was about inbreeding in man and it was giving her more information than any other book that she had seen. It was very specific. She read about inbreeding causing dwarfing, digital malformations, harelip, cleft palate, hereditary cataracts, ichthyosis or scaly skin, defective hair and teeth, diabetes insipidus, an affection of the nervous system called Huntington's chorea, imperfectly developed sex organs, and more.

Suzanne came up for air. She gazed out across the quiet room where the tranquil faces peered into books and the rotating fans hummed with serenity. She was reading her worst fears. How could the atmosphere of this room be so peaceful? Blood pounded in her temples with a pulsing that hurt. She was afraid to read more, but she knew that she must. She read:

> *Some of these abnormalities are extremely rare and for various reasons are not likely to increase except through inbreeding. Among them may be mentioned pigmentary degeneration of the retina, Friedrich's ataxia, and xeroderma pigmentosum.*

Suzanne needed to look up these words and abnormalities because she had no idea what they were, but she was sure that they were going to be ugly. She continued:

> *But there are others, which well may give some cause for dismal foreboding—hereditary feeblemindedness and some forms of epilepsy and insanity. These characteristics may be put down as largely hereditary, and probably transmitted as single Mendelian units...*

Suzanne felt light-headed and got up to drink some water. Perspiring and sick to her stomach, she went into the bathroom and began to retch. As she leaned against the door to the bathroom stall, she realized that she couldn't go on reading. "What am I to do?" escaped her lips. Bumping against the door of the stall, she stooped down, hugging her knees to her chest and dropping her head to her knees. Her child was cradled inside, forming innocently inside her. She saw a hand without all the fingers, and then scaly skin, and eyes without pigment. "Or a perfectly beautiful child could be born...feebleminded," she whispered. The silent tears dripped onto the tiled bathroom floor. She remained in this position though she noticed her legs going numb.

Thoughts of David drifted into her musing mind—the first meeting in the drugstore and working on his stamp collections—and then she regressed to other childhood ways, hoping that wishes could come true. She wished she could go back in time to change the course of events. She prayed for someone to help her innocent child. She called, in her mind, *Mommy, what can I do?* Adrenaline surged! Her Mommy wasn't her mother. *Claire is not my mother.* This made her aware of how alone she was. No one knew. She was pregnant with her brother's child and no one knew. Who could she tell? No one can help! She was alone. *Not really alone because the baby is here with me. Yet one is always alone."* She felt delirious.

Her nose was running, making a tickle that was impossible to ignore. Suddenly she stood from her cramped stoop. Her legs stung. She smiled, shook her head, and almost laughed. *It takes my nose, tickling me, to distract me from all those crazy thoughts.* She reached for her handkerchief and blew her nose. Then she rubbed it to stop the itchiness caused by the dripping. She rubbed and rubbed until it was red. Finally the itching stopped. Her head ached. Before opening the door to step from the stall, she ran her hands down her mussed pleated skirt and straightened the scarf tied at her neck. Some composure returned. At the basin, she splashed her eyes with cool water. There were no towels so she washed the handkerchief she had used for her nose and wrung it out before patting her face dry. Looking in the mirror, she felt her face looked almost normal, and taking a deep breath, she felt she looked okay to walk out. After returning to the table for her notebook, she left the library. She could take no more reading. Anyway, she knew enough.

Learning the possible problems of inbreeding didn't have any effect on her feelings for David. In fact, their love wasn't worrying her. She had no doubts about the love they shared. She had found no reasons to wonder whether David and she would spend their lives together. She was confident and secure about their love. She knew they needed to make some decisions, and their life wasn't going to be as she had thought; they wouldn't have lots of children. "But we'll find a way." She could never love anyone as she loved David.

During the walk to the bus stop she stopped thinking about David and the baby. She had two choices for a bus ride home. One bus route went south and wound around in the downtown area before it turned west toward Park Avenue; the other went directly west and then required a transfer to a second bus for the southbound leg of the trip. The corner to get the transfer was near the place where her father Tony fought his last fire. Suzanne took the bus going west, and peering through the window just before she got off, she had a direct view of the building that had killed her father. Without hesitating, she stepped onto the curb and started walking toward the site. When she chose this route she knew that she'd walk over there. Over the years since his death, she had come several times. The brick warehouse looked nothing like the night of the fire, when it had been dripping with icicles, but the place still gave her a chill. Slowly she walked around the reconstructed building—a mausoleum for her father. Her internal vision looked to a place deep inside, beyond and beneath the new bricks, to where her father had flown into the air and vanished. Poof! He had melted and then evaporated into the atmosphere.

She whispered, "Daddy, I know you're here, floating somewhere." A warm breeze touched her arm, lifted her hair, and crept around her with the scent of her father. "Help me if you can, Daddy." She hugged herself, and when a gust wrapped the wind around her back with more force, there was the touch of his hand. She stood quietly with her eyes closed. After a while she turned and walked toward the bus stop. "Oh, Daddy, I love you even knowing what you did. I'll always feel you're my father. I miss you so much."

On the transfer bus, she was worrying how to tell David about the baby. There was no easy way to do it. Thinking about what she was going to say was driving her crazy as she planned one approach and then another. But thinking about how David would answer was the real worry. Whether she'd talk with David about all the inbreeding was on her mind and if she should talk with him about their future bothered her, but how to resolve the problem of the pregnancy was worst. By the time she got off the bus, she had thought and worried excessively, leaving her with an upset stomach and a headache. And it was suppertime.

CHAPTER 17

Suppertime in St. Louis was at six o'clock in the evening, or thereabouts, and Claire had supper ready when Suzanne arrived from the bus—stewed chicken cooked with peas and carrots and served over rice. It was one of Suzanne's favorite meals, filling the whole house with savory aromas. It had been a favorite with Tony, too, so the conversation over this meal usually was filled with happy talk of Tony. Tonight, the kitchen was filled with tensions between Claire and Suzanne. Suzanne had no appetite.

"Why aren't you eating?" Claire asked.

"Oh, I don't know," Suzanne said with a frown.

"You always love this meal," Claire insisted, starting to get irritated, "and you told me that you haven't eaten since breakfast. Now, two bites and you stop. Are you sick?"

Suzanne had sat down at the table hoping to avoid an argument such as this. She had known that her mother would be irritated. "No, I'm not sick. My stomach is queasy tonight. I'll eat some later after I talk to David. I might be better then."

"Why? Is there something wrong with you and David?"

"No, Mom, I haven't seen him all day and just want to talk to him."

"You said that you went to the library. What were you doing there? I thought you were finished with your exams and classes. Did you have some unfinished assignment? I had hoped you'd help me in the store today. Didn't we talk about that?" Claire was vexed and expressed her exasperation by asking multiple questions. When Claire did that—asking one after the other—it was hard to answer.

Suzanne tried to remember the first question as she sat, staring at her plate of food. What was the sense in answering any of them? Then, the telephone rang and she jumped up. "I'll get it in my room."

"You don't even know if it's David," Claire shouted as Suzanne disappeared up the stairs, two at a time.

It was David. "Hello, Suzanne," he mumbled.

She sat on her bed leaning against the wall. "Oh, David, it's good to hear your voice. I've missed you so much. How did your studying go?"

"Okay, I guess." A silence prevailed on the telephone line as Suzanne waited for some details and none came.

Suzanne broke the silence with the question, "Are you doing okay?"

"Yeah," was all David added.

With that one word she could hear an upset in his voice, a strain in his manner. "What's the matter, David?"

"What do you mean? You know what's the matter. Oh, by the way, I found old photographs in my mother's chest of drawers. There were two boxes of photographs of my sister and me. I mean, of you and me when we were little. Seeing the photographs makes all this so real. I guess that's what's wrong. You're acting like everything is the same as before. Don't you know that everything has changed?"

"You're being negative, David. You always tell me to look for a bright side or to think positive. I had hoped that you'd be..." Suzanne stopped and couldn't finish her thought because she realized that she must tell David about the pregnancy. There was no bright side to that topic. She inhaled deeply and solemnly began. "I need to tell you something."

"Yeah?"

Suzanne explained, "It's hard to say, and I know it'll make things worse, but I can't solve this problem without you."

"Yeah? What are you talking about?" David's voice showed exasperation, impatience, and frustration. What now? All day he had suffered and he was trying to just get by. He had this exam and he need to do well on it, but it was difficult to study. He wanted all the problems to wait, or go away, while he finished his studies. He was trying not to think about his relationship with Suzanne. He willed himself not to think about it. He had told himself that he had to control all those feelings. He reasoned that a doctor must be able to see pain and suffering and yet pull himself above it to function rationally and methodically. As a doctor, he must control himself to be able to accomplish important tasks. For the present, it was this exam. In the future, it could be a patient's life. He adamantly believed this was how he must be.

Suzanne hesitated and then decided to blurt it out in one breath. "I'm pregnant."

"What?" He shouted. He couldn't have been more surprised. "How did you let that happen? Aren't there enough problems?" Suddenly he realized that he had responded without absorbing exactly what it meant for Suzanne to be carrying his child. All the implications were becoming apparent and he gasped, "Oh, my God!"

Suzanne was crushed. What did he mean? She didn't let it happen. It just did! He was the one who didn't use the Trojan. She thought, *How could he blame me?* Her skin felt cold and sweaty at the same time. She paled and her lips looked blue. She was lightheaded and dizzy and started breathing rapidly. She opened her mouth to speak and it stayed open with no words.

David asked, "What are you going to do?"

She collapsed onto the bed and pulled the bedspread over herself. What did he mean? He should have used the word *we*. What are *we* going to do? She felt alienated and pushed aside. He seemed hostile, unfriendly, and indifferent. She was alone, really alone.

"Well, say something! Are you sure? How do you know?"

Softly she responded, "I know. There's no doubt. I'm pregnant."

"What are you going to do, Suzanne?"

She meekly began some ideas, "I don't know…I had hoped that you could help since you know doctors and medical people. Surely there is someone to help abort…"

David's interruption was vehement. "What? You're talking about a procedure that's against the law! There is no such thing as a legal abortion so you're asking me to jeopardize my career and the career of another person? I'm not through Pre-Med, Suzanne; where is your mind?"

Suzanne was having difficulty absorbing all the statements. She was having trouble thinking. Her head hurt. Was this David talking? A throb of pain. How could he say these things? Another surge behind her eyes. Do I not know him? No, I do, I do! She pressed her fingers at her temples to lessen the throbbing. I've known him for over eight years. Her bedroom seemed to be swaying as she continued to try and find reason in his words. They had grown up together, had been in so many situations together, how could she know that he'd act like this? She must be misunderstanding. Misunderstanding the meaning of his words.

David was thinking similar thoughts about her. He knew he was being practical and logical. *I'm being realistic. She's talking nonsense. She had always seemed unlike other women because she was more practical and intelligent. But an abortion? What's she thinking? I have no idea about abortions and don't know anyone who does. Even if I did, how could she ask me to do something that's illegal? Besides, she was supposed to be aware of her menstrual cycle and should have told me when not to make love. How could she be so careless? I take precautions by wearing prophylactics. Her responsibility was simpler, she needed to count and watch the calendar. Look what she has done!*

Her head was undulating in confusion and she thought, *He's angry, but I guess he's talking like this because he wants to have the child.* As a pre-medical student he must know more than she did, and it was true that the information she learned at the library was outdated. He may have reacted because he'd still love his child, even with imperfections. Then again, there was a chance that there'd be no problems.

She asked, "Do you mean, when we're married you'd accept the child no matter what problems there are?"

"Suzanne, are you mad? You're my sister! We can't marry!"

It took her breath away. She hung up. She sat up among the rumpled bedspread, wrapped around her shoulders and tangled in her feet, gave a shiver, and stared at the telephone as if it had caused all her problems. It rang. She picked it up and dropped it dramatically back on the cradle then leaned toward the disconnected apparatus and stated emphatically, "Hang it up! What more could you say, David? I don't want to hear anymore." He had made it clear that it was her problem, not his. She was alone. This time the realization that she was on her own seemed to give her strength. She got to her feet and untangled herself, and then flipping the bedspread into the air, she let it float down onto the bed without a wrinkle. A rosy color returned to her lips, a furrow appeared in her brow, and she was no longer chilled.

If only I could untangle my world as easily as this bedspread. She turned and looked out her window and then got the impulse to talk to Bobo as she used to do as a little girl. She knelt and pushed her bed aside. Up came the loose floorboard and out came the hatbox. With her fingertips, she caressed the flowers on top of the hatbox and the pretty dancing girls on the oval sides before lifting the lid. "Hi, Bobo, want to hear my latest troubles? They're worse than ever."

While seated on the floor she rested her head on her bent arm that comfortably fit to the height of the low windowsill. She looked out at the people and cars below. The ball was against her cheek and she moved it back and forth to feel the ridges of his cap and little nose. The smells of Bobo, rubber and ground-in dirt, seemed to relax her. Ten or fifteen minutes passed as Bobo and she shared the problem, in silence, and searched for a solution. Bobo offered much, like always. First he had provided smells and tactile comforts, and then he filled her with memories of happiness, and finally he whispered, "With me you're never alone."

She came out of her daydreaming and decided, "It's back to the library to learn about abortion. Also, I could make an anonymous call to a doctor to see what he'd say. I know that abortions are illegal, but I might learn something to lead to another solution." She sighed and continued talking quietly to her little friend, "If Mr. Bartlett wasn't David's father, I'd probably talk with him." As soon as it was said, she realized that she was talking about her own father. She froze in her movements for a second or two as she thought about Mr. Bartlett and how much she had always loved him. Then, continuing with her monolog, "Okay, Bobo, back to your beautiful life inside the hatbox. Wish I could join you."

Claire was waiting on a customer when Suzanne went downstairs to say she was going to the library. She hesitated on the last step and peered at her mother while thinking. "Should I tell Mom? Perhaps she could help. No! How? Mom can't help me." But Suzanne decided to ask anyway.

Claire finished with the customer and turned to see Suzanne approaching. "Mommy, I have a problem I'd like to talk about. Could we go upstairs and…" The confectionery door jingled and three people came in.

"Suzanne, let me wait on these people. I'll be up as soon as I finish with them." Claire saw that her daughter was upset, but figured that it was a lover's quarrel. There was no emergency in discussing a lover's quarrel. She planned to finish quickly with these customers and talk to Suzanne.

Calmly Suzanne withdrew her pending question, "Never mind, Mom."

Claire had no time to respond before her daughter went out the jingling door and headed to the bus stop.

Suzanne had reconsidered that impulse to talk with her mother. It was complex. "How would I begin? Start talking about the kidnapping? Start with David being my bother? If Mom doesn't know that David is my brother, how would she understand the real problem of the pregnancy? More importantly, talking with Mom wasn't going to undo anything or solve the problem. By telling her, I would've made another person upset. I need to find someone who can really help."

She took the bus route that required no transfer and headed east on Park Avenue before it started north, twisting and turning on many streets. Looking out the bus window, she saw spring, and she forgot her troubles. She loved spring in St. Louis when the trees were in what Suzanne called "their fuzzy stage." The sycamores, maples, elms, and cottonwoods rushed passed the bus window—leafless, but with little buds poking out, starting to open. From a distance, the bare trees looked out-of-focus or fuzzy. This stage lasted, more or less, for a day if it was sunny, and each spring Suzanne watched for this moment when the trees were ready to open their leaves. The bus turned on Broadway, and in a vacant lot under a cluster of sycamores, she saw the gypsies.

Spontaneously Suzanne got up from her seat and pulled the cord. Buzz! The driver stopped at the corner, and she got off. As the bus passed in front of her, blocking the view, she asked herself what she was doing. She could give herself no answer, and when the bus finished passing, the gypsy camp appeared again across the street.

How different this camp was than the one she had seen with her father, during their best-outing-ever, when there had been a dozen mushrooming tents striped in reds, yellows, and blues and growing out from a cleared, barren tract of land. Back then, old Cadillacs, battered Lincolns, stolen Packards, and tired LaSalles were parked around the tents. Now, one small tent was here on a grassy site with trees and, surrounding that one central khaki-colored tent, were three large shiny aluminum trailers and two small twenty-foot trailers. Also, eight gleaming cars were parked among the trailers—three spanking clean 1950 Fords, one Mercury, and some different models of Chevrolet. Now, like then, there was a multitude of gypsies everywhere—walking, sitting, laughing, talking, and cooking.

Suzanne crossed the street. After she stepped up on the curb, there was a moment of hesitancy before she stepped onto the grass into the gypsy campground. She knew that until she stepped there, no one would know if she was merely passing or if she was actually going to see the gypsies. As her foot landed on the grass, heads turned and much talking stopped. She proceeded forward toward the closest group of people, sitting on ordinary household chairs next to their small trailer. Two small coffee tables had been brought out, too, and had some glasses on them. They watched her approach. The men were a range of different ages and mostly dressed conventionally in white shirts and khaki pants. One older man had on a suit, his hat, and a dress shirt buttoned to the top, but he was without a tie. Two of the three women were wearing ordinary clothing but had added colorful beads around their necks and dangling earrings. One older woman wore a long flowing dress that was made from a yellow sunflower cotton print with a red background. It brushed the ground as she walked. A pig was roasting on a spit over a bed of coals. Suzanne had never seen someone cook a pig in this way. It smelled so delicious.

"Hello," Suzanne began, "I'm looking for Valerie. Could you tell me where I might find her?" She was nervous as the three women came closer with hands on their hips and a strut to their gait. Without comment the older man in the suit slowly raised his arm across his chest and pointed to a distant trailer.

Immediately Suzanne started in that direction. "Thanks," she called out and waved goodbye without looking back. There was no hospitality in the faces of those three women. She was heading toward one of the large trailers and, of course, a larger group of people. She sighed and tried to give an authentic smile to some people staring at her as she approached. Then Valerie appeared. In relief Suzanne greeted her, "Hi, I'm sure glad to see you. People sure do stare here, don't they?"

"Yeah, don't worry about it. It's our custom. Come on over here." Valerie turned and Suzanne followed while noticing that the gypsy girl was wearing a straight skirt the same as hers with a kick pleat in the back. Where the tan skirt ended, mid calf, were white bobby socks and penny loafers, leaving only an inch of leg showing. That was the style. Today, Valerie's blouse was white cotton, and she had a pink cardigan sweater draped on her shoulders. That, too, was the style. Valerie turned as she started up the steps into a trailer. "So, you're surprised to see me dressed so…normal," she said with an impish smile.

Suzanne didn't know how to respond. Did Valerie read her mind?

Valerie eased the unsaid thoughts with, "Glad you came by. Let's go in our trailer and get out of everyone's view."

Suzanne was surprised that the inside was similar to a regular house. In the living room, Valerie plopped on the sofa while Suzanne took an overstuffed chair and said, "Hey, this is nice."

"Thanks." She grimaced and then asked, "So you didn't expect me to live somewhere nice?"

"Oh, I'm sorry. I didn't mean it that way. I've never been in any trailer, and it impressed me that it looks just like a house. Well, it *is* your house, I know.…I'm going to shut-up. I just wanted to say that it's neat. I'm making it worse."

Valerie smiled and nodded, "I'm sorry, too. I'm overly sensitive because people misjudge us all the time. I know you didn't mean to be insulting. Years ago when you saw me I lived in a tent. Hey, I'm really glad your here. What made you decide to come?"

Suzanne laughed, "Listen, this is embarrassing, I didn't really plan to come. I was on the bus going to the downtown library. Suddenly I saw this gypsy campground and remembered that you had invited me. So I got off." They both smiled. "So I don't know why," she stammered. "It's hard to explain. I seem to know you. I even felt something special toward you that day when I was with my Dad." Suzanne stopped her talk. They both remained silent for a moment. Though neither girl spoke, both were deep in thought, thinking similar ideas. Suzanne couldn't understand why, but she was comfortable talking here. "I don't have a best girlfriend right now. She moved away. I know it seems strange, but for some reason, I'd like you as a friend, and I barely know you. Gee, I'm talking a lot." Suzanne stopped again and then, with a tease, said, "Is this some kind of gypsy spell you've put on me?"

"Wouldn't that be nice to have such powers? I wouldn't be here if I had that magic. Ha! I'd be a character in a fairytale." Valerie had reason to be uncomfortable with this topic. She asked, "You didn't really mean that stuff about a spell, did you?"

Suzanne got serious as she noticed the unusual expression on Valerie's face. "I meant everything I said except the comment about the spell. Sorry, again. It's just that I used to imagine all kinds of things as a kid. After I met you, I imagined things about you seeing the future, watching me in a crystal ball, and making spells. It was silly, but I thought a lot about you and since I knew nothing about gypsies, I imagined whatever I wanted. You were so different that day, if you remember."

"I know, I was a smart aleck. I've changed…grown up. We gypsies have changed a lot, too." Valerie voice was somber as she asked, "What's wrong?" Valerie didn't need to be a gypsy to notice that Suzanne was worried. She didn't need to be psychic to know a deep dilemma was drawing Suzanne to seek help; nevertheless Valerie had inner visions, some kind of unknown communication from certain people. Valerie knew more about Suzanne than she should. Ever since Valerie was young, she had known more than she wanted to know about many situations. Only her Grandmother had noticed Valerie's gift. The old gypsy knew how much her granddaughter wanted to be normal, so she kept Valerie's secret between them.

"Now, why do you say that? I said I hadn't planned to come. I came by accident." Before Suzanne could say more, the door opened.

"This is my Grandmother. Gran, this is Suzanne." Valerie saw a jerk of Suzanne's head and knew she was surprised to hear that her name was known. Valerie explained. "I saw your name and your Dad's picture in the newspaper when he died. I don't read minds," she professed with a grin. "But I do have a good memory. Am I correct? You are Suzanne?" A nod verified the name.

"People think we can do things that we can't. We practice hard to learn any trick we have. We're no different from you."

Valerie's Grandmother in a soft-spoken voice and a gentle accent said, "Now, Valerie, you make a mistake. We different and you know that. I also know you say things because you don't want to be different. You dream. You like to be same as Suzanne, but you not erase your Romani roots."

Unlike the other gypsy women Suzanne had seen, the Grandmother was regal looking in a long black skirt with soft pleats at the waist and a frilly blouse with white ruffles on the cuffs and at the neck. A dark maroon waistcoat made a perfect background for her simple jewelry—pearls on her ears and one string around her neck. The slightly stooped old woman looked to her guest and smiled pleasantly as she sat down beside her granddaughter and began to talk. "My granddaughter say things right that we are a simply people. Our clan from Spain have more than five hundred years of tradition behind us, playing music for coins, dancing, or telling fortunes, but we also trade and did some tinkering." The old woman smiled and confessed, "Yes, yes, we also learned to pilfer and pick a pocket or two. The world chooses to remember that we earn money by trickery alone…"

Suzanne listened to the old woman tell of the mysterious gypsies. She learned that even gypsies couldn't explain from where they'd come. No one knew. Over the generations they had forgotten or lost the knowledge of their origins.

"Long ago, people guess we come from Egypt because we have dark looks. The word "Gypsy" came from that mistake," Grandmother laughed. "You hear our people talk when you pass them outside? We speak our own tongue we call "Romani." It the language of the Gypsy. In Spain they call us "Gitanos" but we call ourselves "Romanies" though no one knows where such a land ever was. Maybe it's our secret." The grandmother patted Valerie's leg and rose from the sofa. "Enough tales from old woman. I see you two want to talk. Please come again, Suzanne, and stay as long as you like. We have a party later tonight and you welcome to join us, if you wish. For now, please excuse me." Though slightly stooped, she walked with an ease that made her seem younger than she appeared. Her creased and patterned face was a map of the many roads she had traveled.

Suzanne turned to Valerie and whispered, "Wow!"

"Yeah, my Grandmother is quite the storyteller because she came from the old country, and then she lived in Spain. Let's go out to walk," Valerie suggested. "Don't worry. There should be a lot more strangers arriving for the party. It's a wedding that we're celebrating. With so many people coming from other states as well as around here, no one will notice you. I'd like to learn more about you"

"You and your Grandmother are so beautiful with your black eyes and high cheek bones. I bet she had the same silky black hair as you." Suzanne and Valerie walked in silence for a few minutes. "I find your life interesting. Mine is plain compared to yours. You know my Dad was a fireman and…"

Valerie interrupted, "No, I didn't mean for you to talk about your family. I want to hear about you. You! Who was the guy you were with at the restaurant? Are you in school? Why did you come here? You know. I want to hear about your life."

Words came easily for Suzanne as if this new friend was an old friend. Listening to Suzanne tell all, Valerie confirmed some of her suspicions that she sensed through her inner vision. They sat under a tree for a while and then, as the narrative passed into the second hour, walked from the campground into the neighborhood and into a quiet St. Louis spring evening. Unlike the reaction of David, there was no blame or judgment as Suzanne told of her pregnancy. When she explained the kidnapping in depth, she had no shame telling that her parents had kidnapped a child. Suzanne expressed her fears for having an imperfect child and Valerie understood. The gypsy girl listened and nodded and made little agreeable sounds that seemed to say, yes, this was part of life—difficult, but life. By telling Valerie, the problems seemed less, though they still existed. Suzanne even was comforted by the mathematical notion that her problems reduced to half because Valerie was here to share a part of them. Suzanne knew this gypsy girl was hoping to help. Suzanne felt better.

Valerie sensed something was not correct in Suzanne's story. She took Suzanne's hand as they walked, hoping the contact would help her clarify the discrepancy in the story. The answer did not come.

During the evening Suzanne relaxed more and more. Learning more about these gypsies distracted Suzanne from her problem. She heard about the ridicule, prejudice, and persecution that these people had endured through the centuries and these stories put Suzanne's problem into a more realistic perspective. A whole different way of living existed right here in St. Louis, and this intrigued Suzanne. Gypsies had been coming to St. Louis to spend the winter every year for decades and were accepted by the people of this city. Suzanne remembered that *Nónno* had told her father many different cultures had come together and accepted each other in St. Louis. The few incidents the police had had to control were minuscule compared to a crime like the holdup she had experienced the other night.

Valerie told her, "Most tribes of Romanies…oh, I should use the word gypsy for you. As I was saying, most tribes of gypsies, known to be pickpockets, were rare in St. Louis."

Suzanne concluded, "That must be true because I've never heard anything about the gypsies. If there had been problems, it would've been in the news."

"Some of those troublesome tribes might've come here in the past, but the police probably told them to go elsewhere," Valerie guessed.

Finally Suzanne began to share her expectations and what it meant to her to be a woman. Valerie began to talk as well and they discovered how much alike they were. Valerie's mother had died before Suzanne's father, "My Grandmother moved in with my father and me to help us."

Suzanne recited her poem, *Going in Circles,* that expressed how important it was to be a wife and mother yet to be able to use her intellect to its fullest. "We can be what we want at this time in the world. I really believe that." Suzanne declared.

"I know what you mean. That's why I must go to college and learn more," said Valerie. "That's why I want to change my destiny. We travel here for the winter and then to Florida or other places for the rest of the year. We do it every year! I can't live like that anymore. I have always been accepted into schools here even though they knew I couldn't be here the whole year. I love to learn. My teachers say I'm smart. I want to go to college and learn about all the things I've read. I want a job. I want to have a deeper meaning to my life. I want to talk about intellectual ideas. I want to grow as a person." Valerie stopped and they walked in silence for a while. "Gypsies can't do these kinds of things because we're on the move. I know it sounds like a simple problem for me to solve, but...it isn't.

"Our way of marriage is different. It's difficult for a woman like me to do what I want to do because parents arrange the marriages. I was betrothed to a boy when I was five years old and we were to marry next year, but he died. That means I'm free." Valerie hugged herself and twirled on the sidewalk with that comment. "I told my father and Grandmother my ideas about an education, and though they don't completely understand, they know that our ways are changing. They've agreed to help me do it."

The two girls seemed content from all the exchange of ideas and topics. Then, casually, Valerie broke the solitude, dropping an unexpected comment, "Sometimes our women abort their babies without instruments. Are you interested in trying this?" She clarified her offer, "I don't know exactly what's done. I only know that herbs are used and that you must stay on your back for two days."

"You make it sound easy," Suzanne exclaimed.

Valerie laughed, "That's because I don't know much of anything about it and told you nothing. It might be complicated. Want to talk with my Grandmother about it?"

"Of course! I've been going crazy not knowing what to do. You know, to think that I've created a child that could suffer all his or her life is killing me. I can't stand the thought." Suzanne never would have guessed the gypsies could help her. She was happy to have made a friend to talk to. Words came easily with Valerie.

And she had no difficulty telling the Grandmother the story either. The Grandmother listened, understood, and said, "We can try." Being an old woman, she had seen the results of inbreeding, time and again. She knew it could cause sadness for a lifetime.

Suzanne went to the corner drugstore and called her mother. Suzanne said that she was going to stay overnight with a girlfriend.

Claire was full of questions, "Why did you rush out of the confectionery, Suzanne? We could have talked. Did you think I was putting you off?"

"No, Mom. It's all right." Suzanne confided that she and David did have a serious disagreement, as her mother had thought.

Claire understood that her daughter needed time to think and time in a place where David couldn't reach her. "No, David didn't call." Hesitating, Claire asked, "Suzanne, where'll you be?" It occurred to Claire that she didn't know of any of the new girlfriends Suzanne might have made at the university.

"She doesn't have a phone. I'll give you the address, Mom." After a slight hesitancy Suzanne changed her mind, "Oh, I think I it's best I don't because David might talk it out of you. I need some time to think without talking to him. He hurt me a lot. You understand, I hope." With that said, the plan was set with a bit of a deception, but Suzanne knew her mother wouldn't have gone looking for her, anyway. "I might stay two nights, Mom, and I promise to bring Valerie by the house to meet you after this disagreement with David is over. Okay?"

Claire accepted the idea and was happy knowing that Suzanne had a girlfriend. Claire also knew that her daughter had reached a time when she needed to be independent and have her own freedom. Suzanne had finished her first year at the university. "It's time to untie the apron strings," Claire told herself when she hung up the telephone.

Suddenly, Claire jumped as the telephone rang before her hand moved from it. It was David calling. Being true to her daughter, Claire told him that Suzanne had gone out and, "I don't know where or exactly when she'll be back."

"Please tell Suzanne I called." He hoped the telephone calls would indicate to Suzanne that he was sorry.

When the girls returned to the trailer all was ready. The Grandmother, who would perform the procedure, had purchased a large amount of parsley that she prepared with other ingredients. Suzanne would be sharing Valerie's bedroom and was asked to bathe and get ready for bed.

While Suzanne bathed, Valerie sat on the bed and touched Suzanne's clothes, hoping for an inner vision of what was going to happen. Blackness came to her— no message. From past experiences, she knew that blackness conveyed something was wrong, yet Valerie could not force an explanation to appear.

When Suzanne was ready, the Grandmother explained, "You going to be in bed for two days and you can't get up. So I have a bedpan for you to use." The Grandmother asked, "Do you have any questions?"

"Yes, I'd like to know what will happen. Will it be painful or dangerous? I was wondering if it always works or not."

"All questions good ones and I try to explain. I going to put some herbs in your vagina. Of course, I don't explain what they are because I don't want anyone to try doing this. That is all I do. I use herbs, no medicines or chemicals. They irritate your insides and you miscarry because of this irritation. We know it work if bloody clumps come out. Of course, I must be careful that everything come out, so I going to inspect those bloody clumps. It could start in twenty-four hours up to forty-eight hours. Sometimes it not work when the child is too strong and doesn't want to give up its life."

Suzanne was surprised, "It may not work?"

The Grandmother shook her head and said, "Yes, that right. It may not work. Listen, it works most the time, but not always. I thought you need to know this. If it not work, I take out the herbs and clean you with sterile water. Have I told you enough?"

"I think so. It seems simple. I hope it works, that's all"

The Grandmother continued with her explanation. "Now, you also asked about pain. When we begin to see any bloody clumps, I'll press on your belly to help get rid of everything. This is a bit painful. I'll push hard. You should have no real pain until then. It the same as bad cramps. Well, very, very bad cramps. It tolerable. Now, any other questions?"

Suzanne had noticed the Grandmother spoke with conviction and confidence, explaining well. She seemed intelligent. Suzanne was embarrassed to ask, but did, "Have you done this many times before?"

With that Valerie laughed. Her Grandmother confided, "Let me just say a 'Yes' and, I will add, 'successfully many times.'" She patted Suzanne's hand. "By the way, don't worry if you hear someone come in trailer, that father of Valerie. He's busy with wedding for tonight and will be in and out, but he not come in bedroom of Valerie."

Later that night, as Suzanne sprawled on the bed, she listened to the festivities through the small open windows in the trailer. Only sounds and smells floated in, but from time to time Valerie came to tell her what was happening.

"Oh, Suzanne, you should see my cousin Philip dancing." Valerie was kneeling on the bed while she gazed out the little window, "He has on this bright red sash and a black hat. He is so good. I had no idea that he even liked to dance. When we were growing up he was a bore."

The music sounded like a tango to Suzanne who closed her eyes to imagine Philip dancing.

Valerie was excited, "I've got to get out there and see him. People keep blocking my view. Hey, I'll be back later!" she shouted at the door before it slammed.

Suzanne smiled and knew she wasn't going to sleep much that night, *Thank heavens, I don't have to be bored in bed*, she thought as the music became sad and intriguing. The violins pulled feelings from her chest and then, people began to cheer. *Philip must have done something special*, she reflected as the cheering continued. The music intensified, then ended. Applause and more cheers followed.

The music changed through the night. Sounds of guitars and singing surrounded the trailer, sometimes profoundly tragic music drifted in, but most the time it was music for the audience to accompany with finger snapping, clapping to the beat, or shouts of "olé." Suzanne heard continual laughter and loud conversations in Romani; that seemed to be a part of the music. As she listened, she smiled.

Valerie came in again and again to explain with giggles and laughter about the drunks trying to dance, the flirts making fools of themselves, the gluttony of the crowd, and the beauty of the bride. They even eavesdropped on a conversation, coming from two lovers who, thinking they were away from ears and eyes, stopped to lean against the trailer to talk and kiss.

"Oh, listen to that music," Valerie gushed on one of her trips to be with Suzanne. "Romas love to dance. We call this one the *baile grande*; it has movements like dances from India." With Valerie's explanations of the music, she'd stand in front of Suzanne and show movements of the dance. "Oh, they're starting the flamenco…do you know it? Well, it's from Spain. Oh, just listen to it! Isn't it romantic?" Valerie raised her arms and twisted her hands as she danced the flamenco, but she still talked, "Gypsies from Andalusia were the people who started the flamenco. We like more guitars and violins, but other tribes have different gypsy music played with the accordion." After a few minutes, with her black eyes sparkling and the dark hair flying, she ran to the door again. "I've got to go out and dance."

Suzanne welcomed not only the sounds, but also the smells drifting in the window—savory food, scents of expensive perfume, smoke from exotic tobaccos, and smells from the night air. It was an entertaining night, and Suzanne slept most of the next day, as did Valerie.

The first twenty-four hours ended with no signs of success. The second twenty-four hours began with an evening filled with sounds of insects; the male cicadas were playing their mating music throughout the night. "Listen to those locusts," Suzanne commented and turned onto her side. She was tired of being in a bed and it was to be a long night since neither girl was sleepy.

Valerie spent time relaxing on the bed with Suzanne while they talked endlessly about their lives and dreams. Casually, Valerie turned and her leg brushed against Suzanne. Valerie froze! A flash of a scene came to her. It was one of her visions, like when she saw that Tony was going to die in a fire. This time she saw Suzanne and blood—lots of blood around a motionless Suzanne. Valerie concentrated, trying to see more and understand what it meant. Then it was gone. Valerie looked to her friend and convinced herself that it was a sign that the abortion was going to work. She was so drowsy and Suzanne was drifting off to sleep. It was three in the morning and they soon were both asleep.

Waking at 11:00 in the morning of the second day, Suzanne was sure that nothing was to come of this attempted abortion. All her apprehensions and fears started to return. She could endure being an unwed mother, she thought, but to have a child that was not right was her greatest fear. She imagined how the child might be simple-minded, with missing appendages or a carrier of strange diseases. She realized that she wouldn't know until after the child was born, and until then, she'd drive herself crazy imagining all the possibilities. *My mother will be disgraced at the pregnancy so I'll need to move away to save her from that shame. But I can't stay away from her forever. Someday everyone will see the child. What am I thinking? I have two mothers that I will shame. I can never let Mrs. Bartlett know who I am. What a disgrace I'd be."*

Suzanne could no longer lie quietly and control her fears. She turned in the bed and buried her face in the pillow to cry. Soon she drifted into a light sleep, dozing off and on. Upon waking she'd continue to torment herself with worries about the unborn child. Her lack of sleep only made it worse. Her anguish went on and on in her waking moments and in her dreams. She dreamed she gave birth to a baby boy who appeared normal, and then years passed, and he started having horrible diseases with welts and pustules. The child was in pain and became grotesquely twisted. Suzanne awoke in a sweat and then fell back to sleep from exhaustion. Finally, in the early afternoon, the Grandmother came.

As Suzanne had feared, the abortion attempt had failed. Grandmother cleaned Suzanne and had nothing more she could do except to give some words of reassurance that a healthy child is harder to abort, but the comment didn't lift Suzanne's spirits. On the contrary, Suzanne was depressed more than when she arrived; raised hopes fall harder and penetrate deeper. Departing the gypsy camp, Suzanne's trepidations were apparent to Valerie.

The two girls walked toward the bus stop. Valerie tried to give her new friend some support while inside she felt a panic about what her vision had meant. Her grandmother had told her to use the gift to help people because there was the possibility that the future could be changed. She had no idea how to prevent the scene from her inner vision. "My Grandmother knows a lot, Suzanne. She's probably correct that your baby is healthy and normal. Please try to relax and talk to David. He must share the responsibility with you." Valerie didn't know what else to say.

Suzanne sagged with sadness as she walked and didn't say anything until the bus pulled up. "Thanks for all you tried to do and remember you said that you're going to come to my place tomorrow to meet my mom. I promised her I'd introduce you. Thanks for everything."

As they hugged, Valerie tensed. A gypsy slipped up the steps into the bus ahead of Suzanne. Valerie recognized her. With Suzanne in her arms, an inner vision appeared again behind her eyes in tones of reds, showing Suzanne frantic and in distress. As they pulled apart, it vanished. What did it mean? Valerie talked fast as Suzanne boarded the bus, "Listen, Suzanne, promise me that you won't do anything drastic. We'll talk tomorrow when I come to your house. Okay?"

Suzanne just gave a nod and turned into the bus. When it pulled away from the curb, Valerie could see the gypsy woman moving from her original seat to sit by Suzanne. Though the bus and its occupants were growing smaller in the distance, Valerie was sure she saw them facing each other. That would mean that they were talking. Valerie ran back to her Grandmother.

"Gran, I saw Dolores Chowchki get on the same bus with Suzanne. Does she know what you tried to do for Suzanne?"

"I don't know. Let's find out." It took only minutes for the two to walk around the camp, talking to people, to learn if anyone had told Dolores about Suzanne. No one would admit to talking with Dolores. Her reputation was equated with pigs mired in dirtiness and swilling on the mishaps of others. Who'd want to be seen with her? However, a few people had noticed her during the festivities the other night. Dolores had been observed behind a tree eavesdropping when Grandmother and Valerie had been talking.

"Most our talk was about Suzanne. If Dolores heard us she could know about it. Gran, you know what that could mean? What can we do? Where is she camped?"

Grandmother responded, "We talk with your father!" They knew that it was possible that Dolores might offer to abort the baby with instruments. Dolores had done it before. It was a better business than telling fortunes. Dolores could earn in minutes all she needed for the month. "Come, we need him to drive us to find Dolores. I don't know where, but we must find her. I think of two places to start."

They guessed that Dolores was at the camp on Lemay Ferry Road three miles south of the city limits. Valerie's father, Nick, thought that was where her people were. Valerie worried, "Dolores may work from another campground to hide her trail from the authorities."

"Maybe you're right, Valerie, but it's a place to start."

They also knew that Dolores worked fast so the girl wouldn't have time to change her mind. Dolores was ahead of them by twenty to thirty minutes.

"Nicholas, go right to the King and speak. Others might try and hide Dolores. Do you think?" Grandmother still called her son Nicholas, though he preferred the Americanized name of Nick.

"Of course, Mother. I know what to do. You stay in the car in case she isn't there and we must leave quickly. Valerie, you come with me in case your friend is there. She doesn't know me and I don't know her. Tell me about her. Would she have money on her to pay for this? "

"Maybe. She was careful to have her purse under her pillow the whole time. That usually means that something valuable is in it, but I didn't ask. She did say that she has a lot of money in the bank from an inheritance. So, yes, she could pay for it."

Her father continued to talk and drive. "I want to have a better under-standing of the circumstances. You seem to like her a lot. You've been so happy the last two days with her here, and I haven't seen you this happy for a long time. So tell me about Suzanne." Glancing casually at her son, the old woman understood the wisdom of his words. The talking was going to take Valerie's mind off her fears, and the trip would go faster. Broadway connected directly to Lemay Ferry Road, but the traffic was heavy. They were consoled by the fact that the bus had the same traffic to push through.

Hurrying from the car, Valerie noticed how different the Yugoslavian gypsy camp was. Some of the families still used the large, colorful tents filled with mattresses and curtains to partition areas. The camp was cluttered, and debris was everywhere. Within minutes Nick learned Suzanne's whereabouts. Everyone Suzanne had passed had noticed the stranger, a *gorgio*. So Suzanne was there! Within minutes of their arrival, they learned it was too late. Delores had worked fast. They found Suzanne in a tent and on a regular dining room table with dirty towels and an old bedspread between her legs. Everything was soaked red. Dolores wasn't anywhere to be seen.

"Suzanne!" screamed Valerie as she went to her friend. "Papa, what are we going to do?"

"Calm yourself, Valerie," he insisted as he scooped Suzanne into his arms. "Let's get her to some help. Time is on our side. Stay calm and clear the way for me." As they rushed to the car he spoke directions, "Open the back door and get in so I can put your friend in the back with you. Scoot across and her head can rest in your lap." As they started back to the city he asked Valerie where Suzanne lived.

"Papa, we need her to go to a hospital!"

He demanded, "Valerie, stay calm and let me make the decisions. Tell me her address and I'll decide if we go there or to the hospital." When he heard that Suzanne lived on 3001 Park Avenue he decided to take her home. "Can you understand, Valerie, that we don't want to be involved with this crime? She lives minutes away from the City Hospital, and we'll not jeopardize her or our-selves by taking her to her home. This is what we'll do. We'll take her to the first room in the house. Ask Suzanne what room would that be."

Valerie leaned over, stroking Suzanne's moist forehead and asked, "Suzanne?"

Suzanne had heard the conversation and answered in a whisper, "The kitchen."

With a raised voice, Valerie's father asked, "Is there a phone in the kitchen?"

"Suzanne nodded her head 'Yes,' Papa," Valerie responded.

"Will someone be in the kitchen?"

"She said, if not in the kitchen probably her mother will be downstairs in the confectionery, Papa."

"Good, I'll put her down in the kitchen and call an ambulance. You talk with your friend and make her as comfortable as possible while you remove the towels and coat. We don't want to leave them. You find other things to use in the kitchen for the blood." Then he stated, "When the call is made, we leave."

"We'll need to tell her mother down in the confectionery."

"Yes, of course. You call to her mother as we leave. Give me 30 seconds to get to the car and start it. Then you shout, 'Come quick, Suzanne needs help!' and leave immediately. Can you do that? It's for the best, Valerie."

"Yes, Papa, but I want to know how she is. Can I call the hospital?" He answered his daughter in Romani, and they continued to speak in that tongue. They spoke in soft compassionate voices. Valerie's Grandmother joined the conversation, and Suzanne entered into shock and fainted.

They arrived and did as planned. Valerie bent over Suzanne just before leaving and one of her tears fell to the hollow of her Suzanne's throat. Some blood smeared there began to mix with Valerie's still-warm tear. The blood swirled and curled within the small single drop until Suzanne wore a ruby red gypsy's teardrop in the hollow of her neck, just like the necklace from her graduation night. A real Gypsy's Teardrop!

When Suzanne regained consciousness her mother was leaning over her on the kitchen floor. Blood was smeared everywhere

"Call David, Mommy," she whispered.

Kneeling and cradling her daughter's head Claire was frantic and confused. "What has happened? Where are you bleeding? Don't pass out!" Wide-eyed and near hysterics Claire continued to talk, but it was a conversation with herself because Suzanne wasn't hearing. "I need help." Rising from the floor Claire looked at her blood-covered hands, but took no time to wipe them before grabbing the phone.

Claire called David after she had called an ambulance. Surprised, Claire was informed that one had been requested earlier. It was arriving with wailing sirens while she spoke with David. "David, Suzanne is bleeding badly and an ambulance is coming. I can't explain what is wrong or where we are going. You must come here. I'll ask the ambulance people where we are going and write a note for you."

When David arrived to the kitchen and found the bloodstained floor, he knew instantly that Suzanne had had an abortion. The moment was accompanied by an electric-like reaction as all the significance of this scene was burned into some crevice of his brain. All the spilled blood! More than he had ever seen was smeared in various areas of the red and white linoleum tiles and globbed on an overturned kitchen chair, the telephone, the sink, and doorframe. A violent heat rushed through his legs, his arms, and into his head. Overwhelming pain and fear followed! These feelings that flashed in an instant would stay with him forever. Feelings endure longer than things. People think photographs are permanent, but they fade or crumble with time. Favorite toys disappear into places unknown. Only feelings are forever. Often in future years David would have a jolt upon seeing a red and white pattern. He would avoid Italian restaurants, not because he and Suzanne had frequented them, but only because the red and white checked tablecloths would bring back the pain of this moment. The memory would always pain him deeply. Feelings are forever.

The note on the table told David that they were taken to St. Louis Hospital. He left.

At the hospital and upon finding Claire, David blurted out, "Mrs. Scaglione, do you realize what has happened?"

"Yes," she groaned as she struggled to stand from the waiting room couch that sat too low to the floor. "Suzanne explained that she had your child aborted today. Aborted by some gypsy woman. My goodness! Why didn't she come to me?" Claire's heart jumped and she hesitated in her conversation with David. Speaking those words, Claire realized, for the first time, that Suzanne *had* come to her and *had* asked to talk when she had wanted to go finish with some customers. Claire dropped her head into her hands, crying.

Claire looked to David, "Those people live in such filthy conditions. Oh, David!" She threw her forehead onto his chest. He hugged her as she cried. Quickly, she forced the tears to stop because memories of Harry started to enter her mind, and she didn't want to think about him. How ironic it was that this secret of her past was being repeated with Suzanne.

No more crying! Claire demanded of herself and turned to David, trying to be calm. "The doctor claimed she might not make it through the night so I gave permission for him to operate. Only seventeen! She's too young for this! He needed to open her to stop the bleeding and evaluate the damage. She's lost too much blood." Claire voice gave out. She took a deep breath and continued explaining that the operation could take hours. "It all depends on the damage inside of her." She started to sob again, and the back of her hand went to her mouth. Blinking away the tears, she whispered, "She may never be able to have children."

David sat. He was in shock. He put his head against the wall and began to think about Claire. *Claire doesn't know that I know anything about the kidnapping. About the truth!* As David continued his wait with Claire, the lightheadedness subsided, and the immensity of the situation was becoming clear. It was complicated. He and Suzanne hadn't made any decisions on what they should do next because he had gotten irritated when she told him about the pregnan-

cy. He knew Suzanne had found a way by herself because of how he had reacted. She had asked for his help and hadn't gotten any. *I should have known she'd
go and try to find a way!* With the knowledge that her life was at stake, David
found he was having difficulty thinking. He was scared. He was sad. He could-
n't sit here. He was angry.

His anger started to expand. Inside his head, he screamed at himself, *What
kind of person am I abandoning her when she asked me for help?* He was angry
with his parents for hiding the knowledge of Elizabeth. No, again it was anger
with himself that he should have known about his sister. Still thinking, he
wondered, *My parents had to know I didn't remember. How could they never say
one thing? I'm a man, not a child, why didn't they tell me? What were they waiting for? Suzanne deserved to understand as well as I did. My sister, Suzanne! Jeez!
I still can't believe she's my sister. Poor Suzanne, she wanted answers that only my
parents could give.* He was crazed with these thoughts. He decided to go for the
hatbox. He wanted to have the ball and gown to show his parents. He was
determined to get the answers.

Claire was up pacing.

He said, "I need to tell my parents about Suzanne. I'm going to call my Mother.
Afterwards, may I to go to your house to get something from Suzanne's room?"

Claire knew it was better to be moving and doing something. "I'm on pins
and needles here. I'll go with you. Nothing's going to change in the twenty or
thirty minutes it takes us to go and return. I want to get a fresh change of
clothes for Suzanne, and instead of her using the hospital gowns, it'd be nicer
for her to have one of my nightgowns. I'll get her slippers and robe, too. Let's
go! You can call your mother from my house." She informed the nurse of the
short trip, explaining that she thought it best for them to do something,
instead sitting and waiting.

As David and Claire were leaving the hospital, Detective Frank Wharton
was coming in the entrance toward them.

"Good evening, Mrs. Scaglione and David." The detective nodded with an
extended hand. As Claire shook his hand, David looked dumfounded.

"What are you doing here?" David asked with surprise.

The detective removed his ubiquitous cigar and smiled, "Ha! I'm always
here. This is the gunshot hospital for St. Louis. No, the question is 'Why are you
here?' and I hope there hasn't been another holdup with someone injured."

Claire watched this man and found him to be a contradiction. His rough
manners and cigar smoking were not who he was. She had seen the gentle way
he had handled Suzanne at the drugstore after the holdup, and now she saw
more than concern. "Suzanne is here and in serious condition," she told him.
"We are on our way to get some things from the house for her."

Detective Wharton frowned, glancing quickly to David and back to Claire, "May I stop by her room later on to see how she's doing?" He planned to talk with the doctor and get the real scoop on Suzanne. He knew all the doctors in surgery because he was here officially, day in and day out, for police work.

Claire replied, "Of course, that'd be nice." As the three of them stood in the silence, the detective and Claire's eyes were locked. David, eager to leave, kept looking over his shoulder and rocking on his feet, oblivious to the attraction between the other two. Claire found it easy to gaze into Frank's eyes with the heavy blond lashes. Finally, Claire ceded to the silent messages this man was sending her and lowered her eyes, "Well, we must be going."

Claire and Detective Wharton shook hands goodbye. He thought how attractive she was, nevertheless at the same time, he wondered if he'd ever learn if she was involved in the kidnapping. It's his job to know criminals, and he couldn't believe she had anything to do with it.

At the confectionery Claire unlocked the kitchen door, and they proceeded directly up the stairs to Suzanne's room. As Claire went to the closet she puzzled as to why David was moving the bed. She stopped to watch while he lifted the floorboard and, to her surprise, removed the hatbox.

The hatbox! "What are you doing with that?" Claire demanded. Claire hadn't seen it for over a decade. As always in the past, the loss of Sue Ann rushed into her chest and jabbed at her heart. Not once had she wondered where it had gone; she had forgotten completely about it.

Lifting the cover, David grabbed Bobo and the yellow gown. Shaking them at her, he seethed, "Suzanne and I want to know about these, as well as the newspaper article about the kidnapping." He stood, returned both to the hatbox, and tucked it under his arm. Leaving the bed pulled out from the wall, he hustled down the stairs, "I'm going down to call my mother, and then I'll go to get my father at the drugstore. I'll return for you as soon as I can." His last remark was made with a raised voice, for now he was at the bottom of the stairs.

Claire grasped the night table and slowly sat down onto the bed while her mind whirled, trying to assimilate the comments that David had made to her. *He said "the kidnapping" as if it were an event that had transpired last week, not almost two decades ago. This is the beginning of the fifties. How could something that occurred in the thirties cause these nauseating sensations in me? What's going on?* Down deep inside, she feared there was a relationship between the hatbox and why Suzanne was in the hospital.

Claire could hear David's voice, not all the words, coming from the kitchen and drifting up the stairs as he talked to his mother. Suddenly, loud and clear, "You're coming with me! She may be dying!" ricocheted up the stairwell.

Claire froze. She was stunned. A dread began to expand from within her body, creeping up her spine, leaving her torso and limbs numb while her mind panicked. Slowly she began to piece together some ideas. Heavy with dread and unable to move, she found herself petrified, realizing that it was time for her secrets to be told.

Down in the kitchen David finished the conversation with his mother. "…and we need to go see her right away. I'll explain when we're together." He screamed, "Just listen to me! I can't explain now. There's not enough time. I'm going up to the drugstore to get Dad, and then we'll drive to the house for you. Please be ready to go."

Quickly he went to the staircase and shouted a good-bye to Claire. "I'll be back in ten minutes for you. Please come out when you hear the horn honk."

As he drove up to the drugstore, he glanced at the hatbox sitting on the seat next to him. He knew with a lift of the lid, it was going to come alive with long-held tales waiting to be told. He placed his hand on the lid, feeling the power in its secrets.

David parked, entered the pharmacy carrying the hatbox, and walked directly to the back office where John was preparing a prescription using the balance scale. David circled to the opposite side, wanting to face his father, and placed the hatbox from the crook of his arm onto the counter. From John's lack of response, David knew his father had never seen the hatbox.

However, when David opened it, taking Bobo with one hand and the gown with the other, John reacted by dropping the spatula from his hand. His eyes went from the ball to the gown to the eyes of his son. He saw his son's pain and wasn't sure what it meant. His hand went out to touch the ball, and David pulled it away from him.

"Where did you get those?" John exclaimed with a puzzled face.

"Suzanne had them. She has had them for as long as she can remember," David answered with animosity. As John started to speak again, David blurted, "Suzanne is at the City Hospital." His voice cracked and he put the two distasteful objects back into the hatbox. "She may be dying and we want to know about all this. Come on." He waved his arms in an awkward gesture. "All of this here at the drugstore can wait because Suzanne isn't going to wait. I have the car outside. Mom is ready for us to pick her up and go to the hospital, too."

Time paused for them. In that empty moment, John tried to assimilate what his son had said. In that void, David's face filled with hateful looks and he exploded, "Are you coming or not?"

Without comment, John removed his white coat and went to get his jacket. As they left, he told the person working with him to call the substitute pharmacist to come in. "I have an emergency at City Hospital and don't know when, or if, I'll be back. Can you close the store tonight for me?"

First they drove to Claire's place. With a honk of the horn she rushed out and entered the car. John nodded a greeting. No one wanted to talk. John had guilt for not telling David about Elizabeth. Claire thought they both knew that Tony had taken a child.

Upon arrival at the Bartlett home, David asked his father to drive, "I'm too upset and shouldn't be driving."

David, Ellie, Claire, and John began their trip to the hospital knowing it would be a difficult journey carrying them deep into the past. Without speaking, words swirled in their minds. For now, each was mired in thoughts. Each was weighing the words that needed to be shared. Each was thinking on a different aspect of the situation. Each was trying to decide how to confess his or her own sin. How does one begin to tell of events that have been sealed within for years? How does one tell secrets?

In his mind, David blamed both his parents for never mentioning his sister Elizabeth and also himself for forgetting her. Why were there no memories? Had he consciously wiped thoughts of his sister from his mind? It seemed that a three-year-old should remember something as important as a little sister who had spent every day of her life with him. He had known her for 16 months. *I was an old enough kid and should remember if, all of a sudden, my sister disappeared from my home!* There were subtle clues that he should have noticed, like the difference between his age and his brother William's age—five years. All the other siblings had a two- or three-year difference. This should have prompted a question to learn why his parents didn't have a child for five years and then were always having one. He felt stupid.

David was next to his mother in the backseat of his family's new 1950 Mercury. His head dropped against the side window, and he groaned in agony. He couldn't blame anyone except himself. He had gotten his sister pregnant. *I got my sister pregnant!* he thought over and over. *I did it. I got her pregnant. And, I didn't help her when she asked for my help. I don't know how I would've helped, but I wasn't there for her. I was angry with her. I was selfish and worried about an exam. An exam! A life—no, two lives—so I could pass an exam! I thought we could solve the problem after the exam, but I didn't say that to Suzanne. I only spoke incriminations. I left her alone with this situation.*

Perspiration was across David's brow and the back window was steamed where his head rested. Anguish contorted his face with each memory. *If only I had controlled my lust. Suzanne and I would've seen the newspaper article about the kidnapping and learned we couldn't marry. Oh, my God, I love her. I still want her and she's my sister! What kind of man am I that I desire my sister? Here I am*

*a man going into medicine, and I didn't do enough to stop myself from impreg-
nating her.*

He dropped his head into both hands. His mother touched his head and he
brushed her off. "Leave me alone," he sobbed aloud and returned to his private
thoughts. *How will I live if she dies? It was my sin. Please she can't die for my sin.*

His mother put her arms about him, pulled her son closer, and rocked him.
This time he didn't pull away. "Oh, I can't lose her, I love her so much," he
mumbled.

Upon entering the car, Ellie had slid into the seat next to David, and she had
seen the open hatbox with Bobo and the nightgown. Though she didn't understand exactly what was wrong, she picked up the yellow nightgown, and as she
fiddled with it, she was blaming herself as well, thinking, *We never should have
kept this a secret about Elizabeth. David needed to learn about the kidnapping
from us. He's right to be angry with us. He told me on the phone that Suzanne had
the ball and gown. I can't imagine how the Scagliones got Bobo and Elizabeth's
nightgown. Perchance we're all going to learn something about the abduction
from Claire and Suzanne. I hope they'll be able to resolve the questions that we've
had for all these years. I don't want to try to imagine what Claire is going to tell
us. My goodness, roughly seventeen years have passed.* She shook her head. *I
never imagined I'd ever see Bobo and that gown again.* Then her heart turned to
the problem that was more severe. *Why is Suzanne in the hospital? David says
she could die. I'm afraid to ask what's wrong. Did she try to take her life? Oh, I
wish we'd get there. I must see Suzanne myself. I can only hope he's exaggerating
the severity of her sickness because of his love for her.*

David realized that his parents might not have assimilated the fact that
Suzanne was Elizabeth, but he wasn't going to talk about any of this at this
moment. *Not while we are riding in the car, I can't see their faces! I want to see
their reactions!* He knew his parents must really be frightened to be presented
with Bobo and the gown after so many years. Yet, he had little compassion.
They had kept this secret from him. Besides, he needed to be with Suzanne
when explaining that he had gotten her pregnant and when telling about the
abortion. What about their grandchild? The baby might *not* have been retard-
ed or deformed, but the child was dead and Suzanne might die. Aloud he said,
"Oh, how has all this happened?" Then he threw his head back again onto the
car seat and shouted, "Can't we go faster?"

Claire jumped with his shout. She had been listening to the anguish coming from the back seat and was trying to not cry herself. She had no idea the
Bartlett's child was kidnapped, but she assumed that everyone knew that Tony
and she had taken a child. In her shame she couldn't talk. Claire wasn't sure
whether the Bartletts knew that Suzanne had aborted David's child. She could-

n't worry about what they might or might not know. She must be able to talk calmly and tell her whole story. In her mind she was trying to decide how to begin, what details to tell. *I must start with the trip and Sue Ann's illness,* she decided, *because they must understand our state of mind. They must know the loss we felt and that we weren't thinking clearly. We had just buried our daughter. No one here knows that I had a daughter before Suzanne. I must tell them. I don't want them to blame Tony completely, because I am partly to blame for the kidnapped child.* Claire directed her unspoken conversation to Tony. *Oh, Tony, we're paying for our wrong.*

Claire knew that David and Suzanne were aware that the ball belonged to the kidnapped child. She didn't realize that the two of them thought Suzanne was David's sister. Since Claire didn't know that the Bartlett's daughter had been taken, she was confused why her daughter aborted the child and risked her life. *Was Suzanne so ashamed of her father and me that she decided she wasn't good enough to have David's child?* It was obvious to her that Suzanne had gotten the abortion without David's knowledge and consent. He had been so shocked. *Perhaps David accepted our crime from long ago more than Suzanne. Maybe he could live with it. Obviously she couldn't. I never thought we would have to pay in this way for our actions from long ago. It seemed done and over.* Claire was content that Tony wasn't there to suffer. *Before he died he was happy. I'm glad that he was happy. I'd rather bear this suffering for him than have him here.* Then she spoke to Tony from her heart. *Tony, if you can hear me, you're going to learn how I wronged you with Harry and then kept it a secret. Please forgive me. I'll bear this for both of us because I never told you about Harry and the money. It seems fair.*

John's thoughts were on the memory of his son's face when David came into the pharmacy with the hatbox. John saw over and over the hate in his son's eyes when the gown and ball were lifted from the box. *The anger! Why did I never talk with David about the kidnapping? He was there, though young. It's obvious that he wasn't aware of the kidnapping. A child of his age wouldn't understand. I assumed that it was best not to speak to him. I was wrong. I made excuses to avoid the unpleasantness. David is angry with me for not telling him. I wonder if he has memories of his sister. Probably not. What can I remember about my life before I was four? Nothing. I should have talked with him. I failed him by not letting him know the truth. I lied to him with my silence. The whole incident didn't exist for him because of my silence. His sister was a part of his life as much as she was a part of mine. He and Elizabeth were close. Have I no sense of honor or integrity for my own son? He deserved to know from his mother and me. What a pity he learned by accident. I failed in all I've taught him and in all I believe. And*

Suzanne, what has she to do with all this? Has my failure caused a chain of events that has put her into the hospital? Oh, I'm afraid to know.

The shape and lines of the 1950 Mercury were rounded and bulky, heavy and dreary. The trip was just as heavy and overbearing with all these dismal thoughts. The atmosphere within the car was as stifling as a submerged voyage deep within the sea. The dark blue Mercury was like a large submarine gliding deep in waters, undulating with personal scenes from the past. Visibility was limited and clouded with the unknown. Soon every one of them would be doused with realities that would smother their souls. Some would gasp for air and try to swim up from the depths of disbelief. For others, a part of them would sink like a stone to the bottom.

CHAPTER 18

The hospital was sterile and bright. The drive had been dismal and dark. Both places were colored with the same pain. The Bartletts and Scagliones sat in the waiting room. Claire was completing forms when she remembered that she hadn't given David the envelope that Suzanne passed to her before the ambulance came.

Reaching into her purse, Claire said, "David, Suzanne had this envelope that she wanted to give to you. Sorry, I forgot until now."

It was another poem. Suzanne had written it while in bed at the gypsy camp.

A Poem On Holding and Being Held
Hold me, David, forever—please
Maybe not as now because
I'll not be there
But hold me in your eyes
As you do when in your arms
And hold me in your heart
As I feel you are in mine
And though there'll be No touch
No time
I'll know I'm being held
As only you can hold.

David's eyes begin to fill, and then a salty sadness spilled over the rims and streamed along the crease of his nose and cheek to the edge of his mouth. His tongue subconsciously went to the corner of his lips and licked them away. He didn't want to move; more importantly, he didn't want time to move. He feared what lay ahead. His eyes went back to the poem he held and he read it again. Only his eyes moved. Like a six-year-old he played a mind game. *Don't move! Be like a statue. Freeze! And I'll put Suzanne's fate on hold by remaining motionless.* Nevertheless, his tears continued to flow, and finally he could no longer delay movement and reached into his pocket for his handkerchief to blow his nose…and the clock began to tick again.

Right on cue, the operating room doors opened and David wanted a miracle to emerge, but instead a man dressed in green scrubs came toward them and explained, "Her situation is still grave, and she's weak with all the blood loss, but her youth should help. She'll be brought to her room in a few minutes and you'll find her conscious because I used local anesthesia. I feared putting her under. The room is number 320, but only her mother should be with her."

Claire held both arms of the chair to steady herself as she stood. She pressed her fingers to her temple and took a deep breath before approaching the doctor. She felt weak, but determined, thinking, *They shouldn't have to wait any longer to hear the truth.* Claire stepped forward, wanting to explain enough of the situation to make the doctor understand the importance of the group talking to Suzanne. "We must speak as a group with Suzanne. Doctor, I insist. She needs to know some important facts about her family. I'm certain it will raise her spirits to know these things." And Claire finished with a thought she couldn't verbalize: *Then again, if we are to lose her, she'll be more content having heard what we tell her.*

After thinking a bit, the doctor agreed to the request. He knew that the state of mind of a patient affected the healing.

However, if Claire had known that the child Tony had kidnapped had belonged to the Bartletts, she might not have made this request. Claire was sure her secret was the only secret. Claire was thinking that everyone was waiting to hear her story and nothing else. Within the hour, Claire would learn how complex and intertwined were the lives of the Bartletts and Scagliones.

David rushed up to the bed. Suzanne's eyes were closed and she looked ashen—lifeless. He collapsed onto the mattress, trying not to make any contact that might hurt Suzanne. Claire wanted to hold her daughter and yet dared not, with each arm having intravenous connections. Claire sat in a chair on the side opposite from David and took Suzanne's hand into hers.

Suzanne stirred, "Hi, Mommy." David stood and carefully placed a kiss on Suzanne's cheek and her eyes turned to him. "I'm tired and feel so weak."

David took her other hand and told her that everyone was there. The Bartletts brought chairs closer and were seated one on each side. It was hard to begin.

While gazing at her daughter Claire tried to start, but didn't. Everyone was quiet. The shock of seeing Suzanne this helpless made it harder.

David couldn't contain his frustrations and began talking. He turned to look back at his parents, "We want to know why you kept the secret of Elizabeth's kidnapping from me. To learn that Suzanne was my sister in this way has been devastating. I'm sick and tired of being treated like a child instead of an adult. I deserved to know."

Claire was confused, "Who's Elizabeth?"

John calmly held up the hatbox and opened it to make his point, "David is referring to our daughter Elizabeth, who was kidnapped in 1932 with this night-gown and her ball, Bobo." Although John was trying to clarify who Elizabeth was to Claire, he realized that he, himself, was confused in another way. David had mentioned something about Suzanne and called her "his sister."

John turned to David and began, "David, I…" only to be interrupted.

"*No!*" Claire gasped after assimilating John's comments. She couldn't believe what she was hearing. "That cannot be! The child was your daughter?" Claire's frantic exclamations were hardly noticed. Confusion filled the room.

John ignored Claire's words because he needed to understand what his son had said, and David was starting to stand and look angry again. John demand-ed, "David, you have to calm down. I can't make heads or tails out of your comments." Then John continued, "You said you learned that Suzanne was your sister?"

Each of them was confused.

Ellie tried to absorb what was being said. She knew less than anyone and finally asked, "Tell me about Suzanne. Why is she here? Please tell me what's wrong with her."

David started to speak with an angry face, and Claire quickly reached across the bed and grasped his arm. She shook her head, and he realized he needed to calm himself.

Claire looked to Ellie and explained, "Suzanne had an illegal abortion. It was David's child." Ellie and John were appalled. They hadn't been prepared for this explanation.

Claire used the moment to continue, "I know we each need to say things, but I want to go first. I have the first part of the story that needs to be told. I hope things will start to fall into place after you hear it. I'm as confused as each of you at this moment. I'm amazed that the kidnapped child was yours."

Others started to respond, and Claire blurted, "No, don't say anything! Let's take this in order to resolve all that has happened. My story is long and it's important for Suzanne to hear. I need to start." Turning to her daughter, Claire implored, "Suzanne, please tell me if you need the doctor at any time. Talking will weaken you and I don't want you to talk. If you must, squeeze on my hand or David's, and I'll stop to listen to you. We won't let go of you."

Suzanne closed her eyes while listening to her mother. She understood and moved her head in agreement.

Claire whispered to Suzanne, "Please remember through my entire story that I love you more than you know. I'm sorry I didn't always show you my love."

Claire took a deep breath and the room became quiet. No one moved. She turned to the Bartletts and apologized for the personal and intimate subjects that were to be told, "Actually, I have two stories I need to tell my daughter. I need to talk to Suzanne and tell her many things." Claire turned back to Suzanne. "The first story is an explanation about the money that was left to us. When your father died and you learned that money had been given to us, you always wondered and often asked, but I could never bring myself to talk of the situation. I should have told you. It was..." Claire found herself starting to make excuses. "You didn't seem old enough to comprehend. I was wrong. I can't think of any easy way to say this. I'm going to just blurt it out quickly." She thought for an instant then continued, "You see, this man named Harry raped me and I became pregnant. I had the child aborted." Claire started to become emotional, could barely control herself, and then her voice became a held-back sob of a whisper. "Just like you."

"Oh, Mommy," Suzanne cried out and tried to move. David put a hand to Suzanne's shoulder and begged with his expression and a shake of his head for her not to move.

Claire reached deep within and found the underlying power of her personality that had carried her through the years. She repeated in a voice for all to hear, "I had the child aborted just as you did. I lost a lot of blood, too, and was very ill, like you, but I never went to a hospital. The man who did the abortion, though he was a doctor, did a poor job and left me without the ability to bear another child. Since I was so ill, Mrs. Stein came and took care of me. I never told Tony what had happened. He thought I was having some female problems that he didn't need to know about. Your father never understood why we didn't have another child. He wanted one. I couldn't tell him. But I should have told you. I feel badly that I never did. It would've prevented this. If you had known I had had an abortion, you would've come to me."

Claire was now talking only to her daughter. She seemed unaware of the others. "I want you to remember that I didn't think you were old enough to understand. I was shocked when I learned that this Harry had money and left it to us when he died. He had always claimed that he loved me. I can't explain about that and don't want to try. He had no reason to love me. I never gave him any reason to even like me. It was dirty money to me. Years passed and I never touched it. Then, finally I realized that it wasn't the money that hurt me. I came to understand that my family could use it to improve how we lived. That is when I bought the confectionery." Claire stopped again to decide whether to share more of the experience or not. She saw no need to let the Bartletts know that their home was next door to the site of her forced relationship, or that Harry had threatened to kidnap Suzanne as Tony and she had done to Elizabeth. She decided these facts were not necessary to say. She'd tell Suzanne someday, but no one else. She hoped she'd be able to tell Suzanne someday.

"Now to the second story, the long one, the one that's important to all of us. When we were coming here to the hospital, I tried to decide where I needed to begin to make clear what happened. Please, have patience with me because I think I must go back many years."

Claire began with their trip from the West. "We left California in November of 1932 with our daughter Sue Ann. She was my first child."

"I had a sister?"

"Yes, Suzanne," Claire gulped. A lump formed in her throat. Claire stroked Suzanne's hair and regained her composure. "Just listen," Claire pleaded in a soft voice close to tears, "and you'll hear many things you've never known. I don't think you should use your strength to comment. Try to relax and listen. Please understand that many things are hard to say, and I need strength to tell it all."

The tale unfolded with all the details, starting with Sue Ann's first fever and then telling of the happiness of the natural sights of the West. She told of the horror of the Dust Bowl, the second occurrence of the fever, Doc Moore and his diagnosis, the death, the long drive with her dead child, and the strange secret burial before arriving in St. Louis without Little Sue Ann.

"I had no memory of going to bed in that motel. Tony told me later that he put me there. I had totally collapsed. Upon waking, there was this precious child sleeping with me in the bed. She wore that yellow gown with the pink rosebuds that matched the pink in her cheeks. She was an angel, I was sure, or I was still asleep and dreaming. Tony was asleep and I couldn't absorb what was occurring. The child stirred and began to wake up. She cried and I automatically nursed her. My breasts were full since I hadn't nursed Sue Ann since the day before. As she drank, she studied my face and I talked with her as I had always done with my daughter. Then I changed her diaper. She reached out for her blanket, and as I gave it to her, she smiled at me. Such a moment." Claire hesitated, swallowed, and reached for her handkerchief. Everyone could see she was back in that motel room reliving the impact the child had had on her after losing Sue Ann.

Ellie was blowing her nose, too. Hearing these facts after so many years was releasing all the anguish she had been suppressing. John reached over and took Ellie's hands.

Claire continued, "She slept again and I endlessly stared at her. She had the same basic features as Sue Ann—the curly blonde hair and blue eyes, the chubby cheeks and flawless skin—but of course, she was different. In that one moment when she smiled, I could see that her personality was different. Sue Ann had always been shy and fearful. I saw a completely different child."

"When Aunt Maria saw her that day, no one thought she was anyone except our Little Sue Ann. No one in St. Louis had met Sue Ann before, so why would anyone think any different?"

"Now I hear that the child's name was Elizabeth. For obvious reasons, I called the little girl Sue Ann, and she filled a place inside me with something that began to heal the loss of our daughter. With this child I realized that I could love another child, give to another, and that our lives would go on.

"I'm getting ahead of myself or off the subject. Sorry. I asked Tony who the child was, and he told me what had happened. He had left me sleeping and had gone for a drive. He stopped and was having a cigarette while leaning against a lamppost when this child emerged from a vacant lot. She was holding the ball, Bobo, and dragging her blanket. She climbed into the open car without a comment and then insisted that they go, 'Bye Bye.' He said that the neighborhood was quiet and dark. Every house was dark. There was no way for him to know which house she came from. As he thought a bit longer and was looking around, the child became irritated and insisted on going."

John was shaking his head and affirming that that was how his little girl would've acted. Enveloped in the emotions of that night, Claire talked on. "No lights came on in any home, and he circled the block to give them some time. When nothing changed, he didn't want to go knocking on doors or to leave her with the police, so they went for a ride."

Claire was explaining the story as she had come to accept it. Over the years her mind had arrived at ideas that she accepted as words of Tony. They weren't, but she no longer remembered what he had said and what she concluded. She believed she was telling facts, even though too much time had passed for her to distinguish the facts from her conclusions. "He told me that he figured that he could go to the police, but it'd be a horrible experience for a little girl. He decided that he could return when it was light and knock on doors. Before the light of day, things had changed. When the child rested her head on his thigh, put her thumb in her mouth, and fell asleep, his heart burst with a love for the child and probably it eased the pain of his loss, too. He decided to bring her to me. He had thought he could decide what to do in the morning." Claire stopped to catch her breath. She was trembling.

Ellie used the quiet pause to explain, "In the morning when I learned she was gone I guessed that she went out because she had left Bobo in the vacant lot. I remembered in my dreams that the ball was still outside. I heard the *thump* of the door when it closed. Do you understand? I heard it in my dream at the moment when Elizabeth must have left the house. I heard the door make a thump and didn't get up to check for the noise. I didn't know she was gone, and I didn't put everything together until the morning. It's good, finally, to know the complete story."

Claire began again. "In the morning, we put off making a decision. We read the paper to find if there was any notice of a missing child and that day there was nothing."

"After we got to the home of Aunt Maria and Uncle Vinny, we had complicated the situation. We weren't thinking too clearly. And then, days went to weeks, and the weeks we lived with Aunt Maria went to a month. At some point, Tony came home one day with a newspaper that discussed the missing child. It didn't mention the family's name, and we were too scared to contact the police or newspaper. It was approaching Christmas when we talked again about how to solve this situation."

"What I'm about to tell you is as close as I can get to the truth. I don't know what we would've done if I hadn't learned that I was pregnant. My periods were never regular, and with planning for the move from California, I never noticed that I must have missed a period in October. I noticed after we got to St. Louis. When I knew I was really pregnant, it shocked me from my grief and, more importantly, I realized I was clinging to another woman's child. I was going to have my own baby. We decided that we needed to get the child back to her parents. There was the problem of how to explain this child and the death of Sue Ann to Aunt Maria and others. We had to figure out what to do, without implicating anyone else.

"There was another problem that was bothering me. The idea that Little Sue Ann was buried in some wooded place disturbed me. I wanted her to have a regular grave with a headstone and to have a place that I could visit.

"Tony devised a plan."

Suzanne moved slightly. "Mommy, I cannot believe all this." Her eyes had darkened circles around them, and she spoke with a whispered strain.

"Just listen, there is much, much more." Claire continued, "The week before Christmas, we told Aunt Maria that we wanted to spend the weekend with some friends in the country. We left her house early on a Saturday morning, around six o'clock. I had the child dressed in Sue Ann's clothes because it was December and too cold for a nightgown and bare feet, which was how Tony had found her. When we got to her neighborhood, Tony circled the block to show me where he had parked that night when she climbed into the car. The place was a short block from Kingshighway, so this time he parked the car down on Kingshighway. He took the child and left me inside the car. We had left early hoping that everyone would be sleeping. The neighborhood was quiet. He figured that by now everyone in the neighborhood knew where the child lived because the family and police had to have knocked on doors to ask if anyone had seen anything unusual that night. Tony was going to take her to a door, put her down, knock, and run. That's what he did. He ran away from the direction of our car and went down a back alley before coming to me, in case someone saw him. He figured that he could get down to me and drive away before anyone could follow. He had parked so I had a view of the house he had chosen. My job was to observe what happened to the child after he put her down. We were to drive away quickly when he got back to the car if I had seen the child recovered into someone's arms. We didn't want her walking into the street after him.

"I not only saw the door open and the child picked up, but I saw that first man run across the street with her to a flat and beat on the door. It opened and I was sure that I was seeing the father and mother take the child. I could see and feel their happiness. At the same time I was ashamed that we caused someone else, this mother I saw, the same kind of grief that I had had. I had caused her to experience how it was to lose a child." Claire's shame and anguish showed as she pulled her lips tight, rolling them into her mouth, and put her fist there to control herself. She looked to John and Ellie. "I can't believe it! It was you I saw."

Ellie was crying.

Claire took a deep breath and started to speak again. "There is much more that I want Suzanne to know. I need to continue."

David sat with a puzzled look on his face. He couldn't respond. He was confused. He sat trying to absorb what this story meant.

"Mommy, that means I'm not David's sister? I thought I was Elizabeth. I…"

Claire's eyes showed horror as the significance of what she had done to her child seeped into her mind. Ellie and John reacted as well, realizing what David and Suzanne had thought. There was no need to explain aloud. Everyone understood that David and Suzanne had read that article in the hatbox and had assumed she was Elizabeth. Minutes passed. With regret, everyone now understood about the desperate abortion.

"If I'm not Elizabeth, where is she?"

"I don't know. I can only tell you my part of the story. Please, I must continue…"

"But, Mommy, Dad's cousin Lenny from California said I danced at his wedding. I have photos of me in his arms in 1932," Suzanne pleaded.

"That was the Bartlett's little girl." Claire could see it'd take a while for Suzanne to assimilate all the facts. "He had come to St. Louis to have his wedding. We never saw Lenny again until Aunt Maria's funeral. It was natural that he thought you were the same little girl." Claire hesitated momentarily, and then said, "Let's get back to my story.

"Now we needed to account to Aunt Maria and everyone else where our real little girl was. Right? We drove to Bourbon. Remember, I mentioned earlier that Little Sue Ann was buried there. Oh, I have a photo of her with me on the trip." Claire released her hands from Suzanne and reached into her purse for the long-hidden photo. "This is from the Grand Canyon where we had a photograph taken with an Indian chief. It's the last photograph I have of her." She took it from her purse, studied it a moment, and then passed it toward Suzanne before continuing with the tale. David held the picture for Suzanne to see her sister.

"We had some breakfast at the Diamond's Restaurant; you probably know it on Route 66. We thought that it would've been too early to arrive in Bourbon and find a doctor. Our idea was to talk with a doctor to see if we could dig up the body and have him issue a death certificate. Also, we hoped that he could help us get Sue Ann buried properly in Bourbon. Then, we could show people the certificate and we could visit the gravesite and take others, like Aunt Maria. It'd be normal.

"In Bourbon it was apparent that farmers get up early, and we could go straight there. The main street was busy when we got there at eight in the morning. It was easy to find the doctor. The first person we asked pointed to his house. I guess we were lucky that in such a small town there was a doctor. He was Doctor Connelly, who lived behind the main street across the railroad tracks. He had a nice wooden two-story house, painted white. He lived with his sister because his wife had passed on some years ago. Anyway, he listened to our story about the trip from California and the death. You know, the same version you just heard. He took compassion on us.

"He needed to do an autopsy to determine the cause of death for the certificate. That is when we told him that we still had the paper Doctor Moore had given to us when he wanted us to contact the doctors at the Joplin Hospital. We had never used it, and Doctor Connelly took the paper and said he could contact Doc Moore with that information. It worked out well."

As Claire continued the story, it was like starting a reel of film, clicking on the projector, and in the Technicolor of her mind, reliving the day again. Although Claire summarized the event to those at the bedside, she heard Old Doctor Connelly's voice speaking with its country nasal sound. She said a few sentences and saw the whole scene silently in her mind.

"Why, Mrs. Scaglione, you just stay here with my sister, Jenny, while your husband and I go out into the woods and get all dirty. It'll take some time to dig your little girl out of the soil. It's probably frozen a few inches down. Good thing you didn't wait until February 'cuz I couldn't have dug up anything by then. The cemetery people dig up a few graves in the early winter to be ready for any customers that show up during the winter." He raised his hands as he saw that Claire was about to object. She noticed the enlarged joints and stiff fingers of an old arthritic man. "Now, now, I won't let you go, so don't complain. Besides, Jenny here is making homemade apple butter and pies today. She could use some help." With that said, Dr. Connelly turned and took Tony's arm to direct him toward the door. They left before Claire could comment or object.

The doctor's sister started talking to distract Claire. "Oh, I sure could use someone to talk to while I work. You don't need to help if you prefer not to. Come on now, let's take your coat and hang it up and let the men go do what they must do," Jenny coaxed. "The good doctor will take care of your husband when they're gettin' your little girl. Come on down to the fruit cellar with me to get whatever bad apples I have. Here's a basket for you. You know you have to check about every month and work the bad ones out or the others will go bad, too. When I say bad ones I don't mean that they're no good; they just need to be used in cooking right away 'cuz there's a bruise or wormhole. Last month I made applesauce and put up about ten jars. I figured I'd make apple butter and some pies today. The doctor loves apple butter. Then we could make two pies and send one home with you. How does that sound?"

Jenny went on and on like that the whole time the men were gone; that was about three hours of nonstop talking. Claire found the talk soothing, and she didn't have to say much of anything. She was glad of that. Claire learned the gossip of everyone in town, and then the history of the doctor and the death of his wife, as well as Jenny's explanation of what it was like to be an old maid in Kansas City, Missouri before she had come to live with her brother.

They were putting the last pie in the oven when the men came back. Sue Ann's body had been placed in the doctor's office.

"Now there's no need for you to see your daughter, Mrs. Scaglione, if you're thinking about that. The little girl you know is up in heaven. You leave the scientific investigation of her remains with me. I wasn't about to let your husband open the blanket either. You take my advice. Now then, let's have some lunch. Hope there's more than apple butter, Jenny. Why, we worked up quite an appetite, didn't we?" The doctor talked as much as his sister, Claire thought. It was their way to keep us from thinking too much about Little Sue Ann.

While the men went to wash up, Jenny took some fried chicken from the cupboard where it was waiting covered with a clean white cloth that had appliqués of white ducks with orange legs and black beaks on each end. Then she opened the icebox and took out some potato salad and other 'fixins,' as she called them.

"I always have to make lunch before I start workin' with the apples. The doctor starts smelling the cooking and gets so hungry that he can't wait for me to make up anything," she twittered. She was delighted at her own ingenuity.

The doctor gave his next set of directions as they began to eat. "Now you two are going to go back the way you came into town the first time today and you'll find the undertaker's place. You can't miss it. I wrote up a little note for you to give to Jed. He's the undertaker. You need to buy a plot of land. He takes care of all these arrangements, you see. He'll take you over to the cemetery and show you which plots are ready. You look around and think about how you can plant some flowers, a tree, or some bushes. That'll help you decide which one you want. Well, you get the picture. While you're working on that, I'll do my job with the autopsy and contacting your Doctor Moore. I don't think we'll get all of these tasks done today, so Jenny you prepare the spare bedroom for them. Now, now, we won't take no for an answer, will we Jenny?"

"Land sakes, no! Why, I enjoy company, and Claire has been a joy to be with all morning. We'd love to have you spend the night. No need to go to that motel on the highway, I've been told that it smells horrible. Mold or something! They just don't know how to clean." And on and on Jenny talked during the lunch.

"Oh, yes, I nearly plum forgot," the doctor replied as they were starting out the door to the undertaker's. "You need a coffin. I gave it some thought and I figured this way. Why pay Jed the gall'd darn prices he asks for those plain old wooden coffins for your little precious girl. I got a real good idea. Jenny, remember that real pretty hand-painted hatbox covered with flowers and things? My wife had it back…. Well, you won't remember because you weren't here."

"Why, I know what you mean. I wasn't here when she used the hatbox, but I know where it is in the attic. It's the prettiest box. Made from the thinnest slivers of curved wood. And big! It must have been for one of those big hats at the turn of the century," she went on.

"That's it! Jenny, now you go get that hatbox. I thought what better way to use it than as a coffin for a pretty little girl. It's wood and covered with flowers and things, if my memory serves me," the doctor repeated, as he often did.

"You're absolutely right, that's how it looks. I'll go get it as soon as I clear the table. Oh, didn't our pie turn out good, Claire? Since we've finished our dee-serts, you two go on up to Jed's and then come on back and I'll have the hatbox ready for you to see. If you don't like it you could always go back and talk to Jed again," Jenny suggested.

"Oh, you'll like it," the doctor insisted as he faded down the dark hallway to his workspace. "I decided that's what we are going to use. My wife would've been real happy with this idea of mine. Talk to you later."

"When Tony and I returned from the cemetery," Claire continued as she rejoined the present, "I saw a most elegant hatbox. It was an exact replica of the small one John has in his hands and yet big enough for one of those outlandish hats of bygone days. You know, from those times at the turn of the century when a woman wouldn't step from her house without a hat. We found this little hatbox inside the big one. The Doctor didn't remember that it had existed. He insisted I take it with me and suggested that I put some mementos of Sue Ann inside it."

Claire shook her head. "After the burial, when we started for home, I found Bobo and the gown in the car, so I filled it with Elizabeth's things. We had forgotten to return them with the child the day before. We had been so nervous. So I put the newspaper with the article about the kidnapping at the bottom and then the gown and Bobo on top. On the drive back to St. Louis, the little hatbox sat on my lap and was a comfort. I thought of it as a symbol of my little Sue Ann. I don't think there has ever been a more beautiful coffin than that big hatbox. Doctor Connelly was right; the hatboxes eased my sadness. The beauty of this small one was irresistible; as I touched the smooth-painted flowers, passing my fingers over the silky paint in yellows, pinks, and green, it soothed me. The idea that my little girl was to be forever in a special hatbox, like this one, was a blessing.

"Then I tried to forget about it all. Suzanne wouldn't let me. As soon as she could scoot and get into things, she found the little hatbox in the bottom of my closet and she fell in love with Bobo. I couldn't keep it from her. At some point, when I thought she had forgotten about him, I'd find where she was hiding him. It was impossible.

"Oh, I got away from my story again." Claire stopped for a time. "That was about all, anyway. We told Aunt Maria about Sue Ann getting ill and dying, not quite the truth, and said that the doctor insisted she be buried right away. Then about a month or two later, when a gravestone was ready, we went with Aunt Maria and Uncle Vinny to have a memorial service."

"Years later, Tony's coffin, with his uniforms and helmet, was buried next to Sue Ann. I thought you might see her grave when we buried him, but they draped all his flowers over Sue Ann's headstone because it was so close to his gravesite. It would've been an opportunity to tell you, Suzanne, about your sister.... I was too distraught with your father's death and...." Claire left the sentence unfinished.

John spoke up and asked, "What did your daughter's autopsy reveal?"

"Oh, it was yellow fever. Ole Doc Moore in Oklahoma had saved some of the vomit that Sue Ann had expelled in his office. He went over to the Joplin hospital himself to have it tested and found out. He had tests started the day after we saw him; that's how he knew his guess was correct. Ole Doc Moore had figured that Sue Ann had died but was glad to get a confirmation from Doctor Connelly. He expressed an appreciation to have an ending to the incident. The death certificate was issued. It worked out well."

John was really curious. "How did Sue Ann get yellow fever, an African disease? Did anyone ever figure that out?"

"Yes, Tony remembered something. We went on an all-day picnic to the beach before we left California. It was a place that had some standing water that could have had mosquitoes breeding. In the evening as we were getting ready to leave, some men speaking a foreign language passed us. It was a group of seven or so. I don't remember them at all. Tony thought that they could have been sailors without their uniforms because their skin was dark, like men from the Middle East or that area. Doc Moore reported this to the health services in San Diego and Los Angeles."

"Now that you ask that question, I remember that Doctor Connelly in Bourbon had a booklet that he took from his shelves to show Tony and me. It was about an incident of yellow fever in the 1870s in a place not far from where the Mississippi River meets the Ohio River—near Cairo.[3] Yellow fever right across the river from Missouri! It was a study that listed everyone with the fever, showing who survived and who died. About 150 people died. A steamer called *The Golden Rule* came into town for only twenty to thirty minutes and the passengers strolled around town while the captain sent a telegraph. That was all. The steamer had come up river from New Orleans with the fever on board and a mosquito bit a sick person while they were stopped. Then it bit this boy who was down at the riverfront selling apples on the landing. Amazing how it spread: the boy's sister contracted it soon after he did, and people kept getting bitten after the boat left. *The Golden Rule* left people in Memphis and Vicksburg with yellow fever, too.

"About Sue Ann's yellow fever: Tony called Doctor Connelly a month later to find out if anyone else got it in California or near where we had traveled down Route 66. There were no reports, and the doctor mentioned that it wasn't so strange because we had gone into a desert where there weren't any mosquitoes and it was November. The Cairo, Missouri incident took place in the hot, muggy summer near the river, where mosquitoes were found in great numbers." Claire sighed and looked to Suzanne.

Suzanne seemed to be staring at nothing out across the room. She began to speak, "When I was little, in fifth or sixth grade, I'd stare like I am right now while I listened to the teacher talk as you were talking." It seemed irrational to hear Suzanne's voice drone in a monotone about this completely unrelated topic. Suzanne continued, "It was the strangest thing. Such an illusion! I only remember seeing it in my classroom, until now. Anyway, my eyes would fix on something, the teacher or her desk, and then suddenly my eyes were locked. I could not move my eyes away. Slowly the teacher and the desk started to shoot away from me. They got smaller and smaller and smaller. Suddenly the smallness froze at a very tiny size and didn't get any smaller. It was as if I was looking into the wrong end of binoculars. I called it my 'reduction stare.' It was such a pleasing sensation. I remained in the reduction stare, until I was forced to end it by the teacher asking me a question or something. That would make me break the spell. My reduction stare happened over and over when I was in grade school then it just stopped, until now." Suzanne paused. "I was staring and thinking that I always wanted to investigate what it was."

Everyone was quiet. Claire thought Suzanne was delirious.

John saw a lot of meaning in her statement. He surmised that Suzanne was saying that it's important to learn about anything and everything that occurs to us. If Suzanne had known about the kidnapping a year ago, a month ago, or even two days ago, everything would be different.

David understood that Suzanne was thinking about something else entirely. He thought that she knew she was going to die and was thinking about the little insignificant things that she wanted to accomplish during her life. David could find no words. He sat in sadness. How could he and Suzanne have understood all they learned and been so wrong? He was numb. He was defeated. It should have been a joy to know she wasn't his sister. Not now; all was changed.

Claire broke the silence because time was passing and she wanted to learn all that had happened. She also didn't know whether Suzanne understood everything or not. "John or Ellie, why don't you talk and tell us why there is no Elizabeth in your lives? We did take her back to the right place, I hope."

John began, "Yes, Elizabeth became a Christmas present three days before Christmas. We were overjoyed. I immediately called the police to let them know that she had mysteriously arrived on a neighbor's doorstep. The man I spoke to at the station was offensive. When the call went through, the detective on our case wasn't at his desk and another answered. He immediately started talking defensively, saying that they were understaffed and overworked and didn't have enough time to work on the case. He said something like, 'If you'd please not call, we'll be in touch when there's some information to tell you.' I hung up on him and didn't tell him that we had Elizabeth mainly because he really didn't give me a chance. I never heard from them again.

"We picked up our lives and went on in the same manner as before the abduction. It bothered us, but we figured there was no way to ever know what happened. Then, less than one year later, Elizabeth got pneumonia and died. She was here one day and gone the next. Ellie and I couldn't accept it. We had lost that little girl two times and it didn't seem fair." John's eyes started to mist and he stopped to clear his throat. "The way we dealt with our emotions was to not talk about her. Ellie put any photos we had into the back of a drawer where we'd never see them unless we wanted to see them. Becky has been good for us. We finally have a daughter. She kind of healed a wound that had been open and festering for years." John stopped briefly to look into the eyes of his wife, and then he continued.

"There is really nothing more I can say or explain. We were wrong not to talk to David when he was older. He saw his sick sister taken away, and when she died, he didn't know that she had died. We told him that she had gone to live in a beautiful place. He accepted that. We meant heaven, but he must have thought we meant someone's beautiful home. I don't know. At that time, he had another brother and didn't ask questions. Later on Ellie and I never took the time to discuss whether we should tell the children. We couldn't find a way to talk to each other. We didn't have the emotional strength, and it was easier to say nothing." John looked to his son. David made no eye contact, and no words were passed between them, but they each knew what the other was thinking.

John went on, "Now, finally we are to the present. I don't know what is going on here with you and Suzanne. David could you please explain?" Everyone except Suzanne looked over to David.

David took his hand from Suzanne's and stood as he began to speak. Soon he was pacing the room to help vent his anger. His first comments were accusations and expressions of his own guilt. He tried to explain about his exams and not helping Suzanne. He had no sequence to what he was saying. He wasn't telling his story clearly. While the Bartletts were listening to their son, Claire heard Suzanne and turned away from the others.

"Mommy, Mommy," Suzanne murmured.

Claire leaned her head over the bed and put her face on the sheets to be face to face, only inches apart. "I'm here, Suzanne. Try to rest."

"You never lied to me. I thought you had. I'm sorry, Mommy."

Claire stroked her daughter's hair again and squeezed her hand. "Don't, Suzanne, it's okay. You need to be quiet and rest."

Suzanne's voice was weak and barely audible so the others could not hear. "No, Mommy, I was so wrong. I imagined many things that were not true. I thought you lied to me. I was selfish not to consider that you had sad reasons to be as you are. I'm sorry that I never tried to talk to you. Did Daddy tell you that I asked him why you didn't have any more kids?"

Claire was startled by the question and was beginning to lose any composure that remained with her when she answered, "No, he didn't." Claire thought for a moment, and then asked, "What did he say?"

"He said, 'I don't know, I don't know.'" Suzanne whispered. "He didn't know, did he, about why you couldn't have another child?"

"No. I never told Tony about Harry and the abortion. I should have. I was going to tell you one day. I always planned to tell you, but it was hard to tell until tonight. Isn't that funny? I just told it all to people who are not my family, and I couldn't tell you or Tony. I'm sorry, Suzanne. Sorry that I wasn't a better mother. You have been more than I could have ever wanted in a daughter." Claire continued to talk in this manner, hoping that Suzanne would quiet herself.

Suzanne didn't hear the last words. Her abilities were fading, and her mind was dwelling on her own thoughts of shame. *All the misunderstandings! Mr. Bartlett tried, but I didn't learn well enough all the ideas he tried to teach me.* She saw his teachings—the words *truth, integrity,* and *logic* hanging in the air. She wanted to reach for the words and hold them. *Yes, if I hold them in my hand I'll remember to use them. I need to put them in my purse to take with me wherever I go. His words were so important and I forgot.* In her disorientation she tried to analyze whether there was any fact or clue that could have led David and her to the truth. *How easy it was for us to think we understood,* she thought and then whispered aloud, "but we didn't." She slipped from life while trying to put into order the events that had led her to this hospital bed. At least one aspect was clear to her: David and she had made assumptions before learning the truth.

Claire saw her daughter die. She knew the moment when her Suzanne relaxed into death. She didn't interrupt David's talking. The little strength that had held Suzanne's hand to hers wilted. When Claire peered into the face of Suzanne, she saw her expression ripple and relax into calmness.

David sensed something, stopped talking, and saw her lifeless. Her poem came to him.

David, Hold me…
Hold me in your heart
And though there'll be no touch, no time
I'll know I'm being held
As only you can hold.

EPILOGUE

Grief is a lonely suffering. One needs to wallow in the pain of grief to ease the guilt caused by still being alive. Grieving is a slow and lengthy process. For some, like David, grief is endless.

Claire had grieved before, but this time she learned from it. Her thoughts and ideas started to change. In the future, her private talks of the mind with Suzanne would be filled with sharing her happiness. Claire would see how precious it is to be alive. Claire would find beauty in the world, in people, and in her past. She slowly returned to being the carefree woman Tony had met, his "five foot two, eyes of blue" woman full of exuberance. Learning from the loss of Sue Ann, Tony and Suzanne, Claire knew that life was to be cherished and that sorrows can add beauty to life.

The gypsy girl Valerie came to Claire's house to recount the last two days of Suzanne's life. Claire and Valerie learned that they needed each other, and Claire offered her home as a place for Valerie to live while going to college. The two grew close, spending many an evening talking of Suzanne. In this way, they built happiness into their lives.

However, David could not talk about Suzanne. His medical school and work took him away from his family, and he rarely returned. He became a doctor and found another to marry. However, when holding his first-born child, Suzanne was in his thoughts. With time, David became sadder. No one filled his arms, his dreams, and his lust as his Suzanne had done. Over the years, he became known for his daily evening walk—always alone. Yet unknown to all, these were his walks with Suzanne; she was beside him always. When he finally reached his final night, Suzanne and their love were to be his last thoughts. Suzanne remained forever in David's mind, and he died in old age, knowing that Suzanne was his only real love.

Life is a story, a mural of faces and scenes that can be told in words. Some people try to understand why things happen as they do. Others want to justify the events of life. A few accept what life brings them. One might want to claim that Suzanne's death was not caused by the abortion, but instead, by the shame, guilt, and secrecy that one found in St. Louis in the middle of the twentieth century. On the other hand, the 1950s would see the beginnings of changes that could have prevented the circumstances that led to her death. Conservative ideas would be overthrown, emphasis was placed on communication, educational institutions soon accepted the responsibility for teaching about sexual reproduction, and laws were made to legalize the choice of abortion.

Suzanne's life ended in tragedy with a child lost, a love unfulfilled, and a mind extinguished. But then, loss of life is a part of life. A story was painted of two families who met and merged like the two rivers that come together at St. Louis. And like the rivers, the meeting formed a turbulence that left them forever united in their mural of memories.

SCRAPBOOK

BY

Ellie Bartlett
1947–1973

EVENTS OF INTEREST IN UNITED STATES

February 1947

The Age of Computers was beginning. The first electronic calculator called the ENIAC was built at the University of Pennsylvania and delivered for use at the Aberdeen Proving Ground on 'February 1947. Then, the following year, IBM completed the SSEC, which used punched cards to feed the data into the machine. It could calculate 60,000 multiplications of two 14-digit numbers in 20 minutes. This was a task that would take a person more than five years to complete.

June 1948

A television receiver with a 10 inch screen could be purchased for $350 therefore many homes were starting to own this new entertainment device. There were some television receivers with larger screens, but the price became one for only the well to do with a range from $500 to $2,500.

January 12, 1949

Coaxial cable made television reach from the Atlantic coast to Missouri.
Then in August of 1949 RCA Victor announced that it had a viable color television.

January 19, 1949

President Harry S. Truman was re-elected and on the day before his inaugural address he signed into law that the U.S. President's new salary would be $100,000 per year.

March 1949

The Heavyweight Boxing Champion of the World, Joe Louis, retired and created an argument among the fight fans and officials of the world as to whom the title would pass. By the end of the year there was no agreement...to the people of the world no one could take the place of Joe Louis.

October 26, 1949

President Truman signed a law to raise the minimum wage from 40 cents per hour to 75 cents per hour.

Baseball 1949

Heading into the National League pennant the St. Louis Cardinals seemed likely to take it, but the Dodgers managed to nose out the Cards by one game. That put the Dodgers up against the Yankees of the American League. The Dodgers had stormed into this annual series five times since 1916 and again they wouldn't win. Even though Joe DiMaggio had a bad heel that had given him trouble all season as well as there were 70 other injuries to the New York players, the Yanks took the World Series. Manager Casey Stengel of the Yankees said that the Series was won from the bullpen, the difference between the two teams being the relief pitchers.

But St. Louis made its place this year when Roy Sievers of the St. Louis Browns was made one of the rookies of 1949 by the Writers Association of America. Jackie Robinson of the National League and Ted Williams of the American League were named the most valuable players. Williams placed second in the league batting averages with .3427, had 159 runs-batted-in and led the league in home runs with a total of 43.

December 1949

The Battle of the Decade in the Music Industry concerned—Which speed should a record turn? Columbia had invented machines to run a long-playing 33.3 revolutions per minute (rpm) that delivered thirty minutes of music per side while RCA Victor had designed a single record for 45 rpms with less than five minutes of music. Prior to these two new record sizes the standard had been for 78 rpms. The Battle ended in

December when RCA Victor announced that it would make phonographs that play all three record speeds.

1953

The study of Heredity and Genetics reached a high point when Watson and Crick presented the concept of DNA (a class of nucleic acids found in the nucleus of human cells). With this discovery there would emerge explanations and definitions for major genetic, biochemical, and structural characteristics of hereditary material. This was to be the beginning of a focus on the enormous intricacies and complexities involved in the functions of DNA.

Abortion Laws: 1940–1973

In the early forties a movement began to legalize abortion in Japan and the Eastern European nations. (Russia had legal abortions in 1920.) The movement slowly spread in the world, but it wasn't until the late sixties that the United States began to eliminate those statutes prohibiting abortion. In fact, it wasn't until 1973, in the case *Wade vs. Roe,* that the Supreme Court declared unconstitutional all the statutes in any state that forbade abortion.

AUTHOR'S NOTES

¹ <u>Al Capone</u>

Historical literature writes that Al Capone entered prison for an eleven-year sentence on tax evasion in May of 1932 and was not released from Alcatraz prison until 1939 for syphilis-related dementia. Nevertheless, I found a front-page story in the St. Louis Post-Dispatch from November 18, 1932 that has a photo of Al Capone with hat in hand and a huge smile on his face; the caption under the Associated Press photo states:

> "SCARFACE" AL CAPONE
> CHICAGO'S "Public Enemy No.1" now serving a 10-year sentence in Federal prison for income tax evasion, leaving the Federal building at Atlanta, Wednesday, after Federal Judge Marvin Underwood had taken under advisement his plea for freedom. Capone contends he is imprisoned illegally because the statute of limitations has run in his case.

There were several details that were confusing, such as:

1) Capone's sentence was for eleven years, but this front-page story says ten years.
2) He was sent to prison for tax evasion that occurred in 1925, 1926, and 1927. The statute of limitations was six years when he was indicted on June 1, 1931. I do not see that the six-year statute had expired.
3) I found no record of this November 18, 1932 release.

One needs to see this photo from the St. Louis Post Dispatch and read about Al Capone to decide what happened. My guess is that Al Capone is in handcuffs behind his handheld hat. He is smiling because he had a sense of humor and probably told the reporter taking the photograph that he was free, but more

291

than likely he was being transferred to another jail or prison facility. Historical details discussed above were read in many places of which I no longer have notes, but when the copyeditor questioned the event I confirmed the facts in the book:

Kobler, John (1971). CAPONE The Life and World of Al Capone. G.P. Putnam's Sons, New York.

In the above book the difference between a ten-year and eleven-year sentence was discussed. Al Capone had a ten-year sentence for the federal prison facilities and another one-year sentence to be served in the Cook County Jail in Chicago.

2 Information on inbreeding and incest

It is statistically unlikely that one instance of inbreeding in a family would result in problems with the offspring. It's something that develops over sever-al generations. But I was demonstrating that the books that Suzanne would have found in 1950 at the St. Louis Public Library would not easily explain this. Like Suzanne, I went to the St. Louis Public Library and with the help of a librarian I checked out all books we could find on incest and inbreeding (ones dealing with plants were omitted) that were published before 1950, as follows:

1. Elvins, Kells (1941). *A Case Study of Forty-four Incestuous White Feathers of Texas.* University of Texas at Austin (Thesis M.A.).
2. Layard, John (1945) *The Incest Taboo and the Virgin Archetype.* Rhein-Verlag.
3. Raglan, FitzRoy Richard Somerset, Baron (1933) *Jocasta's Crime: An Anthropological Study.* H. Fertig.
4. Weinberg, Samuel Kirson. (1942) *Incest Behavior and Family Organization.* University of Chicago (Thesis Ph.D.).

In this novel, there are indented quotes from these books. I realize that some of this information was vague and misleading, but that is the point. Suzanne read what I read in these books. But she was reading subject matter new to her, information that was never presented to her in her family or in school, and topics that lacked informative books. She was misled.

3 Background on Yellow Fever in Midwest United States

A man making a geological survey in Kentucky, in 1879, heard about a yellow fever epidemic in an area 38 miles south of the confluence of the Mississippi River and Ohio River at a place called Cairo, Illinois. He investigated the total incident from its origin in New Orleans to Hickman, Kentucky and wrote elaborate details (e.g. number of cases of yellow fever, if white or colored, the numbers who died, and more) for thousands of victims. Through interviews and using detailed notes taken by a judge and doctors, the author John Procter wrote about the kind of day, who was on the dock when the Steamer *Golden Rule* came in, what the captain was doing, etc. The document was obtained at the St. Louis Public Library-Main Branch:

Procter, John R. (1879) *Geological Survey of Kentucky with Notes on Yellow Fever Epidemic at Hickman, Kentucky 1878.*

978-0-595-36323-0
0-595-36323-7